Then There *Was You*

A CEDAR POINT NOVEL

D.L. LANE

This book is a work of fiction. Names, characters, businesses, organiza- tions, places, events and incidents either are the product of the author's imagination or are used fictitiously. Any resemblance to actual persons, living or dead, events, or locales is entirely coincidental. Scripture quotations from The Authorized (King James) Version.

Fiction and Literature: Inspirational

www.dllaneauthor.com
Book and cover design By Faith Publishing
Edited by Red Penn Services Ltd.

ISBN: 978-1-64921-302-0

"And now these three remain: faith, hope and love. But the greatest of these is love."

1 Corinthians 13:13

Prologue

Before

RAIN PELTED DANICA as she slogged her way along the slick, black road, tears streaming down her cheeks, mortification becoming her and her rage's new BFF—a real fun trio they were.

With stilted movements, she swiped her face, but it was a losing battle. The salty-anger mixed into the water dripping from her lashes, running off the tip of her nose, weaving over trembling lips, and dropping from her quivering chin. On the off chance he would try to find her, she hadn't taken the direct path home, but every stupid decision she'd made that night, including putting her trust in Matt Jordan, was costing her. Not only was she going to be soaked to the bone by the time she walked through the front door of her house, but it had to be way past her eleven-p.m. curfew.

I'm so dead.

The thought had her crying harder as she rounded the bend. But if there was any solace to be had, at least she was closer to town.

Just a little bit farther.

Danica's head throbbed so hard she could have sworn her temples pulsed, and her stomach decided to give up on the churning, staging a severe revolt.

Bending over, she heaved—the muscles in her body protesting as cramp after cramp struck.

All of this seemed like a nightmare, but unfortunately, it wasn't.

Wiping her mouth with the back of her hand and straightening, a slice of light cut through the trees—a welcome reprieve from the darkness. Then the momentary relief morphed into worry.

Who's coming?

Head whipping to the left, wet hair slicked to her neck, Danica considered the wooded area, knowing she could hide if she had to, but visions of the last *Jason* movie bounced through her thoughts, sending a shiver of fear up her spine.

Who would be worse? she wondered. *Matt or some freaky masked madman?*

"Matt," she mumbled, squinting, lifting a shaky hand in front of her face as the bright headlights hit her full-on, and the vehicle stopped in front of her.

Heart pounding in her ears—two seconds from bolting—she heard, "Danny?"

That sandpaper-smooth voice enveloped her, making everything come to a halt—feet, panic, even her breath.

A second later, a slamming car door echoed, and then something warm—his letterman jacket?—went around her shoulders. "Danica? What in the hel-heck is going on? Gage touched her arm, causing her to suck in air through her teeth. "Are you hurt?"

She was, but she wouldn't be copping to that.

Blinking up into the shadowed face that starred in her dreams, she shook her head and whispered, "I'm not hurt."

Gage palmed her cold, wet cheek, sending an electric current through her. "Have you been drinking?"

"Maybe."

He scowled. "Maybe?"

"Matt gave me a red solo cup of something."

"Something?"

"I think he called it jungle juice."

"How many cups did you have?"

"Three or four." She shrugged. "I'm not sure."

"You've definitely been drinking, Danny." Gage sighed. "Come on and get in the car, you are drenched, and I'm getting there." Taking her small hand in his much larger one, he tugged.

A few quick-steps later she was inside his dry GTO, watching him run around the front of his vehicle, cutting through the downpour, then slipping in behind the wheel.

"I'm getting your seat wet," she said in a low voice.

"Don't worry about the seat." Combing his fingers through the wet strands of his midnight-colored hair, water flew. "You want to tell me why you were drinking with Jordan?"

Because I thought you'd be there, skipped around in her aching brain. "Matt invited me to a party at his parents' cabin by the lake."

Even in the dim light coming from the instrument panel of his car, his astonishing silver eyes flashed. "And you thought hanging with him, and the brainless crew of seniors who worship at his feet, was a good idea?"

Danica held her forehead. "I don't know, Gage. It was something to do."

"You can't date until you turn sixteen. Isn't that what your father has said, oh I don't know, ten-thousand times?"

She mumbled, "It wasn't a date."

"Did your sister or Jill know about this invitation?"

"No," she muttered, feeling like total roadkill.

"So, you went to a party with a bunch of as—" He cleared his throat. "No one knew you were with that group of jerks?"

"I guess not."

"Look at me."

Peeking up, Danica watched the muscle in Gage's tight jaw jump. "Why were you walking out in this rainstorm at almost midnight?"

"Why were you driving this way?" she countered.

"It's not important." He tapped the steering wheel. "So why are you out here?"

"Can we just drop the interrogation?"

"Nope."

The sound of a million bb's fell on Gage's cherry-red ride as she stared out the windshield, the wipers hypnotically going back and forth. "Take me home, please?"

"We're not going anywhere until you tell me."

"Gage, I don't feel well."

"After four cups of hard liquor mixed with fruit, I'm sure you don't."

Another bubble of nasty came up.

Danica went for the door, opening it, leaned out, and puked—the chunky *splat* onto the wet pavement made her stomach convulse more.

Gage's gravelly, "I'm going to kill Jordan," would have sent needly chills over her if she hadn't been dying. But even with her head pounding like a bass drum, cold and looking like a drowning cat while evacuating the entire contents of her stomach in the pouring rain, Danica Lorry knew she was safe. Gage would take care of her. He was good at that.

Righting herself, she shut the door, the sour taste in her mouth sickening. "Sorry."

"It's bad enough to go home late, but in this condition..." Reaching, he slicked aside some of the damp strands of hair from her face, causing a riot of sensations to dance across her skin. "You will need to sober up some and dry off before you meet the wrath of Mr. Lorry."

"I've got some clean clothes at J.J.'s. You can take me there."

"You'll wake up the entire household at this hour," he said.

"I know where the spare key is. I can sneak in." Danica's wheels turned. "In fact, I can stay there with her and let my parents know time got away from us, and I'm going to spend the night."

A shaky smile formed on her face as she turned to look at him.

Just like he had the day she crashed and burned on her new bike, a significant wipeout, scraping her knees and hands when she was eight, he dried her face of tears, only this time he used his big hand instead of his *Star Wars* t-shirt. "All right. I'll take you to Jillian's, but I want to know why you didn't call someone to pick you up, instead choosing to walk in this rain?"

She nodded, not wanting to talk about her bad judgment, but agreeing to if it meant she could avoid the trouble waiting for her at home.

"And Danny?"

"Yeah?"

"I want to hear all of it. Including why you winced when I touched your arm."

There it was, his brotherly protective mode.

Danica knew, without a shadow of a doubt, what she always did. She loved a boy who saw her as nothing but a little sister, causing a new pain to pop up, but not in her head. No, this hurt pummeled her, causing a desperate yearning deep in her breaking heart.

Pounding on the door, Gage seethed. The music inside thumped so hard the windows shook, making him beat the wood harder, ready to kick it in. Less than an hour ago, he'd been chilling, dry, and warm, reading a Tom Clancy book as reruns of the *Simpsons* played on his TV, until the phone in his room rang.

"Hello?"

"Hey, Gage," came the greeting.

"Phillip. Hey, man. What's up?"

"Listen. I just got home from a party at Jordan's. Well, it was at his parents' cabin."

He didn't know why he should care, but said, "Cool."

"No, it wasn't."

"Okay," he said, unsure of what to say.

"It wasn't my scene, and I left."

"Sorry, dude, but Matt Jordan is in a class all of his own, and not necessarily a good one."

"Danica's there."

Those two blurted words had Gage white-knuckling the handset and sitting up, rolling off his disheveled bed. "Danny?"

"Yeah, man. I asked her if she wanted to go with me, I'd give her a ride home, but she said no. The thing is, I don't think it's a good place for her to be. Especially when Breck and Mase aren't there."

"You're right."

"Anyway. I know you're like a big brother to her," Phillip said, "and I thought maybe you should know."

"Thanks for telling me."

"Sure. Catch you at youth group?"

"Yeah. See you then."

The moment he hung up the phone, Gage grabbed his coat and keys, and then dashed down the stairs, only to be stopped by his dad's, "Where are you going, son?"

"I have to check on something."

Dad's eyes narrowed. "In this weather?"

"It's important," he said, palming the back of his tense neck.

"It's raining."

"I know, but I have to go."

"You be careful, and don't stay out too long. I know you're seventeen, but it's getting late."

"I will, and I'll be back as soon as I can," he said, then went out the door, hopped into his car, and headed toward the lake.

Coming across Danny walking down the back road in the middle of the night during a storm had been crazy. Why he'd chosen to take that particular path, he wasn't sure, but he had.

Extreme relief when he saw her was his first emotion, quickly followed by annoyance when he jumped out in the deluge and put his jacket around her. Oh, he wasn't annoyed at being in the bad weather, but by the fact *she* was. However, his irritation transitioned into anger when he realized her condition.

After watching Danny toss her cookies, he had convinced her to tell him what happened. When she did, it took all of his strength to maintain his cool, but when Gage saw the evidence left behind, he had to close his eyes and mentally count his way to serenity. It didn't work, but somehow, he'd managed to take her to the Donley's place, made sure she was safely inside with Jillian, then all attempts at calm civility vanished. He tore down the street, too reckless, with one destination in mind.

Now, there he was, two seconds from putting his foot through the door when it opened, and a smirking Matt Jordan stood there, swaying, dark hair mussed, his glazed mocha eyes narrowing. "Gage!" He hoisted up a cup, clearly on his way to drunk. "You're a little late, but come on in, we're partying 'til dawn."

Quick as a cobra strike, he grabbed the creep by the neck, and pushed him.

Stepping inside Gage slammed Jordan's back against the far wall of the little foyer, Matt's drink dropping somewhere along the way. "I'm going to rip off your head and spit down your neck!"

"Chill out, dude." He tried to break Gage's hold.

The guy might be a year older, but *he* was bigger.

"Somehow, you lured Danny here, plied her with alcohol, then tried to take advantage of her," he gritted through his teeth.

"She wanted to *come* if you know what I mean."

"She's fifteen!"

"And she's built like a—"

"Shut up! You put your hands on her. I saw the bruises around her upper arms!"

Gage squeezed, making the pissant cough out, "You're chok-choking me."

"I'm going to do a whole lot more than choke you!"

"Noth-nothing happened," Matt spluttered, drool on his lower lip and chin, face turning a deep shade of crimson.

"Enough did!"

A crowd had gathered to witness the first punch, some girl he didn't see screaming the moment Jordan's blood splattered. Like a bull seeing red, Gage whaled on him, feeling the satisfying crack of his nose before he went limp, slithering down the wall into a pathetic pile on the floor.

Chest heaving, knuckles bloody, he turned on the group.

"I'm going to call 9-1-1," Courtney threatened.

"Go ahead," Gage countered.

"Don't," Vic Cordova said, voice cracking in panic as he wiped his face with his palm. "If I get another strike, I'm up shi—"

"You all make me sick!" Balling his fingers into a fist, Gage advanced on Vic, the guy stumbling back before he glared at every one of Jordan's crew, rage over what happened to Danny consuming him.

"I had to go to the bathroom, but someone was in there," Danny said. "Matt told me to follow him so I could use the one in his parents' room." She glanced down at her lap. "That was my second mistake."

"Second?" Gage asked.

"My first was going out to the lake with him."

A bad brew of anger and trepidation made him grip the gearshift. "What happened?"

"He closed the bedroom door behind us, then locked it. I asked him what he was doing, and he smiled at me, but not in a nice way. I tried to leave, but he wouldn't let me. He started touching me. I told him to knock it off and move, that I wanted to go, but it was like fighting off an octopus. When he grabbed my—" Danny bit her bottom lip.

"Tell me."

"He grabbed me, and when I slapped him, he got mad. He wrapped his big hands around my arms and pinned me to the door. He said dirty things about how I'd love it, beg for more… He tried to kiss me. I kneed him in the, you know." Her cheeks flushed. "He howled, and let go of me, and I managed to get out of the door. When he started yelling I was going to pay for what I'd done, I ran down the hall, into the living room."

She went silent.

"Danny?"

"That's when I heard the others laughing, and Vic asked if it was his turn, grabbing his crotch. Other guys chimed in, saying something about circling me and doing dirty stuff. I don't— I just—" She shook her head. "The looks on their faces wasn't good. I didn't know what to do, so I took off."

The anger inside of him flared to new heights by the way they'd treated her.

Attempting to locate a tiny slice of calm, Gage glowered at the group around him. "You guys saw how upset Danny was, but instead of helping her, you made rude comments, sexual threats, and laughed at her. You all sat back and watched her leave here during a rainstorm in the dark. She was walking into town, completely drenched. What if something had happened to her out there?"

Just saying the words made a shudder roll along his frame.

"Since when did we become the designated babysitters of the perfect princess?" Courtney sneered.

"Since when did you lose your decency?" he snapped back.

Disgust twisted her face. "What Danica does or doesn't do, isn't *my* problem."

"So, if that were your little sister, you'd be fine with what happened?" Gage watched her, seeing her arrogance fall, pink lips turning down.

"And how about you, Vic? Would you want Cornelia here with Jordan?" He pointed to the heap on the floor who had started to moan.

"And you, Stephens? You wouldn't have a problem with a bunch of guys making nasty threats to Amy?"

"Did you kill him?" Jerry Collin's asked, eyes wide.

"He's still breathing." Gage left them to their mutterings before he started in on another beatdown, mumbling under his breath, "Unfortunately" as he went out the wide-open door, the night welcoming him back with a *crack* of lightning illuminating the sky.

Chapter One

"THANKS FOR WATCHING the babies," Danica said.

"I love spending time with them," Mom assured her, bouncing Ari, then cooing, "Isn't that right, baby-girl? Oh, you're so pretty."

Arianna grinned and blew spit bubbles.

Smiling at her daughter and her mother, she unloaded the two oversized diaper bags.

"Look at those cute little lips and that lovely pink bow in your curly blonde hair. Grandma loves you, cutie pie. Yes, I do. I really, really do."

Bending down to tug out a couple of toys, Danica felt the burn. At least she could say all the squats, lifting and moving of things—high chairs, stroller, playpen and such—did wonders for her midsection, biceps and leg muscles. Not to mention all the laps she'd done that week, pushing her babies in their double stroller when they didn't want to sleep.

It was like weight training and cardio, rolled up into one excellent daily busy-mommy workout.

"Do you hear that?" her father asked Aaron, who he hoisted up in the air, giving him a smile when her son broke out into a fit of giggles. "You don't need baby talk, do you?" Up and down, up and down, her father lifted him, then flew him around the living room, making silly humming sounds before the "V-r-o-o-m" started.

Danica shook her head, "Is Aaron a car or a plane?"

"We're a Transformer," Dad said, completely serious. "Optimus Prime. No wait, I don't think he can fly."

"Okay, well." She grinned. "I'll leave you guys to your playing. If you need anything—"

"We won't, dear. We've got this." Her mother's thin, smiling face turned to her granddaughter. "Don't we, Ari? That's right. Your grandparents are the best."

Arianna started giggling and waving her chubby fist.

"See," Mom said. "Ari agrees."

After placing her daughter's favorite Lucy the Lamb doll into the playpen, then Aaron's giraffe, Danica went over, leaned down, and kissed her little girl on the forehead. Then she placed a quick peck on her mother's soft cheek, before going over to her Dad and son, doing the same. "All right. I'm going to go."

Her parents didn't bother to look her way, just said in harmony, "See you later."

Running a straightening palm down the bell of her hip, Danny left her family behind, and stepped out the front door, melancholy striking her even though it was a beautiful day. With a lift of chin, the sun hit her face. But instead of lingering in the warmth, Danica plucked the Dolce & Gabbana's off the top of her head, putting the sunglasses in place.

As she stepped onto the sidewalk, yellowing leaves floated down in front of her, and the *hum* of a lawnmower, or maybe a leaf blower, started in the distance.

She glanced across the familiar street and waved at Mr. Groves, who was sitting on his front porch in his rocking chair, then shifted her attention to the mailman slipping a handful of envelopes into the box next door.

"Hey, Danny!"

"Hi, Joe!"

"Beautiful day, isn't it?" The wrinkled skin of his weathered face lifted when he grinned.

"Sure is."

He put his hand above his eyes, creating a visor. "I bet those babies of yours are getting big."

"They are."

"How old are they now?" Joe asked.

"Ten months."

"I remember when Kylie was that age. Such a handful."

"A handful times two," Danica said.

"I bet." He bobbed his head. "Well, I'd better get on with my route. You have a great one, and it was good seeing you, dearie."

"You, too," she said, then sighed.

Everything was different, but the same, and for some reason, the consistency of Cedar Point that used to comfort her had become a mighty stranger—aloof and eluding.

Trying to snap out of whatever was bothering her, she slipped behind the wheel of her Escalade, started it up and pulled away, deciding to turn left instead of right when she came to a stop at the sign. Passing house after house on Downy Street, she slowed when she came to the little bungalow with its blue-green paint, and flower pots staggered up the sides of the steps that led to the wooden front door with its inlaid stained glass.

She frowned, working her bottom lip over with her teeth.

Why she drove by the old Willis place was another mystery. Not only because she knew she had no reason to be there, but because *he* wouldn't be there.

What are you searching for? That was the million-dollar question, one she shouldn't be asking herself.

With a shake of her head, Danica looked away, gripped the wheel, pressed the gas pedal, and left her stupidity, as well as the house, behind.

Chapter Two

Before

DANICA SHUT HER locker door—the rattle of metal hitting metal blending into the laughter of her best friend. "I told Phillip, no. Can you believe he asked me to the homecoming dance? As if."

"Maybe you should have said, yes, J.J."

"Are you kidding me?" Jillian flipped her long, strawberry blonde hair over her shoulder. "Why would I do that?"

"He is a nice guy," Danica said.

"Now, maybe. But he used to wad up paper and spitball me with that nasty straw he kept in his pocket."

"When we were in the first grade. But…" Danica's gaze slipped past her best friend.

"But?"

"*Hmm*?"

"Uh, hello? Earth to Danny."

Danica frowned.

"You're not even paying attention to our conversation."

"I am," she said absently, trying to decide why Gage was showing interest in Britney. She was stick-thin with dull-brown hair, brows that needed a good tweezing, and plain, unremarkable features.

J.J. turned in the direction Danica was staring. "No, you're busy watching Gage flirt with Britney Willis."

"You think he's flirting?"

"Duh? The moment Jenny left for college, he started flirting with everyone."

Yeah, she thought it was strange since Gage and Jenny Lansing never 'officially' dated, but the beautiful, older girl with the long sable hair who looked like a cross between Catherine Zeta Jones and Shania Twain could crook her finger, and he would go running. But once she left, Danica had hoped he'd finally notice her. And sometimes he did. Or she'd thought so.

"Have you seen how he smiles at the new Home Ec teacher, Ms. Anderson?" J.J. asked. "She's got to be, what?—thirty-something?"

Danica tore her attention away from the laughing pair and over to her bestie. "Does he flirt with you?"

Her friend's perfectly arched brows pulled together. "Well, no, but still."

"I'm going to go ask him for a ride home," she said, "Breck and Mason are a no go, and he should have some time before football practice starts. Do you want to come with me?"

"Can't. I'm going with my sister. We're heading over to our aunts on an intervention."

"Intervention?"

"She broke up with Morris, again."

"Oh. I'm sorry."

"Yeah, but a few cartons of Ben and Jerry's will cheer her up."

Danica grinned. "Amazing how that works."

"Isn't it?"

"All right. I'll call you later."

"Later, Danny-D," J.J. said, giving her a quick hug, then spun around, Phillip watching her friend go, looking like someone kicked his puppy.

Poor guy.

Taking a deep breath then straightening her shoulders, Danica made her way over to where Gage and Britney were still talking by his locker.

"Oh, stop it," Britney said, play-slapping his muscled arm and batting her stubby lashes.

"Hey," Danica greeted them as she walked up.

"Hi." Gage gave her that slow, crooked grin of his, making her heart miss a beat.

"Oh, hi, Danny." Britney had a saccharine smile.

"Hi." Shifting her attention back to Gage, she asked, "Do you think you could give me a quick ride home today?"

"Sure."

"Oh, could you please give me a ride, too," Britney whined.

He nodded. "I'll take you both."

"That would be great, Gage." Danica attempted to be upbeat, but the thought of a third wheel didn't make her happy.

"Yeah," Britney said. "Super!"

"Well"—he shoved his hand into the front pocket of his Levi's—"let's roll."

A few minutes later, they were on their way to Britney's house, and Danica attempted not to grin, but a slight smile might have appeared. Soon, she would be alone with Gage, without the irritation of the other girl who'd been blathering on about her porcelain cat collection, and she could sit in the passenger's seat instead of the back like an afterthought.

"Okay, Brit," Gage said, pulling into the driveway of the Willis' place. "I'll catch you later."

"Right." Britney didn't sound as syrupy as before. "Thanks for the ride."

"Welcome." Gage changed the station on the radio, not giving her another glance. And the fact he wasn't paying attention to the sophomore sent a tendril of satisfaction through Danica.

Britney huffed a breath and got out, not quite slamming the door closed, then stomped toward the front door of her house with all the grace of a rampaging rhino suffering from malnutrition.

Turning to look at her, Gage jerked his head. "Get up here."

He didn't have to tell her twice; Danica wasted no time scurrying over the seat. It wasn't very dignified, but hey, she was in the passenger's spot, next to him.

"I love this," she said, doing a little bounce, then reached and turned the knob to increase the volume, singing along with Jewel's soulful voice about "Foolish Games."

She lost herself in the words of the song, then realized her eyes were closed, so she opened them.

Gage was watching her with an expression on his face—*Wistful?* No, that wasn't quite right. *Yearning?* Danica didn't think that was it either. Perhaps… *Regret?*

Aah! She wasn't sure. She couldn't read him.

His silver eyes glittered, making her fumble, but she recovered and finished.

He placed his hand on her left denim-clad knee.

She sucked in a breath, both from the buzz shooting up her leg and the cut, swollen condition of his knuckles. Carefully, Danica brushed her fingertips over the damage there. "So, the rumors are true. You're the one who busted up Jordan's face?"

"Yes."

She glanced at him. "Why did you do that?"

"No one has the right to hurt you, Danny. Let alone get away with it."

"You didn't fully answer me."

Gage shook his head.

"What is it?"

"Nothing."

"You're not going to tell me, are you?"

"You have a great voice," he said, completely changing the subject, making her swallow hard as he palmed her warm cheek—thumb swiping back and forth on her cheekbone. "So pretty."

Every single part of her wanted to nuzzle into his hand, but she looked at him, not sure what to say, not totally understanding him, but hoping for—

Tap, tap, tap.

The moment broke, making Danica realize they were still in the Willis' driveway, and Britney stood outside Gage's window.

Straightening, he turned away to roll the glass down. "Yeah?"

"Did I leave my bag?"

"Don't know." He glanced over at her, then at the floorboard. "Looks like it. Danny, can you grab that?"

She bent and picked up the small quilted purse, handing it over to Gage, who passed it on.

"Thanks," Britney said.

"No problem."

The girl didn't move.

"Well," he said, "we better go."

"Okay." Britney took a step away.

He twisted to look behind him, checked the rearview and driver's side mirror, and when he was sure the coast was clear, Gage backed up.

It was quiet for the rest of the ride, Danny wondering how to get the tender side of Gage back with her, but she wasn't sure how to do it. Those moments, when he'd see her not as too young and someone in need of protecting, were few and far between, but when it happened, they were precious.

When he pulled his GTO in front of her house, she asked, "You want to come in?"

"Better not," he said. "I'm already late for practice."

"Oh, I'm sorry. I didn't mean to make you late."

"It's okay, Danny. I'm sure I'll only have to do wind sprints until I can't feel my legs."

Her eyes went wide. "Are you serious?"

"Naw"—he shook his head with a little grin—"don't worry about it."

She clambered out, then turned around to peek inside. "Gage?"

"*Hmm*?"

"Thank you."

He nodded, the light streaming in the windshield highlighting part of his sculptured face, making her want to stay right there and do nothing but look at him—the length of his black lashes, the perfect shape of his nose, that masculine line of his jaw…

Gage squeezed the steering wheel, and her gaze went to the cords of his forearm dancing before she managed, "Bye" and closed the door.

Cemented in place, Danica watched him go with a wave of her fingers, a longing she couldn't rid herself of proving yet again to be her constant companion.

Chapter Three

TIRED. THAT ONE word summed things up nicely. Gage might be thirty-nine, but sometimes he felt like a crotchety old man, and everything about his life generally bothered him. In some ways, he'd become anesthetized to the constant struggle to keep on keeping on. But this current feeling of exhaustion had changed into something different. Something he couldn't quite pin down.

Scrubbing his face with his palm, he sighed, then glanced around the six by eight-foot office with its mint-green walls and all the awards hanging in a symmetrical row. They were neatly encased within walnut frames, highlighting his glory days at Quantico. With a rub to his forehead, his gaze bounced to the bookshelf. Taking precedence in the middle was the reason for receiving salutations and adoration, a real-life hero, they called him. *Ha! That's laughable.* Hero's got the bad guy *and* saved the day, right? But that inconspicuous twisted metal shard had been embedded into his lower spine—the proof he wasn't one, reminding him daily why he no longer worked for the FBI. Due to one piece of shrapnel, Gage had undergone several surgeries, months of physical therapy, and specialized rehab.

I should consider myself lucky, he thought. Not only did he rid himself of a wheelchair, he could walk and maneuver almost as good as before the event, but Field Agent Rothman, his friend, and long-time co-worker in the bureau, died in the blast Gage survived.

He turned in his swivel chair, then glanced out his one small window. Deloris Kramer, the town's biggest gossip, and president of the ladies auxiliary was strolling along the sidewalk, short graying hair styled like *Leave it to Beaver's* mom, signature pearls around her neck with that nose of hers up in the air.

He yanked back the cuff of his long-sleeved black uniform and glanced at the time on his watch. *Straight up noon.*

Deloris would be off to complete her duties at the auxiliary, joining her much younger vice president, the stunningly beautiful and vibrant, Danica Lorry-Harding.

"*Mmm…*" he hummed under his breath and closed his eyes.

The last time Danny stood in his office, smelling of cinnamon-spiced apples and sin, talking to him about the annual fundraiser for the fourth of July and asking if the police department would join with the fire department, had been five months ago. She assured him, with the two departments help, they could raise twice as much money, allowing Cedar Point to put on a more prominent fireworks display.

"Almost two-hundred years as a town is a huge reason to celebrate," she'd said, ending the speech then adding her thousand-watt smile.

Pretending to give her proposal some serious thought, which he did to keep her in his office a bit longer, he finally sighed, acting as though he'd caved. However, to steal a quote from *Jerry Maguire,* Danica "had him at hello." Gage would do anything she'd asked, but as usual, he played it cool, figuring the woman didn't need to know the power she held over him.

"Gawonii?"

Only two people used his given name. His mother when she was upset with him, and from time to time, Danny when they were alone. He'd asked her once why she didn't just call him Gage like everyone else did, and she shrugged. But as it did when they were kids, that sweet, sing-song voice made his heart pick up the pace.

Shifting his attention to the door, he grinned, then sobered.

"Danica." Gage took her in, marveling. He'd just been thinking about her, and there she was, in the flesh. "You look"—*ticked off, livid, gorgeous*—"lovely," he said. "What brings you in today?"

"Sorry," said officer Davis, appearing winded and disgruntled as he stepped inside. "Dixie was on the phone, and I told her you were busy, but she breezed on down the hall, ignoring me."

Gage held up a hand. "It's fine. I always have time for old friends."

Once the officer left, he gave Danny his undivided attention, and doing so wasn't any hardship.

"Wendell Gibbs," she said, putting a hand on her curvaceous hip.

Gage raised a brow. "What about him?"

"He came stumbling out from the bar, sloppy drunk, stopping to relieve himself on the shrubbery."

"Sounds plausible."

"You need to do something about him. What if I had the babies with me today?" Her blue, blue eyes sparkled. Snapped. Narrowed. "What kind of a man whips out his private parts in the middle of town and does that?" Danny shook her head, making some of the golden strands of hair that had escaped the elaborate twist caress her overheated cheeks.

And that mouth. Oh, Gage wanted to taste that mouth of hers. Press past those straight white teeth and spear her with his tongue. Feel the velveteen softness of her flesh twining with his. He'd kiss and caress her until she lost all her sensibilities and moaned his name. Until she begged—

She's married, you jerk!

"Hello?" she said, snapping her French tipped fingers, "are you listening to me?"

"Every word," he assured, hoping he hadn't been staring at her cleavage, the plump, perfect mounds he—

"Well?" Danny asked, still peeved.

Gage locked his eyes on hers. "I'll make sure to speak with him. Give him a warning."

Her lovely glossed-pink lips parted. "That's it?"

"What would you like me to do?"

"I-well-I'm…" Danny tossed her hand up. "I don't know, but something!"

He smiled. He couldn't help it. Fuming mad or not, she was phenomenal. "I will make sure he understands his actions won't be tolerated, and if I get another complaint, he'll be spending his sober up time behind bars instead of in front of one. All right?"

"I suppose," she said, some of her fire dying down.

"Are you on your way to the auxiliary?" he inquired, knowing the answer.

Danica nodded, her gaze shooting up to where the too loud ticking clock on the wall *used* to be. "What time is it?"

Gage glanced at his blessedly silent watch. "Almost ten after."

"Great. I'm going to be late."

The woman spun for the door, giving him a fantastic view of her backside covered in that tight, tan, was it called a pencil skirt? Did it even matter? Whatever it was called, he liked it. But, knowing Danny, tan was probably the wrong word choice as well. It was likely something more along the lines of almond cream or pale fawn.

Okay. The fact he was stuck on the particulars of her clothing was just weird.

Maybe I've lost my mind?

It was a valid question.

His gaze dropped lower.

Oh, hello there. Those calf muscles were popping, taking his impure thoughts on another journey.

Whoever invented high heels should get a gold star, or at the very least, a heartfelt 'thank you' with a congratulatory slap on the back.

"It was nice seeing you!" Gage bellowed as she hurried out.

"You too!" came her response.

Taking a deep breath, he glanced down, then frowned. He didn't need to be lusting in his office about a woman who he couldn't have. And he sure didn't need to be turned on while at the police station. But that religious, angel-faced blonde with those Kim Kardashian curves just did it for him.

Always had.

"Oh, hey!" Danica popped her head back in. "Don't be late tomorrow. We have the rehearsal at six."

"I'll be there."

"Okay. See you then."

Before he could respond, she was gone.

Chapter Four

Before

HE SAW HER the moment he stepped out of his car, standing there by the batting cage in, Lord help him, Daisy Duke's—the shimmering rays of the sun finding a home in the blonde hair piled on top of her head in casual disarray.

Unbidden, his gaze lowered to her mile-long legs.

Gage almost groaned, wondering why she wanted to torture him, but knowing she didn't have a clue she was.

"You're late." Danny huffed, crossing her thin arms, pushing those bountiful breasts up, creating perfect creamy-white cleavage within the V-neck of her faded blue t-shirt. Something Gage shouldn't notice, but boy did he.

Danica Lorry had been an early bloomer, her body making her appear older. When she was twelve, she started drawing the attention of the opposite sex, even grown men would watch her. Mr. Lorry, her father, took Gage aside one day and said, *"Son. I need you to keep an eye on Danny for me. Make sure she doesn't run into any trouble. Too many male eyes are on her lately, and it will only get worse, I'm afraid. Do you think you could do that for me?"*

His response had been immediate; he didn't need to think about it. *"Yes, sir, Mr. Lorry, sir. I'll keep her safe. I promise."* He'd already been unofficially watching out for her anyway, but as the years passed, things changed. He started to 'look,' and it was troubling. Gage couldn't break a promise and become the very thing Mr. Lorry wanted to protect his daughter from. So even though she was a freshman now, still too young to be lusting over, he waged daily war with himself because he couldn't ignore his attraction to her.

But you're going to try. Gage adjusted the strap of the equipment bag on his shoulder, making sure to keep his focus on Danny's beautiful face as he strode toward her. "Sorry, but I'm here now. So, let's do this thing."

He opened the door to the fenced fortress and allowed her to step inside first, closing them in and putting the bag down behind her.

"Are you sure this is going to help?" she asked.

"Well, look at it this way. The practice couldn't hurt."

"I'm just not very athletic." Danny shifted her weight and bit her lush bottom lip.

The sight had him unpacking the bats, giving him something to do other than thinking about nibbling that lip for her. "You're a dancer."

Get a grip, he told himself, tugging out a helmet.

"That's different."

"Here," he said, "you need to put this on."

A frown creased her brow as she glanced at his proffered hand. "That is totally ugly."

"It's not a fashion show."

"Yeah, but—"

"Nope. This will help protect you." Gage waved the helmet at her. "The balls come out of that pitching machine at a good speed."

"All right." Danny blew out a breath and took the black helmet, then put it on. "This isn't going to work." With a tug, she pulled it back off then released her hair.

In reality, it took seconds, but in his mind's eye, everything slowed down into a frame by frame shot. Golden silk falling around her face. The way it fluttered in the breeze, caressing her shoulders, the ends brushing across her chest. That subsequent shake of her head, turning everything into one of those shampoo commercials, highlighting long, lustrous hair before she combed her fingers through the strands.

Okay, moron. You need to snap out of it. "Good?" he asked, once her helmet was where it should be.

"I guess."

He picked up a bat and handed it over. "How does this feel?"

"I don't know. It's a bat, how should it feel?"

"Too light? Too heavy?"

"It's fine," she said, rolling her baby-blues.

That was probably the best he was going to get, so he stepped closer. "You need to hold your hands like this." He took the bat and demonstrated before he gave it back. "Now, you do it."

She did, but it wasn't quite right, so he helped her adjust her grip, then gave up and stepped behind her, way too close.

Danny was tall, but not as tall as his six-foot-two frame, so she fit into the bow of his body with the curve of hers just right.

"You want to relax your stance some." He adjusted her hips, wanting to keep his hands there, but moved, putting them over hers. "Keep your attention on the ball at all times, and swing like this."

He helped her through the move, then closed his eyes, breathing her in—sweet cinnamon-spice with a splash of vanilla, and a dash of sunshine.

"Good," he encouraged. "One more time."

With him guiding her, his mouth came closer to her ear, voice lowering. "Make sure you follow through. That's right. Nice and smooth."

"Gawonii?" Her tone was soft.

"Yeah?"

"I think I've got it now."

With parts of his body intimately touching parts of hers that shouldn't, he snapped back to his senses, let her go, and moved away. "Okay. Let's hit some baseballs."

Going over and adjusting the speed on the machine and doing all the things he needed to do, Gage finally glanced back at Danny with her pink cheeks, watching him. "Get in your stance and keep your eyes on the ball."

"Right," she said.

She had done a pretty good job with the position of her hands on the bat.

"Ready?"

"Yeah!"

"Here we go." Gage turned on the pitching machine, then almost had a heart attack when she stepped into the path of the ball.

"Move back!" he yelled.

She dropped the bat like a hot potato, then she went down, squatting, covering her head—the ball whizzing overtop her.

After turning off the machine, he jogged over and bent beside her. "You okay?"

She peeked up at him. "Yeah. But that thing is a death machine."

He smiled and gave her a hand which she took.

Helping her up, he said, "Maybe I need to pitch."

"No. I'm going to do this." Her pointed chin came up as her hand went to her hip. "And the next time the youth group plays, I'll hit one out of the park. You'll see."

After six more heart-stopping frights, Danica finally connected the bat with the ball, allowing Gage to settle down and not hover, afraid she was going to end up in the E.R.

By pitch ten, her movements were much more fluid.

"Hey, look," she said, completely taking her attention away from what she was doing. "It's a robin. Isn't it prett—"

"Danny!" he yelled, tossing himself in front of a speeding bullet.

She screamed, helmet flying off her head when he grabbed her.

The ball slammed into his side.

His "*Ompf…*" of pain took his breath.

"Gage?"

He placed a palm over the ache as if that would help.

"Gage? Are you hurt?"

Panic riddled Danny's voice, her eyes wide as she gripped his biceps, nails biting into his flesh.

"Talk to me," she said, getting louder.

"Give me a minute," he managed.

"Did you get hit?"

"Yeah."

"Let me see."

"I'm fine, Danny."

"I'll be the judge of that." She touched the hand he'd positioned over his throbbing right side.

"Be careful."

"I will, but move your hand."

When he did, Danny lifted his shirt, then sucked in a breath. "Oh…" Gentle fingertips skimmed along his ribs, under his arm. The feather-light softness of her touch made the ache disappear and a chill of pleasure to take its place until she stopped.

"Why did you do that?" Her question came out in a mix of breathy concern.

"I told you not to take your eye off the ball."

"I know. I'm sorry. My stupidity hurt you."

"I'll be okay."

Her gaze went up to his face. "You never answered me. Why?"

"I didn't want you to get hit. Better me than you."

"Gage," she whispered, fisting his t-shirt, then placed her forehead on his chest. "Getting hurt should have been my consequence, not yours."

"Is everything okay here?" came the gruff voice of coach Ames. "I was doing some paperwork in my office and heard someone screaming bloody murder."

"Gage got hit by a ball," Danny offered, straightening up and stepping back, her warmth leaving him.

Coach came into the batting cage, went over to the pitching machine that was still tossing out balls, shut it off, and strode over to them. "Where did the ball strike you, son?"

"My side." Gage lifted his shirt to show the man.

"It's already leaving a bruise. You think you broke a rib?"

"Maybe."

"It's broken?" Danny asked, clearly horrified.

Gage shrugged, and the doing sent another spike of pain through him.

"We better go get that checked," said the coach.

"I'll have my dad take a look." Gage dropped the material of his shirt, the cotton slipping along his skin even irritated him.

"Take a deep breath for me."

He did.

"Does that hurt?"

"Not too bad," he lied.

"Well, let's hope you don't have a break, but regardless, you're going to be sore, so make sure you ice it, and get some rest. I'll call Doctor Harrison and see if he thinks you'll be able to play in next Friday's game."

"All right, coach."

"You need me to take you home?"

"Naw. I can drive."

The man gave him the squinty-eye of suspicion. "Are you sure?"

"Yeah, coach. I'm good."

"I'll make sure he is." Danny smiled up at him then over at coach. "And that he follows his dad's orders."

"All right. But no more weekend batting practice for you two. Got me?"

"Got you," Gage said as Danica nodded.

Chapter Five

"CHIEF?" DIXIE'S SOUTHERN drawl came over the intercom. "Your mother is on the line to remind you about lunch."

He was sure this latest invite was his mother's way of setting him up on yet another blind 'look who I brought with me' date. Mom wanted him settled, reminding him every chance she got, and he didn't have the heart to crush her dreams.

"You're so handsome, intelligent, a hero. Women love you, son. I don't understand why you don't make more of an effort," his mother would say, patting his cheek.

Leaning forward, he pressed the intercom button. "I'm trying to finish something up. Will you let her know I won't forget?"

"Will do."

For an intelligent woman, Gage marveled at his mother's naiveté, because for the most part, those well-educated women who held fancy degrees, alumni of places like Harvard and Brown she introduced him to, became confused. One look at his high cheekbones, caramel macchiato skin with a dollop of cream (Danny's words, not his) and his pitch-black hair, gave away his mixed Native American heritage, but then they would stare at the enigma when they saw his liquid-silver eyes. His biological mother had been Cherokee, which explained his more exotic features, his father some no-account red-neck who added to the Caucasian side of the gene pool. Where his unique eyes came from, he didn't know.

Gage blew out an irritated breath. He'd lost count of how many times he explained his two white parents, Ronald Sean Harrison, Cedar Point's local and only M.D. and his adoring wife, the retired Honorable Judge Debra Ann Harrison to those who didn't know him. And the women his mom brought home were oblivious until the "I was adopted as a baby" talk took place. But even if they decided they were 'interested,' it wasn't anything more than the physical. One woman had said once they were alone, "I bet you're a *savage* in bed."

Yeah. Wasn't that a great reference to his biological mother's people.

And if they did want something more than a quick tumble, they tended to bore him to tears. Those dates became operatic music and snooty cocktail parties, where they would greet their other female friends with "Darling" doing those cheek-to-cheek air kisses and talking about Botox or their latest trip to the Caymans.

"Oh, Chief?"

"Yeah?"

"Lee called in. He said someone spray-painted graffiti on the back of the store, and he's blaming it on those Parker kids."

"Let me guess. He wants Stanley to take the report?"

"Yep."

"I'll take care of it."

"All right."

Gage stood and adjusted the gun in his hip holster. *Lee Warner and the rest of his merry men of bigots can kiss my—*

"Chief?"

He bent and pressed the button on the com. "Yes, Dixie?"

"Don't forget, I'm leaving at two today. I'm helping out with Danica's adorable twins so she can get ready. I might not be here when you get back."

"Got it."

Gage headed for the SUV, happy his office was close to the back of the building, near the rear exit. He could come and go without anyone the wiser, and when he finished up at the Food Barn, then went to grab a bite to eat with Mom, he was hoping to call it a day. After all, he had an important date with a tuxedo.

Stepping outside, he took in a deep breath. Autumn had arrived, and with it, the hubbub of the local Farmers Market drifted his way, along with the scent of roasting corn.

With the breeze rustling through the turning leaves of the trees and pinpricks of sun casting dancing patterns by his feet, he smiled, unlocked his door, and slipped behind the wheel.

Suddenly, he had the overwhelming urge to turn on his siren and flashing lights, then speed to the grocery store. Perhaps he'd buy a pack of gum and flirt with Lee's pretty brown-eyed daughter before he took the vandalism report.

Shawna will giggle and flutter her lashes, making the hateful old guy squirm.

Yep, even if everything else stunk, some days, it was good to be Chief.

"Everyone," the D.J. announced from his position behind the mic on the stage, "May I present, Mr. and Mrs. Mason Miller!"

As the crowd clapped and cheered, Danica's heart swelled with emotion. Her beautiful sister and the man she loved took the dance floor, which was the basketball court in the high school gymnasium since it was the only place big enough to accommodate all their guests for the wedding reception.

The two of them had talked about eloping, doing a quickie ceremony in Vegas, but Mom and Dad said everyone in town would be disappointed if they didn't 'do it right,' and Breck agreed, though it took a few days for Mase to cave. Her sister even gave Danica enough time to get back to her 'before giving birth' body. God bless her.

The church overflowed with large arrangements of cream and the palest of pink roses, dozens of flickering candles, tulle and silky ribbon. It had been a beautiful evening event, and jam-packed, turning into standing room only for some of the guests as the two of them exchanged their vows, "To have and to hold, from this day forward." And when Breckin said, "I do," Danica's gaze swung to the best man, who glanced back at her.

Perfect timing.

It was wrong; she knew it. Her heart shouldn't flutter. She was a married woman with two wonderful babies.

Yes, her life was full. She had a beautiful family, a lovely home, and anything she could ever ask for, given by a man who'd gift-wrap the world for her if he could. But even with her handsome husband looking on from the crowd, and regardless of where they were, the entire universe seemed to fade away as she stared into Gage's eyes.

He was always able to do that, make everything around her disappear when he looked at her. And for a moment, however brief, he *saw* her. Then the mask came down, and he stared forward, the magic that couldn't be one-sided, broken.

He'd perfected that, too—the ability to shatter her heart, and like an idiot, she would fall right back into the same old loop, letting him.

Getting her mind back on the celebration, Breckin and Mason were holding each other as they swayed to Alicia Key's singing, "That's When I Knew." They looked at one another with abiding love and a sizzling heat so visible a blind man could have seen it.

When Mason whispered something in Breck's ear, then gently placed his lips on hers, Danica put her hand to her mouth, fighting back the happy tears.

This was a long time coming, but the two of them were finally where they needed to be.

"Danica?" Marcus called, striding to her with a drink in hand, which he offered, and she took. "I'm sorry, honey, but I have to head out to the hospital. Emergency heart surgery."

Her face fell. "Oh, no. We haven't even danced yet."

Bending to place a kiss to her cheek, he said, "I'll make it up to you later."

Brushing her fingertips down his lapel, she sighed. "You better."

Danica knew marrying a sought-after surgeon would have its challenges, like all the time he spent away, but lately, he was gone more than he was home.

Marcus winked, and she couldn't help it, she grinned. "Make sure to thank Dixie for taking care of the twins during this shindig, and have your Dad take you all home."

"I will," she said, "but maybe we should start taking two cars to things since it seems we can't do anything anymore without the interruption of the hospital calling."

A scowl formed on his brow. "I can't help this, Danny, so don't give me grief."

"I'm not trying to."

His whiskey-colored eyes sparked. "But yet, you are."

"I'm sorry," she said, not wanting to upset him.

"It's all right, just stop pouting, okay?" Marcus scrubbed his jaw with his fingers.

She nodded and attempted to act like the thirty-seven-year-old grown up she was.

"Thank you." He placed a quick peck on her forehead. "Don't wait up. I'll be late with this one."

As he turned to go, she stopped him with a hand on his tense arm. "I love you."

He glanced back and smiled, then Marcus weaved his way into the sea of people, leaving her standing there alone—her prior good mood taking a nosedive.

He didn't even take the time to say, I love you, too.

"You're looking as handsome as ever, Gage," Krystin Jennings Gunthery/Salinger, now Porter said, batting her feathery lashes.

"Uh…thanks." Gage lifted his glass of punch and took a sip.

"Black is your color." She laughed. "You should wear a tux more often."

"No real need for that," he said, gaze darting around the gym, catching his waving mother. "If you will excuse me, Mom is summoning."

"Oh, okay. Well, it was *great* seeing you."

Krystin's little sex-kitten voice might have been a draw to other men, but it made him itch like he had a bad case of the hives.

"Yeah. Nice seeing you, too," he lied, pushing back the urge to scratch his neck, leaving the maneater and making a beeline for freedom, only to stop when he saw Danny in a less populated corner of the gym.

Since she was the maid of honor and he the best man, the two of them had walked arm and arm down the center aisle of the church. He had to admit; it was hard to keep his eyes off her.

It still was.

His gaze meandered over her in that light, blush-pink dress, fitted lace bodice, the long, chiffon skirt flowing but cut with a slit showing off her shapely leg—those sparkling, peep-toe spiked heels.

Her dress was a little bit different than the other brides' maids, making her stand out, however, her garment would have been eye-catching on any woman, he suspected. But on her, the formal attire showcased every single dangerous curve she possessed. And while she'd put on what his mother called a pashmina, covering up some, she was elegantly gorgeous.

With a pinched brow, Gage knew something wasn't right. Danica was the life of the party. A social butterfly. *So, why is she by herself?*

"Hi, Chief Harrison, would you like a new drink?" Jake and Maggie's oldest daughter, Alli, asked, always so polite.

"Oh…" He glanced at the tumbler then at her. "No. I'm good. But would you mind getting rid of this for me?"

"Happy to." She snagged the empty glass with a smile.

"And tell Berta those little bacon-wrapped hors d'oeuvres you served were fantastic."

Breckin and Mason had asked Berta, the owner of The Snack Shack for as long as he could remember, to cater their big event. And of course she'd jumped at the chance, closing down the restaurant for the day, bringing all her staff as servers.

"Will do."

"Thanks, Alli," he said, then started in a new direction.

Keeping his attention on Danica, he wondered where her husband was, though the thought wasn't anything new. Marcus had been at the wedding, but the last time he'd seen the two together was when Breckin threw Danny a baby shower months ago. Other than that, he was like a ghost. The man wasn't even around when he and Mason went to visit her in the hospital after having twins, for cripes sake. Not to mention being a no-show at other family get-together's Mase had invited him to, and all of the pre-wedding activities like the rehearsal dinner, and such.

It seemed the hotshot surgeon was M.I.A. quite a bit, or at least it appeared that way to him.

"Hey there," he said, coming to her side. "What are you doing over here all by your lonesome?"

"Feeling sorry for myself, I suppose."

"Why? What's going on?"

"Marcus was called away again." She glanced up, sucker-punching him with those sad eyes. "But I should be used to it by now."

Gage wasn't sure what to do. He wanted to cheer her up. To pull her into his arms. He wanted… "I hear dancing is good for the soul. Do you want to?"

"Dance?"

"Yeah."

His gaze dropped to her lush lips as she gave him a slow, sleepy smile. "Really?"

"Really." He placed his palm on her lower back. "Come on."

"Danny-girl!"

The familiar scratchy voice made him stiffen.

"Don't you look stunning this evening," Matt said, stepping around them, his smarmy smile in place.

Why had Breck and Mase invited him? Well, maybe they hadn't specifically since the whole town had been extended a general invitation to the reception in the local paper.

Danica didn't give the perv a response, just stepped into Gage's side.

Curling a protective arm around her, he snarled, "Alderman Jordan."

"Chief Harrison," the scumbag returned, then ogled Danny, licking his thin lips, proving he had a death wish.

Reminding himself this was a celebration, he kept himself restrained. "Excuse us." Gage took the object of the man's desire with him.

As if she'd been holding her breath, Danny's body relaxed when they'd joined the others who were dancing. She looked up at him. "Thank you."

Pulling her into his chest, he bobbed his head, willing away the need to turn around, go back and give Jordan a beating he wouldn't forget, though since the man used his position on the town council as a thorn in Gage's side, he doubted Matt had forgotten the first one.

Chapter Six

Before

LIGHTS DIM, BALLOONS floating, music mixing into the chatter around him, Gage didn't know why he'd come to the homecoming dance. It wasn't as if he liked dancing or even had a date. Oh, he could have had one, he just didn't *want* one. Well, he did, but—

"Hey," Phillip Granger greeted, striding up.

"Hi."

Gage and Phillip bumped fists. "The game was a close one tonight, but we pulled it together in the end."

"Yeah, it was too close."

"Sorry you were benched. How are your ribs doing?"

"Better. Another week, and I'll be back on the field."

"I just don't get it," Phillip said, tweaking his stubbled chin between his fingers.

With a frown, Gage asked, "Get what, man?"

"J.J.," he said, taking their conversation in an unexpected direction. "I asked her to this dance, and she said no, she didn't 'do' the dancing thing, but there she is, over there with Danny."

Danny? That perked him up. "Where?"

Phillip pointed.

Gage looked in that direction. Breck and Mase were cuddling on the dance floor, Krystin was with Jerry the jerk, and…"

There she is, looking like an angel in red.

"Girls are complicated," he said, keeping his attention locked on Danica Lorry as she talked animatedly with a group of friends.

"Tell me about it. I've been trying to get Jill's attention forever…"

Phillip was still saying something, but Gage had stopped listening, focused on the guy in the corner who was staring at Danny in a way he didn't like.

"Gotta go," he said abruptly, hearing Granger's, "Uh, okay, dude."

His first thought was to go smash Matt's face in, again, but doing that on school property would cost him, so he directed all his attention and energy into maintaining his temper and getting to Danica.

"Excuse me." Gage tapped her bare shoulder then smiled as she turned, glanced up at him with parted lips, eyes rounded in surprise.

"Hi," she finally said.

"Would you like to dance?"

She blinked, once, twice, three times. "You want to dance with *me*?"

"I do." When he gave her his grin, a pretty blush overtook her cheeks.

"Go on, Danny," Jillian encouraged.

Gage extended his hand.

Danica's gaze went from it to his face, then carefully she slipped her smooth, warm palm into his, the slide of flesh against flesh feeling extraordinary to him. "I'd love to."

He curled his fingers around hers and led them out to the section of the gym used as the dance floor—Mason giving him a lift of head greeting, which he returned.

The song changed, and the D.J. said, "Were going to slow it down with this one."

A second later, "How Do I Live Without You" by Trisha Yearwood started.

"Ready?" he asked, pulling her supple body into him, hoping he didn't step on her feet.

"Yeah." When her palm slipped up his arm, those long lashes lifted.

Lost in the color of Danny's eyes, they started swaying, so any worry he had about flubbing up faded away, thinking of nothing but her.

Chapter Seven

WAS SHE FLOATING on cloud nine? Oh yes. Yes, she was, but Danica figured she needed to put some distance between her and Gage. It was the right thing to do.

When the third song came to an end, she said, "Thanks for getting me away from Matt and for dancing with me, but we should probably call it good."

Then the fourth song since they'd been on the dance floor started, and her heart twisted. It was the first song she'd ever danced to. Well, that wasn't technically correct. Her mom enrolled her in dance classes when she was eight, but that was the first she'd ever danced to with a boy.

"You can't go yet." Gage's sandpaper-smooth voice strummed her like a physical touch. "This is our song."

As Trisha Yearwood sang the question, "How do I get through one night without you?" her shoulders relaxed, and she melted back into the warmth of Gage's big body, a place she felt secure.

His palm slipped along the curve of her back.

"All right. One more dance," Danica conceded, breathing in the scent of him, never sure what brand of cologne he wore—leather, freshwater, and hints of the summer sun, it hadn't changed.

"It's that time," The D.J. said. "Time to toast the bride and groom. Best Man. Maid of Honor, come on up."

Gage placed a claiming hand on Danica's back. Though he didn't have the right to lay claim, he had no intention of moving it as he directed their path to the microphone, then glanced down at her. "Would you like to go first?"

"You go ahead," she said in her sweet voice.

One of Berta's staff came over with a silver serving dish, two sparkling flutes of champagne on display, offering him a glass, then Danica, which they took.

Stepping up to the mic, he smiled. "Hello, everyone. I'm not a public speaker, so I hope I don't mess this up."

"You can do it. Just go for it!" someone, he thought Jake, yelled, a chuckle rolling through the crowd.

"Right. Just go for it," he said, then glanced down at Danny, who was smiling up at him encouragingly. "Well, Mason is like a brother to me, and so it follows Breckin is like a sister. Since back in the day, it has always been Mase and Breck. Breck and Mase. You couldn't think of one without thinking of the other."

Gage shifted his attention to the glowing couple. "Growing up, I remember watching you two, thinking how extraordinary your connection was. How much you both loved each other, and I'll admit, a part of me hoped I would one day find what you two shared. What you still share. You guys are an inspiration."

Mason grinned, and Breckin held her hand to her heart.

"It took us all a while to get here, but tonight everything is exactly right. So, I guess what I'm saying is, I'm honored to be a part of this celebration with you. And I wish you both all the happiness in the world."

"Love you, brother!" Mason shouted.

"Back at you," Gage responded, then turned his attention to the crowd, lifting his flute. "Please join me in raising your glass to the happy couple!"

Arms rose as a collective, "To the happy couple!" rang out, then he and Danica pinged their glasses together before they took a sip of the bubbly.

"That was lovely," Danny whispered as he moved aside so she could take the spotlight, knowing without a doubt, she would shine.

Chapter Eight

Before

CHATTING QUIETLY WITH Mason, they sat in the second row of the large auditorium at the performing arts center with Breckin, Jillian, Danny's grandparents who flew in from Colorado, and Mr. and Mrs. Lorry rounding up the entourage of supporters.

"And now, for our first competitor in the singles jazz category, coming from our very own Vibe Studio here in Seattle, please welcome, Danica Dawn Lorry," the announcer's deep voice rang out from hidden speakers.

The clapping echoed around him, then died down.

Gage sat up when the lights on the stage dimmed some, taking on a blue hue, and the intro to, "I Put A Spell On You," started.

Then, there she was, hips swaying, foot in front of foot strutting down the middle of the stage—the blue/black sequined top she wore adhered to her like a second skin, sparkling.

Wow!

His eyes went wide when she put her hands into her lengthy hair, mussing it up in a sexy tussle with a look on her face that was nothing but pure seduction. She stopped walking, but her body never quit moving, her tight hip-hugging leggings thingy devoid of shine, but it was her bare midriff that snagged his laser-focus next.

When Danny started circling her hips, as if she was spinning an invisible hula-hoop around her waist, Mr. Lorry cleared his throat. "Ahem…I'm not happy about this," he complained in not quite a whisper.

"Hush, Samuel," Mrs. Lorry said, "watch our daughter shine."

Oh, and she did. Popping her chest, shaking her hips, going down into the splits, then rolling into a sitting position, knees up, palms on the floor behind her, body arched.

Holy…

Gage squirmed but didn't pull his eyes from her as she shot a leg up in the air, put it down, then did some type of body wave up to her feet, undulating, then spun across the stage in a mix of ballet and modern dance moves that worked in rhythm with the sultry jazz song.

He'd seen her dance before, having gone with Mase and Breck to some recitals, but what Danny was doing up there was a whole new level of remarkable.

Then came a few wolf whistles when she shook her perfect booty, making him scowl—Mr. Lorry starting in again on his fatherly complaints, Danica's mother smacking him in the arm and telling him to be quiet. He tuned them out. Fire could have consumed the building, and he wouldn't have moved a muscle. Gage was mesmerized by Danica. She was a dichotomy, the innocence of a girl appearing to be a sensual goddess of a woman.

Not sure when she'd last been so ecstatic, Danica gripped her first-place trophy and skipped her way to her smiling mother.

"Ooo…" Mom held her arms out wide, allowing her to step into the embrace. "You were wonderful, baby-girl."

"So fantastic," Breckin said, turning the hug into a three-way stretch of swaying joy.

"Let me in there." Her grandmother wiggled her way between them.

"Me, too," Jillian added, the hug expanding into a huddle. "You rocked it, sister!"

Danica chuckled. "Thanks, you guys."

"I'm so proud of you," Mom said, making her feel as if she could fly.

When she stepped back, she noticed her father's unhappy face as he took off his brown suit coat. "Daddy?"

"I'm going to be talking to your dance instructor." He stepped up and tossed the jacket over her shoulders, making sure he covered her up.

"Oh, stop it, Samuel," her mother admonished, then looked at her. "He won't be doing any such thing."

"Watch me, woman. Our daughter about gave me heart failure with that routine."

Her parents started in, arguing as her gaze shifted over to her grandfather, who's lined face didn't look any too happy either. Then she looked at Gage and Mason. They were doing that thing they do—having an entire silent conversation with their eyes and body language as they stared at each other.

"Guys?"

They looked at her in unison, aqua blue eyes, and stunning silver.

"What did you think?" Biting her lip, she waited for the verdict.

"You were pretty awesome," Mason said, taking hold of Breckin's hand. "Congrats on winning."

Her heart swelled. "Thanks."

She looked at Gage, who didn't have any expression at all as he said, "You did an amazing job, Danny." His was the opinion she wanted to hear the most, so she smiled wide until the, "But, your dad has a valid point. It was a bit risqué for someone your age."

Someone your age.

Just like that, all her buoyancy left—a hole punched into a tire, she went flat.

"Exactly!" Dad patted Gage on the back like a proud father agreeing with a son.

Chapter Nine

BOUNCING A FUSSY boy who was hanging on her hip, listening to his sister start to whimper in solidarity from her highchair, Danica was warming up some leftover green beans from the dinner she had made for Marcus the night before. The dinner he didn't make it to. It had been three days since he'd left her at Breck and Mase's wedding reception, and she'd scarcely seen him at all.

"Ya, ya, na!" Ari screeched, little palms slapping the tray of the chair.

"Hang in there, love," Danica said.

"Ba-ba." Aaron's chin started to quiver, a sure sign of doom.

Putting a little dance move into the bounce, hoping to settle her baby down, she watched the carousel go around inside the microwave, taking the beans with it. Once done, she'd smash them with a fork and put the veggies into the divided plates, making sure not to get them mixed into the soft carrots, or cut up hotdogs. If she did, Ari would scream bloody murder. Baby girl didn't like any of her food to touch.

Aaron arched his back, and kicked his feet. "Aaahna!"

"Hush, now." She took the bowl out of the microwave. "Mommy is hurrying as fast as she can."

All that did was make him cry, big fat tears falling down his angry face.

"Look," she said, opening a kitchen drawer and pulling out some utensils, allowing them to *clatter* because he usually liked the sound. "We're almost done here, then you can eat."

"Na, na!" Ari bellowed, reached and pulled off one of her socks, curling her tiny toes.

"Mommy will take you guys to the park later to play. Wouldn't you like that?"

A disgruntled squawk was her daughter's response.

Trying to make quick work of destroying the texture of the green beans, the double whammy came. Both of Danica's children were bawling and vocalizing at the top of their lungs.

She loved her babies with all her heart; she did, but sometimes she just wanted to run and hide out in a nice, quiet place, maybe do nothing but stare at the wall. A couple of months after the twins were born, there was only one word to describe her. Exhausted. It was bone-deep, a result of the wake-up cries coming over the baby monitor. They arrived at all hours of the night, and she was the only one to get up and handle whatever the crisis was—dirty diaper, needing a bottle, etc. so due to her lack of quality sleep, she had a horrible pounding headache.

"Marcus, my head is killing me," she'd said. *"Could you watch the twins? Maybe read them something from one of the children's books Breckin bought them so I can take a bath?"*

She had been envisioning a long, languorous soak in her jetted tub, but he had paperwork to do, and so came the words she would hear time and time again. *"I can't right now, honey,"* before shutting himself up in his home office.

Just one fifteen-minute bath would be a luxury at this point. Danica even had daydreams about being surrounded in warmth and bubbles but had resorted to taking showers so fast it was if she were on water rations. And alone time in the bathroom to do her other business? Yeah, didn't happen.

"Babe," she'd said, barely keeping her eyes open one evening when he was home. *"I'm so tired."*

Marcus kissed her forehead. *"You need to learn to nap when the twins do."*

Sounded reasonable, right? She'd tried a few times, but the moment she would lie down, she'd need to get back up and take care of one or the other crying kids, sometimes both at the same time. So, naps? What were those?

From day one, Marcus had never so much as changed a diaper, and she wished he'd help with something.

During the summer, she'd come down with a nasty flu and was seriously worried, not knowing how she was going to take care of Aaron and Ari since it felt as though her head had turned into a swollen pumpkin and her throat flamed. When the vomiting started, all she wanted to do was curl up and die. But Breck and Mase, God bless them, came over and took care of things so she could burrow under the covers in her bed.

Danica's days were filled with bottles to wash, mountains of laundry to do, toys to pick up and sanitize, floors to clean, bedding that needed changing, dishes to pop into the dishwasher, then take out and put away, diaper pales to empty, baths for the babies. And don't even get her started on the monumental chore of grocery shopping!

Aaron's high-pitched squeal of discontent pierced her ears, followed by Ari's accompanying shriek.

Danica blew out a breath. "Sometimes, Mommy wishes she could clone herself."

If she were lucky enough to see her husband before going to bed that night, she was finally going to talk with him about hiring someone to help her; sure, he'd be okay with it.

The thought of assistance made her smile.

Putting a wiggling Aaron into his highchair was a task, but she managed to get him seated and the seatbelt on, then went back to get the plates. She knew from experience not to place them on the trays—small hands would grab, lunch would go flying or end up smooshed into their hair, so from her position in front of them, she sat, forked a bite of food, blew on it to make sure it wasn't too hot and started in on the 'event' of feeding her children.

Her babies were having a bad day, which meant she was also. Nothing seemed to settle them down, reading, cartoons, soothing music—their favorite, "Clair De Lune" by Debussy. However, no matter what she had tried to get them to take a nap, it was a no go. So, Danica loaded everything into her Escalade (diaper bags, a few toys, snacks, stroller), put the twins in their car seats, and went for a drive, taking the long way into town, thinking that would surely work.

It didn't. It had become a fuss-fest of tears. She even wanted to cry.

Pushing them in their double stroller around the park was going to be her next attempt at calming Aaron and Ari down, and she prayed they would nod off to dreamland.

Now they were parked, the babies still upset. After telling them to give her a minute, Danica clambered out, went to the back, the power liftgate a blessing, and started fighting with the stroller, trying to get it out of her vehicle. One of the wheels had somehow become entangled into the strap of the backpack full of clean baby clothes she carried in case of disasters, which had happened. Another thing learned the hard way after changing both of them out of the mess of dirty diapers that oozed nasty out of the legs. It was like she needed a biohazard suit; it had been that bad. But she washed them up as best she could in the restroom sink at the Food Barn, and put a fresh change of clothing on them—two new outfits she'd purchased for them that day or else they would have been in nothing but diapers. Of course, that then meant she had to disinfect everything not only before but after the sink bath. So, besides the extra clothes and baby wipes, Lysol wipes were another of the many items Danica always carried. Oh, and hand sanitizer!

Irritated, she couldn't get the wheel untangled, she grumbled—the twins screaming at the tops of their lungs. After two more yanks, she stopped, turned around, slumped her backside down, resting precariously upon the carpeted area, and put her head into her hands.

Danica and Marcus had tried for years to have children. It never happened. He suggested fertility treatments when she was twenty-eight, something she didn't want to do after witnessing all the expense and disappointment J.J. had gone through when those treatments didn't take. So, when she had hit the big three-oh, she gave up on the thought of being a mother and asked God to help her accept it. Eventually, she did, busying herself with multiple committees around town and at church. She would have gone to work, maybe putting her Fine Arts degree to good use and teach dance, perhaps open up her own studio. However, Marcus didn't want her to work, and she tried to make him happy, so she was a stay at home wife.

When they found out she was finally pregnant, her surprised joy had been overshadowed by Marcus' concern.

"You're over thirty-five," he'd said, deep lines overtaking his brow.

"Are you saying I'm too old?"

"At your age, it will be considered a high-risk pregnancy, Danica."

The thing was, she hadn't had a single issue. Everything went smoothly from the beginning to the end. It wasn't until those first few weeks after the birth of her twins, when she was home alone, she couldn't help but wonder if she was in over her head. Though if she was, Danica could do nothing but tread water. And she had done a whole lot of treading.

"Yah-ma, ma!" Ari screamed in harmony with Aaron's, "Gaaa!"

On days like that one, Danica considered maybe she *had* been too old.

I'm sorry, Heavenly Father. I shouldn't be having a pity party. I know you knew what you were doing when you gave me the gift of twins. I just need a miracle today.

Gage was on his way back to the station when he saw Danica's vehicle under one of the large trees that dotted the edge of the park, doing something at the back of it. Well, maybe struggling with something was more like it as the top half of her seemed to be inside, her backside out, wiggling. It was a nice view, especially since she was wearing what appeared to be yoga pants (got to love those), then she stomped her sneakered foot and started wiggling again.

What is she doing, fighting a bear?

He slowed, and when she turned around, not wearing a stitch of makeup and uncombed hair in a knot of a twist, multiple tendrils loose, but not in a deliberately messy way, more like she'd been in a catfight, he had no doubt something was wrong. While she was just as stunning without all that stuff she wore, it was out of character. She usually looked as if she just walked off the pages of a fashion magazine—poised and polished.

Not today.

No, she appeared to be on the verge of an earnest cry. Then she sat down and dropped her face into her hands. He didn't need to think about it, Gage pulled over, hurried out of his SUV, and went to her, listening to her twins cry as if the world were ending.

"Danny?"

She peeked up at him, her soft, "Gawonii," doing something to his chest.

"What's wrong?"

"What isn't."

"Are the babies sick?" He stepped up and looked inside, seeing the back of their heads, the two of them secured in their car seats.

"No. They're mad, and I can't do anything right today. No matter what I've tried, they won't settle down. Taking them for a walk in the stroller was going to be my next strategy, but I can't get the wheel untangled from the strap of my backpack."

Tears started streaming down her cheeks in silvery lines.

"Danny." His heart hurt as he swiped the glistening moisture away with his thumbs. "Don't cry. I'll fix it."

She took him in, her gaze going from his head to his feet. "Shouldn't you be at work or something?"

While he shouldn't enjoy the appreciation he saw in her expression, he did. "I'm at work, just getting back from a late lunch. I spotted you here and thought I could help."

"Oh."

"Come on. Get up, and I'll take care of the stroller for you." He gave her a hand which she took, and he tried to ignore the zap of sensation at her touch. "Go see if you can quiet the twins some," he said, then grabbed the stroller, working at the tangle of the wheel and strap, freeing it rather quickly, then tugged it out, doing what needed to be done to get it unfolded and assembled into the rolling position.

"You got it!" Her voice had some life to it as she held a squirming and teary Ari.

"Give her to me and get Aaron," he said, taking the little blonde girl from her.

A wet palm came to his cheek, and blue eyes, just like Danica's, looked up at him with glistening tears on her lashes. She locked her gaze on him as if he were the most interesting thing ever.

"Hi there, cutie." Ariana's little bow lips turned into a smile. "You sure do take after your mommy."

She cooed and rocked her small body in his arms, legs kicking.

When Danica came back, her own beautiful lips were parted as she stared at him.

"What?"

"How did you do that?"

His brow creased. "Do what?"

"She's giggling."

He shrugged and looked down into the angelic face. "You just think I'm pretty darn awesome, don't you?"

When Gage gave Ari a little bounce, she squealed, but unlike the banshee he'd heard when he first arrived, it was one of pure delight.

"Wow." Danny put Aaron into one of the stroller seats. "You are a miracle worker."

"Naw."

"No. Seriously. I had just asked God for a miracle, and here you are."

Gage frowned. "I'm not a miracle."

"So, you think He didn't send you to my rescue?"

"No."

It was Danica's turn to frown. "Why not?"

"God and I haven't seen eye to eye for quite some time, Danny. So I'm positive he didn't, or *wouldn't,* send me." *Especially to you, a woman I shouldn't crave.*

"That's why you don't come to church anymore? You're mad at God for something?"

Not just something. A lot of things. "Let's not talk about it, okay?"

She studied him, saying nothing for a long moment then nodded. "All right. If that's what you want."

"It is." Taking her daughter over, he placed the little one in the other stroller seat, then tapped Aaron on his red-from-crying nose. "Hey there, buddy. I think the whole neighborhood heard you were having a bad day."

Her son smiled, and Danica punched Gage in the bicep. Not hard, a tap really, but he complained with, "Ouch," anyway. "Don't you know assaulting an officer of the law is a Class D Felony?"

She rolled her beautiful blue eyes, making the corners of his mouth twitch. "I've been trying everything, and you get the babies to smile, coo, and giggle for you."

"I'm just something more interesting to look at than the back of your Cadillac seats," he teased. "Give me the stroller, and I'll take them for a lap around the park."

"You don't need to do that." Danny shook her head. "I'm sure you have better things to do, like arrest someone or something."

Gage chuckled. "Luckily, arresting people around here doesn't happen too often. So, no, I don't have anything pressing I need to do at the moment," he fibbed, and off they went, him pushing Danica's twins, her at his side, the afternoon breeze rustling the leaves and blowing the scatter of yellow on the ground across their path.

Halfway down the long stretch of sidewalk, all was quiet, and Danica whispered, "Thank you for this."

He stopped their progress and glanced at her, a thousand thoughts on his mind, the first and foremost, *Does Marcus make you happy?* Followed by, *Is he good to you?* "Danica, does—" Gage paused, fought himself, kept his hands white-knuckled on the stroller bar, then smiled. "You're welcome."

They started their journey once more, then slowed when they came to the white, wrought iron bench on the outer edge by the swings and sandbox. "You want to take a breather?" He only asked because Danny seemed tired in a way that concerned him.

"Sure." Without saying anything else, she started in that direction as memories rolled over him.

Chapter Ten

Before

THE MUSCLES IN his legs were 'loving' him today as they protested half-way through his run. It might have been the first of October, but cool it was not. No, the sun beating down on Gage's back wasn't doing him any favors either.

As he passed the baseball diamond, the burning claws of exertion dug in, but he pushed past it and kept on going. Football practice during the week and weight training put him through the paces, so he probably didn't need to jog, but Mase insisted they did. Although he was solo, which meant he could have stayed home and maybe taken a hot tub since last night's game bashed him up some. However, he didn't do the lazy thing.

"You boys need to give your bodies some downtime," his father had said on many different occasions. *"Rest is important too. Essential for repair."*

"That's what Sunday's are for, Doctor Harrison," Mase would say.

Though his best friend usually joined him on this three-mile jaunt around town, he'd passed up their mutual torture that week since Breck had a rare Saturday afternoon off from work at the book store.

Flying down the street, he was finally in 'the zone,' and nothing would stop him. Or so he thought until he saw *her*.

Curled up on one of the benches in the park, sitting sideways, a book in her hand she wasn't reading, Danny appeared to be far away in thought.

Slowing, he jogged up, took a moment to catch his breath, and then, using his t-shirt, lifted the hem of it and wiped the sweat from his face.

When Gage dropped the damp material, she was looking at him in a way that took any pain his body might be feeling and turning it into a specific ache of want.

"Hey," he said, pushing his need for Danica into the box where it belonged, sealing it up tight with an entire roll of heavy-duty duct tape.

"Hi." Her cheeks flushed pink before she diverted her gaze.

"What are you doing?"

"I have to write a paper for English Lit class."

"Oh, Mrs. Thompson." He shook his head and ran his fingers through the sweaty strands of his hair. "She was a tough one, as I recall."

"Yeah, but I like her."

"Do you mind if I take a seat?"

"No." Danica dropped her feet, turned, and sat up straight, allowing Gage to flop down beside of her.

"Sorry if I stink."

There came that melodic giggle of hers. "You never stink."

"I'm sweating like a pig, so I probably do." His gaze shifted from her face and that sweet mouth to the text in her lap. "What's the paper on?"

"The meaning behind Edgar Alan Poe's poem, *A Dream Within A Dream*." She brought the book up and glanced at it. "Do you want to hear it?"

"Sure."

"Take this kiss upon the brow!

And, in parting from you now,

Thus much let me avow—

You are not wrong, who deem

That my days have been a dream," she smoothly read, causing every cell in his body to focus on nothing but her.

"Yet if hope has flown away
In a night, or in a day,
In a vision, or in none,
Is it therefore the less gone?
All that we see or seem
Is but a dream within a dream.
I stand amid the roar
Of a surf-tormented shore,
And I hold within my hand
Grains of the golden sand—
How few! yet how they creep
Through my fingers to the deep,
While I weep—while I weep!
O God! Can I not grasp

Them with a tighter clasp?

O God! can I not save

One from the pitiless wave?

Is all that we see or seem

But a dream within a dream?"

When she finished, she glanced over at him. "What do you think?"

"It's beautiful if not sad, but what are your thoughts?"

"I think he's talking about coming to the end of his life, and how it has been fleeting. A dream he can't quite hold on to. A series of events and our perceptions of time." She shrugged, the pink strap of her bra showing when the collar of one of her oversized dance t-shirts she wore when she practiced slipped over her creamy left shoulder. "I could be wrong."

"You're not," he said, then unable to help himself, swiped a strand of hair from her cheek before he scooted the material of her shirt back in place, covering the temptation.

"So, you think I'm right?" Her eyes locked on his, that need somehow slipping out of the box he'd secured, making him place his hand over top hers.

"Yeah."

She turned the hand not holding the book until they were palm to palm, fingers twining into his.

The rhythm of his heart *tha-thumped* hard behind the cage of his ribs, and it had nothing to do with his run.

"Danny…" Moving closer as if a strange force was pulling him, his face inches away from hers, two seconds from giving in to the longing to put his lips the one place he wanted them to be, a beastly H-O-N-K interrupted!

Gage jerked, straightening, then glanced over at *Krystin*, who was leaning on her horn with one hand, the other out the window waving like an insane person.

His tense shoulders didn't relax until she stopped the horn.

"Hey, Gage! I'm having a thing tonight. My parents are gone for the weekend so, you know. Party! It starts at eight, but come by anytime, okay?"

He wanted to strangle her. "I don't know. Maybe."

Danica had let loose of him, the warmth of her leaving.

"You can come too, Danny," she said, then added as if it pained her to extend the invitation, "if you want."

"Thanks," Danica said just as enthusiastically as the offer had been given, "but I've got homework, so I doubt I can come."

"Aw…too bad." Krystin smiled, but if it were sincere, it would only be due to Danny not attending. Danica tended to garner more male attention than she did without even trying.

"Okay, well. Catch you later, Gage!" Krystin tucked her head back inside the open window, then popped back out. "Oh, and I guess Jenny will be there. She and my sister are home from college for the weekend."

He and Jenny had a casual hook-up thing going for a while, but Gage had decided a few months ago, when he'd finally admitted to himself he cared deeply for Danny, and not in a brotherly kind of way, he was done with the whole Jenny thing.

"Yeah, all right," he said with a head lift, having no intention of seeing her or Jen if she was back.

"I better go." Danica abruptly got to her feet.

"Uh, okay." He frowned. "Do you want me to walk with you to your house?"

"No. I'm good. Finish your run."

Gage, unsure of what had happened, wondered if someone had smacked him. "I'll be happy to walk you home, Danny."

"It's okay. I'm sure I can manage. Bye." Her words had been stilted and rushed.

Gripping her book, she took off in a dead sprint.

Girls make no sense most of the time. He palmed the back of his neck. Danica leaving the way she did had probably been for the best since he was about to cross a line with her, which he shouldn't.

"Son. I need you to keep an eye on Danny for me." Mr. Lorry's words always came back to haunt him.

"Yes, sir. I will, Mr. Lorry, sir."

"Yeah," he muttered, getting to his feet. "I will."

Chapter Eleven

WITH TWO PERFECTLY contented babies, Danica pulled into her circular drive, seeing Howie come around the garage, leaf blower strapped to his back, waving. Once she parked, she rolled down the window as the kid came her way.

"Hi, Mrs. Harding," he said, then smiled with a mouth full of metal.

"Hi, Howie. How are you today?"

"Pretty good." His smile fell. "I'm sorry I'm late, but I got held up at your parents' house, trying to help your dad with that shed he's building."

Danica grinned. "It's not a problem."

"Doctor Harding wanted me to shape the shrubs again, but I don't know if I will get to it this weekend.

"There's always next weekend if the good weather holds."

"Yeah." He shifted his weight. "Do you need help getting the twins inside?"

She almost said no, but changed her mind. "You know," she said, "I could use the help getting all their stuff inside."

"Sure." He wiggled the leaf blower pack off his shoulders, put it down, then went around to the back of her vehicle as she pressed the button to lift the hatch. She then clambered out, going to open the side door, seeing two smiling faces looking at her.

"Gage sure has the magic touch," she mumbled under her breath, then started in on unbuckling Ari from her car seat.

Thirty minutes later, the twins had gone down for a late afternoon nap, but regardless of the hour, Danica was pleased.

Walking into the kitchen to get the leftover lunch dishes out of the sink and into the dishwasher, she glanced around and frowned. The kitchen looked as if a bomb had gone off, highchairs askew, cabinet doors and drawers open, the wheat bread she had started to make herself for breakfast that morning still standing in the toaster, untoasted.

With a sigh, she went to the appliance, grabbed the stiff, air-dried food, then tossed the pieces into the trash, her attention snagging on the movement outside the bay window.

Howie was raking leaves around their covered pool.

Nothing about the gangly blond with braces reminded her of the younger version of Gage, and she would be a complete sicko if it did. So, it wasn't the boy but the yard work that pinged her memory.

The *hum* of the leaf blower started up.

Grabbing the kitchen cloth, Danica began wiping down her marble countertops, but she couldn't help herself, her mind drifted to other places. *To him.*

Chapter Twelve

Before

THE SOUND OF the lawnmower starting made Danica's heart pick up the pace. She smiled at her reflection in the mirror before she put her lip gloss tube into the drawer, got up from her vanity, and went to her bedroom window.

Part of her wanted to open the daisy patterned curtains wide, but she didn't want to be obvious so, instead, she carefully slipped one panel to the side some and peeked out.

Gage was powerwalking the mower in front of him, having already done a couple of swipes to the front lawn that fast. At the pace he was going, he'd soon make quick work of the grass, moving to the back, meaning her spy game would be a bit harder to achieve, but she'd find a way. She usually did.

Why he'd chosen to do yardwork for a summer job, she didn't know. Especially since he didn't need to work. Gage's parents were well to do and pretty much gave him anything he wanted, including a shiny red GTO when he turned sixteen. But that was the year he'd decided he wanted to do manual labor, and the year Daddy hired him, something she would have thanked him for if it wouldn't have been suspicious.

Over by the birdbath, Gage stopped—the *ppppppp* of the mower still running, and tore the damp gray t-shirt he wore up and over his head, leaving his jet-black hair in a tousle.

Danica's eyes went wide, hoping to seer the vision of all those working muscles in his back and the sweat beads glistening on the smooth span of his tanned neck into her brain. She'd never seen anything as beautiful as him and doubted she ever would again.

Slightly turning, he used his shirt as a towel, rubbing it over his rock-hard chest and rippling abs.

Her gaze slipped, taking in the way his basketball shorts rode low on his hips, showing the start of a deep cut to the muscle above his right one.

She blinked rapidly, placing a hand to her pounding chest, tasting an explosion of the berry flavor of the gloss on her lips, something putting a quiver in her tummy.

Then he fully turned, his head tipping up, looking at *her* window. She caught the start of a crooked little grin on his face before she dropped to a squat, hoping he hadn't seen her, but the swaying curtain probably gave her spying position away.

"Crackers!" she spluttered just as her bedroom door opened, and Breckin stepped in.

"What are you doing, Danny?"

Trying to think fast, she spied one of her socks, reached and grabbed it. "Just getting this." She held up the purple thing as evidence.

"Okay." Her sister shook her head, long ponytail swishing.

"What are *you* doing?" Danica shot back.

"I was coming up to see if you wanted to go with Mase and me to the lake later. We're going to have a cookout, and he wants to fish."

"Just you guys?"

"I think some of the others are going, too."

Like Gage? She didn't ask aloud. "When are you going?"

"Sometime around noon."

Getting to her feet, lone sock in hand, she shrugged. "Sure."

"All right." Her older sister looked at her and what was probably the remnants of heat on her cheeks. "Are you feeling okay?"

"Yeah. I'm fine."

"You sure? You look a little flushed."

"Just hot," she said.

"Really?" Her sister arched a chestnut brow. "It's like, sixty-five degrees in here."

"I was doing sit-ups earlier," she lied.

"Oh." Breck looked at her a bit longer then said, "Make sure you bring your bathing suit. Some of us are going to go for a swim before the summer goes for good."

"Okay. I'll put it on under my shorts."

"All right." Her sister's green eyes went from her face to her hand, gripping the sock in a stranglehold. "I'll leave you to whatever it was you were doing." Breck turned and went out the door—the sound of the lawnmower moving to the side of the house.

Tossing her head back, she stared at the ceiling, letting the cotton slip from her palm, going over her swimwear options. *What would snag*

Gage's attention the most? Sure, Danica couldn't be positive he would go, but, if he did, she wanted to make an impression.

Mind made up, she went to her dresser, tugged out the drawer, and plucked up the two-piece pink polka dot one.

"If this doesn't work, nothing will," she said under her breath as she closed the drawer with her hip, and then headed for the bathroom.

Chapter Thirteen

AFTER PUTTING HER hair up, Danica plucked one of the art deco earrings out of the black velvet box, bent her head, slipped the post through her pierced ear, then attached the back.

"You look stunning," Marcus said, striding up behind her.

She met his gaze, the two of them framed in her vanity mirror. "Thank you."

His warm palm curled over her shoulder then slipped down her bare arm. "Blue has always been your color, and this outfit is a particular favorite of mine. It turns your eyes into sapphires."

The dark blue dress *was* gorgeous, with beautiful pearl detailing around the neckline that continued as an attached tasseled necklace down the open back, tickling between her shoulder blades when she moved.

Marcus kissed the side of her exposed neck, making a shiver traverse the canvas of her skin. "You never said where we were going tonight."

She had been surprised and pleased when he'd come home early, saying to get dressed, he'd made arrangements for a baby sitter and was taking her to dinner.

"Canlis," he whispered before his lips caressed her once more.

"I love that restaurant."

He smiled. "I know."

After more than a few pounding rounds to the heavy bag, Gage stopped, ripped off his gloves, grabbed the water bottle from the stand, and downed it. Mase was his usual gym companion, but since he and Breck were on their honeymoon in Maui, he was solo.

"Hi, Chief Harrison," the new owner of the antique store, Felicia Sands said, hips swaying in her capri yoga pants, the bottom of her tied off graphic t-shirt showing her tight midsection as she sauntered his way. "You're looking good."

"Thanks."

Gage was known to flirt. A lot. At first, he did it as a cover, a way to disguise the fact he was captivated by a too-young Danny, but as the years wore on, it became a sort of blanket, a way to stifle the pain. But after his unexpected visit from Alderman Jordan late that afternoon, who grilled him as to why the department needed new Kevlar vests, he wasn't in the mood for anything.

"When was the last time our guys on the force needed those?" the jackass had asked.

"The fact none of my men haven't been shot at really isn't the point of having them, now, is it?" came his response, before the stupid discussion continued.

"Do you realize how expensive those things are?"

"I do."

"Then why bother with new vests? Who in Cedar Point would pull a gun?"

"You never know what might happen. We do get visitors, and the occasional vagrant passing through."

The scumbag had chuffed.

"Point being, Alderman Jordan, the proper safety equipment is necessary for law enforcement on the off chance someone does shoot at us."

"I've always wanted to try the punching bag, but I'm afraid I don't know what I'm doing." Ms. Sands' voice pulled him from his musings, his attention shifting back to her. She was glancing up at him from beneath her lashes. "Maybe you could teach me?"

Oh, he caught the vibes she was tossing his way; he wasn't obtuse, he just chose to ignore them, instead wiping the sweat from his face with the crook of his arm. "I'm not a very good instructor."

"I *doubt* that."

He didn't say anything.

"Well, how about you and I grab a bite to eat or maybe a cup of coffee? The Choc-Oh! Cottage makes some of the best brews around. They even have the fancier stuff like Cappuccinos."

"Yeah—"

Her face lit up. "Great!"

Gage lifted his palm. "Hang on, Ms. Sands."

"Felicia." She cocked a shapely hip. "No need for Ms."

Gage put his empty water bottle down. "I was going to say, 'yeah, they have great coffee' but I can't grab a cup with you."

"Oh…" She pouted. "Do you have to work this evening?"

"No, but I do have plans." He didn't really, not unless you counted feeding his fish, ordering take out, and watching Monday Night Football on his big-screen TV plans.

"I'm sorry to hear that." She grinned, not put off in the least. "Perhaps we can get together another time?"

"We'll see," he said, though he should have crushed her interest in him. He had to be almost twelve years her senior, meaning she was too young for him, everything Danica wasn't with her short black hair sticking up in spikes around her pixie face, and sleepy bedroom milk-chocolate eyes.

He was insane, he knew it. He'd never find a woman even remotely close to Danny, and he'd long ago decided not to try, knowing, even if he found a replica of her, the woman would be just that, an imitation—not *her*.

Ms. Sands placed her hand on his damp forearm. "I'll let you go, but I hope to see you again soon."

The woman wasn't unattractive; however, even if he overlooked the significant age difference between them, her good looks didn't matter. What put him on his guard when he was around her was a straightforward thing. She hadn't been afraid to let people know she was, in fact, on the hunt for a husband, and being one of those was something he'd *never* be.

Seated at a table positioned in the corner of the wall of windows at Canlis with her handsome husband, Danica and he had an excellent view of Lake Union—all the boat lights lighting up the water like a dark mirror.

Danica slid one of the votive candles aside. "Thank you for this."

"Don't thank me. I have a lot to make up for."

"So, this is a make-up dinner?"

"Sweetheart, I know I've been gone a lot. I'm sorry."

"You have an important job. I get that. But I have been missing you."

He reached and grabbed her hand. "No matter how busy I am, you and the babies are always on my mind."

She glanced down. "I know, Marcus."

"Danica, what's wrong?"

Her head lifted, their gazes locking. "I know I said I didn't need any help after the twins arrived, but I was wrong. I can't do it all, and I think I need someone to come assist."

His brow furrowed. "You want to hire a nanny?"

"Oh, no. Just someone who could come a few hours a week. Help me out around the house, maybe take care of the babies when I need to go out."

"Doesn't your family help when you go to your meetings?"

"They do, but it would be nice to perhaps run errands without packing the entire house to take the kids with me."

He nodded. "If you need help, go ahead and hire someone."

"Thank you, Marcus." Danica's shoulders lifted, a weight falling off them as she leaned over and placed a soft kiss to her husband's lips.

"Doctor Harding?"

Danica turned to the sound of a lilting feminine voice.

"I thought that was you," the young woman said, tucking some of the auburn strands of her long hair behind her ear.

"Yes, it's me."

She glanced at her husband, a strange smile on his face, the look of confusion on his brow.

"Well," said the woman, "aren't you going to introduce me to your lovely wife?"

He cleared his throat. "Ahem… Danica, this is—I'm sorry, I don't remember your name."

A little laugh rang around them. "I'm Rosland. Rosland Strickler." She held out a hand that Danica shook. "I work at the hospital with your husband."

"Oh… It's nice to meet you."

The shake stopped. "You as well. I've heard a lot about you."

"You have?"

The woman's burnt umber eyes slid to Marcus, a smile stretched across her attractive face. "He talks about you and your twins often."

"What is it you do at the hospital?" Danica asked.

Marcus chimed in, drawing her gaze to him with, "Ms. Strickler is one of the new nursing staff in the cardiac unit."

"Ah…"

One corner of Rosland's mouth turned up. "I better leave you two to your evening. I just wanted to come by and say hi."

"I'm happy you did." Danica grinned.

"Yes," Marcus said. "It was good seeing you."

Once the nurse left, Danica gave her husband her full attention. "She seems nice."

He shrugged. "I don't really know her well other than to say she has a good bedside manner with the patients."

"That's important."

"It is." Marcus tapped his knuckles on the white tablecloth. "Where is our waiter?"

"I'm sure he will be here soon."

His whiskey-colored eyes came to her. "Are those earrings new?"

She reached up and touched the right one with reverence. "No. I've had them forever."

"I haven't seen you wear them before?"

"I'm sure I've put them on a time or two."

He squinted. "I don't think so."

"Huh," she said. "I have a lot of jewelry, so maybe I haven't. I don't know."

Chapter Fourteen

Before

BEEP…BEEP…BEEP…

Grumbling, Gage rolled over and slapped his alarm clock, putting an end to the screeching beast, then scrubbed his palms down his face, hoping to go back to sleep for a little while, then froze. It was August 17th, his eighteenth birthday, which meant it was Danica's sixteenth!

She can date, officially.

Wide awake now, he rolled out of bed. He'd take a quick shower, then head for *Second Chances*, the antique store, and pick up those earrings sitting in the display window she'd been admiring the other day.

Scratching his bare chest, he smiled. "She'll love them, maybe hug me, and I'll ask her out."

Wrapping the little box with particular care, Danica grinned. When she saw the masculine ring sitting in the display window of *Second Chances*, she knew she needed to get it, regardless if buying it would wipe out every dollar from her babysitting funds.

"This was worth it." She popped a red bow on the top of the shiny silver paper, figuring she'd build her savings up again, so it was no big deal.

Tap, tap, tap…

Shifting on her bed, she yelled, "Yeah?"

The door opened, and her father stuck his head inside. "You ready, Princess?"

"I guess so."

"Well, come on then, or we'll be late for your party at the Harrison's."

Ever since she was small, her parents, Mason's folks, and Gage's would take turns throwing her, Eddie Miller, and Gage a mutual birthday party since they were all born on the same day and were good friends. But this year, it was the Harrison's turn to host.

Her heart fluttered.

Eddie wouldn't be there since he hadn't come home from college for the summer, so she and Gage would be the only two. And while people would surround them, something about the two of them sharing this day on their own seemed different. Intimate.

When the doorbell rang, Gage came bounding down the curved staircase, smiling when his father opened the door, letting the Lorry's in.

"Samuel." Dad patted the other man on the back. "Ella. Breckin, Mason, and Danica. My, don't you look all grown up."

Gage bounced his gaze over everyone, landing on Danny, who smiled at her father. She wore a little peachy sundress, the hem fluttering around her toned thighs, making him halt on the bottom rung.

"Gage!" Danny's dad greeted, pulling him out of his stymied stupor. "Happy birthday, son."

"Thank you, sir."

"Eighteen." He shook his head. "I don't know where the time has gone."

"You and me both," Gage's father agreed before he said, "Come on out back by the pool. Our housekeeper will get the door for the rest of our guests, and we can relax, maybe have a cool drink."

"Happy birthday, bro!" Mase stepped up to give him a fist bump.

"Thanks, man."

"Happy birthday, Gage," Breck echoed.

"Thank you."

As the group trailed behind Gage's father, Danica paused, glanced up at him, and said in an almost shy little voice. "Hi."

"Hey." He lifted his head in a nod. "You look nice."

Her cheeks blushed. "Thank you." She held out her hand, giving him a small, pretty box. "Happy birthday."

"Thank you. Happy birthday to you too." He took the present, then grabbed her delicate wrist, taking her with him into the family room where the table of gifts was.

"What are you doing?"

Glancing over the festive packages, he grabbed the one he'd bought for her, then offered it up. "For you."

"Aw…" she cooed, taking the gift. "The wrapping is so pretty."

"I didn't wrap it," he admitted, heat meandering up his neck. "Mrs. Hollis did."

"So, you got this from Second Chances?" Her smile widened.

"I did, why?"

Danny shook her head. "Great minds think alike, I guess."

"Huh?"

"I got your gift there too."

"Oh… That's cool." He grinned, pointing. "Well, go ahead and open it."

"Now?" Her brows pulled down. "Maybe we should wait."

He picked up the hand gripping the box he'd given her, lifting it. "Go on. I don't want to wait."

"Okay. But only if you open yours too."

"Deal."

The two of them started tearing off bows and shredding paper. Then came her gasp of breath.

Her "Oh…these are so beautiful," accompanied Gage's "Danny. This is—"

"Do you like it?" She asked.

"Yeah, it's awesome." He plucked the ring out of the box. "I don't think I've ever seen anything like it."

"Mrs. Hollis said it's sterling silver and Koa Wood." She took the ring from between his fingers. "I had it engraved. See?"

He read a flowing script of *Gawonii,* feeling as if his heart would explode. "This is really great."

"Here." She slipped the ring onto the hand that didn't sport his class ring, but would one day hold a wedding ring. "It fits!"

"It does." He reached for the 1920s art deco diamond and sapphire earrings. "Let me help you put these on."

Stepping so close he could count every one of her long lashes, he was glad she hadn't put earrings on that day.

With his heart pounding in his throat, Gage slipped the right post through her cute little lobe, then did the left, her hand covering his, trapping him in place as she looked up at him with eyes that said so much.

Tell her. She's sixteen now. Tell her how you feel about her and ask her out. "Danica—"

"There you are!" His mother's voice hit him in the back like a sledgehammer. "We've been looking for you two."

The moment had shattered. Danny dropped his hand, backing away before he turned around to see his Mom's furrowed brow.

"Did you already start opening presents?"

"Just the ones Danny and I exchanged with each other." He shrugged, attempting to settle his body down.

Mom shook a manicured accusatory finger at him. "Gawonii Harrison, you should have waited."

He went over and kissed his mother's cheek. "Don't be upset, Mommy," he said, knowing that one last word would melt her, even though he was way too old to say it.

She reached up and cupped his face between her soft palms. "I'm not upset, my beautiful boy."

Gage smiled as his mother's gaze went to Danica. "Sweetie. You look lovely."

"Thank you, Judge Harrison."

His mother let loose of him then bent to kiss Danny's cheek. "I'm not 'Judge' Harrison to you." Once she straightened, she spun on her designer heels. "Come on, you two. We'd better greet our guests. We can't very well have everyone waiting on the birthday kids, now can we?"

You'll find the right time to tell Danny. This isn't it. Be patient, Gage told himself as Mom led the way to the pool.

Chapter Fifteen

IF THERE WAS one thing Gage disliked about his job, it was all the schmoozing—City Council meetings, fundraisers, various charity events. He'd never been the guy who loved to mingle, so sitting there with a plate of roasted chicken while at the Chamber of Commerce luncheon wasn't on his top ten list of things to do. *Except…*

He looked at the person seated across the round table from him, who glanced up and smiled demurely, making a warm sensation spread within his chest.

While she wasn't a business owner, she was a volunteer member, and since this was another one of the many town functions Danica attended, he supposed he could revise his 'dislike' items.

Pulling his attention from the woman who he didn't need to be staring at, he caught Courtney Riddle giving Danny the evil eye until her focus bounced to him. She'd never liked Danica, probably petty jealousy due to the notice Danny garnered from the opposite sex back in the day, and still did. But no matter how much time had passed, he could see her smug face that night in the cabin with Matt Jordan, saying, *"Since when did we become the designated babysitters of the perfect princess?"*

Gage clenched his fist at the memory.

Clearly deciding she wasn't going to win the scowling contest happening between the two of them, Courtney looked away.

John's deep voice rang out with, "All right, thank you to everyone who took the podium here today," and Gage tried not to sigh in relief at those words. He'd made it through the introductions of new and renewing members, guests, and visitors, a twenty-minute speech from the keynote speaker, Berta Collins, and thought perhaps it might be a short meeting. But no. Then, a ten-minute business/organization spotlight, a quick non-profit highlight, followed by any suggestions for next year's Founders Day, but now, John Donohue, the president of the chamber, was giving the final wrap up.

"Hope to see you all next month," the man said, blessedly dismissing them.

The sound of people shuffling around as they rose from their seats, ready to exit the back event-room at The Snack Shack, mixed into his movements before Phillip Granger stopped him.

"Chief Harrison."

His former classmate and teammate had used his official title instead of 'Gage,' so he knew whatever it was he had to say, it would be city business-related.

"Mayor, Granger," Gage returned.

"Alderman Jordan would like to call a special meeting with the town council to discuss the necessity of adding to the budget."

"Let me guess. To talk about the need for new vests?"

"You've got it."

Gage sighed. "When and what time?"

"This Thursday. Seven p.m."

"All right. I'll see you there."

"I'm sure this will be a short one," Phillip said. "No one else believes the added expense to be 'frivolous'."

Gage nodded, the two of them shaking hands as their final farewell.

"Chief Harrison?"

The sweet feminine voice fell over him like a cool breeze of fresh air, though yet again, this greeting set the tone of the conversation to come.

Turning, he met Danica's gaze. "Mrs. Harding. What may I do for you today?"

The corner of her spectacular mouth inched up, and if they'd been alone, he was positive she would have rolled her eyes at him. "Wendell," she said. "He's been at it again, only not relieving himself in front of the bar but in the sandbox at the park. I'm sure I don't need to tell you how disgusting and inappropriate that is, let alone unsanitary. Children play in that sand, and it shouldn't be used as a litter box."

Gage frowned. "I'll take care of it."

"You will?"

"Of course. I'm in total agreement with you."

Her eyes widened. "You are?"

"Really, Danica? Did you think I would be all right with something like that?"

"Well, I don't guess so."

"Then, why do you look surprised?"

She shook her head. "I'm not."

He lifted a brow but remained silent.

"I'm *not*," she said, a little more emphatic.

The room had emptied, and he stepped a little closer to her, close enough to feel her body heat and breathe in her intoxicating scent. "Don't try to lie to me. It hasn't, doesn't, and never will work, Danny."

Her perfectly arched brows beetled down. "I'm not lying to you and never have."

You've been doing it to yourself and to me for years, he thought but didn't allow the words to escape his tongue.

Chapter Sixteen

Before

GAGE WATCHED THE clock on the wall, that slow *tick, tick, tick* of the second hand as it inched closer to the last period bell. When class let out, he was going to find Danny and ask her over to his house to watch a movie.

Yeah, it was a Thursday, not the usual date night he supposed, but they had an out-of-town football game tomorrow night anyway. And, yes, he supposed he should probably take her out, like maybe to the theater or something, but he wanted to be alone with her so they could finally have 'the talk'. Well, he was going to talk, let her know he wanted to go out with her—make Danica *his* girl—and Gage was ninety-nine-point-nine percent sure she wouldn't turn him down.

He glanced at the ring she'd bought him for his birthday, curling his fingers, and recalled the tender expression on her face as she'd slipped it on him.

Okay, he was one-hundred-ten percent sure she *wouldn't* turn him down.

After grabbing his Calculus book, Gage was out of his seat a second before the harsh, *Brrring* started, then through the metal door, breezing past his locker and heading to hers. For the past couple of weeks, every time he'd tried to talk with her, just one-on-one, they'd been interrupted. So, he was 'seizing the moment' as it were.

Getting to his destination, he didn't see who he wanted to see. But sometimes Danny took her sweet time leaving, too busy chatting with J.J. and some of the others who hung around together; so even if he were late for their first after-school practice of the year, he'd wait for her. Running wind sprints 'till he dropped would be worth a tardy arrival.

Resting his shoulder against her locker door, he bobbed his head in greeting as some of his teammates and friends passed him in the hall—laughter and chatter becoming a buzz of sound. Then, he saw her, a smile on her face, listening to Granger as he talked, no doubt trying to pick her brain about Jillian.

Gage straightened up when she noticed him and grinned.

"I'll talk to you later, Phillip," she said, leaving him behind and hurrying over to where he stood.

"Hi," he said.

"Hey. What are you doing?"

"I wanted to ask you something." His heart was *bang, bang, banging* in his chest.

She blinked. "Okay. Ask."

"Do you want to come over tonight and watch a movie? My parents are going to be in Seattle for some charity event, so it will just be the two of us," he blurted out, not bothering to take a breath.

Danica stared at him as if she hadn't heard what he said, then she gave him that slow, sleepy smile and nodded her head.

"Yeah?" he asked.

"Sure. I'd love to."

"You'd love to what?" Breck asked as she and Mase came strolling over—hand-in-hand.

Danny turned to look at her sister. "Huh?"

"You'd love to what?"

"Oh, uh…" She glanced at Gage then back to Breck. "I'm going to watch a movie tonight with Gage."

"Oh, hey, man," Mase said, his eyes shifting to him, "you're going to that new action flick?"

"Naw. I was thinking about watching something at home. We've got our game tomorrow, and since we've got practice, we couldn't make it until the late showing and"—Gage shrugged—"just doing the movie night thing at my place."

"Cool," Breck said, "what time should we be there?"

All of his excitement drained from him. Not that he didn't love Breck as a friend, but he didn't want company, yet, he couldn't be rude. "Um, I don't know. Seven-ish?"

"Sounds good," Mase said, holding out a fist to bump, which he did.

Gage's gaze jumped around the group. "It's settled then." He started to go, maintain the chill attitude that he didn't feel when a thought hit him. "Oh, hey. I can come to pick you up, Danny."

"It's okay," Mase said. "She can ride with us."

Another blow to his plan, but he wasn't going to let his disappointment show. "All right." He looked over at Danica, who was smiling, but he knew her well enough to know she wasn't as happy either. "I'll see you later then."

"See ya," she said.

Mason gave Breck a quick kiss. "Meet you after practice, babe."

"Have a good one," she said.

"I will. Love you."

"Love you, too."

After one more kiss, a bit more lingering, Mason pulled back, tapped the tip of Breck's nose with his fingertip, and then joined Gage as the two of them headed to the locker room.

Danica had taken extra time getting ready to see Gage. Starting with going over her clothing options, which putting all the rejected items back into her closet was going to take forever. Regardless, she was happy with what she finally picked—too-tight jeans and a pretty pale blue cashmere V-neck sweater. After an hour at her vanity, her makeup was perfection, and her long, flowing hair looked good.

While she'd occupied her time with clothing, makeup, and hair, Danica had to admit she'd been a nervous wreck the whole afternoon, and still was as she, Breckin, and Mason walked into the large foyer of the Harrison's home. It wasn't as if she'd never been there before; she had been, many times, but this time… Well, this time was different.

He asked me out! Okay, maybe not technically, but she was going with it.

"Hey, guys. Go on back to the media room," Gage said, shutting the door behind them.

Breck and Mase were doing their usual cuddle-walk thing they did, but Danica lingered back a bit, waiting…

"Danica?"

That sandpaper-smooth voice wrapped around her like a warm blanket as she turned. "Yes?"

"You look"—those silver eyes took her in, from the chunky Sketchers on her feet, up her denim-clad legs, waist, chest, and loitered a moment before inching up to her chin, lips, eyes—"gorgeous."

Heat zipped up her spine, overtook her neck, and spread across her cheeks. "Thank you," she said as she did the very same to him, starting with his black Jordan's, up to his muscled frame, and ending on his extraordinary eyes. "You look"—s*moking hot*—"good."

Aah, I'm so lame! You look good? Really?

Gage's lips twitched. "I'll take 'good'."

"Hey! You guys coming or what?"

Her sister's voice made her bristle. *Why are you interrupting our moment?*

Putting a pleasant smile on her face, Danica spun around. Breck was sticking her head out the archway down the hall. "Coming!"

Mase and Breck were cuddled up on the end of the sectional; a blanket tossed around their shoulders as Mason absently played with the ends of Breckin's hair. Without paying any attention to what she was doing, Breck plopped some popcorn into her mouth—the two of them engrossed in the movie.

Gage's attention went to Danny, who was seated next to him, on his left, but at a respectable distance.

He sighed. If they'd been alone, they could have had 'the talk' already and could be snuggling. Or maybe even kissing. Who cared about the movie if that were to be the case? All the clashing swords and screaming would blend into the background.

Heck, if his lips were on hers, all the sound would probably disappear.

When Danica brought her sock-covered feet up, arms wrapping around her knees, he glanced over at her. Her eyes were wide, obviously watching something he hadn't been paying attention to on the big screen in front of them.

"You okay?" he asked.

Her blue, blue gaze slid to him. "Yeah. It's just sort of— I don't know."

"Scary?"

"Not really."

She wasn't a good liar. Danica was freaked.

"Come here," he said, holding out his arm for her.

Her manicured brows lifted. "Really?"

"Sure. I'll keep you safe."

"From a bunch of vampires?"

He chuckled. "Come on, Danny."

She put her feet down, then scooted closer until he had her curled up beside him. When the warmth of her body met his, Gage tried hard not to smile, but he might have been failing as he glanced at her. "You good?"

"I am," she said in her sweet voice, right before she put her palm on his chest. He wished he wasn't wearing a shirt so he could feel the sensation of her flesh against his.

Breathing in the candy scent of her hair, he attempted to keep his concentration on the actor who was going primeval on some vamps, but more times than he'd like to admit, he dropped his attention to her.

Maybe I should just tell her now. We're not alone like I'd hoped for, but I could whisper how I felt by her ear.

They were halfway through the movie when he pulled his gaze from the TV and looked at her for the nine-hundredth time. He frowned. Danny was sleeping, a peaceful, contented expression on her face.

Gage smiled, love for her expanding in his chest. Danica looked like an angel, and she'd fallen asleep in *his* arms. No, he wouldn't wake her. He'd let her rest. They had time, and he'd find a better moment to tell her what he wanted to anyway.

BANG! BANG! BANG!

At the sound of something hitting the glass doors behind them, Gage and Mason both jumped up, dislodging the girls they'd had in their arms.

"What the—" Spinning around, ready to murder someone if they were dumb enough to break in, Gage rounded the sectional with Mase on his heel.

"Who is that?" Breckin screeched.

Gage could see someone dressed in black, white palm smacking the glass, making growling noises. Then, when he got closer to the door, he saw who it was.

"I'm going to kill him," Gage grumbled, unlocking the French doors, and opening them up, the outside motion light going off when he did.

"Oh, man. The look on your faces was priceless!" Phillip Granger hooted as he strode over to the open door, slipping the hoodie off his head.

"What are you doing here, acting like an insane person?" Mase asked, his face still stone-cold serious. "You scared my girl!"

Gage glanced over his shoulder at Danny, who was on her knees, chest against the back of the couch, peeking over with a pale face and wide eyes. "It's okay," he said. "It's just Granger."

Turning back around, he got in Phillip's face. "You frightened Danica, too, and that's not cool, dude!"

"I'm sorry." Phillip held up his hands. "I heard you guys talking about watching movies tonight, and thought scaring you would be funny."

"It wasn't."

In the distance came the sound of sirens.

Gage shook his head before scrubbing a palm down his face. "You better get inside, Phillip."

"Why?"

"I'm assuming you jumped the fence to get into the back yard, and when you did, you set off the silent alarm."

Phillip's topaz eyes went round. "No way!"

"Yep. I'd say we've got two minutes before Cedar Point's finest arrive, and you should be inside, not out here in the dark dressed like a serial killer."

Grabbing the idiot by the front of his dark zip-up, Gage pulled him inside, knowing all his plans for the night were, once again, going down in flames.

Chapter Seventeen

WITH THE GAME blaring on his TV, Gage grabbed the fish food and dumped a few flakes into the water—the googly-eyed goldfish darting to the falling food, tail fanning.

"I hope that stuff tastes better than it smells, Spike."

Yes, he named his fish something silly, but whatever. Since his therapist suggested he get a pet, and he wasn't home enough to take care of a dog, he'd grabbed a few fish from the pet store in Seattle. Two of them didn't last but a few weeks, although the one he had left had been swimming around the large bowl for six months. And the truth was, watching him glide through his underwater kingdom was relaxing.

Ding dong!

"That would be my dinner."

Like the fish cared.

Ding dong!

The sound ground on his nerves. "I'm coming!"

Five quick steps and he opened the door. "Hi, Chief Harrison," Jerry the Jerk's teenage son stood there, smiling, a large box from The Snack Shack in hand.

"Hey, Jimmy."

"Here you go." The boy handed the cardboard square to him, which Gage took, then twisted to place it on the console table by the door so he could grab his wallet and pull out a few bills.

Once he had the money, Gage handed it over.

"Thanks," the kid said, counting out the stack, his brows knitting. "This is too much. The pizza was only eleven eighty-nine."

"I know. The rest is your tip."

"Really?" Jimmy's brown eyes went wide.

His father might be a giant pinhead, but he was a good kid and was never in trouble.

"Really, Jimmy."

"Thank you, Chief. I'm saving to get my own car, so I don't have to use my mom's."

"You're welcome. And that's a noble goal. Keep working, and you'll get there."

"I will."

"Have a good night, and be careful driving. It's supposed to rain."

"Yes, sir. You have a good night as well."

Making sure the kid was back in his car, Gage watched him pull out of the driveway, then he turned off the porch light, shut the front door, grabbed his box and took his meal to the couch, yelling, "Can't you catch!" when the Seahawks wide receiver fumbled the ball.

Flopping down on his leather sectional, he flipped the lid open, taking a whiff of the spices, grabbed a large slice, and grumbled under his breath, "They pay you way too much," as if the player who messed up could hear him before he took a perfect bite of pepperoni with extra cheese.

When the commercials about trash bags started, Gage went into the kitchen, grabbed a two-liter of Coke from the fridge, then took the entire bottle with him. Why bother with a glass when he was the only one there?

Stepping back into the living room, he paused, catching a piece about one of Seattle's landmark hotels, but it wasn't what the commercial was about that held his attention but the spokeswoman.

Jenny.

Chapter Eighteen

Before

"SO, SON. HOW are your classes going?" Gage's father asked one evening over dinner.

"Pretty good."

"Senior year, it will go by fast."

"I just can't believe my baby will be graduating and heading off to college soon," Mom said, a note of sadness in her tone.

"Speaking of college." Dad put his fork down and met Gage's gaze. "Have you given any more thought to your major?"

"I'm thinking of criminal justice." He shrugged. "I don't know, though."

"That's a fine choice," Mom said, then took a sip of her iced tea.

"Whatever you decide, your mother and I will support you," Dad said.

"Thanks. I know you will."

His father cut a piece of meat. "So, what are your plans tonight?"

"I'm going to go get Danny and take her to youth group."

We'll take a detour by the lake, so we can finally talk.

"Doesn't she usually go with Mason and Breckin?" his mother asked, picking up her glass of wine.

"She does, but Breck is sick with the flu or something, and Mrs. Lorry is in Colorado helping her mother who's had some kind of back surgery. I guess Mr. Lorry is working late, so Mason is going over to stay with her." Gage grinned. "You know him. He worries about Breck all the time. But I guess I would want to check on my girl too, if I had one."

And I soon will.

"Aw, I'm sorry to hear she's not feeling well." Mom frowned. "But it's good she has Mason if her parents can't be there to take care of her."

Nodding, Gage slipped his gaze to his father. "If she's not better in a day or so, I'm sure Mase will insist she come and see you, Dad."

"I'll make sure to tell the front desk to fit her in if she calls for an appointment."

"You're that busy?"

"Colds and flu are raging, son, so yes, the clinic has been inundated."

Gage traced his fingertip down the condensation on his glass.

"What is it, honey?" Mom asked him, always the observant one.

Tell them about Danny and what your plans are. "I've been thinking—"

One of the pocket doors into the dining room opened, and Sonoma, their housekeeper, stepped in. "I'm sorry to interrupt, but someone is here to see you."

Dad leaned back in his chair. "I didn't hear the doorbell ring?"

"No, sir. I was taking the trash out and ran into her pulling up to the gates."

"Ran into who?"

"Young Ms. Lansing."

Gage started to rise. "I'll go see what she needs."

"Sit and finish your dinner." His father's green eyes went from him to Sonoma. "Tell Jenny to come join us, and will you please get her a place setting?"

"Of course, sir."

"You were about to tell us something, Gage. What was it?" his mother asked.

"It's nothing we can't talk about later."

"You sure?"

"Yeah, Mom."

Jenny walked in, a tentative smile on her face. "I didn't mean to interrupt your dinner."

"You haven't, dear," his mother assured. "Come, have a seat. Sonoma is getting you a plate."

"Oh, okay." Her gaze shot to Gage. "I guess I can eat if you don't mind?"

"We don't mind in the least," Dad said.

Gage got up and pulled out a chair for her, which Jenny took. "Thank you."

"You're welcome."

Sonoma came back in bearing china, a crystal glass, and silverware, which she placed down for Jenny. "Thank you."

"You're welcome, Ms. Lansing."

"Everything smells wonderful," his friend commented.

"Don't be shy. Grab a bowl and serve yourself." Dad picked up the platter of beef. "Would you care for some roast?"

"Yes, thank you."

Gage and Jenny had hung out over the years, but having dinner with him and his family was a first, and he couldn't help but wonder why she'd stopped by. He hadn't known she was back in town, and when she wanted to see him, she usually called.

"So, dear," his father said, "how is your mother doing?"

"Much better than she was a few months ago when I came home to help her out after knee surgery."

Dinner began again, chit-chat swirling around the table, Jenny talking about taking summer classes, wanting to get ahead of the game, which his father thought to be a useful endeavor.

"I didn't have a break since the fall semester started, but that's okay." She grinned—the dimple on her right cheek appearing.

"What brings you home to visit, then?" Mom had asked the question he was interested to know.

"I'm pregnant," Jenny blurted out, and the room went deathly still, including Gage's heart. In fact, the only clue he had that he was indeed alive was when he dropped his dessert fork, the *clatter* meaning his ears were working, so he must be breathing.

After a few heartbeats, his father asked, "How far along are you?"

Jenny looked at Dad, then over to Gage, to his mother, then back at his father. "A little over three months."

Gage's mind whirled into the calculations, knowing there wasn't any way around the numbers and his monumental mistake. A mistake fueled into flames by his feelings for Danny. She had called him in late May, panic in her voice.

"Gage?" Danica's voice quivered, making him grab the remote, turn down the volume on the TV, sit up straight, and grip the handset.

"Danny? What's wrong?"

"Do you think you can come over?"

"Of course, but are you all right? Is everyone okay, Breckin, and your parent's?"

"Everyone is fine. But something happened, and I'm home by myself, and I-I—" She sniffed. "Can you just come?"

"I'll be right there."

The moment he hung up the phone, he raced out of the house, hopped into his car and sped to the Lorry's, Danica meeting him at the door with tear-filled eyes.

Hugging her, and stepping inside the foyer, taking her with him, he asked. "What happened?"

"The door," she said into his chest.

Not happy about doing it, he let her go, turned and closed the front door, then took her chilled hand, leading her into the den where they took a seat on the couch. "Tell me, Danny."

"I was walking home from the Vanderpool's place; they needed me to watch the boys today. A car started following me. At first, I didn't think too much about it, until it turned when I took a left on Ash Street, then again when I went onto Downy."

Fury flamed from Gage. "Did you see who it was?"

She nodded. "I finally slowed and looked."

"Who was it?"

"Jordan, only he wasn't driving his car, but one I've never seen before."

Dynamite detonated inside his head, blinding him with fury for a moment as he got up and headed for the hall.

"Where are you going?" Danny was behind him.

"To go smash Jordan's teeth in."

She gripped his arm. "No. Don't leave me."

Her soft voice, those pleading words, stopped him. Then her sad face as she came around his large frame and looked up cemented Gage in place. "Danica."

"Please, stay with me."

Gage grabbed her around the waist, lifted her feet off the floor, and took her lips with his. Danny was hesitant at first, then she gave to his will, allowing him entrance on a breath.

She tasted of butterscotch candy.

He groaned.

In the back of his mind, he knew their first kiss should have been nice. Slow. Soft. This, more than likely her first kiss, should have been respectful, gentle, not the hard, almost punishing kiss he was giving her.

Gage almost came to his senses, but when Danny kissed him back with just as much passion, wrapping her arms around his neck and her shapely legs around his waist, any thought of how it should have been left his addled thoughts and became nothing but all-consuming need, burning him to the bone.

Spinning, Gage put her back against the wall, mouths working, tongues tangling, teeth clashing, one of his hands gripping the back of her head and neck, fingers fisting the silk of her hair, the other hand riding dangerously low on the sweet curve of her spine.

As he ate at her, something insisted, *Stop!*

He ignored the little voice of reason, growling low in his throat when Danny's nails bit into the flesh of his neck, but that one word became incessant, *stop, stop, stop*, and wouldn't shut up until he wrenched his mouth from hers, chest heaving, and put her down.

"I'm sorry, Danny." A tumult of emotion ranging from want, remorse, need, anger at Jordan, at himself, lust, so much lust, all of it whirling around inside of him like a tornado made him stumble back.

Looking dazed, she touched her glistening swollen lips and whispered, "I'm not."

He had three more months to go before Danny could 'officially' date, and if he did what he wanted to do, and crossed the line, they'd never get to the dating part or doing things properly—respectfully in order. No, they'd jump right into the physical.

Gage welded his eyes closed. He'd started this fight with himself when she turned fourteen, and he got it—if he touched her again, there would be no going back. How she'd always looked at him hadn't gone unnoticed. The way she watched him when she thought he wasn't paying attention. He knew she had the same aching attraction for him he felt for her. The same yearning was evident as they'd consumed the other just moments before.

If I kiss her again, she'll let me.

She would, no doubt. But he wanted more, there was no denying it, so he wouldn't quit at the lip lock, and she wouldn't stop him.

You can't go there with her. Not yet.

Eyelids lifting, Gage said, "I have to go" while backing farther away, every muscle in his body protesting, not wanting to move.

"No, don't!"

Smoothing his features, pulling that blank mask down, he shook his head. "Lock the door behind me, and don't worry about Jordan. He won't be scaring you again."

With that, he stormed out of her house just as fast as he'd stormed in, came across Jenny, picked her up, went to a secluded spot on the far side of the lake, and used her in a way he shouldn't have in order to slake the hunger for the too young Danica Lorry coursing through him.

"…assume you are telling us this because you believe Gage to be the father?" Dad asked Jenny.

Blinking, Gage wondered how much of the conversation he'd missed.

"Yes, Doctor Harrison."

"Son? Could this be true?"

Gage's attention went to his mother, who looked ashen and was so stone still he didn't see her blinking, then over to Jenny who didn't look much better, and then to his father, who wasn't happy by any means, but was maintaining his cool. "It could be. Yes, sir."

His stomach balled so hard he thought he might puke.

Dad shook his head and steepled his fingers.

Rubbing the throbbing pain in his temple, Gage said, "I'll do the right thing," though saying the words was like spitting up shards of glass. "I'll marry her."

Every dream he'd ever had about Danica was crushed under the boot of his stupidity, and ground into the pavement by his monumental mistake.

His father held up a hand. "No, that's *not* happening. You *will* take care of your obligations, but you will not jump into marriage at eighteen."

Mom had yet to say a word.

"Jenny." Dad's green eyes swung to her. "I'm not trying to be harsh here, but I will insist on a paternity test."

"Okay," she said, then bit her bottom lip.

"We could have an amniocentesis done anywhere between fourteen and twenty weeks, but there is a small risk factor for the baby, so I won't ask that be done. But, when the baby is born, I will insist on a test then."

"All right."

"If it turns out that Gage is the father as you have said, then we will discuss what will be done next, but that in no way means he—or *we* won't help you through this time." Dad looked at him. "Do you agree, son?"

Feeling numb, he nodded.

Chapter Nineteen

"I'M SO HAPPY you told me you'd like this job when I mentioned it during our welcoming committee at the church the other day, Mrs. Beil." Danica's face beamed as she looked at her once-upon-a-time Sunday school teacher, who reminded her of Elizabeth Taylor—only not as blinged-up glamourous with jewels and furs.

"Well, sweetie, I did retire last year from the school district as a bus driver and have the time. Besides, after raising six children of my own and being the proud grandmother of a whopping fourteen, I figured I would qualify for the position."

"I couldn't have dreamed up anyone any better."

Mrs. Beil reached over from where she was seated next to Danica on her snow-white couch and patted her hand. "Thank you for that."

"No need to thank me, Mrs. Beil, it's the truth."

"Since this is my first *official* day, what would you like me to do?"

Ari squealed from the playpen as Aaron tossed a stuffed toy over the top of the enclosure, then clapped his chubby hands in victory while rocking his body back and forth on his little bottom excitedly.

"The twins are just darling," Mrs. Beil said.

"Thank you." Danica stood, went and picked up the lion, putting it back into the pen only to have it tossed right back over, so she left it. On her way back to the couch, she said, "I thought I'd talk about our weekly schedule and daily routine." Her cheeks flushed pink. "I guess I should say; I *try* to keep to a schedule and daily routine. You know, wakeup times, feeding times, playtime, naps, etc., but honestly, I don't do a perfect job. The other day our early afternoon naps didn't happen until four in the afternoon."

"With all the demands of active twins, it's understandable."

"Active would be the word for it."

"Ga-ga!" Aaron babbled loudly.

"Let's see, what was I talking about?" Danica pursed her lips.

"Schedules and routines."

"Right. Thank you. I haven't had much sleep lately, and I'm a bit scatterbrained." She waved a hand and took a seat. "Marcus is out of the house in the mornings by six. And while I'd love to be snoozing, I get up and make him something for breakfast before he leaves for the day. Ari and Aaron are up anywhere between then and eight in the morning. But it is more likely than not, they are up. All the stuff like changing diapers and things happen, then their breakfast, followed by morning baths. By then, depending on their moods and how long it takes, it could be getting close to lunch."

Mrs. Beil nodded.

Danica tucked a piece of unkempt hair behind her ear. "So, I guess what I'm saying is, you could come at any time during the mornings, and we'll be up in some stage of readiness for the day. Though I must apologize for my appearance this morning, I didn't have a quiet moment to myself."

The woman took her in with a critical eye. "You do appear to be a bit… tired."

You have no idea, she thought. "I am, Mrs. Beil."

"I could be here by seven-thirty if you think it would be helpful."

"That's not too early for you?"

"Not at all. I'm an early riser, but I do need time to get Harvey out the door, bless him. My husband said he was going to retire two years ago, but he's still part of the daily grind commuting to Seattle."

"Oh, okay, then. If seven-thirty works for you, I'm thrilled about it."

Ari started fussing, and Danica hopped up. "I better get her. If she starts to cry, Aaron will join in the lament, and we will have two grumpy children."

"Let me get her," Mrs. Beil said, getting to her feet. "In fact, why don't you go draw yourself a hot bubble bath and enjoy a few quiet moments of relaxation."

Danica's eyes rounded. "Are you sure?"

"I'm sure, sweetie. A little alone time soaking in the tub will do wonders for you. You'll see." Going to the playpen, she bent and picked Ari up, *shh*-ing her, patting her small back with gentleness.

Her daughter quieted, placed her cheek on the top of Mrs. Beil's shoulder, and closed her eyes.

"Go on now. Take as long as you need," the wonderful woman said, "things here will be fine."

Feeling as if she'd won the lottery, Danica rose from the couch and headed for her en suite, her anticipation for a real bath instead of a fast-as-a-heartbeat shower making her move her feet quicker.

Once she closed the bathroom door, she slumped against it, glanced up and said, "Thank you, Lord," before she straightened.

Walking over to the tub, Danica turned the faucet on, dumped two capfuls of bubbles in, and watched the water churn the liquid into pretty, white froth.

Mrs. Beil was a godsend.

"Chief?" Dixie's voice came over the intercom, and Gage stopped reading last night's activity report to answer.

"Yes?"

"You have a call on line three. Mrs. Vanderlyn."

He frowned. The name didn't ring any bells. "All right. Thank you." Tapping the blinking light for the line, Gage picked up the handset and put it to his ear. "This is Chief Harrison; how may I help you?"

"Gage," the sultry female voice said, and he knew at once who it was, though it had been a while since he last heard it, so he needed to make sure he was correct.

"Jenny?"

She gave a breathy little laugh. "Yes, it's me."

Gage and Jenny stayed in touch, for the most part, their correspondence having turned into the periodic e-mail and text message, but chatting via phone didn't happen often. "It's good to hear from you, but I have to ask, what's going on?"

"Nothing horrible or pressing. I just wanted to let you know I've moved back to Seattle and thought, perhaps, we could get together for drinks or something. It's been a long time, you know."

"It has been," Gage agreed but didn't commit to drinks. "What brings you back this way? Last I knew you were living in Arizona."

"I guess I didn't tell you, but I married someone. It only lasted a few months, and I've been through a pretty awful divorce and wanted a new, or perhaps I should say, familiar change of scenery."

He was surprised Justin hadn't mentioned this that last time they spoke on the phone.

"Ah… I'm sorry to hear about the divorce. Those can get pretty bad, from what I hear."

"How about you? Mom told me you were the police chief there now. Are things going well?"

"They're going," he said.

"Good or bad?"

"The jury is still out on that one," he teased, her laughter tickling the shell of his ear.

"I know you've never married, but are you seeing anyone special?"

"No. I'm not seeing anyone."

"I'm not asking in an attempt to wheedle my way back into your life, just want to know if you are happy."

"I'm…" It took him a minute to come up with an answer, "okay," he said.

"*Hm*… That says a lot now, doesn't it."

A pause.

A breath.

"Look, I'm coming this weekend to Cedar Point to visit Mom, and I'd love to see you. What do you say?"

Gage squeezed the back of his neck. "I might have some time on Friday around two if that will work."

"Fantastic! I'll see you then."

"All right, see you this weekend."

"Oh, and Gage?"

"Yes?"

"It was terrific talking to you."

"Yeah," he said with a nod, then hung up the phone when the buzz of the line going dead hit his ear.

Chapter Twenty

Before

"THANK YOU FOR coming," Jenny said from her prone position on the examination table. Her small rounded bump protruded on her usually flat stomach as the technician squeezed something that looked like goo on her before placing the wand in the gel substance.

Gage rested his palm on her forearm. "You needed me, no reason for thanks."

A second or two later, the quick *thrum, thrum, thrum* of something rang out in the room, then the lady performing the ultrasound grinned. "That's your baby's heartbeat. Strong and steady."

While interesting, Gage didn't feel what he supposed a father to be should—a sense of wonder and connection. But maybe that was because he'd been detached for the last few weeks, trying to come up with a way to break the news to Danny. He'd told Mase, of course, who promised he wouldn't say a word to anyone, not even Breck, and he'd keep that promise. Mason wasn't one to blab anyway. And as far as he could tell, the gossipmongers around Cedar Point didn't have him and Jenny as the topic of their nattering either, which was a good thing. He didn't want his business and epic mistakes to be making the rounds and getting to Danny before he could somehow locate the courage to tell her.

How am I going to do that?

Closing his eyes, he heard Jenny and the tech talking. Apparently, everything looked okay, which was good news. He didn't want there to be anything wrong with the baby; he just didn't want to be the father.

"Gage, are you all right?"

Jenny's question had his eyes popping open. "I'm fine. Why?"

"You look as white as a ghost, that's why."

He glanced down at his perpetually tanned arm then back at her. "I think white would be quite a feat for me."

She grinned. "You know what I mean."

"Yeah, I'm good. Just haven't had much sleep lately. Homework, football, and stuff." He shrugged.

"*Mm-hm.*" She was looking at him with skepticism in those hazel eyes but didn't call him on the lie.

The whole truth and nothing but the truth? Gage hadn't been sleeping soundly. And it started the night Jenny dropped her bombshell announcement at his parent's dinner table. So he very much doubted his tossing and turning 'til the wee hours of the morning would end anytime soon.

Chapter Twenty-One

"SORRY I'M LATE," Danica said as she came bustling through the door connecting the garage with her kitchen. "The meeting at the auxiliary ran a bit over, and then I had to stop and get gas since I was driving on fumes."

"Not a problem, sweetie." Mrs. Beil grinned, her twins sitting nicely in their highchairs, eating orange popsicles, the bibs stained more than their clothes.

"I don't know how you do this?" Danny glanced around her spotless kitchen in awe. "By this hour in the day, the place usually looks as if the Tasmanian Devil twirled through."

"I was able to do a bit of cleaning while Ari and Aaron took their nap."

"It's been a month of on-time naps." She shook her head. "I'm beyond impressed."

"Well, I'm not doing anything special." Mrs. Beil's brows knitted.

"What's wrong."

"I didn't want to say anything, but…"

"Tell me."

The woman worried her hands. "The first check you gave me bounced, and so did this last one."

"What?" Danica's voice hit the octave of shrill, making Ari's chin quiver. "Oh, baby, it's okay. Mommy's okay," she said, going over to place a kiss on top of her curly blonde head, then looked at Mrs. Beil, dumbfounded. "*Both* of your paychecks bounced?"

The woman nodded. "I'm afraid so."

Since she hadn't set her Michael Kors bag down, she quickly plucked her cell phone free, tapped the icon, and put the device to her ear.

"Hi," her husband said, sounding tired, maybe, not to mention it wasn't his usual 'Hello, sweetheart' greeting.

"Marcus, we've got a problem." She got straight to the point, not bothering to ask what was wrong with him.

"Are the babies okay?" His question had a little more life to it.

"They are fine. No issue with them."

"Then what is it?"

She tapped her Jimmy Choo. "The checks I wrote Mrs. Beil bounced. Both of them."

It was quiet. Too quiet.

"Are you still there?"

"Yes," he said, "it's got to be some mix-up at the bank. I've been moving money around lately, setting up a college fund for the twins. Don't worry though; I'll take care of it."

"Okay. I figured it must be some mix-up, too." The concern she'd felt lifted. "I'll pay Mrs. Beil from my grocery money, but please find out what is going on."

"I will."

"Are you okay. You sound…off."

"I'm just exhausted. Back to back surgeries are wearing me down. I'm not in my late twenties anymore. But I'm fine. Just getting old."

"You're not old."

"Older than you," he countered.

"Forty-three isn't nursing home bound, Marcus. But maybe you should think about slowing it down there at the hospital."

"I'm already giving that some serious thought."

That made her smile. "You are?"

"I am. I've been a resident surgeon a long time, and I've been talking with another colleague of mine about the possibility of opening up a private practice."

"Are you serious?"

"Yes. Nothing has been decided, though."

It didn't matter, just the thought of him being with her and the twins more was a gift. "Will you be home for dinner this evening?"

"I don't know. Let's play it by ear, okay?"

"All right. I'll let you go."

"Kiss the babies for me and tell Mrs. Beil I'm sorry for the mix-up and that I'm calling the bank as soon as we hang up."

"I'll tell her. Love you, Marcus."

"Listen, I've got to go. I'm being paged."

"Okay, bye," Danica said, but he'd already disconnected.

Sitting her bag on the counter, and putting her phone down beside it, she pulled out her wallet, riffled through the bills, happy she just had enough to pay Mrs. Beil, then handed the money over. "Marcus sends his apology for the issue and says there's some sort of mix-up at the bank, but he will take care of it."

The woman's cheeks flushed as she took the cash. "I'm sure he will, and I'm sorry as well."

"Don't be. The bank should be the one apologizing, but I wished you would have said something to me sooner."

Mrs. Beil nodded. "It was kind of awkward, sweetie."

"I understand. But don't worry, nothing like this will happen again."

Unable to sleep, Danica sighed, rolled over in bed and looked at the time on the clock. 12:13 A.M. stared back at her in red, and Marcus still hadn't made it home. Of course, she'd been listening for the telltale sounds of the automatic garage door engaging, the door lifting before her husband pulled his newest Mercedes into the third bay next to his SUV, instead of praying, then nodding off. But regardless of her exhaustion, she wouldn't be sleeping until he was home safe and sound.

Tossing the sheets back, she rolled out of bed, slipped her feet into her fuzzy slippers, and went into the en suite to grab a glass of water, not wanting to make the trek into the kitchen and possibly disturbing the twins. From the sound coming over their baby monitor, all was well, and Danica tried to keep it that way.

Flipping the light on in the bathroom, she walked toward the double vanity then stopped. Unsure why she hadn't put that box back into her jewelry cabinet weeks ago, she reached out, picked it up, and lifted the lid.

Beautiful diamond and sapphire art deco earring's twinkled. She smiled.

With a gentle brush of fingertips over the precious stones, she let out a breath. The gift Gage had given her on her sixteenth birthday hadn't been taken out of its tomb for years until last month, when for some weird reason, she'd felt like putting them on.

While clasping the box shut, the four-carat emerald cut diamond set in a platinum band sparkled on her left hand. However, as beautiful and important as the wedding ring was to her, those earrings were the one piece of jewelry that had always been priceless.

The sweet moment turned into a bitter pill as she took the jewelry to put away correctly. "Soon after Gage sent your dumb little heart aflutter with his thoughtful gift, your world came crashing down."

Chapter Twenty-Two

Before

TAPING HER FEET, Danica was in the two-car garage her father had transformed into a smaller version of the Vibes Dance Studio, ready to put all her emotions into the new piece she'd been working on. Standing and bending her toes, she tapped the button to start the song. Moving into first position, swaying to Alanis Morissette's "Uninvited," arms weaving into port de bras, she broke out into a pirouette before twirling across the floor. As she danced, Danny's worry didn't subside, so she channeled it into the routine.

Leg extending out behind her, then transitioning into a cambré (the bending at the waist to the front, fingertips on the floor, leg going up in the air still behind her), she closed her eyes and let the music move her.

She hadn't heard a thing from Gage. Oh, she'd seen him around school, at church, and youth group, but he acted as if she didn't exist. His bizarre behavior not only confused her, but it hurt, badly, like someone had stabbed a knife in her chest and kept twisting. But for the past couple of weeks, he'd completely stopped coming to church and youth group, and she knew, deep down in her gut, something was seriously wrong.

Go see what's up with him. Ask him what's going on.

When the song ended, she went over and shut off her stereo, grabbed a towel, and dabbed her sweaty face; mind made up to see him.

As if on autopilot, Danica hurried inside the house and up to her room. Rushing, she grabbed a pair of pants she used as a cover-up for her leotards, tossed on a t-shirt, then slipped her feet into a pair of slip-ons, not even taking the time to cut the tape off.

Not bothering with her hair or anything else, she thundered down the stairs, tugged her windbreaker off the coat rack, and opened the front door, gasping—hand to throat. "Gage! You startled me."

He'd been standing on the stoop, the expression on his face so sad, it almost made her cry once she really looked at him. She wanted to grab hold of his muscled body, plead and beg him to tell her what was wrong, but she held herself still. "I was just heading out to see you. What are you doing?"

He didn't answer.

"Gage?"

"Your mom's car isn't in the driveway. Are you here alone, or is Breck with you?"

There was something off with his voice. Almost flat.

"No one is here."

"Can I come in?"

"Sure." Danica stepped aside, allowing him entrance then closed the door behind him. When she spun around, saying, "Gage," his, "We need to talk," blended in harmony.

"Okay." She tossed her jacket and took his hand, but he pulled away, the stabbing sensation in her chest flaring to life once more. "Do you want to go into the kitchen? Maybe have a snack and talk? Or maybe a drink? We've got—"

"No."

She frowned at his abruptness. "All right. Where do you want to go?"

"The living room."

She was surprised, figuring they'd go into the den. They always went to the den.

"Okay. Let's go." Danny took the few steps it required to get to the couch and took a seat on the edge, Gage sitting in the wingback chair across from her, obviously putting as much distance between them as he could.

She rubbed at the pain in her breastbone. "What's going on? I've been really worried ever since you called me a few weeks ago and said you couldn't take me to youth group because 'something came up'. You haven't been talking to me, and well, fine, but you haven't been in church either," she rushed out, peeved overtaking the ache. "It's like you've decided to be a ghost or something. I wouldn't even know you're alive if I didn't see you at school. And thanks for ignoring me, by the way, it's been so much fun!"

"Danny." His usual sandpaper-smooth voice was nothing more than a hoarse whisper. "There's something you should know, and I'm not sure how to tell you."

Gage bent, put his forearms on the worn-white thighs of his jeans, and glanced down at the carpet.

With a sense of doom looming, Danica swallowed the lump starting to form in her throat. "Whatever it is, just say it."

"Jenny."

The name was enough to do her in, but she asked in a low tone, "What about her?"

"She's…" He paused, set up, rubbed his forehead, looked at her with an expression she'd never seen before, and said, "She's pregnant and says the baby is mine."

Danica was expecting him to say they were dating or something, and that would be horrible enough, but not that she was… She was…

Had someone sliced her open with a samurai sword? Was she bleeding out?

A heartbeat passed. Then two, and three, as the life drained from her.

"She's-she's—" Danica couldn't get the words out of her parched mouth, they seemed to get stuck in the sand.

"She's pregnant." Gage's brows pulled down. "I just came from the ultrasound and knew I had to tell you. I didn't want you to hear this from someone else."

Standing to her feet, she swayed like a sailor on a ship in the middle of a storm.

"Danny?" Gage stood.

Head spinning as if she were going to faint, she held up her hand, palm out. "Get out!"

"Danica, I—"

"Leave, Gage." With her heart shattering, she somehow held back the tears threatening to overflow.

He rounded the coffee table and stepped up to her, reaching. She jerked away from him. "Don't touch me. Don't *ever* touch me again!"

"I'm sorry," he said, voice broken. "I never meant—"

"You never meant to what? Send me mixed signals for years, finally kiss me, hold me on your couch, making me think maybe, just maybe we could—" She shook her head, straightened her spine and let all the hurt, anger, disappointment, and heartache churn into a venom spewing from her lips. "No more, Gage! I'm done. From this point forward, you *don't exist* in my world."

Turning, she made her way to the stairs, briefly glanced over at the boy who had single-handedly torn her apart, and said flatly, "Lock the front door when you go."

Devastated in ways she never thought possible, she went straight up to her room, slammed the door shut, fell onto her bed in a limp heap, and let the torment in her soul scream its way past her trembling lips.

Chapter Twenty-Three

"GAGE!" JENNY SASHAYED into his office, wearing a long, red, cashmere coat, a huge smile on her face as he stood from his chair and came around the desk. Grabbing his biceps, she leaned in and kissed his cheek. "It's so good to see you."

Making sure to take a step back, Gage grinned. "It's nice to see you too."

Those hazel eyes of hers scanned him. "You look so handsome in uniform."

"And you look as if you haven't aged a day since I last saw you."

She waved, then adjusted the strap of her purse. "I'll let my plastic surgeon know you think he's doing a great job."

His brow furrowed. Gage always did have a hard time knowing if she was teasing or if she was serious. "Are you joking about the plastic surgery thing?"

She lifted her gaze heavenward. "Yes, silly. I was." She glanced around his office, her attention falling onto his 'reminder,' then looked back at him. At first, he thought she was going to bring up the tragic events in L.A., but instead, she asked, "So, where are you taking me for drinks?" rather too cheerily.

"Since I'm on the job, I'm afraid drinks will be your choice of soda at The Snack Shack or coffee from Mason's place."

"I heard he opened a chocolate shop. Delish!"

"He did. And it comes with a fancy coffee bar. Frappuccino's, Latte's, Mochaccino's…"

"How about plain old black sludge?"

Gage chuckled. "He serves that too."

"All right. Let's go."

The *bleep, bleep, bleep-bleep* of Danica entering her PIN rang out as the ATM clicked, started sorting, and then shot her withdrawal into the slot. They'd never talked about the money snafu further, as when Marcus finally came home, he fell into bed.

Grabbing the bills, happy relief settled over her. Marcus had taken the time to chat with their bank in Seattle, and whatever the problem was had been fixed.

Putting the replacement cash into her wallet, she went over a mental list of to-do's—*Pick up something cute for the babies to wear for Halloween. Drop off the dry cleaning. Make a quick stop at the Food Barn…*

Her thoughts were interrupted by the bell tones of her cell phone, so she slipped it out of the designated pocket in her purse, tapped the icon and said, "Hey, Brecky-boo!"

Her sister chuckled. "Hi there, sis."

"How are the honeymooners?"

Danica could practically see Breckin's green eyes roll. "We've been back for two weeks."

"I know, but isn't the honeymoon continuing?"

"Maybe."

Danica could *hear* the sly grin. "By that wily tone, I'll take that as a yes."

"Being married to Mase is pretty great."

"Aw… I'm so glad you are happy."

"Me, too."

Danica smiled. "So, what's going on?"

"Nothing really. I just wanted to call and see if you are bringing the twins to Trick or Treat Street tomorrow evening."

"I was planning on it. Why?"

"I thought maybe it would be fun to come to the shop and help us give out candy. The twins all dressed up will be a big hit."

"Sure, that sounds like fun. I'm going to go pick up their costumes here in just—" Turning for her vehicle, Danica's good mood dropped like a led weight. "Breck, I've got to go."

She heard, "Danny is everything—" before she pulled the phone from her ear and stood there on the sidewalk, a still life, her open purse dangling off her forearm, white-knuckling her cell while something vile squeezed off her air and noosed around her throat.

With his palm resting between Jenny's coat-covered shoulder blades, Gage directed their path across Main Street, then down the sidewalk. All the lamp posts and storefronts were decorated for the current holiday, he absently noted as the occasional, "Good afternoon, Chief," came their way, people doing a double-take at his companion.

"Do you think they're surprised to see me?" Jenny glanced at him with one corner of her mouth tipped up.

"Whatever would give you that idea?"

Their teasing came to a screeching halt. Well, Gage's did when he noticed Danny just a few feet away, frozen in place, lips parted, with a look of desolation on her face he'd hoped to never, ever see again, let alone be the cause of.

The screams of horrible pain started seconds after Gage heard Danny's bedroom door slam shut —a horrible heart-wrenching sound, as if she was being gutted. And, she was—by him. Every wail mixed into his pain and just about took him down. But when her intermittent sobs became evident, he willed his legs to move to get to her. Poised, there at the foot of the stairs, he stopped.

"From this point forward, you don't exist in my world."

"She means it," he muttered.

Fighting to maintain, not allow *his* tears to escape, he turned toward the Lorry's front door, opened it, made sure the knob was locked, and whispered, "I'm so sorry, Danny." Then the words he'd meant to say for months fell from his lips. "I love you," he whispered, before he shuffled his leaden feet outside, closing the door behind him.

With the finality of that sound, something happened inside of Gage—a fissure formed in his heart. Somehow, he knew with all certainty, the faultline would, in time, shift, becoming more extensive as he took *her ring* off his finger and slid it into the pocket of his jeans.

Stopping in front of the Choc-Oh! Cottage, Jenny asked, "What?" Then she looked in the direction Gage was. "O-o-o-h…"

"Listen, go on in, and I'll join you in just a few."

Jenny's, "Sure" registered, but he was already walking away, heading toward the woman who appeared to be shellshocked.

Just steps from her, she blinked out of her immobile state, turned, and started hustling down the sidewalk, away from her parked vehicle. "Danny!"

She didn't stop or glance back; she just power walked in those too-high heels.

"Danica!"

She ran.

Gage sighed and took off after her, finally putting his hand around her elbow before she rounded the Cedar Point Gazette. "Danica?"

Yanking her arm free, she spun on him. "What?"

"Shouldn't that be my question, but with way less attitude?"

Jerking her purse up, she closed the yawning top. "Really, Gage?"

"Why did you take off like that?" he asked, but already knew the answer—seeing him with Jenny had stirred up her world of old pain.

She clenched her teeth. "Maybe because I didn't want to see you."

"You couldn't have got in your vehicle and driven away?"

Her eyelashes fluttered as if processing his question. "I need the exercise."

His lips twitched; he couldn't help it. "I see."

"You can let go of my arm now."

As he released his grip, she started to leave, so he stopped her once more. "Nope. You're not going anywhere."

"Are you arresting me, Chief Harrison?"

He arched a brow. "Do I need to?"

"If you think I'm going to stay put and talk to you, then I guess you'd better; because I'm leaving."

He went for his cuffs, and those beautiful blue eyes narrowed on him. "You wouldn't *dare*."

"Oh, but I would." Dangling the steel in front of her, he said, "Go ahead and try me, beautiful."

She gaped.

He reached out, placed his fingers under the shelf of her chin, and lifted until those pretty lips shut. "Now, let's get a few things straight."

"Like what?"

"First, nothing is going on between Jenny and me. She moved to Seattle recently and is here to see her mother."

She crossed her arms and glowered.

"She wanted to take a few minutes to catch up," he said, "that's all."

"All right then. You need to get *this* straight. First, I don't care what you are or are not doing with Jenny Lansing."

"Vanderlyn."

Her nose wrinkled in that cute way she had. "Huh?"

"It's not Lansing. It's Vanderlyn."

"Whatever. I don't care."

"You don't?"

Her hand shot up. "Why would I? What you choose to do is your business and none of mine."

"It's not?"

"No, Gage. It's not. I'm a married woman. I couldn't care less who *you* see."

"I'm *not* seeing Jenny. It's just a friendly visit."

Fire snapped in her eyes. "You know. I just don't get how you could still be friends with that, that *woman*, especially after—" She clamped her pretty mouth shut.

"I thought you didn't care?"

"I don't!"

"I think maybe you do."

It was wrong, he got that; but his heart and mind pleaded with her, *Say you do. Tell me you care.*

"Aah!" She stomped around him. "Either arrest me or don't, but this foolish conversation is done."

With a smirk on his face, Gage watched Danny hustle back the way they'd come, totally enjoying the view before he got hold of himself. He cleared his throat, put his cuffs away, and strode down the sidewalk, waving when her Escalade passed.

Amused, he shook his head. He'd swear, by the expression she wore, she'd love to flip him the bird and do it with vigor. But while she might secretly consider it, she'd never actually do it.

Chapter Twenty-Four

Before

WHEN THE BELL rang, Gage shot out of his seat, ready to commence his covert guard dog duties. Everyone knew, when Danny turned sixteen, she could date, so she had been attracting the boys like bees to honey—which meant he'd been doing an excellent job of threatening them within an inch of their lives if they so much as looked at her.

It had worked. One visit from him, be it at school, around town, or after youth group, did the trick—they'd leave her be. Except for…

Gage's eyes narrowed on the new kid who had transferred in from the sunny shores of California—Max Dillon, a junior and golden boy with a big smile full of entirely too-white teeth. Teeth he wanted to bash in, and would if he didn't get his arm from around Danny.

Making his way down the hall, shoulder clashing with someone he didn't notice only hearing a masculine, "Hey, watch it," Gage stepped in front of the pair, eyes laser-focused on his target.

"Get"—Gage balled his fist—"your"—he stepped closer—"arm"—he put his chest against Max's—"off"—he gritted through clenched teeth—"Danny!"

Danica glowered up at him. "Don't be such a jerk!"

Max did the smart thing and removed his arm. But then for some stupid reason, he maneuvered her behind him.

As if Gage would ever physically hurt a single hair on Danica's head!

Gage's attention went to her peeking out from Max's decent-sized frame. "Come here, Danny."

"No!"

"Do it now, Danica Dawn!"

"Dude," Max said, "I don't know what your glitch is, but you're not going to talk to my girl that way."

"Your girl?" he snarled, eyes going to the kid he wanted to pound.

"His girl," Danny said, stepping out, looking at him with pure disgust on her face.

It was that expression, not the shove to his shoulder she gave him, which knocked him back.

"Come on, Max," she said, "let's go."

Danica took hold of the kid's hand, and tugged—the guy not budging for a second, then he turned with her and started to walk away.

Everyone in the hall had stopped whatever they were doing to watch the scene. Of course, the word about Jenny had spread, but keeping his business out of the spotlight had worked for about five months until she came back home for her grandfather's funeral, and he'd become her shoulder to cry on—literally. Coach Ames even called him into his office to confirm the rumors. So, yeah, he was giving everyone more ammunition to fire around town again. But right then, he didn't seem to care.

"Danica!"

She spun around and hit him dead center in the heart with, "I hate you!" causing him to flinch.

She left with Max, leaving him standing there. He wasn't sure he actually could locate his legs since every muscle in his body seized. Nor did Gage think he was breathing.

At some point, he finally became aware of two things. First, the hall cleared out, becoming a virtual ghost town. And second? The bell rang, indicating the start of third period, making him late.

Chapter Twenty-Five

"SHE'S IN LOVE with you, you know." Jenny's soft voice had Gage putting his coffee cup down.

"No. I think to see us together just stirred up some past hurt for her."

"Danica Lorry has been in love with you since you were kids, and she still is."

"She's married, Jenny."

Her perfect brow arched. "And your point is?"

"I guess that *is* my point. She's a married woman, end of."

"A married woman, who's in love with you."

Gage shook his head.

"Do you believe for one second, if she didn't love you, she would have been so upset seeing me with you after all these years?" Jenny picked at her brownie. "Come on, Gage. Buy a clue."

He knew Danica cared for him, even though she tried to hide it, and at one point he believed she did love him until he ruined everything. But now? Their friendship had been mended to some extent, although the thought Danica *could* love him, as in present tense, did something strange to his stomach. Or maybe it was his heart.

"Let's change the subject," he said before he took another sip of his no longer hot but warm-ish drink.

"All right. What would you like to discuss?"

"How is Justin doing?"

Jenny's face lit up. "He is such a wonderful boy. Well, he'll be twenty-one in January, so I guess I can't call him a boy any longer."

"I would imagine he wouldn't like it, no."

"It's hard to believe Justin is all grown up."

"How's he doing in college?"

"Pretty good, though he's probably told you he's changed majors something like four times."

Gage smiled. "He has. It's Philosophy now."

"Yes, but what in the world will he do with a Philosophy degree?"

"Anything he wants to, I suppose."

"Did I send you that picture of him with his new girlfriend?"

A frown formed on his brow. "I don't think so. I haven't received any pictures in a while."

"I would have e-mailed it."

"Then, no."

"Here," she said, pulling out her cell. "I've got a bunch saved on my phone."

After tapping the screen, Jenny held out the little device so Gage could see. "Isn't she cute?"

"Very," he said, his attention going from the tiny blonde girl and locking on Justin's face, remembering the first time he saw him.

Chapter Twenty-Six

Before

GAGE CONSIDERED HIMSELF a pretty tough guy, having survived numerous broken bones in his life, as well as getting bashed on the football field pretty regularly. But, being inside the delivery room with Jenny was testing his notion as she squeezed the life out of his hand with an iron grip!

"Give me the epidural!" Her voice had gone guttural, and he wondered if her head was going to twist on her neck like Linda Blair in the *Exorcist.*

"Jenny," he said, using a soft voice, though it was a total sham; he wasn't calm, "remember to breathe."

That earned him a string of expletives, and some of them were quite creative, he'd give her that.

As sweat beads broke out on her upper lip, he hoped things would get better soon, glad to see the anesthesiologist until he did a horrible thing with a needle in her lower back. Gage squirmed uncomfortably, even though he wasn't the one with a sharp object stuck in him. But, okay, he was still standing… then the doctor came in, and the real eye-opening experience started.

"Son? Are you all right?" He heard the older gentleman, but couldn't locate his voice to speak. "Nurse, make sure he doesn't pass out on us."

Am I swaying? He believed he was, blinking when someone came over and asked him to have a seat, or he thought that's what she said, finally registering, "…or do you think you need to step out for a moment?"

"*NO!*" Jenny's response to the question he'd been asked came fast and hard. "Don't go."

"I'm fine," Gage said, closing his eyes and taking a few deep breaths.

Heck, if Jenny didn't want to use the breathing techniques they'd learned, he would. And it worked.

"All right," said the doctor, "one more large push, Jenny, and we're there."

She grunted.

"That's it, that's it. Good."

Gage made it back to his feet just in time to see a small, wrinkled, slimy blueish being clasped in the doctor's hands. And for some bizarre reason, seeing him bent between Jenny's splayed legs, he thought of the man dressed in a baseball uniform with a helmet, face mask, and a catcher's mitt instead of the green scrubs, surgical mask, and hair cap he sported. "It's a boy!"

A second later, the baby's "Waah, waah, waah" echoed in the room, when they lay the newborn on Jenny's upper belly/lower chest.

He tried to locate something other than the happiness the pain of giving birth was over for her, and the baby was all right—some type of fatherly joy, a stretching of his heart.

Isn't this the moment I should finally feel a connection?

"I did it," Jenny said, exhaustion radiating from her.

Gage smiled down at her, then placed a chaste kiss to the top of her head. "You did."

"It's a boy," Gage announced to his parents a few minutes later as he stepped into the waiting room of the hospital. "Seven pounds five ounces."

His father stood, then clapped him on the back.

"And Jenny. Is she doing okay?" His mother's brow was crinkled.

He nodded. "She's doing great. You can see her in a little bit. Right now, they are doing all the post procedures and stuff."

"Are you all right?" Dad asked, concern on his face.

"Sure. Why?"

"You look a bit dazed, son."

"It was a lot to take in, I guess." Gage paused, wondering if he should say what was weighing on his heart.

"What is it?" Mom asked, coming and taking hold of his hand.

His gaze bounced from her to his dad, then back to her. "I just don't feel anything."

"What do you mean?"

"I mean, shouldn't I have some connection to the baby? Some parental instincts? Instant and unfathomable love?"

"No one says having an instant connection is a hard and fast rule." His father squeezed his shoulder.

Gage raked his fingers through his dark hair. "But… I'm not your biological child, Dad, yet I've heard you talk about loving me from the moment you first saw me."

"It's true," Mom said, "we both felt that way."

"Then why don't I?"

It wasn't until an hour later, when the nurses brought a bundled baby into Jenny's room, and placed him into his arms, that Gage truly *saw* his son. *Justin*, as Jenny was calling him (though the birth certificate had yet to be filled out), had milky-white skin, almost translucent.

He skimmed a fingertip along the little one's soft cheek, studying the child, looking for something familiar that might come from him, like the shape of his nose, the line of his pink bowed lips, the curve of an ear…but… there was nothing of Gage there.

Gently, he took off the blue stocking cap to see a fine sheen of peachy fuzz on top of Justin's tiny head. Touching it must have roused him—the baby opened his eyes. They were blue-green, though he'd heard a newborn's eyes could change color as time went on, but still.

"Jenny," Gage said in barely a whisper.

Her watery gaze came to his.

"Is this baby mine?"

She broke down, crying, she stuttered, "I— I— I don't know."

Getting up and carefully placing the baby into the bassinet beside her bed, he went to her and took hold of her cold hand. "Tell me the truth."

"I am telling you the truth. I *don't* know. But I've been hoping and even praying he would be."

"He doesn't look like me at all."

"I know."

"If he's not mine, then who does he belong to?"

Jenny shook her head, wiping at her wet cheeks. "I don't know."

Gage frowned. "What do you mean? You have to know."

"No. I don't."

"I'm confused here," he said, sitting down on the side of her bed, keeping his attention trained on her face.

"I'd gone to a party with my bestie, Karen. It was like most frat party's we'd attended, nothing any crazier or anything. Then she saw a guy she'd been hoping to hook up with and went off with him. I thought about leaving, but for some dumb reason, I stayed."

Jenny swiped a palm over the blanket, covering her legs.

"You hooked up with someone there?"

"No. I didn't. I hung with a few college friends, some boys I had classes with, and a few I didn't know. Then after having more than a few drinks, I excused myself for the restroom. When I came back, I fell right into the conversation with them again. But soon after, my head started spinning, and the space I was in began to tilt. I knew something was wrong with me and told someone. I wasn't speaking to any one of them in particular. I just said I didn't feel well."

She paused, glancing away from Gage, looking out the window of her room. "I remember a voice saying he would help me, staggering down a long hall, and to what I thought was the front door."

Jenny rubbed at her temple.

"What happened?" A sense of dread for her hit him.

"I think I said something about helping me home, and hearing he was, then I don't know. It was like I slipped into darkness. I didn't dream. I wasn't aware of anything. I was just… gone."

Gage placed his palm over her sheet-covered knee.

"I woke up in my dorm room. The morning light shone in. I winced. It hurt my eyes. I couldn't figure out how I'd got there or when I'd gone to bed, then I tried to get up and realized I was half-dressed and missing some important items of clothing. That's when I felt it. The soreness in places I shouldn't have been sore."

Jenny looked at him. "I think someone slipped me something, took me back to my dorm, and raped me while I was unconscious. I should have perhaps gone to the campus nurse, or campus police and reported it—" Jenny scraped her teeth over her bottom lip and looked away from him. "But I didn't. I just pushed the whole thing out of my head, and then I got the call Mom was going to have knee surgery, so I came home to be with her, and well—" she met his gaze "—you know the rest from there."

Her chin quivered, right before she let loose of the pain.

"Oh, Jenny." Gage held her in his arms while she cried, with deep, body rocking sobs that his body absorbed. "I'm so very sorry."

"So am I," she whispered while he was rocking her.

"*Shh*… You're going to be okay."

Once she settled, she said, "If Justin's not yours, then he won't ever know who his real father is, because I don't. And after what happened, even if I somehow knew, I wouldn't want a rapist in my son's life."

"Don't worry." Gage smoothed the hair back from Jenny's face. "No matter what, I won't leave you or Justin hanging. Even if I'm not his dad, I'll do everything I can to be there for him."

Chapter Twenty-Seven

"I'VE NEVER THANKED you." As she placed her warm palm over the top of his hand, Gage glanced at Jenny's pretty face, his brows pulling down.

"Thank me for what?"

"For being a part of my son's life. You are there for him when he needs a man to talk to."

"It's not a big deal."

"Yes, it is. How about all the times you came to visit when he was growing up? You taught him how to throw a ball, showed up for important events." She shrugged. "Thank you for being a stand-up guy when you didn't need to be. You could have told us, 'See ya later,' but, you never did. So, for all of that and more, I'm grateful."

Her words seemed to soften Gage some. "I've been honored to be a part of Justin's life. Although I know it hasn't been anything like having a full-time father around, I did my best."

"You did a great job under the circumstances."

"I made you a promise, and I always keep them. Besides, Justin was a great kid, so loving him wasn't a hardship."

"He's a great kid because of you, Gage."

He grinned. "Thank you, but I would suppose you have something to do with that too."

"You're right. I do. But he has known from day one he can count on you, and that means the world to me."

Chapter Twenty-Eight

Before

THE MOMENT HE received the results of the paternity test, Gage went to look for Danica. She might not want to see him, but he had to find a way to tell her. Make her listen. What happened after that between them, he couldn't know, but he had to try to repair—at least—their friendship.

After parking his car behind Mrs. Lorry's old clunker in the driveway, Gage clambered out, the late January chill smacking him in the face as he tugged the collar of his coat up to his chin and hurried to the front door. Jabbing the bell, he opened the storm door and waited, shifting from foot-to-foot, hoping someone would show up soon, then gave in and punched the bell again.

"Gage?" Mrs. Lorry had opened the door, a frown marring her forehead. "What's wrong, honey?"

"I need to speak to Danica. It's important. Is she home?"

"No." She shook her sandy-blonde head. "I'm sorry, she's not."

Disappointment stabbed him. "Will you tell me where she is?"

"Come in. It's too cold out."

"No. It's okay. I can't stick around. But I do need to talk to your daughter."

"She's at school. Practicing for that musical she's in."

"Oh, okay. I'll catch up with Danny there. Thanks."

He started to turn, but she stopped him when she said, "Gage?"

He glanced at her. "Yes, ma'am?"

"Don't break Danny's heart again," she said with a quiet authority.

His eyes widened, and for a moment, he didn't know what to do or say. Any heartache Danny felt, she wouldn't have confessed to anyone, not even her mother. Gage knew her well, and she was the mistress at keeping things bottled-up tight.

He realized Mrs. Lorry was watching him process this, with a knowledge only a mother possessed, so with a sincerity that bubbled up from his soul. He said, "I won't."

"See that you don't."

He nodded, then turned, jogged to his GTO, slipped inside, and headed for Cedar Point High.

Danica saw him the moment he walked into the auditorium. As he came down the aisle and took a seat in the middle row, her voice wavered for just one moment while she sang. But by pulling all her attention back to the task at hand, she was able to pretend he wasn't there and continued with practice.

"All right, everyone." Mrs. Bisbee clapped. "That was great, but it's time to call it a day. Don't forget to be here at four-thirty instead of three-thirty when school lets out tomorrow. Be safe getting home."

Taking her time, Danica considered leaving through the backstage exit, but Gage would notice and do what he needed to do to get to her back there. If she did that, the two of them would be secluded, and being alone with him was something she sure didn't want.

She let out a breath.

In a perfect world, she didn't want to speak to Gage at all, but he'd obviously come to talk to her. She couldn't imagine any other reason for him to show up at a practice for the school play.

With a thousand hot needles poking her spine, she followed the rest of the cast, taking the steps as slow as possible, trying to put off the 'up close and personal' with Gage as long as she could.

Danica kept her attention on her feet until she came to the first row where she'd left her coat. As if she were feeble, she picked the thing up from where she'd discarded it in a chair, slipped one arm into the garment, then the other. She pulled her long hair free of the restraint, releasing it—the dense strands tumbling down her back, slipping along the material.

"Danny."

She spun to the sound of Phillip's voice. "Yeah?"

"Do you need a ride home? I'd be happy to—"

"I'll take her," Gage said, striding up to them, making her beating heart stutter before resuming its normal pace.

"Dude." The two of them bumped fists. "I didn't know you where here."

"I came to talk to Danny, so I'll give her a lift home."

Phillip's gaze bounced between her and Gage, then landed on her. "You good?"

"Why wouldn't she be?" Gage sounded none too happy with his friend's question.

"I get you're all 'big brother' protective of Danica, but back off!"

Her eyes widened. She never knew Phillip could put some bite into his words. He was usually a 'go with the flow' kind of guy.

Gage stepped up to him, and Danica put her palm on his chest, stopping Gage from making a butt of himself. "I'm fine, Phillip," she said, then glanced up, avoiding any direct eye contact with the boy who broke her. "And you need to chill. If I want to accept a ride from Phillip, I will. You don't have a say in the matter."

"Dann—"

She shook her head and held up her palm. "Don't." She couldn't believe what she was going to say, but there it was on the tip of her tongue, getting ready to spill. "I'll let you take me home. Emphasis on the 'let'." Danica slid her attention to Phillip. "Thank you for offering, but I'm good."

She wasn't, not really, but whatever, she was going to attempt to pull off the fib.

"Sure?"

She nodded.

"All right." Phillip's gaze bounced between them again. "I'll see you guys tomorrow."

"See you," she said, watching him go before she started to follow.

Gage stopped her with that big hand of his, wrapping over her shoulder, which she shrugged off, eyes snapping as she looked up at him. "Don't touch me!"

He let her go, hand up mea culpa. "Sorry."

Pulling her gaze from him, she made her way to the exit, walking at a brisk pace, Gage trailing along beside her, quiet. He tried to open the door for her, but she pushed on the lock-bar with force, stepping out into the evening air—the chill hitting her.

"Where are you parked?" she asked, her tone clipped.

"Over there." He pointed to one of the lot lights, his cherry-red GTO highlighted by the beam.

Straightening her shoulders, Danica didn't stomp, but she wasn't heading over at a reasonable pace either. Gage jogged to get in front of her to open up the passenger door, the only time she slowed so she could get inside.

She didn't bother to tell him thanks, she just took the seat, looking straight ahead and crossed her arms.

A few seconds later, he was behind the wheel. "Thanks for agreeing to this," he said.

She didn't take the bait, just kept her attention trained out the front windshield, hearing his exasperated sigh.

"Do you think you might look at me?"

She didn't respond.

"Please?"

"You wanted to take me home, so take me," she said.

"I will, but I want to talk first."

"I don't recall 'talking' as part of the deal."

"Danica Dawn, look at me."

His stern softness penetrated the fortress of anger she'd built around her, making her shoulders slump.

"Please, Danny."

She closed her eyes and dropped her head, her hair shifting to form a curtain between them.

"Please," he said again.

"I don't want to."

"I get it. I do, but I want to see you. Don't shut yourself off from me."

It took all of her strength not to cave and look at him, but if she did, she'd fall into the depth of stupidity, and she wasn't going to do that again with him. Ever.

"All right." Gage sighed. "I'll talk. You listen."

The childish part of her wanted to stick her fingers in her ears, but she wasn't going to stoop that low, so she just nodded.

"I know I have confused you with my hot and cold behavior, but I wasn't being a giant jerk, I was fighting a battle with myself."

That did it. She lifted her head and turned to look at him, but remained quiet.

He smiled, but it was sad somehow. "See, I made your father a promise. It was a simple one at the time. I would look out for you, and I've done my best to do that. But somewhere along the way, I developed feelings for you I couldn't ignore, though I needed to."

"Why would you need to?" Danica asked.

"Because the feelings I had were the type of thing your father wouldn't be too happy about, especially since you were too young for me to be having them."

"So you…" She shook her head, confused.

"I didn't want to break my promise to him, but so many times I was on the verge of doing that, of stepping over a line I wanted to cross so badly with you, but if I did—"

"You'd break your word."

Gage nodded. "But, Danny, I came so close to shattering it."

She gave in and locked her eyes with his silver gaze, fastened on her.

"When we kissed," he said, "I was ready to go to places with you that wouldn't have been appropriate. I knew I had to do things right, so I backed off."

"Clearly."

"I was waiting for you to turn sixteen so we could date. So, I could make you my girl officially."

Every part of her body stilled, maybe even her heart.

"But I did something monumentally stupid when I left your house after kissing you." Gage grabbed the steering wheel, white-knuckling it.

"Jenny," she whispered, her gut twisting.

"Yes."

Danica glanced down, the pain slicing into her at the thought of Gage touching someone else with the hands *she* wanted to feel—of him doing *other* things with that girl.

"I'm so, so sorry for hurting you."

She was sorry too, but even though she was hearing he cared for her, any momentary joy she'd felt vanished with the introduction of Jenny Lansing into their conversation. But, wouldn't she be forever part of it, whether spoken or unspoken?

Yes. Jenny will always be the thorn in my side.

With tears swimming in her eyes, Danica said, "Sorry really doesn't fix anything though, does it."

"Maybe not, but there's something you need to know."

"What?" she asked, looking up at him once more.

"The baby *isn't* mine."

She blinked, letting those four words sink in. "How do you know that?"

"It's obvious when you look at him."

"Him?"

"Jenny gave birth to a boy," he said.

Regardless of the baby being his or not, the damage between them couldn't be undone as far as Danica was concerned.

"She named him Justin."

"Oh," she mumbled.

"But, back to your question. I know for a fact the baby isn't mine because my father insisted from the start on a paternity test once the little one was born." Gage started to reach for her, then stopped. "I received the test results today. He isn't mine."

"I'm sorry," she said, not sure if she was or wasn't, but she figured getting the news Jenny had been messing around on him wouldn't have been something he wanted.

"Don't be."

She frowned. "But your girlfriend was unfaithful. That has to be hard."

"She wasn't, and isn't, my girlfriend."

Danica shook her head. "I don't get it."

"You do, Danny."

"Are you saying you have no feelings about her and the baby?"

"No. I'm saying we were never together in a boyfriend/girlfriend type of way."

She wasn't sure if hearing that was worse. "You just had sex with her. That's what you're saying."

Gage looked uncomfortable, shifting in his seat, hand going to the gearshift. "We hooked-up some, but I'd put an end to it when I realized how important you were, and still are to me."

"Evidently not," she spat, anger popping like effervescent bubbles inside of her.

"I already admitted I made a horrible mistake, and I can't undo that. I would if I could but—"

"Take me home," she said, turning back around to stare out the windshield.

"Danny, I—"

"You talked. I listened. Now I'm ready to go home."

"But, we're not done—"

"Oh, but we are, Gage. We've been done since you came to my house and told me Jenny was *pregnant*."

"Justin isn't my baby, Danny. Please."

The pleading in his voice did nothing. Meant nothing.

"Take me home, or I'm getting out and walking."

"Danica, listen to me—"

Quick as could be, she lifted the handle on the door and was out of the car, hearing the echoing slam behind her as she took off running at full speed. If Gage were going to follow her, he'd have to do it on foot since she weaved her way through the few remaining cars in the lot, and jumped the chain-link fence into the football field.

"Danny!" Gage's bellow came, but he wasn't close, and she wasn't going to turn around to see how far back he was either. She just put on more speed, heading for the opposite fence where she'd jump again, escape into the trees.

Chapter Twenty-Nine

THE ANNUAL TRICK or Treat Street the shops put on was happening, so Main Street was buzzing. Gage was glad he had an extra patrol on shift for the night. Tapping his brakes, he slowed and came to a stop at a red light, watching the pedestrians pass by the front of his vehicle—little Bailey Johnson, dressed like a fairy princess, waving at him. With a smile, he waved back as she hopped alongside her mother, holding her hand.

Making an effort to be extra diligent, he drove like a little old lady, putting on his turn signal. He'd park in the newspaper's side lot and then head down to the Choc-Oh! Cottage, see how things were going there with Mason and his crew. Maybe even help with giving out candy, since Dixie and one of his rookies had matters handled if anyone brought their kids by the station. But mostly, people stuck to the downtown stores, and the police station wasn't on the main drag.

After parking, he grabbed a few Tootsie Rolls and some assorted suckers, shoving them into the pockets of his coat, then slid out of his SUV.

He was hit up by one of the kids the moment his foot hit the sidewalk in front of the building.

"Trick or Treat, Chief?"

"Hi, Kallie." He pulled a candy from his pocket and dropped it into her outstretched bucket. "That sure is a pretty crown you're wearing."

She smiled up at him, too cute with her missing two front teeth. "Thanks!"

"You sure are welcome."

"Thank you, Chief," her Mom, Victoria said.

"No problem. You both have a good night and be safe out here."

"We will," the woman said before tugging her daughter alongside her, heading for more loot.

With a few more stops to give out the candy he'd stashed, he finally stepped inside Mason's shop, the smell of chocolate and coffee always a great scent.

Kasey came over wearing a black cat getup. "Happy Halloween!"

"Right back at you."

She grinned and glanced down.

He heard, "G!" and turned to the sound of Mason's voice, the man smiling from ear-to-ear.

"Hey, brother. Where's your costume?"

"You know I'm not the costume kind of guy, but wait until you see Breck." Mason shook his head, an indulgent grin on his face.

"Boo!" Breck yelled, jumping out from behind a display case, looking like one of the zombies on *The Walking Dead*, but she was too happy to pull it off completely.

Gage chuckled. "Now, that's a costume."

"Do you like it?" She spun around for his inspection.

"Very undead."

Breckin clapped and bounded to her husband. "I told you it wasn't too much."

Mason kissed her makeup-smudged forehead. "You're crazy, but I love you."

Gage looked away when they went into their little snuggle-box of two, not jealous, but sometimes wishing he had just a slice of what they did.

"Sorry I'm late!" Danny came through the door, pushing the double stroller, and he grinned. Not only had she dressed up, jet-black hair and all, but her twins were decked out like two of the seven dwarfs, though he didn't remember there being a girl dwarf.

"Gage," she said, coming to a halt.

"*Snow White*," he returned, before squatting to peek in at the babies. "And who do we have here. Sleepy and Doc?"

Ari burst into giggles as he tapped the tip of her button nose, Aaron tossing a fist and grinning.

"I don't know how you do that," Danica said unbuttoning her coat, right as the sirens started.

Gage straightened, listening to the distinctive sound of the fire engines. A second later, a cell phone pinged, Mason's shop phone started ringing, and then the com Gage had attached to him went off.

Concerned, he stepped to the back of the shop, picked up the handset from his shoulder, and spoke. "Harrison here."

"Chief," Dixie said, "there's a fire at Doctor Harding's place. I'm worried about Danica and the babies."

Though he knew they were okay, something twisted in his gut at the word fire.

"They are all fine," he said into the little device, "I'm with them now at Mason's shop." He scowled, looking over at Danica, who was staring at her phone, deep grooves on her forehead. "Is the house on fire?"

"No, just one of the trees on the front of the property. Probably Halloween pranks gone bad, but the fire department was dispatched."

"I'll head over, too."

"All right, Chief. Be safe."

"Will do."

Striding back to Danica, she looked up at him, her face ashen. She held out her phone so he could see the screen. There in front of him, sure enough, he could see one of the large trees in her front lawn blazing. "My security feed from the house."

"What's going on?" Breck asked, coming to her sister's side.

"Someone has set fire to a tree in front of Danny's home," Gage said. "I was just talking to Dixie. The fire department has been dispatched, and I'm heading out as well."

"I'm going with you," Danica said, then looked at her sister. "Will you take care of the twins for me?"

"Of course." She hugged Danny. "You be careful, okay?"

Danica nodded, appearing stunned as she stepped back, then glanced up at him. "Let's go."

He started to tell her no, that she needed to stay put, but she was already heading out the door she'd just come in.

Mason came over after hanging up the shop phone. "Did you hear?"

"Yes." Gage tried not to sound ticked off. "I'm heading over now and taking Danica with me. You and Breck keep the twins happy while we're gone."

"We will." Mason tapped him on the back of his shoulder blade. "Take care of Danny and yourself."

"That's a done deal, brother."

Without wasting any more time, Gage stepped out into the night air, catching up to Danica getting into her vehicle. "Hang on!"

She spun around. "Why?"

"You're riding with me. No arguments or you stay here."

She narrowed her eyes on him but then nodded. "Where are you parked?"

"This way," he said, taking her arm.

It appeared the fire department had everything under control by the time Gage pulled up Danica's driveway. Though her stomach was in knots as she took note of her black as sin tree, once so beautiful but now reduced to a sad char of limbs sticking in all directions, the ground around it scorched as well.

Without a word, she undid her seatbelt and scrambled out of the big SUV, going to Darnell Parker, the captain. "Besides the obvious, do we know how this happened?"

"Danica," he greeted, his dark onyx gaze going to Gage. "This was done on purpose. You could smell the accelerant as it burned."

"Who would do that?" she asked, knowing they wouldn't have a clue.

"Kids out doing things they shouldn't is my best guess," Darnell said.

"Do you have your phone?" Gage asked her.

"Yes, why?"

"You were showing me a security feed. Can we access it from a prior point?"

"My phone captured a thirty-second clip, but we can take a look on my laptop inside by hitting the history."

"Let's go," he said, then glanced at the captain. "Darnell, you want to be in on this?"

"Sure do."

With that, the three of them went to the front door, Gage staying close beside her.

They were watching the feed, Gage's blood boiling as someone tall, wearing black from head to toe, their face even obscured, poured lighter fluid or gasoline out of an unmarked container onto the tree. Stepping back, they struck a match and tossed it, the oak going up in a blast of flames before they scampered out of sight.

"That's all I've got," Danica said.

"How about a different view?" Darnell asked.

She tapped a few keys on her computer, then the view switched, but the shot was from the side of the house, not showing the front lawn.

"Anything else?" Gage asked, raking his fingers through his hair.

"The back of the house."

"Hit it and let's take a look," he said.

Eyes focused on the screen, he watched for something, anything, but nothing but a stray cat walked into view.

"I don't think there's anything else." Danny slumped in her chair. He put a palm on the top of her shoulder, feeling her tense, then relax. "I just don't get why someone would do that."

"Meanness," Darnell said. "Kids being stupid on Halloween? A combination of both?"

"You're probably right." She sounded tired.

"Chief," Darnell said, "I'm going back out to check on my men, but the fire is extinguished, and nothing bounced. It was all contained to the front lawn."

Gage nodded. "I'll let you know if I come up with anything else."

"Please do."

The two of them shook hands, then the captain of the fire department strode away.

"Are you all right?" Gage asked.

Tipping her head back, as he was looking down on her from behind, she said, "I suppose so."

"Is your husband working all night, or is he scheduled to come home?"

Wasn't that the million-dollar question? Gage thought he should have been with his wife and children, celebrating the holiday.

"I haven't heard from him yet, so I don't know." Sitting up straight, Danica inched her chair back, then stood, going over to the breakfast bar—the ankle-length dress she wore swishing like cornstalks in the breeze. "I'm going to make some coffee. Would you like a cup?"

"Sure." He walked over in his long-legged stride, taking off his coat. "Maybe you should stay with Breckin and Mase tonight if Marcus gets detained at the hospital."

"Do you think that's necessary?" She reached into the cabinet, pulling down a couple of mugs.

"I think it would make me feel better if you did."

Danny raised a brow, glancing over at him. "That didn't answer my question, Gawonii."

The hard set to his jaw softened. "If you and the twins are going to be all alone tonight, then yes. I think it is necessary to be safe and stay with them."

"I'm sure it was just a kid thinking it was 'gangster' to light my tree on fire. I doubt it was anything more than that."

"I'm sure you're right, but still…"

"We'll be fine."

"Give me your cell phone," he said.

"Whatever for?"

He held out a hand. "Just do it, Danica."

With a sigh, she pulled it out of her coat pocket and gave it over. Gage tapped the screen, then handed it back. "Here."

"What did you do?"

"I put my cell phone number in your contacts. If anything, and I mean, if you hear so much as a snap that sounds out of place, you call me. No matter the time. Got me?"

Danica nodded, turning on her Keurig.

Chapter Thirty

Before

"DANNY!" HER SISTER'S muted voice called. "Jillian is on the phone for you!"

Glum, she rolled off her bed, feeling like total sludge, while at the same time wondering why J.J. was calling her. After all, she should be at the prom.

Stepping out of her bedroom, she went to the top of the stairs and glanced down at Breckin, who looked just as miserable as Danica felt. "I'm coming."

Breck nodded, and turned around, heading toward the kitchen where she spent most of her time if she wasn't holed up in her bedroom—something she didn't want to talk about going on between her and Mason. Whatever it was, it wasn't good.

After making it downstairs, she picked up the phone on the cordless and went back to her room, before putting the handset to her ear, saying, "Hello?"

"Danny." Jillian sounded upset.

She frowned. "What's wrong?"

"I should be asking you that. Why didn't you show up at the prom with Max?"

"He blew me off." Danica's heart twisted. She'd spent so much money on a formal gown she wore for all but an hour while waiting on him, only to be taken off and flopped over the back of her chair in a splash of powder blue. Not to mention the extra time doing her hair and makeup.

"What do you mean? Did you guys fight?"

"I mean just that. Max said he'd pick me up and never showed. I tried calling him to find out what was going on, and no one answered the phone."

"Oh, he did show up, but with Miranda Burrell."

Fire rolled up Danica's neck. Was every boy she allowed in her life going to burn her? "He's there with Miranda?"

"He was. I heard him say something about heading out to the after-party at the lake."

"Is that right," she said through gritted teeth.

"Girl, I'm sorry."

"Don't be."

"I'll tell Vance I have to go and come over there."

"No, don't do that," she said. "You stay and have a good time with him."

"Are you sure?"

"I'm positive."

"Okay, but I'm coming over tomorrow, first thing."

"All right. I'll talk to you then."

"Love you, Danny-D."

"Love ya, too, J.J."

Hitting the button to disconnect the call, Danica's blood simmered, making her pace the room until she came to a decision.

"You're not going to let another boy walk all over you!" she said rather loudly to the reflection in her vanity mirror.

The handset bounced when she tossed it onto her bed before she went to her closet, slipped on her Nikes, and ran for the door.

Wood popping and sparks flying up into the night sky, Gage and Mason were sitting by the bonfire, talking about how the little bit of the prom they attended pretty much sucked until something caught his attention.

"Hey," he said. "I'll talk to you later. I've got to go check on something."

"Okay, sure, man." Mason was quickly distracted by Phillip's crazy antics.

Getting to his feet, eyes narrowing, Gage walked toward the line of trees in the distance, where he was pretty sure Max just went. Only, from his vantage point, it didn't look like he was tugging Danny along with him, but—

"Maxwell Dillon!"

Danica's loud voice had his head whipping to the right. Sure enough, whoever Max was with, it wasn't Danny. A sense of relief surrounded him, then switched to concern as Danny all but ran up to Max, then pushed the guy. Hard.

"You blew me off so you could take *her* to the prom?"

"Settle down," Max said, holding his hands up in front of him like a suspect about to get nailed.

"Don't you tell me to settle down you rotten piece of pond scum!"

Max gave a sarcastic laugh. "That's the best you've got?

Gage picked up his pace, wanting to get to them before things escalated from bad to worse.

"Oh, I have a whole lot more, I'm just not going to lower myself to your potty mouth level."

"Potty mouth? You never complained about my mouth when I had it on yours!"

"Watch it!" Gage yelled, swooping in beside Danica, his arrival barely registering on her stunningly livid face, too upset with Dillon.

"We made plans to go to prom, and you pulled a no-show on me!"

"Look. It was fun while it lasted, but I need things you won't give me, and I'm tired of playing the choir boy on the slim chance I'll get into your pants."

That was it. Gage balled his fist and swung, connecting with Max's jaw, making him stumble back, and Miranda Burrell, he realized a little too late, screamed as the jerk bumped into her, sending her onto her backside.

Gathering his composure, Max shook his head, then helped Miranda up. "Are you okay, babe?"

"Babe? Really?" Danny asked, crossing her arms, still on fire. "You're hooking up with Miranda because she puts out, and calling her *babe*?"

"Shut up, Danica!" the girl yelled.

"You shut up, Ms. 'I'll do you, just ask'."

Sadly, Danica had the right of it. Miranda, who transferred in two years ago, did get around a lot. Though he'd never touched her and wouldn't, Gage just heard the other guys talk about their conquests.

"You're nothing but an uptight, prissy—"

Smack! His little Danny slapped her right across the face. And it might be wrong, but Gage was proud of her at that moment.

"Why you bitc—" Max grabbed his 'date' by the waist, as Gage grabbed Danny, stopping them both before the catfight ensued and a crowd gathered, which he was surprised hadn't already started since they weren't exactly keeping their voices down.

"*Shh*," Gage whispered in her ear as she squirmed in his hold.

"Let me go! I'm going to snatch her bald!"

Gage chuckled; he couldn't help himself. "I don't think so, Slugger."

Max glowered at her then up at him. "Get her out of here."

"Glad to." Gage started to carry her off, but before he left snarled, "You stay away from Danica, Dillon!"

"You don't need to worry about that!"

Danny was still kicking as he put her down by his car, boxing her in with his hands on either side of her, resting on the roof. "Calm down and take a breath."

Angry blue eyes lifted up to him. "Did I ask for your help?"

"Nope, but you're getting it just the same."

She turned her head, not looking at him while her chest heaved.

"For whatever it's worth, I'm sorry Max did that." *I always knew he wasn't right for you. No one will ever be because they won't love you like I do,* he didn't say.

"*Hmpf.*"

Her grunt of displeasure made him want to smile, but he put his amusement on lockdown.

"And I'm sorry he ruined going to the prom for you, too."

Slowly, she brought her gaze back to him but remained quiet. Well, all but for her heavy breaths, which were, he noticed, doing very nice things to Danny's chest and the cleavage she was showing in the V-dip of her tight t-shirt.

Don't notice! "Do you think you might ever talk to me again?" he asked.

"Take me home, please."

Gage locked his eyes with hers. "I suppose that's a start."

Chapter Thirty-One

SIPPING ON HIS cup of coffee, absently listening to the radio, Gage took his usual morning route to work, watching the clouds roll across the sky, wondering if it were going to snow.

"This just in," the D.J. said in his throaty voice, and something about it made Gage take note, turning the radio volume up when he came to a stop at the sign. "The Department of Homeland Security has issued a bulletin highlighting the continuing terror threats to the U.S, calling for all citizens to remain aware. Today, one of the Al Musa terrorist cells was taken down successfully in Chicago, bringing that staggering number to fifteen raids in the past four years here on U.S. soil. According to our sources, several detailed plans, as well as homemade detonation devices, were confiscated from the scene, making this the latest in Al Musa's unsuccessful plots to take place. Stay tuned for more information as it arrives here on WKJL, the Alternative Heart of Seattle."

Scrubbing a palm down his face, Gage's bad mood, which started last night when some malcontent (and that was putting it nicely) set a tree in front of Danica's house on fire, took a further nosedive into dark territory. Turning on his blinker, he straightened and put his game face on.

"Listen up," Gage said, striding into the station a few minutes later, gaining the attention of his officers in differing stages of their morning rituals. "Meeting in the war room. You've got fifteen to make it happen. Everyone is required to be there."

"Chief?" Dixie stood from behind her desk. "Officer Stanley is still out on patrol."

"Call him in."

She nodded. "Will do."

With that, Gage went to his office and shut the door.

After purchasing gas, groceries, and the twin's first Halloween costumes the other day, Danica had run through all the cash she had on hand, so, on the way to the holiday committee meeting at the church, she made a quick pitstop at the ATM again.

It was cloudy and *too cold*, she thought as she popped her card into the machine, fingertips freezing while she punched in her PIN.

A second or two later, the machine started beeping at her. The sound drew her attention from the weird feeling she had, which made her look behind her, returning to the issue at hand.

Brows pulling down, she stared at the screen as DECLINED blinked at her.

"Huh?"

Taking her card, she brought it to her lips and blew her warm breath across it, not sure why, but thinking perhaps the chilly weather had something to do with the error. Satisfied she'd done what she could, Danica slipped the debit card back into the slot and re-entered her personal identification number.

Another wave of something she couldn't quite pinpoint made the fine hairs on the back of her neck stand on end. Danica once again turned around, expecting to see someone watching her, but there wasn't anybody there.

You're just paranoid after the whole tree thing.

Another series of beeps took place, making her focus on the screen, seeing the same DECLINED blinking at her.

Ticked, she took her card, turned for her vehicle, got inside, cranked up the heat, and pulled out her cell phone.

After five rings, her husband's voice mail kicked in. "Hello, you have reached Doctor Harding. I'm unavailable to take your call right now, but please leave me a detailed message, and I will return your call as soon as possible."

"Marcus. I need you to call me back right away. There's some issue with the debit card. The ATM has declined my transaction twice."

Disconnecting the call, she stared at the sparkle of her wedding ring. She'd asked Marcus to stay home that morning, wanting to talk more about the whole debacle that took place in their front yard the night before, but he placed a kiss to her forehead and told her he couldn't. He had two surgeries scheduled.

A sense of loneliness and confusion hit her in a one, two punch.

Rubbing her temple, her gaze shifted to her iPhone, then lifted to her reflection in the rearview mirror. "What is going on?"

The thing was, the woman looking back at her was just as clueless, and the feeling wasn't very settling.

"All right," Gage said from his spot behind the podium, "I don't know if everyone is aware, but the FBI took down another terrorist cell last night in Chicago. While I get that our mindsets tend to fall into the 'small town' mentality, that doesn't mean things can't or won't ever happen here. I want all of you to be extra watchful. I don't care if it takes you a few more minutes to check something out. If you get that tingle on your skin or the rumble in your gut that says something isn't right, listen and look into it. We've all heard the saying, better safe than sorry. Adhere to it. If you think you have a situation that might need backup, don't be a cowboy. Call it in."

Gage's gaze went around the room, momentarily landing on each of the faces of his men. "Am I in any way unclear?"

A collective, "No, sir," echoed.

"Good. This meeting is going to be short and sweet today, but before you all head out, I also want to mention there was a fire at Doctor Harding's place last night."

"Did you find out who set it?" Stanley asked.

"No." Gage shook his head. "There was some footage of someone, dressed in black from head to toe, face obscured, who clearly put accelerant onto one of the trees on the Harding's front lawn, struck a match, and set it ablaze. But that's all we were able to see from the footage on the security system. Whoever it was, is tall. Slim."

"Could you tell if it was a man or a woman, teen boy or girl?"

"My gut says an adult, but as to male or female, there just wasn't a way to discern." Taking a deep breath to keep his irritation from showing, Gage then rapped his knuckles on the wood in front of him. "That's it for today. Watch your backs, and stay safe."

"Chief," Officer Stanley said, striding up.

Gage didn't care for the man and expected him to go into a spiel about the Parker kids. He was one of 'those'. Other than their darker skin matching that of their father's, he didn't have a reason to always think the worst of them.

"Yeah?"

"I just wanted to let you know I brought Wendell Gibbs in last night. I haven't had time to do my nightly reports yet, but as I'm sure you can guess, he was drunk and disorderly, yelling outside of the bar about the alien invasion while stumbling around. He scared a few people during Trick or Treat Street, so I figured he needed to sleep it off, but he said something that makes me wonder now."

"What was that?"

"He was yammering on and on with that crazy E.T. stuff, then started in a different direction, about someone watching, and I quote, 'That pretty little blonde girl with the blonde babies'." Stanley scrubbed his jaw with two fingers. "I just figured he was rambling, you know, three sheets to the wind and all, but with the whole fire thing… I don't know. Maybe there was something to it?"

A ball of tension formed in Gage's back. "I'll go talk with him."

Stanley nodded and started to go.

"Thanks for telling me, Officer."

The man glanced back at him. "Sure, Chief."

Chapter Thirty-Two

Before

"WHAT'S UP WITH Mason and your sister?" J.J. asked after Danica slipped into the passenger's seat of her car.

Putting the seatbelt on, she shook her head. "I have no idea. If I didn't know any better, I'd say she and Mase broke up, but she's still wearing his rings."

"Why did you leave him standing in front of your house?"

She sighed. "He came to see her, but she's not home."

"What is it? You have that look you get when you have more to say."

"Something bad has happened between them, only Breck won't talk about it."

"Sounds like she's related to you."

Danica frowned over at her bestie. "She's my sister. Of course, we're related."

"That's not what I meant, and you know it, Danny, so stop being obtuse."

"I'm not thick, J.J., so quit using that thesaurus of a brain on me."

"Do you honestly believe I'm oblivious to the whole Gage thing? You're messed up over him and have been for several months now."

"Do we have to talk about him?"

"See. You're just as closed-mouthed as Breckin."

Danica shrugged.

"Okay, Danny. We won't talk about the boy who crushed your heart."

"Good. I don't want to talk about Max."

J.J. snorted. "Yeah, whatever."

Glancing behind her, then down the street as Jillian pulled out of her drive, Danica said, "It's all clear this way. You're good to go."

Once they were tootling down the street, J.J. turned the music on the radio up, but not in an overwhelming way. "Before we go do our nails, do you want to stop by Berta's place and grab a milkshake to go? I've been dying for a large strawberry with whipped cream."

"Sounds good."

"Tomorrow is graduation. Are you guys doing something special to celebrate your sister's big day?"

"I think Mason's parents are throwing a party or something, so I guess we'll go over there. At least, Breck hasn't said she's not going, so if she goes, we will too."

"Don't you think *he'll* be there?"

She whipped her head toward her friend. "You mean, Gage?"

"I didn't say his name, you did." J.J. grinned, pleased with herself.

Danica rolled her eyes heavenward. "God, give me the strength."

"Oh, knock it off with the dramatics before you win the best actress in a daytime drama."

Tucking some hair behind her ear, Danica flipped the visor down to check her lip gloss in the little mirror. "He might be there. I don't know." *I don't know much of anything about him anymore.*

"Well, speak of the devil and all that."

Knocking the visor back in place, she glanced out the windshield, catching Gage helping Jenny out of his GTO, then he did something inside his car for a bit before he came back out with a baby carrier.

Immediately, she wrapped her arms around her midsection in a weak attempt to combat the pain, but it wasn't any use. *"Justin's not my baby, Danny,"* he'd said to her once, but it sure didn't look like any of that mattered as the three of them walked inside The Snack Shack like one big happy family.

"Oh, Danny." J.J. obviously caught the expression of complete and total desolation on her face.

And the thing was, she doubted she could have hidden it, no matter how hard she tried.

"I'm so sorry, girlfriend."

Swiping a single tear that had escaped and rolled along the contour of her cheek, Danica whispered, "It's not like he cheated on me, we were never a thing." But, every single cell in her trembling body said Gage *had* cheated on her and was still doing it.

Placing a supportive hand over the top of hers, J.J's gesture made Danica glance down—the light shining in the side window creating a slant of warmth along her knees.

"I know you're hurting,' her bestie said, "but I don't know what to do to help you get over him."

"There isn't anything you *can* do, J.J." Closing her eyes, Danica didn't know if she would ever recover from what Gage Harrison did to her, because some wounds were just too deep to overcome.

Chapter Thirty-Three

PACING FROM THE formal living room to the dining room, to the kitchen and back, Danica was fit to be tied. It had taken her a while to get the twins down for the night, and she didn't want to wake them with her frantic back and forth, so she'd closed their bedroom door, taking the baby monitor from her room and putting it in the kitchen, turning it up full volume.

She glanced at the clock—2:18 A.M.

Danica frowned. She' been calling and calling, leaving message after message for Marcus, and it was getting late, but what concerned her so much? She hadn't heard anything back from him at all. There were times, yes, it took a bit to get back to her, especially if he were performing surgery, but this, to hear nothing, was sending her to the edge of panic.

Having a tug-a-war with herself, she considered calling Gage, tell him she was uneasy about her husband's complete lack of response, then she talked herself out of it, only to talk herself into calling. Back and forth she went, finally deciding she would give Marcus until 2:30 to either show up or call her, and if not, she *was* going to do something!

Gage was in the middle of one of his night terrors when ringing—*Is it my cell phone?*—roused him from the horrific scene. Rolling over in bed, he grabbed the little device from his side table, saw the number on the lit-up screen, and sat bolt upright.

"Danica? What's going on?" The residue of his bad dream dripped over into his present.

"Ga-Gage." She was crying.

"What's happened?" he asked, his bare feet hitting the hardwood floor.

"Marcus isn't home, and I've tried calling him for hou-hours, but he-he's never returned any of my calls. I cal-called the hospital in Seattle and the gir-girl who spoke to me must be ne-new or something 'cause—"

"Danica. Take a second and breathe for me."

He heard her intake of breath.

"Okay. Slowly, tell me."

"For a moment, she acted like she didn't know who my husband was, but it is late, so there's that too, but she finally told me he's no longer there. When I asked her if she knew when Marcus left, she just said she didn't know and to call back in the morning during regular office hours to speak with the chief of staff." She sniffed.

Gage was putting his jeans on, one-handed. "Did you try calling his parents?"

"No, they are in Brazil, so they wouldn't have a clue as to what is happening here."

It was quiet.

"Danica?"

"I'm sorry to bother you, but I know something is wrong. Marcus might be gone a lot, but he never fails to call me back, and if he's going to be late, he calls me. He hasn't called."

"I told you to get hold of me anytime you needed me, so you will *never* be a bother."

"I don't know what to do." Her voice had gone small, almost child-like.

"I'll call Mason and have Breck and him come over and stay with you."

"I don't want to wake them up."

"*I'm* waking them, Danny."

"Gage?"

"Yeah?"

"Can you try to check on him?" More sniffling.

"I'll make some calls; then I'm heading out. Have you guys had any arguments lately?"

"Huh?"

"Fights. Have you had any?"

"We don't really fight."

He doubted that, but Gage wasn't going to press the point. "So, there wouldn't be a reason he might purposely stay away for a while?"

"No."

"Does he have any colleagues he might go out with?"

"A couple. But one of them is on his honeymoon, and the other, I think he was taking a vacation. I remember Marcus saying something about it."

"I'll be over just as soon as I can. In the meantime, think of anyone Marcus might hang out with to blow off some steam, and write down their names and phone numbers if you have them."

"Okay."

"And, Danny?"

"Yes?"

"I'll find Marcus." *And when I do, he better have an excellent reason for putting you through this,* he thought, ticked. "I'll see you in a few."

"All right."

Chapter Thirty-Four

Before

"I HEARD HE'S going to the University of Washington to be where Jenny's at," Pam said, her voice a low whisper as she spoke to J.J, but the words were loud enough to pierce Danica's already hole-riddled heart. "It's like an episode of *As The World Turns* around here with all that graduating class."

Danica knew that was the truth. First, her sister took off to parts unknown without a single word, leaving Mason crushed, then her Mom and Dad got a call, which she wasn't home for and missed, but was told Breck was in Paris of all places! Then, Jake and Maggie started seeing other people, and now Gage had changed his plans from attending WSU to the university in Seattle to be with *her*.

A sick roll of disgust traversed Danica's spine, and she couldn't even say that girl's name.

"Are you all right?" J.J. asked, pulling her back into the room, and a good thing too since she'd been far away.

"I'm fine."

Her best friend eyed her. "Um-hm. And I have fairy wings and can fly."

Standing by the swimming pool, glass of sparkling water in hand, people mingled all around him, and many stopped to talk. But for the first time, Gage felt utterly alone. Oh, he could lose himself in a crowd, but since Mason had taken off, Breckin was gone, and Danica had stopped speaking to him, he'd fallen into the depths of an ocean of sadness, and was going under. Yet he smiled and said all the appropriate things to the people who had come to this party his mother threw—his going away to college celebration.

Celebration? That was so funny it would hurt to laugh if he'd remembered how.

Even his inner voice sounded sarcastic.

Gage glanced around, hoping, though the chances were slim to none, he'd see *her* walk through that set of open French doors, but while he'd spent the last few hours in the same general area, Danica had never arrived.

"And she's not going to," he said, under his breath.

"Huh?" Phillip asked. "Did you say something?"

"Naw, man."

Danica was up at the crack of dawn, dressed in whatever she'd grabbed, not worried if she matched or not, and had gone out the front door of her house, taking the keys to her mother's car with her.

Honestly, she didn't know what she was doing, other than she had to tell Gage goodbye at least since she never went to his going away party. It would hurt, and it may be the final blow, doing her in, but the thought of him leaving for college, and more than likely not seeing him for a long time, ate at her like a slow drip of acid and had kept her awake all night.

After getting into the hatchback, starting it up, and pulling out of her drive, she headed for the Harrison house, going too fast. One good thing, she wasn't pulled over for speeding.

Dad would love that.

Danica made the final turn onto the street where Gage lived, slowing down, ready to pull through the wrought iron gates. She had the code and could get in. But when she arrived at her destination, those gates were standing wide open—the GTO usually parked in the circular drive wasn't there.

Danica's heart sank as tears threatened to fall, but she finished what she'd started and pulled the car through the gates, parking where Gage usually did. A second later, Mrs. Harrison came out the front door, gently dabbing a handkerchief at the corners of her eyes, and she knew, without doubt, she was too late.

Gage has already left.

Chapter Thirty-Five

HE HAD BEEN in Danica's custom build home on Halloween; however, he'd been so focused on her and what he could see on her security feed, that Gage hadn't bothered to pay any real attention to the place. But that was all different now. He was taking everything in with an expert eye as Breck hugged her sister, the two of them snuggled on the couch, while Mason walked into the living room with a tray of coffee cups.

He'd been asking Danica question after question, gaining some contact information on a couple of people he would be checking with, and he'd already put out a call to his officers, as well a call to the department in Seattle. They were quick calls, asking them to keep an eye out for the doctor and his silver Mercedes, giving them the number on his license plate.

"Danny," he said, not wanting to disturb her quiet moment, but knowing he had to.

"Yes?"

"I need to see your husband's office."

"Why?"

"I might come across something that could help figure out where he might be."

"Okay. I'll show you."

"You can just tell me where it's at, and I'll find it."

Getting to her feet, she ran a palm along the curve of her hip. "It's fine. I need to be doing something."

"All right."

With that, he followed her down a corridor, past a room that appeared to be a home gym, and then she opened a door and flipped on the light. "This is it."

The space was immaculate, with a massive wall of bookshelves, a large mahogany desk positioned in front of that, a few leather club chairs, a putting green, and a big-screen TV.

Gage advanced farther into the room and continued his visual inspection. If he was correct, those were expensive one of a kind paintings from artists, both modern and classical hanging on the walls.

The room screamed, *I've got money!*

"Do you mind if I take a look at your husband's computer?"

"No. Go ahead," she said.

Walking around his desk and taking a seat, he powered up the laptop, then glanced at Danica. She was wandering around the space as if she were lost. "Do you know his password? The computer is locked."

"I think it's dannydawn#1. All lower-case letters."

Gage typed it, and bingo, he was in!

Going to the calendar, he took a quick look through the entries but didn't see anything that would stand out, only stopped when something strange caught his eye. On random dates during the month, there was an R+ or R-. *What did that mean?* Doctor's shorthand, or weird blood types? No, there weren't any R blood types.

"Do you know what this means?" he asked, taking the laptop and turning it around. "Look at the 2nd, 8th, and 19th of the last month."

Danica came over, bent, and frowned. "I have no clue, but probably something to do with his work."

"Makes sense that it would, I suppose," he said, putting the laptop in the correct position, then flipping back through the months, the same notations on different days of September, all the way back to February of the last year.

Gage didn't have a real reason why, but this struck him as suspicious, and he had a gut feeling those R's with the plus or minus had nothing at all to do with being a surgeon. Putting this little tidbit of strangeness to the back of his mind for further ponderings, he started tapping on some file folders, seeing patient notes, which he didn't read, then saw a folder labeled PICS, and opened it.

There on the screen in front of him was a sort of photo collage of Danica and Marcus—their relationship in photographs, from some impromptu pics to more structured photos like what he assumed were vacation pictures. Danica was wearing a tiny red string bikini that made his eyes pop, the wind blowing through the strands of her golden hair as she stood on the deck of a boat.

Something inside of his heart severely bent.

"Is this a boat your husband owns?" Gage asked, pushing the envy he felt toward Marcus Harding aside.

Danica came to him, glanced toward the screen, then smiled. "Yes. He bought that four years ago."

"Does he boat very often?"

"Yacht."

"Huh?"

"Marcus called it a yacht."

"Ah…"

"But to answer your question, not much anymore. For a while, after he first purchased it and I popped some motion sickness pills, we went out quite a bit."

"You have motion sickness?"

"When it comes to sailing, I've got it big time."

That was something he didn't know, but he needed to steer their conversation back to where it needed to be. "If Marcus was upset about something, would he go and hang out there?"

"Upset? About what?"

"I don't know, Danny. If he had an awful day and needed a place to go to get away for a while, would he go there?"

"Like you?" she asked, drawing his gaze up to her.

"Me?"

"You used to go sit out on the dock at the lake when something was bothering you."

He was surprised she knew that about him. He did go out there, and sometimes he still would. "Yeah. I guess so."

"He might." She shrugged, "But I don't know for sure."

Interesting she knew something about him that she didn't know about Marcus, but he needed to focus on the problem, not Danica.

Turning back to the screen, he tapped a different folder and almost, but managed somehow, not to gasp. It was pictures of Danny, dancing. A dance he saw her perform. One of the many things about her he'd *never* get out of his mind.

"Gawonii?" Her soft voice seemed to caress him, making Gage snap to his senses.

He rose to his feet.

"Are you okay?"

"Of course, but I'm going to leave you here with Breck and Mase. I have a few things I want to check out."

"Oh." She blinked up at him.

"Tell me where Marcus keeps his yacht."

"You want to go look there?"

"I do."

"I want to come with you," she said, and he shook his head.

"Not this time. But I promise to call you the moment I locate your husband."

Chapter Thirty-Six

Before

GAGE'S HEART WAS in his throat as he took a seat in the back of the auditorium at Washington State University to see their Spring Show. Well, to see *her.* He'd been reduced to finding stolen moments here and there where he could watch Danica from afar, but this was different. He'd graduated with his degree in criminal justice and was getting ready to head off to the academy in Quantico, Virginia. She would be graduating with her BA in a few weeks, which meant they would both be in different places, but regardless, he'd made up his mind to lay all his 'cards,' as they were, on the table. No matter her response once he did, at least he would have, at long last, told her how he felt.

Glancing around at the sea of heads, he looked for anyone familiar but didn't see a soul. Although, he knew Mr. and Mrs. Lorry and Jillian, Danny's best friend, would be there somewhere, probably front and center in the first row.

All the low chatter in the space died down when a dapper-looking man took the stage. "The Department of Dance welcomes you," he said from his position from behind a microphone. Then, he mentioned the names of the dance director, the assistant professor, the department chair, along with a few facts about the University and the department honors.

The young woman seated beside him spoke to the girl next to her in a low whisper. "Did you see who's first?" She held up a program. "They are so-o-o-o good."

"I know," said her companion, before someone he wasn't paying attention to, hushed them.

"And now," the announcer continued, "please show your appreciation for two of our very best as they dance their last performance here with us. Seniors, Danica Dawn Lorry, and Ryan Walker Feilding with their contemporary piece set to *Gravity* by Sara Bareilles."

Low rounds of applause echoed as Gage straightened his shoulders. He leaned forward in his chair, the curtain lifted, and a gray smoke rolled along the floor of the stage where a dark-haired young man stood, poised in the middle. He was dressed in black with a sparkle of red suspenders hanging off him, wearing what looked to be red Kabuki-type makeup surrounding his eyes and lining the sides of his nose, the rest of his face unadorned. Then the introduction to the song began, and he moved, almost like a robot or street mime. But all of Gage's attention shifted when Danica twirled onto the stage, disturbing the fog at her feet, the flowing white dress she wore reminding him of undulating material taken by a current of water while she moved.

He steepled his fingers together in front of his mouth.

She looked like a graceful angel in motion until she was stopped when her dance partner caught her. They wavered there in slow, back and forth movements, before the dance transitioned into fast actions—him grabbing her and she breaking free, not in a creepy way, but a sad, yet sensual set of holds. Then Ryan dipped her, skimming his nose from the apex of her cleavage to the line of her throat, up the side of her face before they twirled apart, and Danica gracefully went to the floor, rolling; him crawling after her, reaching.

Gage was so entranced he couldn't have budged from his spot even if the apocalypse started.

Over the years, he'd watched her dance, but this, what Danny was doing up there on that stage, was phenomenal. She *felt* the music, each movement translating the story she told. And not for the first time, he saw her—the beauty within, the whisper of soft vulnerability, a hidden strength, that elegance of a woman with the romantic heart of a girl.

Danica was, in a word, stunning.

"Do you know where I might find, Danica Lorry?" Gage asked the Master of Ceremonies once the showcase ended and he stepped out of the auditorium into the large foyer. "She's a friend of mine, and I would like to congratulate her."

"I believe you will find all our performing seniors this evening over there"—he pointed—"in that receiving line."

"Thank you."

"You're very welcome."

The space was crowded as he made his way through the throng, chatter and laughter swirling all around him as he said, "Excuse me" and "Thank you" when people moved out of his way.

Then, as if Moses had parted the Red Sea, he saw her, smiling, shaking hands with people, her partner at her side, doing the same. He thought to stand there a moment and soak her in. The way her hair shone in the light, the feminine curve of her jaw, how her lips moved when she spoke.

Jillian came into view. "You guys did an awesome job! I couldn't keep my eyes off you."

"Thanks," Danny said, the dark-haired guy wrapping his muscular arm around her waist.

"You are both seriously fantastic together, and I don't just mean when you dance."

That made the step Gage was about to take, halt.

Danica glanced up at her partner, who smiled down at her, then looked back at J.J.

"No!" Jillian exclaimed as Danica held out her left hand, a diamond ring sparkling there. "You guys are—?"

"Getting married." Danica beamed. "Ryan asked me before our performance this evening."

His lungs seized.

The two friends hugged and squealed, while yet another crack zipped along the faultline of Gage's heart, spidering off into a jagged configuration.

Without a word, without letting Danny know he was there…that he loved her, he'd always loved her…he turned around, walked out of the building, across the lot, slipped inside his car, and tossed his head back.

"Why?" he screamed, beating his fists on the steering wheel. "Why do You hate me? Why can't I have just one single minute of happiness? Why can't I have her?"

That was it. The moment loneliness so profound, a sadness so fathomless, and desolation so vast pulled him into a dark pit of despair. Right then and there, Gage severed something, cut himself off from the one person he shouldn't—God.

Chapter Thirty-Seven

THE RISING SUN had cast the sky into a shade of wavy purple blending into pink as Gage pulled his SUV into the right lane, ready to take the exit.

The chime of his cell started.

Tapping the screen to send the call over to his vehicle speakers, he answered with, "Harrison."

"Hey, Mack, here."

He'd called his old buddy who was on the force in Seattle once he knew Marcus hadn't shown up or been in contact with Danny, asking him for a favor, the kind that would require him to return one just as significant when the need struck.

"Mack, tell me you've got some good news."

It was silent a moment, then the gruff Sargent said, "Where are you?"

"I'm heading into Seattle now, getting ready to see if Marcus might be on his boat, or maybe he took it out."

"The Rising Dawn in slip eighty-three?"

"Yes, did you find him?"

"We found him."

The tone in the man's voice sent that tingle, a specific vibe of imminent bad news over his skin. "And?"

"I'll see you in a few, Harrison."

With that, the man hung up.

It took Gage fifteen minutes from the time Mack disconnected their call to the time he pulled up to the site of what most assuredly was a crime scene. Police cars were everywhere, a section already marked off with yellow tape, and a vehicle identifiable as the coroner.

Gage's heart and stomach sank at what he would find. At what he would have to tell Danica.

Putting some steel into his spine, he got out of his SUV, showed his badge to the officer who stopped him, and said, "Mack is expecting me."

"Yes, sir," the fresh out of the police academy would be his guess, kid said. "Go on."

Being careful to watch where he walked, he boarded the boat, Mack meeting him with a grim, bulldog set to his face. "He's in the aft cabin. But I warn you. It isn't pretty."

The man handed him a pair of booties to cover his shoes, which he put on.

Making his feet move, Gage went below deck, followed the crime scene investigators wearing jumpsuits and rubber gloves, then walked into the bedroom.

Click.

Flash!

He had to close his eyes for a moment.

"Barnes," Mack said. "Give us a few."

"Sure thing."

Gage stepped aside to let the photographer pass.

"You okay, Harrison?" Mack was watching him.

"Yeah."

Death saturated the air in the room Gage stood, a specific scent, the kind that once you were in contact with, your sense of smell would file the information away as if waiting for the moment you came across it again. When you did, those olfactory functions were triggered, bringing past horrors back to you in a rush.

"You sure? Do you want to go into the hall and take a moment?"

"No. I'm okay."

Four Steps. That's what it took to get to the bed where the body was. Three breaths and Gage started cataloging.

The bedsheets and cover were turned down to the foot, and Marcus lay half propped up on the headboard, slumped, utterly nude with part of his head missing. Blood splatter, and other unspeakable things, were stuck to it, as well decorating the wall behind him in a macabre display of tragedy. But Gage found that place inside of him where he detached from emotion and took it all in. No matter how horrific, he *needed* to see the site before him—and not with the eyes of a man who loved the woman this would devastate, but with those of a former FBI agent turned cop.

In Marcus's right hand, a 44-caliber Magnum revolver was loosely gripped. On the wall of gore, just above the line of the headboard, a single bullet hole had bored into the wood, splintering it.

Gage's attention shifted to the right. The bathroom door was open, light on, and what looked to be a damp towel hung on the hook in the middle of the paneled door.

To his left, a charcoal gray men's wool overcoat was on the hanger of a coat rack. Next to that, Marcus's clothing was neatly folded—shirt, pants, tie, all placed on the chair, his shoes, with his socks tucked in them, sat side-by-side on the floor. His belt was rolled and perched atop his clothing. His suit jacket was hanging over the back of the chair. A wallet, not opened, had been placed on the bedside table, a lamp light shining down on it. Next to the black leather sat a watch—Patek Philippe Grand, with a perpetual calendar chronograph. He knew because he'd seen the man with it on his wrist. A cell phone was perfectly aligned beside that. And finally, the platinum band—his wedding ring.

"There's an empty condom wrapper in the bathroom, but a used prophylactic isn't discarded anywhere," Mack said.

Gage pinched the bridge of his nose and dropped his head before taking another visual sweep of the room. It was obvious nothing had been disturbed, or that Marcus hadn't been in any hurry. Instead, everything looked meticulously placed, as everything about Marcus's life had seemed to be—ordered, and without clutter.

"You thinking suicide?" Gage asked, turning to look at Mack.

"Looks like it. But I'd say the man hooked-up before doing what he did."

As if this wasn't horrible enough, would Marcus being unfaithful in his marriage have to be added to it?

"It doesn't make any sense why, he of all people, would take his life. Let alone use this place as a sex pad." Gage shook his head. "He had everything—wealth, a prominent career, and more importantly, he left behind a beautiful wife and two sweet babies."

"This sort of thing rarely makes sense at first glance, but there's something that pushed him over the edge. We'll find those answers."

Yeah, they would, but the question that was going to haunt him had already started to float through his mind. *Can Danica accept whatever the darkness was that Marcus hid from her once we shed light on it?*

Chapter Thirty-Eight

Before

GETTING OUT OF his rental car, Gage tossed his backpack over his shoulder and walked to the front of the home he grew up in, a thousand pounds of unseen weight holding him down. After his graduation from Quantico, he thought he would save the world; only the world had other things to say about that. It had been a rough couple of years, and even a harsher six months.

Twirling his keyring around his finger, he focused on the jangle, trying not to think about what he'd left behind in California, but failing. He and his partner had been working on a particularly gruesome serial murder case, which ended when they had enough evidence to arrest their suspect, but they were too late. Entering the fancy Brentwood home was like walking into a horror scene from a movie. This psycho had killed his entire family, placing them in different states of repose around the house—his father at the workbench in the garage, his mother in a rocking chair with knitting in her lap, the wife in the bathtub as if she'd fallen asleep while bathing, and his three children... Gage couldn't think about those kids, the oldest twelve, the youngest only four. The killer had displayed them all like dolls, then took his own life when he was done, with a bullet to the head.

Sucking in a deep breath of fresh air, Gage unlocked the door and stepped inside, then punched in the code on the alarm. He knew his parents had taken a long overdue vacation, so even though they weren't home, he was glad to be there. He needed the quiet time in a familiar place filled with good memories to help clear the clutter of nasty in his mind. Coming home for a few days seemed like the thing to do.

"Sonoma?" he called, but the housekeeper didn't answer, so she must be out.

Going up the stairs, looking forward to being in his old room, the bell tones of his cell made him stop on the landing, pull out his phone and look at the number on the screen. Letting his backpack slip off his arm and land by his foot in a *thump*, he answered the call.

"Hi, Jenny. Is everything okay with Justin?"

"No," she said and sniffed.

The hairs on the back of his neck stood on end. "What's wrong?"

"For some reason, he decided to climb the trellis on the side of the house and fell. He busted up his leg, and the doctor is talking about surgery to put a pin in it."

"Are you at the hospital now?"

"Yes," she whispered.

"Which one?"

"Harborview."

"I'll be there as soon as I can."

"Soon?"

"I'm in Cedar Point. It won't take me long."

"Oh!" She sounded relieved. "Gage, thank you."

"Nothing to thank me for, Jenny. You and Justin need me, so hang tight. I'm on my way."

"Thank you for having lunch with me," Marcus said, his handsome face highlighted by the summer sun streaming in the wall of windows.

Danica placed her palm on his chest, over his name embroidered into his white coat. "That's a silly thing to thank me for."

"No, it's not. You had to make a special trip to accommodate my schedule. But that will change soon. Once we're married, you'll be here in Seattle with me."

She'd never told Marcus she didn't want to live in Seattle, but she would, just later, after their wedding on the sandy beach of Hawaii and subsequent honeymoon. "Since you brought up the wedding," she said, "we need to talk about the issue with the resort."

Marcus frowned. "What issue?"

"The one I told you about last week with the caterer."

"Oh, yes. I think I do remember you saying something about it."

"Marcus," she whined. "Sometimes, I wonder if you listen to me."

He skimmed his knuckles along the line of her jaw. "I listen to every word. I'm also busy, so other things take my thoughts in different directions sometimes, but that in no way means I don't think you, or what you are saying, isn't important. It is." He leaned in close and whispered in that velvet-soft voice. "You *are* important to me, Danica. Never doubt that."

The man had a way of melting her. "All right."

He took her chin between his fingers and lifted. "I have to get back to work, but you be careful driving to Cedar Point." Her fiancé placed a soft kiss to her lips, then let her go.

"I hope your afternoon goes well," she said.

"I'll call you later. I promise."

"Okay. Love you."

"I love you too, gorgeous." He winked then turned—the hustle and bustle of the hospital swirling around him until Danica couldn't see him any longer.

Spinning on her heel, she made her way past the nurse's station, then stopped dead in her tracks.

Gage.

He'd come through the sliding glass doors, looking as if he were chewing on nails.

He's upset.

Part of her wanted to go over there, find out why he was in Seattle, at that hospital, what was going on. While the other side of Danica, the grownup version that hadn't seen him in years, told her not to be ridiculous by running to him.

The battle started. *Go, don't go. Go.*

Taking that first shaky step forward, her heart pounding in her tight throat, she stopped once more when a woman came into view—long glossy sable hair, impeccably dressed, then her attention went to the profile of her face, and she knew.

Jenny.

That old familiar sense of betrayal meandered its way through her chest, turning the pasta she'd eaten sour, stomach churning, blood coursing through her veins transforming into acid.

Danica closed her eyes, willing the horrible feeling to go away, but it didn't. There was only one thing left to do. She would leave.

Turning around, she went in the opposite direction, anguish mixing into the nasty brew of duplicity as Danica popped her sunglasses off the top of her head, putting them on her face to hide the tears that shouldn't be present, but most definitely had begun to fall.

Chapter Thirty-Nine

HAGGARD FROM NO sleep, the hole of worry in her gut growing to a massive pit, Danica hopped off the couch when the doorbell rang.

"I'll get it," Mason said, striding out of the room.

"No. I will. It might be Gage with some news since he hasn't called."

Bypassing her brother-in-law, she all but ran to the front door, unlocking it and flinging the thing wide open. "Gage?"

The man's head lifted, and his silver eyes filled with unfathomable pain locked on hers.

Every bit of blood she possessed drained from her face to her feet. She swayed before she slowly backed up, hands out in front of her as if to stop an invader. "No, no, no…"

"Danica," he said, his voice almost hoarse.

Mason came up beside her, her sister from behind, asking, "What? What is it?"

"Don't say it!" Danica felt as if her head had detached and was floating up, up, up.

"I'm sorry," Gage said, stepping inside and moving forward until Danica's back hit Breckin's front, her sister's arms going around her.

"Shut up, Gage!" she yelled, "don't say another word!"

"Danica." He reached out, placing his warm palm on her ice-cold cheek. "I don't *want* to tell you this. I wish I didn't *have* to. Marcus was found. I'm so sorry, but he's dead."

"No-o-o!" she screamed, her legs giving way, Breckin struggling until Mason and Gage took over. Mase grabbed his wife; Gage took her.

Something inside of Danica snapped, her sanity maybe, and she started pounding her fists into Gage's chest, wailing and saying things. "You're lying to me! Marcus isn't dead! He isn't!"

"I'm so sorry, Danny." Gage held her through the thrashing, taking every blow and absorbing them. "I'm so sorry."

"I hate you, Gage Harrison! You've ruined my life! *Again!*"

Danica's house was full of people, her parents, Breckin and Mason, Mrs. Beil, who was taking care of the crying twins, Pastor Kyle and his wife, but Danny had finally quieted from the state she was in after his father came, giving her a sedative. Gage checked on her twice, relieved she was sleeping.

"Are you okay?" a grim-faced Mason asked, coming to take a seat beside him.

"I don't know how to answer that, brother."

"I'm sure you don't." Mason swiped a palm over his head. "Can you tell me what happened? To Marcus, I mean?"

"It appeared to be suicide, but we won't know for sure until all of the evidence is gathered, and the investigation is completed." Gage wasn't going to say anything about possible infidelity.

"Where was he?"

"On his boat in Seattle."

"That makes no sense at all."

"I know. You wouldn't think Marcus would have done something like this, but from what I saw, it sure looks as if he did. There wasn't anything obvious that would point to foul play."

"I just can't wrap my mind around it."

Gage nodded.

"I know this probably isn't the time, and I'm sorry, but something Danica said is poking at me."

He met his friend's gaze. "What?"

"She said you ruined her life *again*. What does that mean?"

He took a deep breath, then scrubbed his fingers through his hair. "I would imagine it has to do with the fact, for the second time in her life, I told her something that rocked her world."

"What did you tell her the first time?"

Gage rubbed the pulse in the middle of his forehead. "That Jenny was pregnant and said it was my baby."

Mason's brows knit. "What aren't you telling me? I get the news might have been surprising, it surprised me, but why would it have ruined her life?"

"It's a long story, Mase. Let's not get into that now."

Mason clapped him on the back. "All right, brother. But we *will* get into it, one day."

"We will."

Mason stood. "I'm going to go check on my wife."

"Go on." As much as Gage didn't want to leave Danica, sleeping or not, he had to, so he rose to his feet as well. "I've got to get a shower, catch a quick catnap, then head to the station."

The *rat-a-tat-tat, rat-a-tat-tat* of a gun spraying bullets had people screaming and scattering in wild disarray.

"Get down!" Wood fragments and pieces of books rained around his partner as Gage tugged him back, jerking him to the floor, taking cover behind an oak table he'd overturned. It was the best he had. Gage tapped his earpiece and said quickly, "Shooter, second floor of the library, automatic AK-47!"

They'd tailed the subject on foot into the public library—not the best place to be since there were far too many civilians, but he hadn't had a gun. *Where did that one come from? Had he stashed it in there, drew them into that building for some reason?* Gage didn't get it. Nothing made sense.

The security guard who was helping people get to one of the doors was shot in the back, his body falling forward, hitting the floor face first, limbs sprawled, a crimson pool forming around him.

There was no way that man would survive.

Gage tapped his earpiece. "Civilians! They're coming outside, take them to safety. It's chaos in here! A security guard is down! I repeat, a guard is down!"

More bullets sprayed. More innocent people fell as Gage pulled out his weapon and started firing in the direction the shooter was, or where he *thought* he was. He couldn't see the guy, just the massacre taking place as adrenaline pumped through him, all his senses sharpening, things around him slowing down into frame-by-frame pictures of horror.

Pow-pow-pow, pow-pow-pa-pow! His shots rang out, but Gage didn't hit anything, not the monster in the body of a man anyway.

Tapping his com once again, Gage bellowed, "We need backup in here! It's a blood bath!"

Pow-pow-pow, pow-pow-pow! He fired more shots, hearing in his ear, "Backup is coming, hang tight!"

Looking behind him, he glanced at the staircase going up to the second floor, then told his partner, "Lay down some cover fire, I'm going up—sneak around to the back of where I think our shooter is."

"Don't get dead," Agent Rothman said, his gun poised.

Inching backward, Gage belly crawled to the steps then made his way up, being as careful as possible as he headed in the direction he thought the shooter was.

Rat-a-tat-tat!

More screams rang out. More shots were fired. More, more, more of the nightmare whirled all around Gage as his blood raced through his veins, his heart pumping so hard it rattled his chest.

Rat-a-tat-tat, rat-a-tat-tat!

A woman yelled in a heart-wrenching lament, "My baby!"

It all became so much, the overwhelming sound, the horrific pain of people screaming, moaning. Gage's heart beat so fast, sweat broke out on his forehead, and he couldn't move quick enough, he couldn't get to where the monster was to stop this. It was like he was walking in knee-high sand, yet he was going as fast as he could until finally, he saw the man.

Gage aimed his gun and shot.

The guy's shoulder jerked, the gun dropped, the man spun and yanked something out of his boot—a smaller gun.

But, just as deadly, he realized an instant before the *bam, bam, bam!* of bullets were coming his way. He jumped behind a bookcase, waited for a second, then peeked, pulling back, looking out.

Gage no longer saw the guy.

He had to have gone out the back exit.

With gun drawn in front of him, Gage moved forward, following the trail of blood on the carpet to the door, leading out, then down the stairs.

He put on the speed again, catching up to the monster. "FBI! Freeze!"

Bam, bam, bam. Another few rounds came out of the Ruger that spun his way, one bullet grazing Gage's shoulder, but he ignored the flames overtaking his skin, shooting back, missing as the guy ran down the last few stairs, Gage shooting again and hitting!

The guy's body jerked forward, making him stumble out the back door.

Gage jumped past the last steps, going out the same door, taking the man down, putting his forearm along the back of the monster's neck, his knee pressing into the man's lower back, smashing him into the concrete.

With blood trickling down his arm and overtop of his hand Gage tapped his com, saying, "I've got the shooter! Back alley!"

Once the fight went out of the guy, body wilting beneath him, Gage took a breath. *It's over.*

"Al Musa sends their greetings," the shooter said, then laughed—a horrible, evil cackling.

B-O-O-M!

The impact of the blast catapulted Gage forward into a dumpster, slicing his forehead, something piercing his back like a blade. Everything rang, his ears turning into a *woom, woom, woom*… Then, his world went black.

Jerking up in the bed, body shaking like a piece of debris in a tsunami, a cold sweat covering him, Gage sucked in a breath. *It's just a nightmare. It's over now,* he told himself, but when the terror hit him in his sleep, it wasn't; it was happening all over again.

Putting his feet on the floor, he ran a palm over his damp face and took three more fortifying breaths. His therapist suggested counting, but he never did, he just took his mind to other places, other things, mainly the extraordinary blue of Danica's eyes—a tranquil sky on a cloudless day, the irises ringed in navy—and when he did, Gage calmed, his breathing returned to normal. But his life returning to anything close to normal? Well, that was a whole other story.

Chapter Forty

Before

PALM TREES SWAYED, their fronds whispering in the breeze; the sound of the water lapped along the shore. The warmth of Marcus at her back, his arms around her, sent a sense of peace through Danica as she gazed over the balcony.

The setting sun hit the horizon.

"It's so beautiful here," she whispered, her head falling back to rest on her fiancé's chest, the orange glow of the sky spreading a path across the ocean.

"*You're* beautiful," Marcus said before he let loose of her. "Come on."

Danica turned around and looked up into his whiskey-colored eyes, then took the hand he held out for her, fingers twining with his as he led them inside, the breeze blowing the sheer curtains past them in a billow of purity.

When he stopped at the foot of the massive bed, he disentangled his hand from hers, then started undoing the buttons on his Brioni shirt.

She frowned. "What are you doing?"

"I'm taking off my shirt."

"I see that, but why? We need to be downstairs for rehearsal in a few minutes?"

"I want to hold you in my arms, but not standing on the balcony. And I want to feel your skin on mine." He glanced at the bed then back to her.

Marcus had a thing about wrinkles in his clothing, but his suggestion about the two of them laying together on a bed was a first.

"We're not doing anything." Heat infused her cheeks. "Not until—"

"I know." Shrugging the material off his shoulders, he turned, took the few steps it took to get to the desk and put his shirt over the back of the chair.

His body was cut, sculpted into lean lines, a swimmer's physique, alabaster skin shimmering in the light with a birthmark that looked like someone swiped a small oval of bisque foundation on the left side of his rippled abdomen, by his navel. He was sexy, though nothing like—*Stop it, Danica. You won't think about Gage while you're with Marcus. Ever!*

He came to her, positioning himself behind her body. "Did you like what you saw?"

Heat raced up her chest, neck, and over her cheeks. "Marcus, I—"

"Tell me, Danica." *Zip…* He'd pulled the tab on her dress down, making her shiver. "Give me the words.

"Ye-yes."

Softly his fingertips traced up her spine, then over her shoulders, taking the material on her body and sliding it off her arms.

"Marcus, we can't!"

"*Shh*…tomorrow, you will be my wife."

"But, I'm *not* your wife yet." Danica put her arms around her midsection when the garment slipped to her hips.

"You are stunning." Marcus came around her, his gaze hungry as she stood there half undressed, her pale pink lacy bra not much of a covering the only barrier keeping her from exposure. "Please, let me see you."

This was a whole new side to the man she'd never witnessed. Oh, he was loving, but never hungry for her. She'd wondered more than once if they would have the right type of chemistry when it came to being intimate in a way a married couple should be.

Biting her lip, Danica carefully took hold of the slouching dress, stepping out of it and tossed it on the end of the mattress. A deeper flush of embarrassment hit her skin. She was in nothing but her skimpy underwear, and her high heel flower print Prada's—one of the many gifts Marcus had given her.

"Exquisite." He circled like a bird of prey, his fingertip tracing a line from her shoulder to her back, to her other shoulder, before he stepped in front of her once more, taking her face between his hands. "I love you."

Marcus kissed her then, in a way he hadn't done before. This wasn't a soft, sweet, reverent kiss, but a taking of her mouth with his as one of his large hands went to the back of her head, the other to her hip, then around, pulling her into him—claiming.

The few crisp chest hairs he had tickled her cleavage as his taste mixed with the wine he drank earlier exploded on her tongue.

"Marcus," she uttered, her palm curling around the back of his head as he picked her up and lay her back on the bed, his body coming down on hers—hips positioned between her thighs. "I've waited a long time to give myself to the man I love, and I don't—"

"We won't," he said, then put his mouth on the apex of her breasts, the tip of his nose skimming up to her throat, along the side of her neck. "Not until you become Mrs. Marcus Harding." Kiss, nibble, kiss. "Then you'll be mine in every way."

"Marcus," she moaned.

He flicked her earlobe with the tip of his tongue, making her shiver. "*Mm*…you smell so good, Danica."

When he pressed himself into her while gently sucking on a hot-spot she didn't know she possessed beneath her ear, chills traversed her flesh, flames shot along her spine, and Danica knew her preconceived notions about *not* having chemistry flew out the open balcony doors.

Scoring her nails down the muscular contours of Marcus's shoulders, she said, "We can be late. Kiss me."

"I *am* kissing you," he said, then left a trail along the column of her throat, making her arch into the sensation.

Tap, tap, tap!

"Sis!" Breckin's voice came from the other side of her room door. "We need to get downstairs. Everyone is waiting!"

Marcus groaned, then looked into her eyes. "To be continued." He bent his head and caressed her mouth with his, then brushed his nose along hers. "We better go."

Palm resting on his bare chest, she reluctantly said, "Yeah."

Chapter Forty-One

TAKING A QUICK peek at the time on the bottom right-hand corner of his computer, seeing 3:04 P.M., Gage tapped the com on his desk. "Dixie, I'm heading out for the rest of the day. Call if you need me for anything."

"All right, Chief. Are you going over to the Harding place?"

"Yes."

"I'm going to go when I finish up here, but please give Danica my condolences. My heart breaks for her and those babies."

"Maybe you should give them when you go. I'm not sure—" Gage clamped his mouth shut before he could say he wasn't sure she would agree to see him.

"Okay. I will," Dixie said, not going into twenty questions, something he always liked about her.

After rolling his head along his stiff shoulders, he got up, strode to the door of his office, grabbed his coat off the hook, and hurried for the back exit.

Less than fifteen minutes later, Gage was walking into the foyer of Danica's home. Breckin let him in, with a weary expression on her face and fatigue showing in her posture.

"Is Danny awake?" He should have asked about her, how Breck was doing, but he went straight to the heart of the matter.

"She is." Breck tucked some hair behind her ear. "Two detectives were here. They just left a few minutes ago with Marcus' laptop."

"Where is she?"

"In the family room, and won't come out. I've tried to get her to eat something, but she shakes her head."

"I'm going to go talk to her."

"Gage?"

He looked into Breckin's green eyes. "Yeah?"

"Try to get my sister to move. She's been in the same spot since before the detectives arrived."

He nodded. "I'll see what I can do."

With a sensation of tightness in his chest, Gage made his way from the foyer, down one of the corridors, and into the family room. Complete and total silence filled the space as his gaze bounced from the large sectional, to an armchair, and finally came to rest on an oversized piece of furniture positioned by the window looking into the side lawn.

Danica sat there, staring out. Her hair was a mess; bare feet in the seat with her knees propped up, something in her hand.

"Danny?" he called softly, but she didn't respond. Not even a twitch.

He went to her, squatting beside the bulky chair and taking her in from the side of her face, down her arm—to the fingers pressing so hard into the frame of a picture she'd cracked the glass—drops of crimson drip, drip, dripped onto her heather gray lounge pants.

"Sweetheart? I'm going to take this. You cut yourself." Gage pried her fingers loose, taking a look at the photograph. A picture of her and Marcus kissing under the tropical-flowered arch on the beach where they had said, "I do."

That stab of pain hit him dead center, but he pushed it aside, leaving it with the broken picture frame.

"I need to check your fingers," he said, but Danica hadn't budged, she was still gazing out the window, though Gage didn't think she saw a single thing, nor was he sure she even knew he was beside her.

Pulling her hand closer, he studied the small wounds. They wouldn't take stitches but should be tended to. "Danny? We need to get your fingers cleaned up. You're bleeding."

That roused her, and she turned her head to look at him. Nothing. No life in her eyes or on her face. "Huh?"

"You cut your fingers, and they are bleeding."

She glanced at her hand as if she were seeing it for the first time. "Oh."

Her flat tone and affect worried him. "Come on. Let's go get that fixed, okay?"

She nodded, and he stood, helping her do the same, guiding her out the archway and into the first bathroom he came across. "Let's put those fingers under some cool water, what do you say?"

She didn't answer.

Like a lumbering zombie, Gage needed to steer her toward the sink, turn on the water, make sure it wasn't too hot or too cold, then placed her wounded flesh under the stream. She didn't jerk back from the sensation. Danny didn't do anything. She just stood there, absently watching the lines of dark pink flow into the water and swirl down the drain.

Once her fingertips looked clean, he turned the faucet off, grabbed a hand towel, and started softly patting her hand dry.

Danica let him maneuver her like she was a life-sized doll, but never said a word.

Gage didn't think his heart could break since it had been decimated, but the soul-deep pain Danny was in caused the small sliver that still functioned to fracture. With every fiber of his being, he wanted to take her into his arms, tell her everything would be all right, and never let her go. But she wasn't his to hold, nothing would be all right, and he'd unwillingly let her go twelve years ago.

Placing the towel on the countertop, he swiped some hair back from her face, hoping she would look up at him. She didn't. She just kept her gaze on his shoulder.

"Is everything okay in here?" Mrs. Lorry asked, worried lines on her forehead as she stepped into the bathroom with them.

"Danica cut her fingers," Gage said.

"Oh, my." Her mother hurried over. "What happened?"

"She cut them on some glass."

"Glass?" Her gaze lifted up to his.

"A picture frame she was holding a little too tight."

"I ruined it," Danica whispered, but he was just happy to hear her voice.

Mrs. Lorry went to the cabinet, pulled out a tube of Neosporin, and a box of Band-Aids. "Ruined what, baby-girl?"

"Our wedding picture."

"No." Carefully, Gage cupped her cheek, though she still didn't look at him. "You didn't. You'll only need a new frame, that's all."

Ella Lorry glanced up at him and mouthed, "Thank you," before she took hold of her daughter's hand and said, in an upbeat tone he was positive she didn't feel, "Now, let's get those fingers fixed up, and then go get something to eat."

"Not hungry."

"Well, maybe not, but you need to try to eat something. Besides, Mrs. Beil is going to go home soon, and Ari and Aaron need their mommy."

Chapter Forty-Two

Before

STANDING IN THE shadowed corner of a balcony which overlooked the scene below, Gage knew he had gone insane, or perhaps he was a masochist. Either way, it wasn't right. When he'd heard Danica finally set a date to tie the knot, it wasn't hard to do a little bit of detective work and find out the particulars of the location, not sure why it had taken so long for her to do the deed. He found what he needed, then boarded a plane headed for Hawaii, where he booked a suite in the same hotel the Lorry's were staying at and laid low.

As classical music started, the people who had been seated all stood, turning to see the bride walking in on the arm of her father.

Dressed in a long flowing white gown, her hair done up in some elaborate twist, tiny pink flowers woven within, Danica took his breath away. Everything in the world narrowed down to her, the sparkle in the fitted bodice of her gown, the way she moved with an innate sensuality and grace. The curve where her elegant neck met her bare shoulder. The shine of the sun hitting her pale skin. And as much as he didn't want to pull his eyes from her, he did when a man stepped up to the pastor, or whoever was officiating the ceremony.

He was expecting to see the same guy she'd been with a couple of years ago, her dance partner, since he'd overheard her tell J.J., *Ryan, that's his name*, had proposed, but it wasn't Ryan. It was someone else. A man who was probably a few years, maybe four or five, older than her, with brown-blond hair, and looking like someone on the cover of GQ magazine, smiled as Danica came down the sandy aisle to him.

The expression on the groom's chiseled face said it all. Danica Dawn Lorry hung the moon and the stars. Gage knew precisely how the lucky guy felt.

Then the person officiating said, "Who gives this woman to this man?"

The beating of Gage's heart slowed as Mr. Lorry looked at his lovely daughter, smiled, then turned back to the gentleman who had asked the question. "Her mother and I."

With that, he gave his daughter's hand to the person she would marry, while J.J. and Breckin, who he hadn't seen in years, stood beside the couple, with two other men Gage didn't know on the other side as they all closed ranks.

That little voice inside his head said *You should leave now, you've seen enough,* while the crazy one countered with, *You have to see this through.*

So, Gage stayed, while those multiple cracks in his heart all converged, collapsing into a mighty gulf containing the sorrow, as he listened to the woman he loved pledge her fidelity and devotion to another man.

It wasn't until the pastor said, "*Marcus*, you may kiss your bride" that he turned to go, and left his spectators spot.

Walking into the hotel room he hadn't slept in, across the floor, and then opening the door to escape, Gage experienced a pain so deep, so profound, he almost doubled over as he stepped beyond the threshold.

Without looking back, he went down the hall, into the elevator, exited into the lobby, strode through the front doors of the resort, then paused as he said two simple words—the hardest he would ever say. "Goodbye, Danny."

Chapter Forty-Three

PEOPLE HAD SURROUNDED Danica for five days and still were as she watched her husband's casket—the one her mother and sister helped her pick out because she'd been in a fog—being lowered into the ground.

Not for the first time, she hoped someone would wake her up from this nightmare, tell her she was having a horrible dream. But no one ever did. It all just continued.

Shifting her attention to the bruised sky, she wondered, apropos of nothing, if the sun would shine again, then looked at some of the solemn faces who came from the church to the graveside service. She'd seen them all before—the pastor's wife, Mr. and Mrs. Beil, Dixie Newberry, Berta Collins, Kasey Albright, Phillip Granger, Jake, Maggie and Alli, Darnell, Frank Guymon, Doctor Harrison and his wife, some of the staff her husband worked with at the hospital, and *Gage.* He was dressed in his dark uniform, those silver eyes trained on her.

Reaching up, she placed her cool hand over the top of Breckin's who was standing behind the metal folding chair she was seated in, palm resting on her shoulder. J.J., sitting next to her, held her other hand. She glanced to her left, where her stoic in-laws were, each of whom held one of her fussy twins.

Unsure of why she was looking at anyone, she glanced to her right, past her best friend. Mom, dabbing tears from her eyes—Dad, with his arm around her. A movement caught her attention, and she tried to focus on what it was, catching the back of a tall woman walking away, weaving through old headstones. Something about her looked familiar, but it didn't matter who it was or why she was leaving before Pastor Kyle said the final words.

Nothing mattered anymore.

Gage's old injuries were making themselves known, probably because he had put his body through the paces in the gym the night before, brutally punching the heavy bag, then lifting weights until it hurt, pushing past the burn. But even if every part of him was aching, and the slight hobble that only showed when he was fatigued cropped up, he ignored it all as he made his way through the crowd, his singular focus on getting to Danica.

"I'm so very sorry for your loss," Clarise Kyle said, taking hold of both of Danny's hands. "You and the babies are in my prayers."

"Thank you." Danica's voice was robotic, nothing, no emotion discernable.

It was that lack, her being devoid, that bothered Gage on a level he couldn't shake, even if he had wanted to.

"Danny?" Gage stepped up where the pastor's wife had been.

Her eyes lifted to his shoulder. Since the night of her breakdown in his arms, it had only ever been his shoulder, except for a brief moment during the ceremony when she looked *at* him—there and gone.

"I know saying I'm sorry doesn't do a thing to help you, and never will. But I'm here, and I'll be here for as long as you need me."

"You have things to do," she said, still in that same flat, lifeless tone. "You should go."

His heart almost seized. "Danica, look at me."

Slowly, her lashes lifted, her chin coming up, and, *at last,* she locked her gaze with his.

Not caring who saw them or who heard him, Gage pulled her into his arms, her smaller body enveloped by his bigger one as he placed his lips to her ear. "I'm not going anywhere, Danica Dawn, do you hear me? I'm not leaving you."

Chapter Forty-Four

Before

DANICA TOOTLED THROUGH the door of her apartment, the luxurious high-rise she and Marcus were living in until their custom home in Cedar Point was built. They were through the planning stage, and Carter Construction would be breaking ground on a perfect lot not too far from the lake sometime next week. It had been four years of living in Seattle, and as lovely as it was, she missed home. Though she was there a lot, since Marcus agreed they would attend the church where she'd gone her whole life, and for the most part, he tried to follow through with taking her. But on the days he was stuck at the hospital, she took herself to church and then spent the afternoon with her parents.

Tossing her keys on the table by the front door, she took off her sunglasses and made her way into the kitchen, placing them and her purse on the breakfast bar before going to the fridge to grab a bottled water. She'd been working on a part-time basis at Vibes, her old dance studio, helping Madame Doucet with her beginners class, but Marcus didn't want her to work, so this two day a week thing was the compromise they'd come to.

With her hand on the stainless-steel handle of the refrigerator, she stopped, interrupted by the ringing of the phone. She took the few steps it required to get to it, picked up the handset on the cordless, and answered, "Hello?"

"Danny…" There was something not quite right with her mother's voice.

"Mom? What's wrong?"

"Something came through on the prayer chain."

"Oh, no. What happened?"

"Gage," she said.

The name struck her hard enough she had to take a seat at the bar.

"What about him?" Her hands started to shake.

"He was involved in a horrible explosion."

"Is he—" She clamped her mouth shut, tears falling down her face as she licked her dry lips. "Is he dead?"

"Lives were lost, but Gage is in critical condition at Cedars Sini. You need to pray."

All the blood seemed to leave her. "I will," she managed past the numbness.

The moment she disconnected the call, she stood on unsteady legs, made it a few steps, where she didn't know, then went to her knees. "Oh, God. Please don't let Gage die. Don't take him home. Not yet, Lord. He has so much life to live. Spare him. Help him. Heal him. Send Your angels down around him…"

Unable to speak any longer, Danica cried heart-wrenching, body-shaking sobs, her moaning lament of sorrow spilling from her as she bent forward until her forehead rested against the Brazilian hardwood.

Help him, Lord. Please, please, please, help him.

The continuous *beep, beep, beep*, of some machine had Gage fluttering his heavy eyelids open, everything around him a blur.

"Son?"

"Dad?" he rasped, his throat too dry as he tried to focus on the shape looking down at him.

"Oh, Sean. He's coming around, praise the Lord!"

"Mom?" Gage turned his head, but it hurt, and the light was killing his eyes, so he closed them.

"I'm here, my beautiful boy," she said. He thought she patted his leg, but he couldn't be sure. "I'm here."

"Where am I?"

"In the hospital," Dad said.

"Hospital?" His head swam with a jumble of stuff that didn't connect. "Where?"

"In L.A., son."

"You're in L.A.?"

"Yes. We are here."

"What happened?"

"You were severely injured. But… try to go back to sleep if you can. You're still in recovery."

Recovery from what? He didn't have the strength to ask. Sleep sounded good. *I'll make sense of things later when I'm not so....*

His coherent thought faded before everything went away.

Chapter Forty-Five

A WEEK AFTER the funeral, Danica had managed to pull herself together enough to drive into Seattle. She left the twins with Mrs. Beil, telling her sister and her mother that she needed to be alone when they both insisted they go with her. She loved them, she did, but the quiet solitude seemed to be something she needed; so they gave in, letting her leave without them.

Pulling her Escalade into the designated "Doctor's Parking" spot Marcus had at Harborview, she took a deep breath before she shut off the ignition. She had a lot of business to attend to, like going to check on his Mercedes, which the police had impounded, stopping by the bank, and going to start the paperwork process to collect on his life insurance policy… But she thought she would start by going to the hospital to gather Marcus' things from the office he kept there. For some crazy reason, she figured that might be the easier of the things to do.

Why? She had no idea since nothing was easy, not even getting out of bed in the mornings.

Leaving her vehicle behind, she made her way into the building, then down the familiar halls, breezing past people she recognized who had strange expressions on their faces—mouths agape, shock evident, almost as if they were surprised to see her.

Danica kept her focus on the task at hand, which was getting to her husband's office door. Once inside, she could shut it and fall apart if she needed to, but until then, she was just happy she'd put her Dolce & Gabbana's on. The sunglasses would hide the dark circles under her bloodshot eyes.

"Mrs. Harding?"

She turned to the sound of a deep, familiar voice. "Doctor Forsyth. Hello."

"My dear," the white-haired chief of staff said, "what are you doing here?"

She frowned. "I thought I would come to collect my husband's things from his office."

The man just looked at her as if she'd lost her mind, and maybe she had, but she wasn't sure why he thought so.

"You don't know, do you?"

Danica shook her head. "I'm sorry. Know what?"

"Oh, my." The older gentleman rubbed his chin. "Perhaps you should come with me."

"All right," she said, not wanting to, but figuring she must if she wanted to get on with things.

"After you." He held out his arm once he opened his office door, allowing her to step inside. "Take a seat, dear."

Going to the chair by the window, she sat in the spot of sun, watching the man shove his hands into the front pockets of his dark slacks, his lips in a thin line as he looked at her. "I'm not sure there is any way to say this, so I'm just going to tell it to you straight." He glanced down at his feet.

Pinpricks of anxiety started poking her. "Whatever it is, Doctor, please, tell me."

His gray eyes came to her, sorrow swimming in the depths. "Marcus was dismissed from the hospital six months ago."

She gasped, her hand going to her mouth. Of all the things the man could have said, she would never have guessed that. "Excuse me?"

"I'm sorry, but… his employment here was terminated."

"Terminated?" she asked, not sure she was hearing right or even having this conversation. Maybe she was still home, in bed, having a bad dream?

"Yes."

"He hasn't been here for six months?"

"I'm afraid not, dear."

Danica shook her head, disbelieving.

Where has he been going all that time? Where was he when he called and said he was working late? When he said he was being paged?

"I-I—" Danica dropped her head into her hands.

"Mrs. Harding, I'm so sorry to be the one to tell you this. But I assumed, as I'm sure does everyone else, Marcus told you he was no longer here."

"No," she squeaked. "I had no idea. He left in the mornings, as he always did. Sometimes he didn't get home until late."

"Are you alright? Can I get you some water or something?"

She looked up at the man and ignored his question and concern. "Why was he let go?"

"There was a lawsuit brought against the hospital and your husband."

Her heart was pounding so hard she could hear it. "A lawsuit?"

"Yes, but that was only one of his troubles. His focus had slipped, he'd been coming in late, sometimes under the influence of something. He failed an impromptu drug test."

"Drugs?" She waved a hand in front of her. "I'm sorry, but are we talking about the same man? My husband, Marcus Harding? You're telling me he was using drugs?"

"I'm afraid so."

"That's…" She glanced down at her knees. "That's just not possible." Danica had the overwhelming urge to pinch herself to see if she were awake, or maybe she should bend over and vomit in the ficus.

"Mrs. Harding." The doctor came to her and put a hand on her shoulder. "I'm so very sorry. I can see this is all a shock to you, and I wish things were different. I really do."

Gage was on his way to check on Danica over his lunch hour, ready to turn into her drive when his cell phone started chiming. He hit the screen, sending the call over to his speakers and answered, "Harrison."

There was the sound of sniffling on the other end.

"Danny?"

More sniffles.

"Danica? Speak to me!"

"Gawonii," she said in a broken voice, small and tear-filled, making his heart hurt. "I'm just pulling into your driveway now. I'll see you in a few."

"I'm not home."

That got his back straight. "Where are you?"

"I'm in Seattle, and I need you to come help me. I don't think I can drive."

"Why not? Are you hurt?"

"I'm-I'm—" Danica burst into sobs.

"Tell me, what is going on?" he asked, panic hitting him as he took the circular drive out, and was back on the street.

"Marcus," she managed. "He hasn't been at the hospital. He was let go six months ago."

"What?"

"Ca-can, you come to get me?"

"I'm on my way. You sit tight. Are you still at the hospital?"

"I'm in my car, in his park-parking spot."

"Okay. Hang in there for me."

"Gage?"

"Yes?"

"I want to go home, but I ca-can't until I go to the bank and talk to the insurance company."

"I'll take you to do what you need to do. Don't worry."

Her "Thank you" came out in a breath.

"You never need to thank me, Danny. Just hold on. I'm coming."

You'll need one of your guys to go with you so they can take Danica's vehicle home.

The moment he disconnected, another call came in. "Harrison," he clipped impatiently.

"Chief, I—"

"Dixie, I was about to call you. I need you to round up one of my officers and have him meet me at the front of the station in five."

"Oh, all right." She sounded surprised.

He sighed. He'd been rude and needed to apologize. "Listen. I'm sorry I cut you off. What did you need?"

"Cooper Kane called in and said someone's been lurking around his place, and you know how he is. He won't let anyone but you on his property."

Gage rubbed his forehead. Cooper was a former Navy Seal, and due to the extensive burns and scarring he suffered from a mission gone wrong, he had become a recluse. The guy holed up in the big antebellum house on the outskirts of town—a place with several acres of land and a few old cabins deep within the trees his grandfather owned back in the day. But most local kids believed Land's End to be haunted, so he doubted one of them would be sneaking around out there. Regardless though, Gage needed to see him.

"Dixie, call Coop back and tell him I've got an emergency going on, but I'll come by his place when I get free. However, it might be this evening before I can get there."

"I will." She was quiet for a moment then asked, "Are you all right?"

"Yeah."

"But you'll tell me if there is anything I can do?"

"I'll let you know."

"Okay. I'll round up one of the guys to meet you out front and call Cooper back."

"Thank you, Dixie. I don't know what I'd do without you."

Chapter Forty-Six

Before

CONFINED TO HIS wheelchair, Gage closed his eyes, listening to the water trickle down the column of the fountain. This private courtyard was a place he tried to come to as much as possible. The flower gardens attracted butterflies, bumblebees, and birds. There also seemed to be a constant breeze.

He took a deep breath, feeling his lungs expand, recalling a memory of Danica the summer after she graduated from high school. He had come home for a few days and saw her as he drove into town. She had been across from the baseball field in a patch of wildflowers, shimmering in the sun, holding a clump of purple blooms, her head tipped back, the sweet expression on her face, his golden gift from above.

"Gage?"

Henry's deep voice had his eyelids lifting.

"*Hmm*?"

With his buzz cut and square jaw, the orderly looked like a cross between a linebacker and a soldier dressed in pale blue scrubs.

"It's time to get back inside. Art therapy starts in just a few."

Gage groaned a protest. "I am not, and have never been, an artist."

"Well, me neither, but that's not the point. Painting helps improve your hand-eye coordination and your dexterity."

Henry grabbed the handles on the back of his chair, pushing him toward the doors of the rehab hospital. "I hear you've been doing pretty good with your physical therapy."

"I'm still not walking," he grumped.

"But you're moving those legs, something the doctors didn't think you would be able to do."

Gage had made it through two spinal surgeries, and a few skin grafts on his upper back and part of his neck because the heat of the explosion had melted his flesh like caramel in a hot pan. He had healed from a busted femur, six broken ribs, and his fractured collarbone and cracked tibia had mended as well. So, he shouldn't be ticked off all the time. He was alive, while there hadn't been enough left of his partner to bury. And compared to many other patients in the rehab facility, he could be considered doing well. But even though he knew he should be grateful, he was the opposite.

"I've got a surprise," Marcus said, tugging Danica, the two of them all but jogging down the too long dock.

"Slow down. My wedges and this pace aren't the best combination unless I want a sprained ankle."

"We're almost there, just-a-few-more—" her husband stopped. Danica wanted to let out a relieved breath as he dropped his hold on her hand, turned, and smiled at her. "This is it!"

She glanced around, only seeing one thing. "That boat?" she asked.

"Yes, but it's a yacht. Isn't she great? I bought it for our anniversary and thought we could celebrate by having our maiden voyage."

"I thought yachts were huge?"

"Not necessarily. This is a small one. Only thirty feet."

She blinked at the white vessel then back at her jived husband. "Do you even know how to sail?"

"I do, but I haven't sailed since before we started seeing each other." He looked behind him. "What do you think?"

"Well, I don't know anything about boats."

"Yacht." He smiled back at her. "Boats are smaller."

"I don't know anything about yachts, boats, sailing in general, but it looks…nice."

"Nice? Oh, sweetie, you're going to love it. Come on, let's go on board. I've got another surprise waiting for you."

Thirty minutes into their 'maiden voyage' and Danica found out something interesting about herself. She and boating didn't get along. This became evident when she tossed her cookies. Then the dizziness joined the party, leaving Marcus no choice but to turn around and take the yacht back to the slip.

As he helped her off "The Rising Dawn," which was his second surprise—he'd named the thing after her—she'd never been happier to be back on solid ground.

"I'm so sorry, Danica. I didn't know you suffer from motion sickness."

"Neither did I."

"Aw…sweetheart." Marcus kissed her forehead. "I didn't mean to ruin our anniversary."

She patted his arm. "Look at it this way. It will be an anniversary to remember."

Her husband chuckled.

Picking up the cloth napkin from the bistro table where they sat outside the café he took her to, Marcus carefully dabbed at the corner of her eye. "Your mascara is smudged."

"Is that you, Danny?" someone called.

She turned to the sound of her name, seeing Mrs. Harrison coming her way, dark hair in an elegant updo, a smile on her symmetrical face.

She waved. "Hi. How are you?"

"My dear." The woman leaned down and gave her a quick hug. "I'm doing well. How about you?"

"I'm afraid I flubbed up," Marcus interjected.

"How so?" Mrs. Harrison asked straightening and glancing at Danica's husband.

"I thought it would be a good idea to go sailing for our anniversary, and—"

"It appears I get motion sickness," Danny said, "who knew?"

"Aw… I'm sorry. I've never had it, but I hear it can be pretty awful."

"You've heard right."

Gage's mother took her in, gently eying her. "Are you feeling better now?"

Danica nodded. "Much. Being able to sit still has done wonders."

"That's good news, at least."

"Do you want to have a seat with us? We are going to order something. Well, Marcus is, I think I'll go light." Danica moved her ice water aside.

"I'd love to join you, but I'm meeting a couple of colleagues, so I'll be heading inside."

"Oh, all right. But before you go"—willing her heart to calm, she asked the question weighing on her—"how is Gage doing?"

"He's improved, though he's still in the rehab hospital, overall he's leaps and bounds above the point his doctors thought he would be. Sean and I will be flying out next week to see our boy, and I'm hoping for even more improvement."

A small wisp of relief started, then grew. "I'm so happy to hear that. I pray for his full recovery every day."

"Keep praying, dear." She pointed her manicured finger skyward. "He's listening."

Holding the thin paintbrush between his fingers, Gage stared at the same blank canvas from the week before, wondering what he was supposed to do. He could put a few strokes of paint across all that white and call it good, he supposed.

"Mr. Harrison," the woman, Lindsey, said as she came up beside him, leaned down, bracelets jingling, and whispered, "I want you to picture a special memory. Something that stands out. Something that, when you saw it, made an impact. Now, close your eyes and picture it."

He figured why not, and did what she asked.

The memory of Danica dancing on stage at WSU that white dress flowing, her movements graceful as she twirled across the floor, her feet disturbing the fog, came back to him in vivid full-color motion—a picture show of sensuality and sheer perfection.

For a moment in time, Gage smiled.

"What do you see, Mr. Harrison?"

"*Gravity*. I see Gravity."

"Then paint that for me."

Chapter Forty-Seven

"WHAT CAN I do for you today, Mrs. Harding?" the president of the bank asked as Danica took a seat in front of his large, walnut desk, his gaze shifting to the imposing man in uniform standing behind her. "And… Officer?"

"Harrison. *Police Chief* Harrison."

"Police Chief Harrison," Mr. Monroe echoed.

"I'm here as support for Danica."

"I see," he said, his dark eyes coming back to her.

"I'm not sure if you are aware," Danica said, trying to mash down her nerves, "but my husband passed away."

"I had heard. May I give you my condolences."

"Thank you, Mr. Monroe. His death has come as quite a shock for me, so I'm sorry if I seem scattered."

"I'm sure it was a shock, and you have nothing to apologize for, Mrs. Harding."

"Yes, well." Danica fidgeted in her seat until Gage's warm palm rested on her shoulder. "I realize I've never been involved with our banking business, leaving everything for Marcus to handle, but out of necessity, I will be changing that."

The man nodded his graying head.

"I understand Marcus did most if not all of our banking with Chase online, but again, I wasn't proactive, so I will need access to our bank statements for starters. And, before I forget, there seems to be an issue with my debit card."

The man's gaze went to Gage, then back to her. "Would you like your friend to step out while we discuss your business?"

"I see no need for that. I've known Chief Harrison since we were kids, so there's nothing here that I would be concerned about him knowing."

Gage squeezed her shoulder but remained quiet.

Mr. Monroe cleared his throat. "Are you sure?"

Danica scowled. "Yes, sir."

Leaning back in his chair, the man steepled his chubby fingers. "Mrs. Harding, I'll be happy to provide you with paper copies of your bank statements, however…"

"However?"

"I'm afraid the reason you are having an issue with your debit card is due to lack of funds."

She blinked, cocked her head, and blinked some more. "Lack of funds? What do you mean?"

"I mean just that." Mr. Monroe shifted forward, tapped a few keys on a laptop, then looked back at her. "As of now, your checking account is in the red."

"The red?"

"Yes. There is a negative balance of one-thousand-five-hundred-sixty-three-dollars and fifteen cents."

"I-I…" Danica felt the room spinning.

"Are you all right, Mrs. Harding?"

She shook her head.

Gage was there, kneeling at her side, taking her cool hand into his much warmer one. "Breathe, Danny. In and out. In and out."

"Perhaps you'd like some water?" Mr. Monroe asked, but he sounded far, far away.

"Get her some!" Gage snapped.

The man jumped out of his chair and scurried out of his office.

"Danica, look at me?"

Feeling as if she might pass out, she slowly turned and locked her gaze with Gage's.

"Don't freak. We'll get to the bottom of this, okay? Breathe."

As if she were back in Lamaze class, she started pulling air into her lungs, then exhaling.

"That's good, sweet-one. Keep breathing. There you go."

"This is cold," Mr. Monroe said, bringing her a cup of water, which she wasted no time sipping, the tilt-a-whirl sensation dissipating little by little.

Gage stood but didn't let go of her hand. "If there is a problem with Mrs. Harding's checking account, could you have transferred funds from their savings into checking?"

"Yes, well."

Danica glanced up at the man who appeared to be turning a shade of puce.

"Yes or no? It's a simple answer," Gage said.

"We could."

"Then why wasn't that done?"

"We could, Chief Harrison, if the Harding's savings account had the funds."

"So, you're saying both our checking *and savings* is... are..." Danica couldn't find the right words.

"All of your funds with our bank are depleted, Mrs. Harding."

The warble started at the corner of her eyes, then spread, until everything blurred. Danica thought she heard Gage curse, then that was all she wrote, everything turned into lights out.

"Danny?" Something swiped over her forehead. "Danica, wake up for me."

Eyelids fluttering, she opened them. "Gawonii?"

"Yes."

She smiled as she looked into the most exquisite shade of silver she had ever seen, then like an avalanche, it all came crashing down around her. *Marcus. The hospital. The bank.*

"Gage?" She tried to set up, but she couldn't. Not unless he helped her.

"It's okay, Danny. I've got you."

She glanced around.

Danica was half on his lap, half on a couch of some sort, but they weren't in Mr. Monroe's office, which confused her. "Weren't we in the bank?"

"We still are, only we are in the back breakroom, away from all the bustle happening in the front of the building."

Her tears started to fall, and he began wiping them with his fingers. "Oh, Danny-girl. Don't cry."

"I ca-can't help it."

"Please. When you cry, it shreds me."

More streaks wound down her cheeks. "What am I going to do?"

"We will figure it out." Gage swiped the wetness away.

"I don't— Wait," she said. "Help me up." Sniffling, she wiggled until Gage assisted her, allowing her to sit up on the leather loveseat next to him, her feet going to the floor. "Marcus has a trust fund. He told me he had been moving money around for the twins, you know, to start a college fund for them. Maybe he moved things to another bank for some reason."

As she glanced around, wildly, Gage figured out Danny was trying to locate her purse. He picked it up from where he had placed it earlier and gave the designer bag to her. "Here."

"Thanks." She pulled her cell phone out of the pocket, scrolled through her contacts, then tapped the screen and put the device to her ear. "The Harding family finance lawyer," she said to him with her hand over the bottom of the phone, then grinned, slipping it away. "Hello, Laura. This is Mrs. Harding, Marcus' wife. May I please speak with Mr. Davey?"

Pause.

"No. He's not expecting my call, but this is somewhat of an emergency."

Another pause.

"Yes, all right. Thank you." She glanced up at him. While she wasn't crying, and her color was back, he was still worried about her.

"Oh, hi, Mr. Davey. Yes, thank you." She stood and started pacing. "I'm sure I needn't say it has been a horrible shock to me as well."

She listened, nodded.

"Look. I'm trying to take care of some business, and I'm, for lack of a better description, in the dark here."

Danica tucked some hair behind her left ear. "I know Marcus told me he'd been moving money around for the twins. You know, starting a college fund. And… well, I'm wondering if you would know anything about that since you handled his trust."

It was quiet, Danny biting her plush bottom lip, then she glanced down. "No? Are you sure?"

Those pointy-toed heels looked painful to wear, but she walked in them as if they were jogging shoes.

Danica stopped her back and forth, raised her head, peered up at the ceiling, then closed her eyes. "Okay, well, then what about his trust fund? Now that he is gone, how does that work? Will I have access to it, or—"

All the color drained from her face once more, making Gage jumped to his feet and grab hold of her, worried she was going to pass out again, knowing whatever the man was telling her, it wasn't good.

"I see." She rubbed her temple. "Are my in-laws aware of this?"

Danica swayed. Gage stood behind her, afraid she would tumble backward, then she leaned into him.

"Okay. Yes. I'm sorry too, Mr. Davey." She didn't even disconnect the call, the hand holding the phone just dropped to her side, the cell slipping from her loose fingers, slap-sliding across the hunter-green carpet.

Gage walked her back to the seat, had her sit, then went, picked up the phone, tapped the icon to end the call, and put her cell in his shirt pocket. "What's happened?"

"Mr. Davey doesn't know anything about college funds for the twins." She closed her eyes, leaned forward, dropped her head into her hands, and muttered, "Marcus' three-million-dollar trust fund was depleted—a year ago. And, per my husband's instructions, his parents were not to be informed."

"If he's the family lawyer, can he do that, not say anything to the Harding's?"

"I don't know, the trust came from his grandfather when Marcus turned twenty-one, and it was his money to do with what he wanted. But whether or not Mr. Davey's could legally tell his parents or not, they don't know the funds are gone."

If Marcus had still been alive and breathing, he wouldn't be for long. Gage wanted to strangle him with his bare hands.

"And it gets worse," Danica said in a small voice, just above a whisper. "His investments are gone, too."

She went quiet. Too quiet.

"Danny?"

"That's not all."

"Tell me." He placed his palm between her shoulder blades, making what he hoped to be soothing circles.

"Apparently, Marcus cashed in his two-hundred-and-fifty-thousand-dollar life insurance policy around the same time as he emptied what remained of the trust."

"Danica." Gage heard the frog in his throat. "I'm so, so sorry this is happening. I don't know what to say."

She started wheezing. "I-I-I-can't bre-breathe."

He scooped her into his arms, cradling her. "Deep breaths. In and Out. Good, one more time. That's right, Danny."

Limply, she rested her cheek against his left shoulder, her petal-soft palm curling around the side of his neck, the collar of his uniform covering the beginning of his scars there. "I have no idea how…"

"Don't talk, just breathe."

It was quiet for a second, all but for the sound of his heartbeat mixing into her respiration, then she whispered, "I don't know how I'm going to pay the funeral home. How I'm—"

Danica started crying then, the hard, body-shaking kind of sobs, and there was nothing he could do at the moment but hold her tight.

Chapter Forty-Eight

Before

SWEAT POURED DOWN his face, and he felt like giving up, but he wouldn't. He'd push on, and keep on pushing, regardless of the pain.

"One more lap. Can you handle it?" his petite physical therapist asked from beside him. With her pixie features and smiling face, she might look like a sweet pushover, though she was anything but.

"Yeah. I'm good," he lied.

Gage had transitioned from a wheelchair to a walker, but it was as if he were a baby, learning to crawl, who'd decided taking part in a triathlon was the thing to do. Every muscle in his body was stiff, and nothing on him didn't ache, including his head, which was pounding like the drum section in a marching band.

"All right. I'm going to stand back. You're on your own now, Gage."

Making it to the open doors of the therapy room seemed like a thousand miles when in reality, it was only a couple of more feet, but he set his sights on the light shining in from the hallway, making it his only goal.

You can do this. You're not a quitter, became the mantra in his head as the *rattle, thump, rattle thump,* of the walker he was white-knuckling lifted, the legs coming back to make contact on the tiled floor.

Five more steps. Four more. Three, two… *Yes!* He'd done it.

Stopped in the open doorway, Gage took a moment to catch his breath before he turned around and made the trek back.

"Have you seen that poor man who just came in?" someone who he couldn't see in the hallway asked.

"Which one?"

"Room 320."

"Oh, my, yes. He's an ex-Navy Seal."

"What happened to him? It looks like the entire right side of his body melted!"

"Car bomb, I believe. But someone else said a building fire?"

Gage made his way out into the hall to see the two aides who clammed up once they saw him, and scattered like feathers in the wind. But he'd heard enough to make up his mind. He was going to find out about the elite soldier in the room next to his who'd been wounded, and do it sooner rather than later.

"You aren't wearing that, are you?" Marcus inquired as he straightened his striped tie.

"Yes," Danica said, twisting her hair up off her neck.

"We're having dinner with Dexter, James, and their wives. Put something else on. Jan and Shar will look like a million bucks." He gestured toward her body. "You can do better than that."

She tilted her head. "What's going on? You've never commented on my clothing before?"

"You're mine, and I want to show you off."

Danica blinked, letting that sink in, releasing her hair, feeling it tumble down her back. "What do you want me to wear?"

"Maybe the black Dior dress, it's sexy."

She backed up, her husband watching her reflection intently in the mirror.

"Where are you going?"

With a frown, she said, "To change."

He shook his head, turning from his position at the bathroom sink to look at her. "I want to watch."

"You want to watch *me*?"

"Yes. Take off what you're wearing."

This was different. "Marcus."

"Do it, sweetheart."

Taking a moment to consider, she finally unbuttoned, then slid the shirt off her right shoulder, then her left—letting the material flow down to the floor in billowing waves of snow which she stepped around.

The corners of her husband's mouth turned up into a smile.

"The Dior dress will require different undergarments," she said, walking out of their en suite in her La Perla bra and panties, into the bedroom and over to her closet. Marcus trailed behind her, until his fingers wrapped around her arm, above her elbow, stopping her.

"Marc—"

"You're extraordinary," he whispered by her cheek, the warmth of his body against her back. "And you *belong* to me. Never forget that."

Belong? She wasn't sure how she felt about that strange statement as she spun around, glancing up into his hungry eyes in the shimmering color of whiskey. "What's the deal with you tonight?"

"Nothing," he said, an instant before he took her lips with his.

Below the number on the wall was the name, *C. Kane*, indicating who was occupying the room with the door ajar.

Tired from his workout, Gage chose to use his wheelchair as he could wheel himself now, then knocked on the doorjamb.

A raspy, "Come in" floated to him.

Rolling inside, Gage noticed three things. First, the dimly lit room held the taste of despair, the blinds shut tight. Second, C. Kane was a big guy, larger than him since he practically took up the entire bed and then some. And third? He was positioned at a weird angle, half facing the closed-off windows, not bothering to check behind himself to see who was there.

"Hey," Gage said, going deeper into the room. "I'm your neighbor in 318. Thought I'd stop by and introduce myself."

"Neighbor?"

He chuckled. "I figured that's better than saying 'inmate'."

"Why not? We might as well be inmates."

"It feels that way sometimes; I'll give you that."

It was quiet for a moment, the guy still not facing him, only respiration moving his back giving away he was, indeed, breathing.

"So, *neighbor*, what's your name?"

Gage cracked a grin. "Gage. Gage Harrison."

That got the guy to rolling over to look at him, and Gage willed himself not to react at what he saw. "Gage?"

He frowned. "Yes?"

"You're Gage Harrison from Cedar Point."

"Yeah, man. Do I know you?"

"I'm Cooper Kane. I used to come to Cedar Point to stay with my grandfather during the summers when I was a kid. Land's End?"

"Right… I remember a dark-haired boy fishing off the docks in the summer." Gage pictured his beaming face as he pulled a tiny lake trout out of the water. "You're little Cooper?"

The left corner of his mouth—the right-side shiny and thin, the skin pulled so tight he appeared not to have lips—tipped up. "I haven't been little in a long time, but yes. You gave me your minnows once. I'm *that* Cooper."

Gage would agree. He wasn't little. Cooper Kane was built like Arnold Schwarzenegger back in his glory days of *Conan the Barbarian*, who looked as if someone had drawn a line down the middle of his face. The left side pristine, like a male model, with thick ebony hair, the right burned and disfigured, the flesh on his cheekbone so slight he appeared skeletal, with intermittent tuffs of dark hair puffing out over the spot where his ear should be.

"It's good to see you again, Cooper, only *not* under these circumstances."

Chapter Forty-Nine

GAGE PULLED INTO Danica's circular drive—the sun falling below the trees, their ride from Seattle back to Cedar Point a quiet one as he mulled over everything he'd learned in the past few hours.

When he came to a stop and parked behind her vehicle, which Officer Stanley had brought home for her, he turned in his seat, taking in her beautiful profile. "Danny, listen. I know you don't want to believe your husband took his life, but with all of the things we found out today, you realize it gives a strong reason for him doing so."

Silence sliced through his SUV, then she glanced down at her hands, flicking her fingernails against each other. "I can't believe any of it, yet… Marcus did things I didn't *know* about or couldn't *imagine* he would have done."

He watched her close her eyes and wanted to reach and touch her, but he held himself still. "The detectives working on this case will find, if they haven't already, what you did today."

"I know."

"That means they will be able to establish a motive behind his actions."

She looked up and over at him, pain in her eyes. "Nothing makes any sense to me. It's like I didn't know the man I was married to at all." She worked her bottom lip over with her teeth. "You knew Marcus. Well, maybe you weren't close or anything, but you know what I mean."

Gage nodded.

"You've worked for law enforcement for a long time, FBI then for the police, so you've learned to read people, right?"

"I'd like to think I have."

She locked her eyes with his. "Putting aside all the tangled mess today. Do you think Marcus was the type of person to kill himself?"

He thought about it, and it was hard not to take the loss of his job and all the financial issues into account, but he did, recalling what he knew of the man. The way he'd look at Danica. The love in his eyes when he smiled at his wife. He said, "No."

"Then, what happened?"

"I don't know, Danny, but I'll do what I can to find out."

"But whatever happened doesn't fall into your jurisdiction."

"I'll still look into things." Unable to stop himself, he touched the top of her hand. "I promise."

"I believe you." She turned her hand in his, wrapping her fingers around his palm. "I'm sorry for what I said the other day. For saying I hated you. It wasn't true."

Gage swallowed. "It is true. You do hate me."

"No." She shook her head, then looked at him with a sadness that was hard to see. "It isn't the truth."

"In my experience, when we are buried by anguish, we tend to release the truth as we try to ease the pain. And what I told you that morning, hurt you in a way that may never heal. And, Danica, it wasn't the first time I hurt you."

"Maybe during the eye of the storm, I did, but Gage, I get this is conflicting, so whether it makes any sense or not, I *don't* hate you."

"I'm so sorry I had to be the one to tell you something so horrific. I'm sorry you are in such pain. I'm sorry that I wounded you and not just the other day, but for all the times when we were young when I sent you conflicting signals—pulling you close only to push you away. I'm sorry because while we'd never said the words, we *were* in a relationship, one that was implied by our actions and how we felt about each other."

Gage paused, took his hand from hers, and reached up to cup her cheek. "I'm sorry because every single time I made up my mind to tell you what I wanted, how I felt, something or someone would interfere, and I stupidly thought I had time. *We* had time."

He took a deep breath. "I'm sorry for breaking your heart when I told you about Jenny, for all the things I did and all the things I didn't do. Danica, I'm sorry because you meant and still do mean the world to me. I always have—"

She placed her fingers to his lips. "*Shh...* I can't do this. I can't talk about this, Gage." Her eyelids fluttered down, sending a fan of shadows over the tops of her sculptured cheekbones. "I'm up to my neck, lost in a tangled cobweb of confusion, trying to figure out what in the world has been going on in my life, in my marriage, not sure how I'm going to pay for anything, including the burial of my husband.

I have two babies who need me, and no way to take care of them at the moment, money-wise."

"I'll help you. I may not have the kind of funds you were accustomed to, but I have a trust of my own, so I—"

Her eyes popped open, along with her lips. "No, no, not going to happen. I'm not taking money from you."

"Danica—"

She was shaking her head. "No, Gage."

Her expression was somewhere bouncing around the spectrum of disbelief, anger, mortification, stubborn refusal, and tremendous sadness.

Gage sighed. He wouldn't win the argument; he knew it. But that didn't mean he wouldn't win the war. He'd be helping her, regardless.

"Okay." He gave her a reprieve from the talk of assisting her financially but couldn't stop himself from touching her. Gage framed Danny's face between his hands, and when he looked into her eyes, he lost himself in their blue coloration, leaning forward until her breath bathed his mouth.

"Don't do this," she uttered in a low, unsteady tone.

It was far too soon, she wasn't ready, he got that, yet he couldn't let her go.

"Gage." It sounded like a breathy entreaty.

Perhaps he was immoral, after all, she'd barely laid her spouse to rest, but while she wanted to ignore what was happening, that spark between them was there. He knew it. Felt it. Longed to explore this thing between them. Wanted. No, needed.

"Danica, I—"

"I can't handle another thing. So *please*, don't. Not right now."

With his stomach a ball of nerves and his heart in his throat, Gage surrendered, giving them both a momentary retreat when he placed his lips on her forehead, closing his eyes, breathing her in for a long moment, then whispered, "All right, Danny. All right."

Chapter Fifty

Before

BOX OF COOKIES in hand, Danica stepped out of the blazing sun and into the cool air of the fellowship hall. Something about the scent of brewing coffee, as well as the familiarity of the space, put her at ease. If there was one thing she needed, it was peace of mind. Marcus had been acting strangely again last night, demanding—sterner—which wasn't at all like him. Though things seemed well enough this morning before he left for work. He'd given her the usual chaste kiss on the forehead and said he would call her later.

Maybe he had a rough day at the hospital, and when he came home yesterday, he was in a rotten mood? The thought made sense.

Pulling herself into the task ahead of her, she walked toward the snack table.

"Have you heard?" Deloris asked.

Removing her sunglasses, she frowned. "Heard what?"

"Gage is coming home."

Those four words seemed to seize Danica's breath, as well the functions of her brain. So it took her a second to mumble, "Excuse me?" needing the confirmation she had heard the woman correctly.

"Gage"—Deloris patted her arm—"he's coming back to Cedar Point."

"How—" She cleared the frog in her throat. "How do you know?"

"I was talking with his mother this morning—breakfast at The Snack Shack. Anyway, she said he won't be returning to the FBI in any capacity and will be coming home."

Stunned, Danica wondered if she needed to take a seat, but she somehow found the strength to stand there. "When?"

Deloris stopped fiddling with the napkin arrangement and glanced up. "*Hmm*?"

"When is he coming?"

"Oh, sometime next week. They are flying out to L.A. to help him with the move."

"So"—she blinked once, twice, three times—"it's not just a visit?"

"No, dearest. He's coming home for good."

After the surprising news from Deloris Kramer, Danica had gone through the rest of her day as if on autopilot, not recalling everything she'd done. Oh, she knew she'd gone to the ladies auxiliary meeting, though Danica doubted she could say what they discussed. Then she ran a few errands, doing them more so to get her head straight, but it hadn't worked. What had? Her husband's car in the garage yanked her out of the mental fog when she pulled up beside it, making a point to glance at the time on her dash.

4:48 P.M.

"Marcus is never home this early," she said to no one.

Slipping out of her vehicle, she went into the kitchen, placing her keys, purse, and sunglasses down on the marble countertop of the breakfast bar, then set her course to find her husband, never able to stop wondering why he was home.

Deciding to check his office, figuring that's where he'd be, she slowed before she even made it to the hallway. Music, and not the classical he tended to listen to, was blaring.

Frozen, she heard Skillet and their song, "Monster."

She frowned, and for a moment, fear zipped up her spine. But, she had nothing to be afraid of, not from Marcus. So why did that emotion strike?

Pushing that ridiculous, irrational feeling to the side, she headed for the room the music was coming from—her small dance studio. The one Marcus insisted on adding to the design of the home when they were in the planning stages of building it.

Crossing the threshold, her eyes widened. Not only was the music deafening, but her studio with its mirrored walls had been transformed into a home gym of sorts, and a shirtless Marcus was running at full speed on a treadmill, sweat dripping off him as if he'd come up out of the pool and hadn't toweled off.

Heading over to the wall cabinet that contained the stereo system, Danica turned the music down, then spun around to see her husband slow from a sprint to a jog, then a walk, before he shut off the bulky piece of exercise equipment.

Chest heaving, he gripped the side rails, then slowly, almost menacingly, Marcus turned toward her.

"What's going on?" she asked, hand on hip.

"I wasn't done with my jog."

Danica narrowed her eyes. "You haven't jogged for years, not to mention what you were doing couldn't be considered one."

"I've started again."

"Okay. If that isn't bizarre enough, what is all of this." She swiped an arm out like a game show hostess, taking in the weights, the elliptical, *the rowing machine?* "You never said you would be turning my studio into a gym."

"I didn't realize I needed your permission," he snapped, and it was like he'd slapped Danica with his attitude.

"All right, Marcus," she said, trying not to be upset, but she was probably failing. "Whatever this Neanderthal thing is about, I don't know. But when you're ready to speak to me respectfully, come find me."

Telling herself not to stomp, she made her way out and into their bedroom, intending on locking herself in the bathroom. She'd take a long, hot, bubble bath until her fingers pruned. Maybe she wouldn't even make dinner! Then Danica's mind clicked over to her upcoming trip to see J.J. on Friday. Her best friend had opened an art gallery in Hollywood and was having a special showing—a silent auction in which the proceeds would go to wounded heroes and their families, all of them members of the armed forces or some branch of law enforcement.

The time away will do you good.

Two steps from her en suite, long, strong fingers wrapped around her elbow, stopping her. "I'm sorry."

Closing her eyes, she stood her ground. She wouldn't turn around and look at him. "You should be."

Marcus wrapped his arms around her, pulling her back into his chest—his sweat-soaked body seeping through Danica's clothes. "I am. I'm sorry, sweetheart. I've just had a rough week at work, but that's no excuse to be hateful with you."

All the anger seemed to leave, deflating her stiff shoulders.

"Forgive me. I'll send all the equipment back. You're right. I should have spoken to you first."

"No," she said with a sigh, "you don't need to do that. I haven't used the space in a long, long time."

"I love you, Danica Dawn Harding." He burrowed his nose into the strands of her hair, into the side of her neck, nuzzling.

"I love you, too, Marcus."

"You mean everything to me. Everything."

"You do to me, as well."

"I'm such a lucky man."

"Lucky?"

"The moment I saw you dancing up on that stage, I had to make you mine. You were the one. I knew it when I asked you to dinner, and you told me you were engaged and couldn't accept my invitation. I knew you were the one even when you kept turning me down after that crazy guy Ryan broke your heart. You've always been the one, and you always will be."

Chapter Fifty-One

LIKE MAGIC, THE massive wrought iron gate opened the moment Gage pulled his SUV up; Cooper, having most of Land's End dotted with security cameras, would obviously be seeing he had arrived. With no need to roll down his window and push the button on the speaker box, he pushed the gas pedal instead and drove through.

Twilight did give the place an eerie, not quite night, not quite day haze, so he got why the kids around town would believe the property to be haunted. Although, with the substantial ivy-covered wall surrounding the main house, it would be difficult to see.

Glancing up into the rearview mirror, he watched the gate slide to a close as he left it behind, then focused out the windshield, taking in the home. It had been standing tall and proud since 1795.

Cooper had been working on the place—the mansion slowly coming back into its own, Gage noted. All the faded black shutters framing the large windows no longer faded, but repainted, and the white house had a fresh new shade of white, making it pop in the gloom.

Parking by the three-tier fountain, devoid of water and filled with debris and dead leaves, Gage got out of his vehicle and headed for the stairs to the columned front porch. It had been a while since Gage had been there to see him, but he knew the inside of the place should be flooded with natural light during the day, but Cooper kept it all out with heavy velvet curtains pulled shut. However, even within the dimly lit spaces, there were pleasing architectural details like Italian marble mantles, crystal chandeliers, and thick walls of original horsehair plaster.

The *skree* of rusty hinges sounded as the door opened, making Gage think he was headed into the inner sanctum of a night dwelling creature like on those bad, low budget B movies that played on his TV in the wee hours when he couldn't sleep.

"Chief Harrison," Francis McCloud, Cooper's housekeeper, greeted him then stepped aside so he could enter. "He's in the study."

More like his command room, he thought but kept it to himself. "Thanks."

"May I get you anything? Something to drink, perhaps?"

"No, thank you, Francis. I'm good."

She inclined her graying head, then left him to his own devices.

Knowing the way, Gage went past the grand staircase, down a marbled corridor, then into the room that, back in the day, would have been a study but was now a space NASA would envy with an entire wall of monitors.

"Coop?"

The man turned the leather desk chair he was seated in around to face him. "It's good to see you, Gage."

He strode up to the oversized desk Cooper was sitting behind and grinned. "I think I need a little more light before I can say I can see *you*, but since you insist on living in the shadows, I'll just agree for agreement's sake."

Coop chuckled. "Pull up a chair."

Rounding the antique Bergère, Gage took a seat. This close, and with the lights from the monitors flickering, he could tell Cooper had shaved his head. "So, Dixie told me you called in about an uninvited guest on your property?"

Cooper nodded. "Happened yesterday. Late afternoon."

"Tell me about it."

"I'd been down by the pond and was on my way back here when I noticed movement. So, I changed my course, and—"

"Let me guess. You didn't make yourself known but became a ghost in the trees?"

"I wanted to find out who was dumb enough to come here."

Gage nodded. "Go on. Sorry I interrupted."

"The person was dressed in baggy black sweats and an oversized black hoodie, the hood covering their head."

Straightening, the visual struck Gage. "Black?"

"Completely covered."

Those cop instincts sharpened. This couldn't be a coincidence. Whoever Cooper tailed was the same person who'd vandalized Danica's place. "Did you see who it was?"

"Only the back of them, but by the direction they were going, they came from the old cabins."

"Is there anything in the cabins that would draw someone to them?"

"No. They are all empty and in need of some serious repair. Meaning, there's nothing of interest to see or to steal."

"How about a kid scoping out a secluded party place?"

"Maybe, but as I said, they are in bad shape. Some of them open-air since the windows are gone, and the roofs have caved in."

Gage tweaked his chin. "Could you tell if it were a man or a woman?"

Shaded fingertips thrummed a beat on the desktop. "Whoever it was, they were tall, but not very broad of shoulder. So, if it were a man, he's slim. Going back to your kid thought, I suppose it could have been a teenager. But even on the off chance they were looking for a place to party, you know the rumors about Land's End."

"Rumors you'd like to keep perpetuating."

The former elite soldier raised his hand, the angle causing the muted light to sweep over the scars. "Spooky keeps people out."

"You didn't happen to catch any of this on one of your spy devices, did you?"

"Not way back there, but the intrusion has made me make some changes to my camera setup. So, if they show again, I'll catch them."

"Do you have paper and a pen?"

"Sure." Cooper pulled out the middle desk drawer, producing both a pen and a note pad.

"Jot this down." Gage rattled off a number, the man scribbling quickly across the little square. "Call me if you see anyone or get anything on camera. That's my cell. Don't waste time going through Dixie."

"Got it. But, if you don't mind me asking, why?"

"I've recently seen a figure dressed in black on someone else's security feed, setting a tree on their front lawn ablaze, so I'm *really* interested in talking to your mystery person."

"Ah… All right. If I catch anything on camera, I'll call."

Her house was quiet. Too quiet, she realized, as she waited for Breck and Mase to bring her babies home. The whole day had been horrible, finding out the steadfast man Danica could always count on had been someone she didn't know. *Dismissed!* Marcus had been dismissed, had failed a drug test, cleared out their bank accounts, his trust fund, sold his investments, and cashed in his life insurance policy! He had left her by herself to raise their two children, with ten-thousand questions and, not to mention, penniless.

Some of the numbness had worn off, replaced by little wisps of anger. They cropped up one by one and started to swirl inside her head. Danica tried, really tried, not to let them take over.

Perhaps I should watch some mindless television?

She considered going into the family room and turning on the TV, but sitting in there, staring at some random show in an attempt to get her mind off things, didn't appeal to her. Besides, she doubted she'd be able to shut her brain off anyway, so as if a stranger in her own home, Danica wandered.

The *tick, tick, tick* of the mantel clock drew her eye to the marble surround, the empty fireplace, over to the chair her husband had claimed as his own. A spark of insanity flickered then turned into a burn. Spinning on her heel, she stormed to the linen closet, reached in, flung folded sheets behind her, saw what she wanted, then grabbed a blanket—and went back to 'his' chair.

With a whip of material, she covered the furniture so she couldn't see it any longer and took a step back. *Not good enough!*

Danica grabbed the wingback and started dragging it until she maneuvered it out of the room, into the foyer, where she took a second to catch her breath. She opened the door and tugged it out. With the evening air disrupting the strands of her hair, she booted the thing off the rounded stoop, seeing it bounce/slide down the three curved stairs, then tip to its side.

Tired from the effort, yet on the other hand energized by some strange combo of anger and anxiety, she stepped back into the foyer, shut the door, and kicked off her heels. Leaving them willy-nilly, she power-walked down the hall. The movement felt good she decided as she came to the half-open door. Reaching out, Danica pushed it fully open, went in, and flipped the light on in her once-upon-a-time dance studio.

Glancing around the space, irritation joined the mix of emotions she was experiencing. It had been too long, but she wanted—no, she *needed* to dance. However, with all the bulky equipment Marcus had added to the room a few years ago, she wouldn't be able to accomplish that.

"Well," she said to herself, "you tossed the chair; so you can get rid of this stuff."

Going to the weight rack, Danica started pulling them off, then blazed a trail until she made it to the front door. Throwing it open, she heaved.

This became her pattern—to the room, removing what she could, to the front door, pitching it out onto the front lawn.

Back and forth she went until she was as winded as if she'd ran the Boston Marathon.

"Danny?" Her sister's voice registered, but she was too busy yanking on the elliptical to respond. "Danica?"

Breckin sounded upset.

Join the party! Huffing, she finally had the machine out of the corner and in the middle of the room.

"Danica?" Breck was closer, but Danica didn't care. "The front lawn looks like a yard sale gone wrong, and the hallway appears to have been struck by a tornado!"

Puff. Pull. Grumble.

"What in the name of Pete?"

Swiping sweat-damp hair from her face, Danica turned to see Breckin and Mason, their eyes wide, both holding one of her twins, attention locked on her.

"Do you need any workout equipment or know anyone who would like some?" She went back to her yank-grunt job.

"Danica," Mason spoke calmly as if he were a hostage negotiator attempting to talk her down. "You are going to hurt yourself if you try pulling on that thing any longer."

"I want it out of here."

"Okay. I'll make sure to remove it for you, but for now, let it go."

"No! I need to clear this room!"

It wasn't until her babies started to cry that her crazy-town behavior became apparent to her, catching a glimpse of her disheveled and sweating self in one of the walls of mirrors. Her updo was no longer up, but half down. She even had a large tear on her damp, silky sleeve, while mascara ran down her cheeks in lines of morbid black.

She should have gone to soothe her children. She should have taken a breath and gathered herself.

All Danica could do was burst into tears and collapse to the floor, in a mound of undone woman.

Chapter Fifty-Two

Before

"OOOO, DANNY-D, I love that navy blue off the shoulder two-piece cocktail dress you've got on!" J.J. squealed as she hugged Danica. "When you told me your flight had been delayed, I was worried you'd be late."

With her arms around her best friend, they rocked from side to side. "Changing in the restroom at the airport was a 'fun' experience I'd rather not do again."

After the two disentangled themselves, Danica grabbed the handle on her silver luggage, happy she had brought the one with wheels. It had been so much easier to maneuver through LAX. "I should stash this somewhere."

"Your bag will be fine here in my office."

"You sure you don't want me to tuck it into your coat closet or something?"

"No." J.J. beckoned with her fingers, the sequin décolletage of her dress sparkling in the light. "We need to head up front to the main part of the gallery. I'll take you on a full tour later."

"All right."

"Tonight, all the art on display is up for grabs."

"I can't wait to see what's up for auction."

"Of course, you know all the proceeds made here will be going to wounded members of the armed forces or to those who were part of the many different branches of law enforcement, police, fireman, and so on."

"I know. I'm so proud of you for organizing this event."

Her friend smiled, then flipped a section of her strawberry blonde hair over her bare shoulder. "I hope you brought your wallet."

"I've got Marcus' Platinum card ready to swipe."

"Danica, I see someone I need to speak with. Will you be okay on your own for a bit?" J.J. asked.

"Sure, hon. I'm just going to continue my browsing."

"All right. I'll catch back up in a few."

Once Jillian flitted off, Danica rounded a section of the wall while listening to the hauntingly beautiful violin piece drifting through the gallery, her gaze bouncing over some lovely pastel paintings, a few desert landscapes…

As she moved on, she gasped, coming to a full stop in front of an 18-by-24-inch abstract. The arcs, lines, and shades formed motion.

Like a dancer!

Unable to pull herself away and ignoring those wandering around her, she stood captivated, studying the piece, her eyes lowering to the title. "Gravity." Blinking, she shifted, catching the painting from a different angle, seeing the graceful bend of an arm, the shape of a leg, the swishing flow of white material. *My dress.* But it couldn't be her when she danced to the song of the same title several years ago. No. It just wasn't possible, it had to be some strange coincidence.

"Exquisite. Isn't it?"

The sophisticated male voice with the slight Irish accent had her turning to see a distinguished man, perhaps in his fifties, with graying sideburns and a closely shorn goatee.

"It is. Yes."

"The artist captured the movement of sensuality on canvas."

"Do you know the artist?" Danica asked, hoping to meet them if they were in attendance.

"No. But I wish I did. I'm afraid this piece was donated anonymously."

"Danica," J.J. called, sashaying over, then placed a claiming palm on the gentleman's lapel. "I need to introduce you two." Her green eyes glanced up at the man who was smiling down at her bestie. "Collin, this is my best friend, Danica Lorry-Harding." Jillian looked back to her. "Danny, this is Collin Amhurst, the gallery's silent partner I've spoken to you about."

Danica smiled and held out her hand. "I'm so very pleased to meet you, Mr. Amhurst."

He took her offering, placing her hand between both of his warm palms. "The pleasure is all mine, my dear. But please, call me Collin."

Serious gallery-goers, looky-loos, patrons of the arts, and servers with sparkling flutes of champagne swirled all around them. Everyone spoke in low tones, turning the space into a musical buzz of monotone sound.

The man let her hand go, then spoke to Jillian, "Your friend and I were just discussing the Gravity piece."

"Oh, yes." J.J. glanced at her. "Isn't it something? It reminds me of you."

"Her?" Collin asked with a raised brow.

"Yes. Danica used to dance," Jillian said. "She and an old partner danced a contemporary piece to the song by Sara Bareilles with the same title. Collin, I wish you could have seen it. The two of them were something to watch up on that stage."

"You no longer dance?" he asked, bringing his attention back to her.

Danica shook her head. "No. I stopped soon after I married."

"Do you miss it?"

No one had ever asked her that before. "I guess I do."

"Then, perhaps you should consider…"

Collin was still talking, but the broad back of someone weaving his way through the people bustling around them caught her eye, snagged her, and kept her on the edge of breathless.

"Excuse me," she whispered absently, not bothering to consider her rudeness as she started in the direction of the black suit with a sheen that spoke of the high-end expense, bumping into someone she didn't notice. "Sorry," she muttered but kept going, waving off the server she didn't look at who asked if she would like a glass of bubbly, her neck stretching to see, not stopping in her vision quest.

Part of her wanted to call out, make the man stop and turn around, find out for sure if it *was* him, but she had to be mistaken. After all, it had been a long time since the last she saw him, so she couldn't be sure of his stride anymore, and she thought this man had a cane. Not to mention that, of all the places he could be at that moment, it wouldn't be in Hollywood at an art gallery. If Deloris was correct, he should be with his parents, relocating. But…

Lips parted, ready to make a fool of herself if it wasn't him, she focused on the way the light slashed over his big shoulder and shone off the back of his blue-black hair—the ends curling slightly over the collar. Then he went out those doors she was trying to get to before she could utter a sound.

Pushing past a few more people, she finally shoved open the door and stepped out onto the long span of gray sidewalk, the warm evening air bathing her as she looked right, then left.

As if the person were a ghost, he'd disappeared.

Shoulder's falling, Danica stood there. The *hum* of passing traffic faded into the background, and the memories struck. His name filled her mind and tumbled past her lips in a low murmur of sorrowful lament, "Gage."

Chapter Fifty-Three

"COME ON, DANNY, I'm going to start a hot bath for you," Breck said, steering her by the arm into her bedroom.

"I don't think that will help."

"A long soak in the tub fixes a lot of things, sis."

"It's not going to fix me."

"Do you want to tell me what happened today in Seattle, and why you were trashing your house?"

"Not right now." Danica sniffed, every part of her body aching, her head fuzzed and hurting in a way she'd never experienced before. "Maybe I could just burrow under the sheets instead."

"Bath first, burrow later."

She didn't have the will to argue. "All right. At least let me grab a robe. The one I usually leave in the bathroom is in the laundry."

"Okay. You go snag one, and I'll start the water. Do you want one cap or two of bubble bath?"

"Use two of the lavender. It makes more bubbles."

Breck grinned. "Frothy goodness coming right up!"

Shuffling her feet along the floor, Danica went to her closet-cum-dressing room, opened the door, turned on the lights, and came to a complete stop. It took her a second for the scene to come into full focus, as if the connection from her eyes to her brain was faulty.

Hand to mouth, she stumbled over to her jewelry cabinet with the drawers pulled open, but what took her immediate focus was the painting she'd won a few years ago, during the silent auction at Jillian's Hollywood gallery. There, hanging above the tall piece of furniture, her beautiful artwork had been slashed into ribbons of limp canvas hanging off the bottom of the frame, some even turned into long strips of confetti scattered about on the carpet.

Several emotions walloped her at once. Disbelief, anger, fear, confusion, sadness, though as big fat tears rolled down her cheeks, it was that overwhelming sense of loss which seemed to be winning. While the painting wasn't some priceless masterpiece, it was invaluable to her. But someone, whom she couldn't even fathom a guess, had come into her home and destroyed it, turning it into tatters.

"Breckin!" she yelled, not waiting long until Breck came running in.

"What is it?"

Danica pointed. "Look!"

She knew the minute her sister took in the tableau. Breck sucked in a large breath, then bellowed, "Mason!"

Standing on his front porch, with his house keys poised in hand, Gage rolled his head along his stiff shoulders, his mind awhirl with so many things—Danny, what Marcus had done regarding their finances, the vandalism of a tree at their house, the vague, scattered memory of Wendell Gibbs saying he saw 'someone' watching her, but couldn't come up with any real type of description other than baggy clothes, and tall. Then there was Cooper's lurking mysterious person in black. All of it was somehow related, Gage knew it deep down in his gut, he just needed to connect the dots.

The muted sound of an electric guitar went off, so by the ringtone, it was Mason calling. Quickly, he unlocked the front door, stepped inside, tossed his keys on the table, pulled his cell out of his pocket, and tapped the icon for the speakerphone.

"Hey, brother. What's up?"

"G…" There was something off about Mase's voice, which put Gage on alert, not to mention the fast chatter of Breckin in the background melding into fussy babies.

"What's wrong?"

"You need to come over to Danny's. Something's happened."

Heart speeding up and beating against the cage of his ribs, he turned, plucked up his keys, then back out the door, saying, "What's happened?" as he strode to his SUV.

"Someone's been in her house. Destroyed a painting and took some of her jewelry."

"Is she okay? Did you call it in? Didn't her alarm system activate?" Gage hopped inside his vehicle and started it up.

"She's…upset but physically fine. Yeah, I called—"

"Good. I'm on my way now."

"The thing with the alarm, Danny doesn't think she set it before she left for Seattle earlier. Or at least, she says she didn't enter her code when she came in a while ago, but she can't remember."

"Did you check her security feed?" he asked as he tore out of his driveway.

"I went through the whole house, and there's only one area that's been disturbed. The security feed, though, well, that's the thing."

Another lousy feeling pummeled him. "What's the thing?"

"All the outside cameras have been disabled. Danny doesn't have any interior devices."

"Disabled?" Gage repeated, trying to maintain his calm. "Shouldn't something like that trigger the security company?"

"Yeah. I was going to call them next."

"Hang tight. I'm only a few more minutes out. I want to be in on *that* conversation."

"All right. See you in a few."

After disconnecting with Mase, Gage put the pedal to the medal.

"I thought Mason said there was only one area of disturbance?" Gage asked Officer Stanley ten minutes later as he stood on Danica's walkway, which looked like drunk movers had been at her place running amuck.

"Apparently," Stanley said, "Danica did this."

He glanced around. A white, wingback chair was tipped over, half in the shrubs, half on the sidewalk in front of the stoop. Different free weights were plopped all over like lawn darts. A medicine ball was by a small fountain. Workout towels were scattered everywhere, some hanging from the branches of the rose bushes. A black training bench was upside down, legs up in a flower bed…

"Danny did all of *this*?" Gage rubbed the side of his tense jaw.

"According to Mr. Miller, this is what he and his wife came upon when they arrived."

"Gage?" Mason called, causing his attention to shoot to the open door his friend was standing in, backlit from the light as it shone out of the foyer. "Officer Davis isn't having much luck with Danny."

With that, he walked the gauntlet of her front walk, up the stairs, and into the house. "Where is she?"

"Look," Mason said. "When Breck and I got here with the twins, she was in the midst of a breakdown, trying to get everything out of the home gym, and doing a good job of it by herself. Until she crumpled to the floor in a sobbing heap. Breck put the babies in their playpen, then came back to help me with her sister. She finally convinced her to get up and take a bath, then… You'll need to see for yourself. But my point is, she's balled up in that chair in the family room again, and won't speak."

Gage nodded, that too-familiar tightness in his chest came back. "I'll go, then I want to see what's been disturbed in here by someone other than her, and after that, I'm calling about her disabled security feed."

"I already made that call," Stanley said, striding up. "It would seem that, when the first camera went down and didn't come back online, the company, as per their protocol, called here. Someone, a female, answered the phone, saying they were Mrs. Harrison, gave the verbal code, then said she was having her contractor do some work around the house that required the cameras to be disturbed. Said she would be calling them later when the work was completed, to set up a time for the company to place the cameras in new positions."

Gage's brows pulled down. "Someone answered her phone and passed themselves off as her?"

"Yes, sir."

"Danica was obviously tearing things up here. Are you sure she didn't speak with the security company?"

"'No' was the only word we got out of her when we inquired. Other than that, she's been almost catatonic."

"What time did that call from the security company happen?"

"Around eleven this morning."

"All right, thank you."

"Davis was going to dust for prints. I'll go help him."

Blowing out a breath, Gage nodded, then took note of the condition of the house as he made his way to the family room.

There, with only one small table lamp lit, Danica sat in the same spot he'd seen her the week before while holding her wedding picture, staring out the window.

"Danny?" he called, going to her.

This time, she responded by turning her head, meeting his gaze.

Those lifeless blue eyes, filled with tears, hit him like a wrecking ball. Bam!

"They took your earrings," she said in a low voice, then her chin quivered.

"My earrings?"

"The blue art deco earrings you gave me for my sixteenth birthday." The welling tears stopped threatening and flowed, streaking down her cheeks. "They're gone."

He went to her, intending to kneel by her chair. But Danica hopped up, surprising him, then lunged into his body, knocking him off balance for a moment. Gage righted himself, his arms going around her as she burrowed into him, shaking as she cried.

"I'm sorry, Danny," he whispered into her hair. "I'll find out who it was."

"Why? Why would someone do that?"

"I don't know, but I promise you, they won't get away with hurting you."

It was quiet for a long moment, all but for their breathing and Danica's almost silent crying, until she said. "They didn't only just take your earrings, but…"

"What?"

She pulled back, looked up at him, and said as she swiped the moisture from her face, "Come see."

Taking him by the hand, she led him from the family room, past Mason, who just watched with a scowl of concern on his brow, then to her bedroom. He couldn't know for sure since this was the first time he'd been in there, but nothing appeared to be disturbed—until they walked into her colossal room of a closet and he saw Davis and Stanley. One was taking pictures, the other dusting for prints.

"Give us a moment, guys," he said, the two of them doing what he asked, and leaving him and Danica alone.

"They did that," she uttered, pointing to a painting, or what was left of it, but he knew. He knew what painting it was. "Out of all the things they could have done to this house, they struck at the two most important things here."

Being sure not to touch anything, he stepped up, looked into the open drawers of her jewelry cabinet, seeing expensive pieces in there, which didn't look at all like they'd been disrupted. And compared to the jewels on offer there, those earrings he bought for her back in the day wouldn't be as pricy. So, why would someone take them and leave the rest? For that matter, why destroy *his* painting?

Whoever it is, he—she— knows these things are important to her.

"I'll never get that painting back. It's not a reproduction. It was an original, one of a kind." Danny spoke as if it were a masterpiece, done by a famous artist.

"It wasn't worth anything. Not monetarily anyway."

"It was to me." A crease formed on her brow. "Wait. How do you know what monetary value that painting held or didn't?"

Gage locked his eyes with hers. "Because I'm the one who painted it."

Chapter Fifty-Four

Before

"I'M SO HAPPY you came by this morning," Danica's mother said in her sing-song voice, pulling the carafe from the coffee machine.

Taking a seat at the breakfast bar, Danica tucked some hair behind her ear. "I'm sorry Marcus missed dinner the other night. He told me to extend his apologies before I left the house earlier."

Her mother waved a dismissive hand, then poured the dark brew into a cup. "He's a busy man. Your father and I understand that."

"He is, but it seems he is busier and busier."

Mom eyed her. "Is everything okay with you two?"

"Yes. We're fine."

"You don't look 'fine'."

"I guess I'm just feeling sorry for myself lately, but I shouldn't be so grumpy about his job. I knew before I married him, the hospital consumed all of Marcus' time."

"Baby-girl, have you spoken to him about slowing down some?"

"I've mentioned it, but we've never had a serious conversation on the subject."

"Maybe you should tell him how you're feeling."

Danica shrugged as she slid the non-dairy creamer toward her mother. "I'm not complaining; I'm really not. Marcus is a wonderful provider and a man who loves me. I don't need to be the center of his world."

That's not true. You want to be the center of his universe, she thought.

"Oh, I don't know. Don't most of us want to be the main focus of our husband's lives?"

Danica didn't respond, not willing to bring up any of the things that were bothering her lately.

"All right, by your silence, I get it. Change of subject. What are your plans today?"

Placing her palms around the warm ceramic mug, Danica tapped her toe. "I need to do the rounds for the chamber this morning."

"Oh?"

"I'm going to stop by and speak to Karley Robinette, extend a formal invitation to join."

"Isn't that something John should do? He is the president."

"It is, but he asked if I could handle it. I guess he's swamped with family issues lately."

"Yes, I heard about his youngest son. Expelled for fighting again."

Danica nodded. "He's an angry kid, that's for sure."

"Well, it's nice you stepped up to help him out. I'm sure John appreciates it."

"He never fails to express his appreciation for anything I do."

"He's a nice man. Such a shame about him and his wife." Mom blew on her coffee, then took a sip. "Getting divorced after twenty-six years of marriage?"

"That was shocking news, wasn't it?"

"Very. So, what do you think about our newest business?"

"I was surprised when Karley came back home, but even more so when she opened up a gym."

"You and me both."

"It seems strange for Cedar Point to have such a place. It's like we've turned into a big town."

"It's my understanding her gym is going over pretty well, though."

Danica tapped her mug. "I suppose, if you think about it, if you don't have equipment at home, then having somewhere to workout is nice."

"I'm trying to talk your father into joining." Her mother held up her hand and crossed her fingers.

"You mean you're nagging him?"

Mom chuckled. "Pretty much."

Danica stared into her coffee cup, watching the steam waft up, working her bottom lip over with her teeth.

"Danny? What is it?"

"Deloris told me…"

"Told you what?"

"Gage left his parents' place and bought the old Willis house. Have you heard anything about that?"

"I have, and he has. He moved in last week after having the place painted."

Glancing up, Danica met her mother's gaze. "I haven't seen him."

"I know. And, I would imagine you've purposefully avoided it, right?"

"There's just—" She welded her mouth shut, wondering what in the world was wrong with her. She didn't talk about Gage to anyone. *Ever.*

Her mother placed a soft palm on her forearm. "I know we've never talked about him or what happened to split your friendship all those years ago, but I do know you two were such great friends once."

"Mom—"

"I know, baby-girl. You don't want to talk about it. So we won't. But I will say you can't avoid him forever. It just won't be possible to do anymore now that Gage is here."

"Hello, Lyle," Danica greeted, popping her sunglasses on top of her head. "I'm here to see Karly if she's in this morning."

"Sure, Danny. She's here. Last I saw she was over by one of the weight machines."

Since she'd gone to the grand opening ceremony the month prior, she knew the place. "Okay. Thanks, Lyle. I'll head on back if you don't mind."

"Don't mind at all."

"Oh, hey. Do you think I could leave my purse up here with you?"

"Of course. I'll put it behind the counter."

"Appreciate it," she said as she handed over her bag before heading in the direction she needed to go.

Passing a line of treadmills, most of which were in use, she noted, Danica kept on going past the rowing machines and took a left at the stationary bikes, all the while listening to the upbeat music drift from the open door of the glass aerobics room.

She waved at Phillip, who was curling some impressively sized dumbbells. He grinned and bobbed his head.

Danica smiled when she saw Karly all decked out in her tight multi-colored spandex pants, with a neon pink t-shirt with the gym's logo and name—*Iron Rose*—printed across the back, and matching pink streaks in her platinum-blonde hair. Karly had been a couple of years behind her in school, but she knew her well enough to know she'd always been a bit of a free spirit, and Danica liked that about her.

When the woman turned, the corners of her lips lifted, transforming her serious face into a dimpled, bright-white picture of happiness. "Danny! It's good to see ya."

"It's lovely to see you as well."

"What brings you in bright and early on a Saturday?" Karly gazed at her from the top of her head to her bold print dress, to the pointed toes of her Jimmy Choo's. "You don't have a duffle with you, so you're not here to work out in that outfit." She scanned her yet again. "Wow! You are working it too. Who's the designer you're wearing?"

Danica ran a palm over the bell of her hip. "Versace. A gift from my husband."

"The man sure has great taste."

"Thank you."

"So, what can I do for you?"

"I wondered if you might have a moment to chat. Perhaps in your office?"

"Sure. Can you give me a second to move the clutter? Dennis dumped all the shirts I ordered in there, and so I've got boxes all over the place."

"Oh. I don't want to put you out."

"You're not. I need to find you a chair. Right now, they're hidden beneath a city of cardboard."

"Are you sure? I could come back another time."

"It will just take me a minute or two. Feel free to go over to the snack bar to grab something to drink, and I'll be right back to get you."

Karly spun around in a twirl, then off she went.

Though she'd seen it before, Danica took a second to glance around, marveling at the job Deacon Carter did with the place. He took the old, unused theater building and remodeled it into a gym that would rival any of those fancy fitness facilities in Seattle.

With a tilt to her head, Danica listened to the change in music and mood as Anya Marina sultry voice sang, "Satellite Heart."

She liked that song and listened to it a lot when it first came out, picturing a dance routine in her mind's eye that would work with the tempo, but she hadn't heard it in quite a while.

Turning, she ran smack into a wall of a man with an *oomph*, spluttering, "Sorry!" feeling large hands enclose around her upper arms to steady her.

Lifting her head—eyes trailing up a well-muscled torso covered in a white wife-beater shirt that hugged his body like a lover—she blushed. "I didn't—" Danica gasped when she came to the chiseled face with those high cheekbones, her gaze tangling with his.

Everything shifted into nothing but *him*—the floor beneath her feet, leaving. The building surrounding them crumbled to dust. Time and space no longer existed, the years falling away. Paralyzing vines sprouted from the void, held her in place as they wrapped around her ankles, slid up her calves, twisted along her thighs, circled her waist, slithered around Danica's spine, and manacled her hands—sharp thorns *digging* into her chest. "Gawonii…"

Chapter Fifty-Five

MOUTH AGAPE, DANICA stared up at Gage, his words rattling around in her head. *"Because, I'm the one who painted it."*

"You—" She licked her dry lips. "You painted it?"

"Yes."

"But, but…" She blinked, glancing down at her feet. She never knew Gage could paint, or that he did, but her thoughts jumped to, "You were at the gallery that day of the silent auction." Not a question, a statement.

"Yes," he said, going into no explanation.

"Yo-you." Shaking her head, she said quietly, "You titled the painting Gravity."

"I did."

Slowly, Danica lifted her chin, then her eyes, studying his stoic features—the scar that bisected the arc of his right brow, something that hadn't been there when they were kids. The perfect shape of his lips, the dark stubble on his usually clean-shaven face.

"You saw me dance." Again, she hadn't asked a question, the reality of the situation coming into crisp clarity, spilling from her.

He nodded just once.

"You came to watch me at WSU, and I never knew it. Why?"

Gage sighed, then combed his fingers through the black strands of his hair. "This is a conversation for another time. Right now, we need to talk about what happened here. Not the past. Not now."

"But we will. We will talk about it?"

"We will."

An hour later, Gage's men had left the scene. Breckin, Mason, Danny, and he were all sitting in her family room, the full story of what happened in Seattle earlier told to her sister and Mase, but it was she who spilled the information. It wasn't his place to share it.

"I just can't— I don't— It's so hard to believe," Breck muttered, holding onto her husband's hand.

Gage had listened to their conversation, yet still ran through the possibilities of who would have entered Danica's home to vandalize a painting and take a pair of earrings, both of which brought *him* into the scenario. Whoever did this knew, at the very least, Gage was on some level important to her.

"I don't know what I'm going to do," Danny admitted in almost a whisper of breath.

"Whatever it is you need, we'll help you," Mase said.

"Of course we will," Breck chimed in. "You won't be struggling to find a way to pay for things."

"I can't—"

"Nope." Mason shook his head. Emphatic. "Not going to argue about this, Danny. You are family, and I will not leave you, Aaron and Ari dangling in the wind of financial uncertainty."

"I'm on the exact page as Mase," Breck said, getting up to go hug her little sister.

"G?" Mason called, drawing his focus to his friend.

"Yeah?"

"What are you thinking? What happened here, could it somehow be connected to the strange things Marcus did? Maybe he got in deep with the wrong sort of people?"

"It's possible. But there are several things about this whole situation here tonight that bother me."

"Me, too, but tell me what you think."

"First, someone knew about the security here. They not only disabled the cameras, but knew the security code, and impersonated Danica when the company called about those cameras being down. Second, whoever it was must be a woman. I doubt a man could pull off a believable feminine voice, and if it was a man, why not just roll with that?"

"You mean like he was Marcus?"

"Why not? The company that monitors this house isn't local. Chances are they don't know about Marcus."

"But they might."

"All right. For argument's sake, let's say the person who took the call figured they might know about Marcus. That still brings me back to, if it were a man, it would be tough to pull off an impersonation of Danica."

"True."

"The third thing that bothers me," Gage said, "is once inside this house, nothing of real value was taken. There are multiple paintings on the walls in Marcus' office worth something, so why not take those? Also, Danica's jewelry would have been easy and pricy things to grab. Yet only one item of jewelry, with more sentimental value than monetary, was taken. And a painting that held sentimental value for Danny as well was messed with and destroyed. Everything else, untouched." Gage rubbed the middle of his chin.

"So, it's someone who knows Danny," Mase stated.

Gage met his friend's gaze. "Someone who knows her well, and is holding a grudge of some kind."

No more had he said those words when his mind kicked over to *Courtney*. She hated Danica, always had and wasn't subtle about it. But, would she know about the security, the code, the jewelry, and the painting? Let alone have the brass to do what was done? Not to mention the mystery vandal in black. That was tied into this as well, he just knew it.

Gripping the back of his tense neck, Gage said, "Danny, until we get this figured out, I don't want you alone."

Mason nodded. "I agree."

"We'll stay," Breckin offered.

"I'm staying," Gage said before he even took a moment to consider his words.

"What?" Danny stared at him with wide eyes and a red-tipped nose from all her crying.

"I'm staying here."

"You can't do that. You—"

"I can, I will, and I'm doing it, Danica Dawn."

Chapter Fifty-Six

Before

"GAWONII…"

Her voice, that breathy, sensual softness he dreamed about, wrapped around him like a blanket of need as he gazed into the face of an angel. Though he knew he'd run into Danica at some point, he hadn't been at all prepared to see her when he walked into the gym. Unable to stop himself from stalking over to her like a panther on the prowl, he'd startled her when she turned around, her smaller body colliding with his larger frame.

Seconds, hours, or even a lifetime passed while Gage's heart raced, and he fought a battle with himself to let loose of her arms. He wanted to pull Danica close, so close there wasn't any space between them; to hold her tight, inhale her sweet scent, and never let her go—lock them in infinity.

Instead, he willed his fingers to move, broke the contact, steeled himself, and took a single step away. "It's good to see you."

A crinkle marred Danny's brow as if she hadn't expected him to speak, or maybe it was the calm, detached tone of his voice she hadn't been expecting.

"How are you? I heard about—" She pressed her lush lips together and closed her eyes, then pinched the bridge of her nose. "I heard about what happened last year in L.A."

A pause.

A breath.

"I've been praying for you."

Praying? If she had been wasting her time with that, she'd been doing it for almost two years, but Gage wasn't going to correct her.

"I'm perfectly fine," he said, glad he hadn't needed to use his cane that morning and prove him the liar he was.

Danica lifted her head and gazed at him, doing what she'd done just minutes before, taking him in as if studying every line and curve from his legs, waist, arms, to his chest, throat, chin, lips, his nose, locking her stunning blues on his eyes. "I doubt you are fine, Gage."

He stared at her, silent.

She stared back.

The quiet bubble they were in burst with, "Danny? Oh, hi Gage," as Karly came strolling up.

Chapter Fifty-Seven

AFTER RUNNING HOME to grab a few things, shove them into his duffle, change out of his uniform, and feed his fish, Gage headed back to Danny's place. He'd finally convinced Mase and Breck he 'had it covered,' sending them on their way before he did another sweep of Danica's house. He wanted to double-check, make sure all the windows were secure and the doors were locked. He even looked in on the twins, the two of them sleeping soundly in their cribs, their little cherubic cheeks rosy—Arianna sucking her thumb.

Gage smiled and backed out of their room, sure to close the door as quietly as possible, then turned. Danica was just a few steps away, dressed in an oversized shirt and sleep pants, looking weary to the bone as she silently watched him. Yet as tired as she was, she was still the most beautiful thing he'd ever laid his eyes upon.

Going to her, he took her hand, led her down the hall and over to her room. "The house is locked up tight. The babies are safe and sound; everything is quiet. So, you need to go to bed and get some sleep."

"I don't know if I can sleep."

Stopping beside the large bed she'd shared with Marcus, Gage pushed back the stab of jealousy that always struck him when he thought of the man, and forced himself to let loose of her. The task seemed monumental, but he did it. He let go, only to cup Danica's soft cheek, thumb brushing back and forth over the petal-soft flesh. "You're safe. I won't let anything happen to you."

She glanced up at him from beneath her long lashes and sucker-punched him in the gut as she nuzzled his palm. "Gawonii…"

Gage broke the tender moment by dropping their physical connection to tug down the covers on the mattress, saying, "Get in."

Blinking, she stood there a moment, then complied, climbing into the bed, allowing him to pull the sheets back up, covering her.

"I'll be down the hall in the guest room if you need me." Turning, Gage headed for the door. He paused when he heard her voice.

"Sleep well."

Without looking back, he said, "You too, Danny," then made himself step out.

Once away, he took a breath, scrubbed his fingers through his hair, pulled the cell phone out of his pocket, and tapped her icon.

Three rings later, came a sleepy, "Hello?"

"Dixie, this is Gage."

"Is everything all right?" The tone of her voice indicated she was wide awake now.

"Everything is fine. I'm just calling to let you know I won't be coming in tomorrow. So, while I'm not going to be working in the office officially, I will be available via phone."

"Okay."

"Tell Davis to cover anything for me that requires a face to face."

"Will do." She paused then said, "Is Danica all right?"

"Not yet, but she will be."

"You take good care of her and those two babies."

Gage smiled. He hadn't said anything to indicate why he wasn't going to be in, but Dixie knew. "I will."

"Make sure she gets some rest, too. It's important."

His eyes widened. "How do you propose I make sure she does that?"

"You're with her, aren't you?"

One corner of his mouth hooked up. "Yeah."

"Well then, I propose you do what you do best, Chief Harrison."

Shaking his head, Gage said, "Good night, Dixie."

"Good night, Chief." Her grin had its own sound.

Something, a noise, roused him from the start of a bad dream. Scrubbing his palm down his face, it took him a second to remember where he was and why. Then, with complete clarity, it all came rushing in.

Sitting up, Gage grabbed his Sig Sauer from the nightstand and got out of bed. A cold hard lethality settled into his bones.

Quietly, he left the guest room, slipped into the darkened hall, and stealthily made his way toward the bedroom where Danica was. Gage was almost to her half-open door when he heard it again—the sounds of agonized moans, and… *Is she crying in her sleep?*

Pushing the door fully open, he crossed the threshold, gun still ready as his gaze swept the dimly lit space. Once satisfied no one was in the room with her, Gage crossed over, put his P226 on the table by her bed, and watched Danny's body twist in the sheets as if in the throes of a nightmare.

Wondering if he should wake her, he reached out, then stopped, carefully untangling, then removing the covers from her instead. Her t-shirt had rucked up, exposing a sliver of her perfect, pale skin, making a familiar ache start in his chest.

Gage closed his eyes for a moment, took a breath, then solidified his decision.

"*Shh*...Danny," he whispered, sliding in next to her. "I'm here."

Pulling her back into him, he spooned her, holding tight. While Gage didn't believe she had awoken, her movement stilled, and her irregular breathing ceased.

"Everything's okay," he purred next to her ear. "I've got you now. I won't let you go."

Taking in the candied scent of her hair, he burrowed his nose into the side of her neck, allowing his eyelids to drift shut, feeling Danica's muscles relax.

Over the years, he'd fantasized about doing this. Well, not under these types of circumstances. But...having her in his bed, holding her, was something he'd longed to do. And no matter how he'd told himself to keep his baser side leashed, it broke that flimsy thing.

Danny needs the comforting strength of a man, not the animalistic side of a beast.

Basking in the warmth of her, listening to her breathe, now slow, peaceful respiration, knowing she couldn't hear him, Gage curled his bigger body protectively around Danica even more. "I love you. I've always loved you."

Chapter Fifty-Eight

Before

MARCUS WAS STANDING, staring into the open refrigerator as if lost when Danica came in with take out from The Snack Shack. Her morning had been going along just fine until literally running into Gage at Iron Rose. It shook her, but she'd been attempting to push seeing him to the back of her mind as she spoke to Karly about joining the Chamber of Commerce, then did a few more errands before stopping by to talk to Berta and ordering lunch to bring home.

"I'm here," she said, placing the bags on the kitchen bar.

Looking over at her, Marcus grinned. "I'm glad your home, sweetheart. I didn't have a clue what I was going to do about lunch, but it looks like you brought something."

"I did. Though, it's probably not the healthiest choice."

Stepping over to peek in one of the bags, her husband's brows pulled together. "What is it?"

"Deluxe nachos, chili dogs, curly fries, pepperoni pizza slices, and bacon cheeseburgers."

He glanced up at her, eyes wide. "That is an interesting combination, for sure. Not to mention a lot of food. Are we expecting someone?"

"No." Danica sighed. "I couldn't decide what to get, so I just picked a few things."

That wasn't technically correct. Yes, she had a hard time making up her mind since it was preoccupied with thoughts of Gage. But the truth was, she also felt like drowning her melancholy with junk food.

Marcus pulled one of the Styrofoam containers free. "I guess I'll be running a few more miles than usual on the treadmill later."

Her husband was irritating her. It had started the moment she saw him peering into the refrigerator. He was gone most of the time, and when he was there, she waited on him hand and foot. Case in point, making him breakfast, which she brought to him in bed before she left, so heaven forbid that he needed to look for something to eat for lunch.

"You know," she said, pulling the sunglasses off her face and tossing them on the bar. "If you want to complain, then fix yourself a salad. Grab some fruit and yogurt, or warm up some of the leftovers from last night's dinner *I* made that *you* didn't eat."

Marcus stopped his removal of containers from the bags, glanced up at her, and frowned. "Where did that come from? Is it your time of the month?"

"Aah!" She tossed a hand up in the air. "Why do men do that? Believe if a woman isn't happy about something, it must mean she's hormonal?"

Turning on her heel, she took off for the bedroom, ignoring her husband's, "Danica!" as she hurried down the hall.

"Danica Dawn!"

Shutting the door behind her, she stormed into her closet and started flinging her shoes off while taking out an earring. She wanted to undress, slob it in her yoga pants, hideout in the family room and watch an old movie. *Flashdance* on Blu-Ray was appealing.

Long fingers wrapped around her elbow, her husband spinning her around. "Tell me what's going on?"

"Nothing, Marcus."

"No," he said sternly, his whiskey-colored eyes sparking. "That's not happening. Something is going on, and I want to know what."

"Do you ever take a moment to stop and think, maybe I get tired of you being gone all the time?"

"I'm here today."

She looked heavenward at that. "This is the first Saturday in months that you are."

"You're the one who left this morning."

"Because I promised John I would help him."

"You didn't need to. You could have stayed home with me."

"I didn't think you'd be here when I made my commitment."

Marcus locked his gaze on hers, intently studying her. "So, this little outburst is about the hours I keep at the hospital?"

"Yes! No. I don't know."

"Danica, take a breath and talk to me."

Shoulder's lowering, she glanced down, only to look back up when Marcus lifted her chin. "Please." His voice was soft. "Tell me. Is this really about my job?"

"No," she mumbled.

"Then what's it about?"

"It's about me."

Chapter Fifty-Nine

THE BABIES WOKE him. Well, their yammering voices coming over the monitor did. Reluctantly letting go of Danica, Gage rolled over to see the time. 5:34 A.M.

Wow. Those two are crack-of-dawn risers.

Staring at the ceiling for a moment, he took a cleansing breath, then carefully got out of bed, going to turn the monitor off so it wouldn't wake Danny. He took his Sig to leave in the room he *didn't* spend the night in, making a quick pit-stop in the bathroom to take care of business.

When Gage made it to their door, one of the twins was starting to cry. Wasting no more time, he went inside, turned the lamplight on, and strode over to Arianna. She was shedding tears, legs kicking.

"Hush now, little one. I'm here. What's going on to make you so upset this early?"

When he peeked over her crib, she locked her gaze on him and stopped crying, but she didn't exactly stop the uncomfortable squirming. "Hi, there, cutie." He touched the tip of her little button nose.

"Ya-ya-na!" Aaron said.

"Yeah," Gage said, turning to look at him. "It's too early, I agree."

The boy grinned, tugging on the strings of his heart.

Ari fussed some more, but wasn't full-on bawling, though he returned his attention to her. "I'm afraid I'm not very good at this stuff, so be patient with me. Okay?"

She waved an arm.

"Thanks. I appreciate that," Gage said as he picked her up, the smell of something nasty wafting to him, making his eyes widen. "I think I've figured out why you're upset."

Glancing around, he saw the changing table, and a bookcase full of diapers, wipes, baby powder, and other such supplies right beside it. So over he went, putting the baby down, and eying her outfit. It seemed to snap at the legs.

"Genius," he said, getting the bottom of her tiny PJs free, smiling when her chubby legs started working as if she were doing aerobics. "Just hang tight, and I'll grab some stuff."

Plucking a diaper, a package of baby wipes, a container of powder, and a soft-looking, was it a thin hand towel?—he didn't know, but he swiped it up, putting all his loot on the edge by Ari's feet, then wondered if he would totally flub this up.

Looking down into the face of Danica's tiny twin, he said, "I have no idea what I'm doing, but we're going to give this a shot. So, are you with me?"

Ari gave him a gummy smile.

"That's the spirit." Gage clapped his hands together. "Let's do this thing!"

"Ba-ba-ba-ba!" Aaron agreed.

Three mangled Pampers later, and he had both babies cleaned up, the diapers on in the correct position, and their PJ's reattached, never mind it took more than one attempt to get all those snappy things lined up correctly. But hey, Ari and Aaron were clean and dressed, so it was a win, win really.

Carrying a baby on each hip, Gage took his small hitchhikers into the kitchen, wondering what in the world they usually ate, coming to a stop when he heard the front door open, then Ella's worried voice, "Danica?"

"We better go intercept your grandmother before she wakes your mommy," Gage told the twins, leaving the kitchen behind, coming face to face with two concerned-looking parents—their pinched brows giving away their distress.

"Gage!" Mr. Lorry said, his face losing the worry, morphing into surprise. "I didn't expect to see you here?"

"Oh, give me one of my grandbabies." Ella held her hands out as Ari stretched toward her.

After making sure Danica's mother had her grandbaby secure, he shifted Aaron and started patting his back—tap, tap, pause. Tap, tap, pause. "I'm guessing you have a key and let yourselves in since you're here, and you heard?"

"We do. We did, and what is going on in the front lawn? Did the vandals do all of that?" Sam inquired.

"No, sir."

The man raised a brow.

"It's a bit of a long story."

"Never mind the mess outside, I want to know why no one called us yesterday about the happenings here?" Ella looked ticked.

"I don't know, ma'am, I figured Mase or Breck would let you know."

"Stop with the ma'am stuff, Gage Harrison!"

His mouth twitched. "Yes, ma— I mean, okay."

"Breck did call us." Sam palmed the back of his head. "This morning."

"How is my daughter?" Ella stared at him. "What did you find out? Are you going to get whoever broke into her home?"

"Danica is tired but physically fine. She's sleeping. At this point, I have more questions than answers. And yes, I promise you—I'll nail whoever is bothering your daughter."

Mr. Lorry came over, patted his grandson's head, then clamped his hand on Gage's bicep. "I know you will, son. But, I'm still a bit confused as to why you are here, dressed in your sleep pants, taking care of my grandbabies."

"I don't want Danica to be alone."

"So, you're telling me you stayed the night here?"

"I did, sir. Yes."

"What Ella said earlier. No 'sir' stuff."

He nodded.

The man eyed him for a long moment, a silent approval in his gaze, squeezed his arm, then turned. "Well, let's help Gage get our grandchildren fed, Ella."

Chapter Sixty

DANICA'S EYELIDS FLUTTERED open as she came awake, the sun sending a slant of warmth over her cheeks and chin. She had the vague recollection of being held while she slept. Surrounded. Secure. Safe. But while holding her in their sleep was something Marcus did in the early years of their marriage, he hadn't done it in a long, long time.

Blinking, she decided she must have, for some reason, slept in, her thoughts bouncing to, *Did Marcus get up and go to work without waking me?* Rolling over, she slid her palm across his side of the bed. It was cold, but his pillow and the sheets were disturbed. *Maybe he's in the shower? What time is it? The babies!*

At that, some of the sleep fog lifted, and she shot up in bed, glanced at the time on the clock, seeing it was after nine in the morning, and panicked. *Why didn't Marcus' alarm go off at five-thirty?* And her twins. *They should have awakened me long before now.*

Getting out of bed, she went to the baby monitor. Seeing it turned off, Danica dropped it and flew out of her bedroom, down the hall, and heard the chatter of people. The sounds were coming from her kitchen.

"Na-na-na!"

Aaron.

Some of the fear subsided at hearing her son, but she didn't slow her pace, she slid into the kitchen on her socked feet, more than likely looking like a crazed woman with bad bedhead, eyes wide as she took in the scene.

"Morning," Gage said in his sandpaper-smooth voice, those silver eyes locking on her.

Why is he here, dressed in a black t-shirt and sleep pants?

Her gaze bounced from him to her twins in their playpen, to her parents, to Mason, and then over to Breckin. Her sister was at her stove cooking something that smelled fantastic. Then as if a switch flipped in her brain, everything—every single thing came crashing down around her.

Marcus is dead. No money. Someone broke in yesterday. The painting. My earrings...

All the strength left her in a *whoosh* as her stomach bottomed out, the blood drained from her face, and she swayed. Danica grabbed onto the back of a highchair to keep herself from falling, Gage swooping in to catch her. "Danny! What's wrong?"

What's wrong? What wasn't wrong.

Unable to stop the coming storm, her chin quivered.

"Oh, baby-girl," her mother said, coming to her as well.

That's all it took. Danica burst into unmeasurable sobs.

Both her breakdown and Breckin's breakfast was over, though she very much doubted the storm of her insanity had dissipated for good, just had subsided for a little while.

Danica sniffled.

"I've got you, Princess." The low *hum* of her father's voice vibrated against her as he swiped his palm up and down her bare arm—the two of them on the couch, Danny curled into his side, cheek resting on his chest.

"I love you, Daddy."

"I love you too."

"I really should get up and do something."

Everyone else bustled around her house—her mother and Breck cleaning up things, taking care of her twins. Mason and Gage having morphed into moving men, clearing off the disaster she'd made of her front lawn and the exercise room, having told her they would stack 'things' in the garage.

"No, you don't. Let your family take care of you for a change."

"But—"

The sound of her doorbell had her sitting up, and Gage popping his head into the room, saying, "I'll get it."

A few seconds later she did get up and went to the arch that led into the foyer.

"Hi, Chief Harrison," Howie greeted. "I finished up with the back yard, so I'm done."

"Okay, son."

"I need to pick up a check from Mrs. Harding unless you and Mr. Miller need me to help you guys?"

Her heart sank, and that feeling of despair rolled over her as she shuffled forward. She had no way of paying Howie. If she wrote him a check, it would bounce like a rubber ball.

"Mrs. Harding is otherwise occupied this afternoon, but let me know how much she owes you, and I'll take care of it." Gage pulled out a wallet from the back pocket of his jeans.

"Gage?"

He half-turned to look over his broad shoulder at her, Howie peeking around him.

"Oh, hi, Mrs. Harding." The boy smiled.

"Hello, Howie."

Her chin started to quiver as the storm clouds rolled back in with a vengeance.

Her father had come up beside her, put his arm around her shoulders, and she slumped into him.

"I've got this," Gage said to her, his gaze going to her Dad. "Sam, will you—"

"I've got my daughter, son."

Her father maneuvered her back into the living room, over to the couch, her body numb as she took a seat. All of the things she had to deal with started stomping around in her brain. All of the people she would have to tell she could no longer afford to keep. The people and places she owed money to and…

Tears burst from her, "I have to tell Ho-Howie I can't have him do-doing the yar-yard work any-anymore."

"Aw…Princess. Settle down now." Her Dad took a seat next to her, placing his big palm on her back and started rubbing circles between her tense shoulder blades. "Everything's going to be okay."

"No, Daddy. It-it's not go-going to be o-okay!"

When she heard, "Danny, don't worry about Howie. I made sure he was taken care of," body rocking sobs hit her.

"Y-you should-shouldn't have done tha-that, Gage."

"Danny. Don't cry." He took a seat on the other side of her, his hand coming to her knee and squeezing. "Please."

Gripping the bottom of her shirt, because she needed to hold onto something, tears streamed down her face before she started on her word-vomit.

"I can't keep him on, I can't pay Mrs. Beil, need to te-tell her, I'll ha-have to sto-stop our yearly con-contract with the pool gu-guys. The fune-funeral home. Mar-Marcus always paid th-the utility bi-bills and I-I…"

That was all the blubbering, borderline, nonsensical words she could manage before the waves of gray started overtaking her vision. She tried to take a breath as the lightheadedness struck, along with grief, mortification, and a million other emotions. They all won the battle, and Danica blacked out.

Chapter Sixty-One

WHEN DANICA OPENED her eyes, it took her a minute to figure out she was cradled in someone's arms before she shifted her gaze.

"Hi," he said.

She was looking into stunning silver eyes. *Gage's eyes*, and for a moment, just a single moment in time, she was fine. Then her reality came back, as well as a thought—a lightning strike.

"I need to get up!"

"Danica—"

"No. Help me get up." Her voice was manic, she realized, but she couldn't focus on that or anything else at the moment.

With an exasperated sigh, Gage complied and helped her.

When she got to her feet, Danica noticed everyone—her mother, her sister, Mason, and her dad were there. But she made tracks to Marcus' office, all of them trailing behind her one by one.

Once inside her husband's private sanctuary, she went to the far wall where a Monet hung, ran her fingertips down the side of it until she hit the little latch, and swung the door hidden by the painting open, to reveal a safe.

Trying to be careful, though her movements were more jerky than smooth, she punched in the combination to release the door, took a breath, then opened it. When her eyes focused in on the contents, her legs about gave out again, but this time it wasn't with heart-wrenching panic, but of relief, as she gazed at the five half-inch bundles of cash. Grabbing one, she looked at the top bill. *It's a hundred.* Which meant, she had ten-thousand dollars in her hand, and another forty sitting on the shelf inside the safe.

While that was a lot of money, it wasn't going to keep her, although she didn't want to be kept. Her husband was the one who didn't want her to work, insisting his wife never would. But she would find a job doing something. What that would be was another problem to solve at another time. Right then, Danica needed to focus on what she *could* do. She could pay the funeral home, and everyone else.

A little ray of hope lit, her mind became clearer. She had a lot of stuff. She didn't need it. The paintings in her husband's office were worth a small fortune on their own. Jillian dealt in art; she could call her bestie about selling them for her. And her jewelry... Danica glanced at the sparkling ring on her finger. All but for her wedding rings, she didn't need any of the other expensive things. Never did. Marcus was the one who'd insisted on her having them.

I'll sell them, too.

"Honey," Breck said, voice weary as she stepped up to her. "Are you okay?"

Danica realized she was staring into the safe while her mind was working overtime at the beginning of a problem-solving plan.

Gaze sliding over to meet her sister's worried green eyes, she said, "Not yet, but I think I'm *going* to be."

Chapter Sixty-Two

IT TOOK GAGE a little while to convince Danica's family to go home for the evening, assuring him he *wasn't* leaving and would make sure she and the twins were all right.

"We still need to finish our discussion, G," Mason had said.

They had started talking about the past—as in his and Danica's—while they were hauling gym equipment into the garage earlier, only to be interrupted by the arrival of Howie. Then more disruptions by a phone call Mason took, followed by a call on his cell which he needed to deal with, and then two more calls he made. One to Dixie, telling her he wouldn't be back in the office until Monday, and another to his mother to see if she would take care of his fish for him.

"We will, brother," Gage was able to assure Mason eventually.

"Talk about what?" Breck had asked him.

"Nothing you need to worry about, babe." Mason leaned over and placed a soft kiss to her lips, doing that thing he did well—distracting his wife.

But, thankfully, they all left a little over an hour ago, and the house was blessedly quiet.

"Danny?" he called, stepping into the twins bedroom, where she was getting them ready for bed.

"Yes?"

"I need to take a shower. Will you be okay with the babies, or do you need my help?"

Glancing back at him, she smiled. Not her best or brightest, but it was a smile. "Sure, Gage. I do it all the time."

That made him scowl. Hadn't Marcus helped her?

Deciding she wasn't going to do anything by herself any longer, he went to the bookcase, grabbed a diaper, then stepped over to Aaron who was lying on his back, playing with a toy on the changing table.

"What are you doing, Gage?"

"I'm going to help," he said.

She was snapping Ari's jumper thingy. "I'll take care of him in just a second."

"I've got it."

"You know how to change a diaper?"

One side of his mouth quirked up. "I learned this morning."

"You did?"

"I only wasted three, but after that, I got the hang of it. Isn't that right, buddy?" He tickled Aaron's tummy, making the boy giggle.

Danica chuckled, and the sound was phenomenal. "You're good with them, you know. Have you ever thought about having children of your own?"

"No," he said as he pulled Aaron's tiny pants off his legs.

"Why not? You'd be a great father."

Gage paused a moment, wondering if she could handle hearing the truth, then decided he wasn't going to tell her anything but the truth. He stopped what he was doing to meet her curious gaze. "After the whole Jenny thing, I knew I wouldn't have any children of my own."

The curiousness he witnessed earlier turned into… not anger, but sadness he thought as Danny's face fell. "We don't need to talk about it."

"The thing is, we do, Danny. We've always needed to talk about it."

She placed a sweet kiss to her daughter's cheek, put Ari in the crib, turned on a butterfly mobile, then stepped up beside him.

"Danica?"

"Let me get my son settled. Go on and take your shower."

"No." He put a hand on her arm, stopping her. "You started this conversation, and we are going to finish it."

Her blue eyes snapped celestial fire as she looked at him, but her voice was low as she said, "Go, Gage."

"Not happening."

"Aaron can't just lay half-undressed on the changing table."

"I agree. Let's get the little guy ready for bed."

Quietly, the two of them worked together to change the boy's diaper and his clothes, Gage handing things over like a surgeon to a nurse in an operating room, until Danica picked Aaron up. She kissed his cheek, placed him in his crib, turned on his mobile, flipped on the night light, and said, "Goodnight, Ari, and Aaron. Mommy loves you," and out the door she went.

With a sigh, Gage ran his fingers through his hair. "Night, you two. Sweet dreams."

He closed the door to their room behind him and went looking for Danica, seeing the back of her escape into the master suite.

Well, if she thought that would stop him, she was wrong.

Upping his stride, he stopped her from closing her bedroom door with a palm. "We're not done talking, Danny."

"I am."

"I'm not." Stepping inside, Gage shut that door behind him, enclosing them in.

"Gage—"

"Nope. You asked me a question, and I'm going to answer you fully. So take a seat, or stand there with your arms crossed glowering at me, but either way, you will listen."

With a huff of air, Danny dropped her arms, spun around, stomped to a chair in the corner, and took a seat.

He didn't like the distance, so he went to her, knelt beside her, and said, "I told you a long time ago Justin wasn't mine, but you stormed off before I could say much more."

"I don't want to talk about this."

"Too bad, because we are talking about it." Reaching out, Gage took her chin, turning her head toward him. "I made a huge mistake. I admitted that to you then, and I'm admitting it to you now. If I could go back in time and change my behavior when it came to Jenny, I would, but I can't. What I did was wrong. I shouldn't have—"

"Had sex with her multiple times?"

"No. I shouldn't have. But my regrets don't really change anything, do they?"

"They don't."

"Look," Gage said, gazing into her wounded eyes, a wound Marcus wasn't responsible for, but he was. "I came to tell you Justin wasn't my child that day because I was hoping we could work things out. That maybe, in time, you could forgive me, and we could, at the very least, get our friendship back. But what I wanted was more than a friendship. And we *were* more than friends Danny. You know it, and I know it."

She closed her eyes, shutting herself off from him.

"Look at me."

The stubborn woman shook her blonde head.

"Please?"

Finally, she complied.

"Admit to me we were more than friends."

"Gage…I."

"Say the words, Danny."

"We—" She worked her bottom lip over with her teeth.

"Give me the truth. Give *yourself* the truth."

Danica balled her fist in her lap.

Gage placed his palm overtop the tight knot. "Say it."

She blew out a breath, tipped her head back, exposing the smooth span of her throat, then whispered, "I *loved* you, Gage. Maybe I shouldn't have. Maybe I was just a silly girl, but I was in love with you."

He closed his eyes, hearing the finality of past tense, and breathed through the pain. "And I broke you. I broke us. I mangled your love."

"When you told me about Jenny being pregnant, you devastated me in ways I have never fully recovered from. So, when you came to me and said her baby wasn't yours, the damage was already done. You slept with her, did things with her. *I* wanted to do those things with you, and that wasn't going to go away for me."

Looking into her face, he whispered, "I'm so, so sorry I hurt you, Danica. You were the last person I ever wanted to cause pain."

"Whether you meant to do it or not, you wrecked me, Gage. The kind that, well, I don't know I have the words to explain."

"You don't need to explain. I already know. Shattering you killed me. It still does." Gage stared at her, her beautiful face, the slope of her nose, the line of her lips, the way her golden hair framed her cheeks. "You asked me why I didn't want children."

Danica shook her head.

But he gripped her hand and confessed, "I didn't want them because I couldn't have them *with you.*"

Chapter Sixty-Three

"I DIDN'T WANT *them because I couldn't have them with you."*

Gage's soft words had become a broken record, Danica playing them over and over in her mind as she sat in her bedroom, staring off into the distance. That meant he had loved her once; however, she wasn't sure if knowing that made things better or worse. When they were growing up, he had moments where she thought maybe, just maybe, he did think of her as something more than a little sister to protect, then he would do something to make her change her mind, only to make her change it again. But, if she would have known, without a shadow of a doubt, he loved her… *Would that have made a difference back then?*

Probably not. Hearing he had been with Jenny would have crushed her just the same, because regardless of knowing how he had felt, she knew what *she* felt.

Listening to the quiet, she finally pulled herself out of the stupor Gage's confession had put her in, her mind clicking over to the bathroom in the guest suite. The last time J.J. had come to stay, she'd used up all the towels, and Danica knew she hadn't restocked the linen closet in there.

Jumping up from her spot, she went into her en suite, grabbed an arm full of folded, clean towels, and headed for the guest room. Gage was more than likely in the shower, so she'd slip in, put the towels on the foot of the bed, knock on the door to the bathroom to tell him she'd left them for him, and go.

Danica might be caught in a tangle of emotions that both her husband and Gage had put her in, but she wasn't a bad hostess.

Armed with fresh bath towels, she tapped lightly on the closed door, didn't hear anything, so she went in.

The lamplight on the nightstand was on, shining down on a black gun, which she would need to talk to him about. Danica didn't want firearms around the babies.

Her attention shifted to Gage's cell phone and wallet placed beside the scary weapon, then over to a big black duffle bag open, and a scatter of clothes on the bed that had been made, but not very well.

She grinned, remembering his bedroom back in the day being a huge mess. This wasn't that bad in comparison she figured as she went to place the stack of towels on the foot of the bed.

Danica paused when she noticed the bathroom door open, steam coming out. But what held her in place was the mist swirling around Gage like something you would see in a movie dream sequence.

She should go. She really should, but Danica couldn't locate her legs—she was frozen there.

With his back to the door, a blue towel wrapped around his lean hips, low enough it showed off the two dimples on the small of his back, he scrubbed another towel through his wet, raven-black hair. Then some of the vapor lifted.

Danica's eyes widened, and not at the magnificent, seriously muscled body, but by the mass of crinkled, discolored skin covering the entire span of his shoulder blades, continuing up into his hairline on the back of his neck.

Oh, Lord. Gage has been through so much. Thank you for sparing his life. Continue to help and to heal him.

Her heart, if it hadn't already been wounded, would have broken open and bled out at seeing what was usually hidden by his clothing—scars she'd never seen on him before.

Perhaps she'd made a sound, she didn't know, but something snagged his attention, making him turn to face her, the towels she held tumbling from her hold. "Gawonii… your back. Does it still hurt?"

Gage stalked forward. "What are you doing?"

"Towels," Danica managed, her eyes lifting from the deep V-shape on his lower abdomen, to writing. Writing that sidetracked her from the previous question she'd asked.

Slowly, she reached out and touched the dark ink imprinted in his skin. "You have a tattoo," she whispered as she tilted her head, trying to understand what she was looking at.

His hand grabbed hers, putting a halt to her tracing fingertip.

Lifting her eyes to his, Danica said, "Let me see."

He just stared at her for a long moment.

"Gage?"

When he closed his eyes, his long, dark lashes sent spiky shadows across the tops of his sculpted cheekbones.

"Please, Gawonii. Let me see."

Slowly, his eyelids lifted, and he let go of her hand, never saying a word.

Danica went back to tracing the ink. It was a capital D, but it looked exactly like her handwriting. And around that, it read, "A dream within a dream."

"The poem. Do you remember it?"

His question drew her gaze up to his face. "Yes."

"The day you read that to me, I couldn't pull my eyes from you. You were so beautiful."

"I, I—"

"I had this tattoo designed a long time ago. I had something with your signature on it," he said, "so I asked the artist to ink the D in the spot where the baseball that would have hurt you broke my ribs instead."

"You—" Danica's jaw dropped, her head spinning at this newest revelation.

"I loved you, Danica Dawn." Gage framed her face with his large palms, looking directly into her eyes. "I'm still in love with you."

Kiss her, kiss her, kiss her, ran through Gage's head in wild abandon, but he couldn't. Not yet. Danica wasn't ready to go there. He knew that, but his body? Well, that was a whole different issue.

"Danny," he whispered, trying to keep himself in check, "it's getting late, and I need to get dressed."

He dropped his hands from her face and took a significant step back, but she took a step forward.

"You should go," he said.

"Don't."

Gage quirked a brow. "Don't do what?"

"Don't pull me in, then push me away. We've already been there, done that. So let's… Let's not do it anymore."

"You don't get it."

She frowned. "I guess not. So, tell me."

"If you don't leave, I'm going to do something we will both regret."

"Why would we regret whatever it is?"

"Because you are not ready." Gage pierced her with his silver eyes.

"Ready for what?"

"For me."

Chapter Sixty-Four

GAGE COULDN'T BELIEVE he was in church. All right, he could since he'd brought Danica. But still, he'd stopped going when he was eighteen, and he'd never been back. Yet here he was, shaking Pastor Kyle's hand after the Sunday morning worship service, his free hand gripping Aaron's baby carrier that transformed into a car seat like an Autobot.

"It's so wonderful to see you here again, Gage," the man said.

"Thank you."

"And Danica." Pastor Kyle extended a hand to her. "You and your family have been in my prayers."

"Thank you for that. They are needed."

"My wife and I were thinking of coming to see you next week."

"Sure. Come at any time. You're always welcome."

"I'll call you before we head your way."

She nodded.

Placing his hand on her upper back, Gage allowed Danica out the door, he and Aaron taking the rear for a moment, then stepping up next to her. "Do you want me to carry Ari, too?"

"No. I'm fine. But thank you for taking Aaron for me."

"La, la, la, ba-ba!" Aaron chimed in, making Gage grin.

"Hang on!"

Breckin's voice had them stopping, both turning as her sister came striding up, Mason right behind her, followed by Ella and Samuel Lorry.

"I've got lunch already made. I just need to warm up a few things, so you guys come on over to the B and B," Breck said.

"All right." Danny glanced up at him. "I guess I should have asked you first, but is it okay?"

"Of course," he said, making him wonder if she'd had to ask Marcus for approval before she answered something so trivial.

She smiled, then turned her attention back to her family. "We'll head that way."

Mason locked his gaze on him. And Gage knew the man would find the two of them some alone time, so they could finish that talk they'd started on Friday.

"Mama, mama," Ari sang from her car seat in the back of Danica's Escalade, which Gage was driving, making her whip her head around and stare at her daughter, then glance over at the handsome man behind the wheel.

"Did you hear that?" she asked, her heart beating fast.

"I did."

"That's the first time she's said, 'mama'."

"Mama," Aaron parroted.

Danica put her hands to her mouth, telling herself not to cry.

"Danny?" Gage asked.

"I'm okay." She glanced over at him, then back at her babies. "That's right. I'm"—she pointed to her chest—"your mama."

The two started in on a chorus of mama's in harmony, making joy bubble to the surface. Danica laughed. Really laughed.

"I love that sound."

She righted herself in the passenger's seat. "Huh?"

"You're laughing. I love it."

Heat infused her cheeks, and she glanced at Gage askew. "Thanks, I guess."

The man chuckled. "You're welcome, I guess."

Gage knew Mason like the back of his hand, and not too soon after an excellent lunch he took him out onto the large sun porch that wrapped around a section of the B and B, where they finally had 'the talk'.

"Man, why didn't you tell me all of this back then?"

Gage shook his head. "I don't know. It was such a disaster, and then the whole Jenny thing rocked my world. I guess I didn't understand how to deal with it all, let alone talk about it."

"But, you told me about Jenny."

"That was the easier thing to discuss."

"So, I'm assuming Danica knows how you feel about her."

"She does now, but I confused her back then with all my push and pull, hot and cold, and then, as I said, every single time I was ready to tell her, something or someone happened."

Mason put a hand on his shoulder and squeezed. "I'm sorry. I know this is still rough on you. I don't think I could have gone to watch Breckin marry Daniel."

Gage shook his head. "It wasn't one of my better decisions, trust me on that."

"Does Danica know you were there?"

"No. You are the only one who knows all of it." He met his friend's gaze. "She's it for me. Always has been, always will be."

"Is that why you have stayed single all this time?"

"Yeah, brother. Trying to start a relationship with another woman wouldn't be fair to them."

"I totally get that. I do."

Gage bobbed his head.

"Have you told Danny she's it? She's the one?"

"Not yet. It's way too soon. Marcus hasn't been gone a month."

"You're right."

The two of them eyed each other as Breck and Danny came in. "What are you guys plotting about out here?" Breckin came over, bent forward, and kissed her husband on the cheek.

"Nope." He turned to look up at her, pointing to his lips. "Not good enough, babe."

She laughed, bent again, and placed her lips on his.

Gage glanced up at Danica, who was looking at him. "You doing okay?"

She nodded.

"Are the twins taking a nap?"

"Yes. When they wake, we can go, if that's okay with you?"

He reached and took her hand. "That's fine, Danny. You don't need to check with me. When you're ready to go, just say so. Okay?"

"All right."

Chapter Sixty-Five

TWEETLE-DEET!

The sound drew his attention. His cell phone had a message. Something he would usually ignore when he was busy, but putting the report he'd been reading down, Gage snagged the little device and looked at the screen.

Danny-D: *I'm leaving the twins with my sister at Choc-Oh! Cottage and wondering if you have had lunch. If not, I'll bring you something.*

A smile overtook his face as he typed; *Actually, I haven't had lunch. A burger from The Snack Shack would be fantastic. But why are you leaving the babies with Breck?*

He quickly read it to make sure he hadn't fumbled and made a typo and hit SEND.

Like a giddy teenager, he gripped his phone, keeping his gaze trained on it for a response, seeing the little dots dance, an indication she was typing something.

Danny-D: *Two slices of cheese, extra ketchup, no onions, right?*

She remembered. Still grinning like a crazed loon, Gage typed, *Yep.* Then as if he were a teenage girl instead of a grown man, he added a smiley face emoticon and hit SEND.

As if he held the holy grail, he watched his phone.

Danny-D: *Be there in a few, and then I'll tell you why I've dropped off the twins. You want me to grab you a Doctor Pepper, too?*

Danica was staring at her phone.

Gawonii: *That sounds great. But I hope you're not texting while driving.*

She shook her head, a grin on her face as her fingers started tapping, *No, I'm not texting and driving. I might be able to multi-task, but I'm not that talented.*

After she sent her response, she saw the dots bounce, knowing Gage was typing something.

Gawonii: *Okay. Just checking. Be careful, and I'll see you soon.*

"Danny!" The smiling woman with her signature big hair greeted when she walked into the police station. "It's so good to see you, honey."

"Hi, Dixie. Good to see you too." She held up the bag from The Snack Shack. "Bringing Chief Harrison some lunch."

"Aw…isn't that sweet of you. Give me just a moment, and I'll make sure he isn't tied up with something."

She nodded, listening to Dixie tell Gage she was there and hearing him say, "Send her my way."

"Go on, hon."

Running a straightening hand down the side of her dress, she made her way past several desks, Officer Stanley glancing up at her. "Hello, Mrs. Harding."

"Good afternoon. Just taking Chief Harrison something," she said, breezing on by him.

When she arrived at Gage's office, she didn't bother to knock, she just went in, the man standing up from his desk as soon as he saw her.

Wow, he sure looks mega-hot in that black uniform. Danica's heart skipped a beat, reminiscent of when they were teens. *What's wrong with you?*

She stopped her crazy inner monologue, and willed her heart to get with the program, because hot or not, she'd only been a widow for a little while. Her attraction to him just wasn't right. Regardless of what Marcus did to her, she loved him, and ogling another man so soon was disrespectful.

"Hey," he said.

Tingles danced up her spine due to that low, sexy tone of voice.

Danica needed to ignore the feelings Gage invoked in her, so she swallowed, put on a smile, and placed the bag and his drink on his desk. "Lunch is served."

Gage chuckled, and yet again, the sound attacked her heart. "Thank you. I appreciate this." He studied her a moment. "Did you eat?"

"I grabbed a quick bite before I left the house, so I'm fine."

"Well, at least have a seat for a second."

Gage took his seat, then started pulling his burger and, "Thanks—You got me fries *too*!"

"Of course. You can't have a burger without fries, Chief Harrison."

Stop flirting with him, Danica.

"Of course," he said, then popped one in his mouth.

Mesmerized, she watched him chew, the movement of his throat when he swallowed, the way the sun coming in from his one window set the left side of his face into shadow, turning him into a masterpiece of light and dark.

When Gage glanced at her, Danica glanced down.

"So, tell me. Why did you drop the twins off with Breckin? I thought you were going over to your Mom's today."

"I did go, but she got one of her migraines and had to lie down. I need to go to Seattle to take care of some banking business." She shrugged. "I needed a babysitter for a bit, so..."

Gage was mid-bite of his burger when he scowled. "You're going to Seattle by yourself?"

"Well, yes."

He put his lunch down. "Not happening, Danny."

"What do you mean, not happening? I *have* to go. The checking account is overdrawn, as you know, and I need to put the money that was in the safe at home in the bank."

"I get that, but you are not driving to Seattle by yourself. I already told you, until we figure out who was in your home, I don't want you alone for long periods."

"Gage—"

"I'll go with you."

A little crinkle formed on her brow. "You can't do that. You've already been at my house for four days, missing several days of work. You—"

"Don't argue with the Chief of Police," he said, trying not to grin. *Man, when she gets upset, she's way too cute.*

Danica rolled her baby blues at him. "As if *that* will work with me, Gawonii."

Aw…there she went, using his given name. "You do realize I get what I want, don't you?"

"You might *think* you do."

"I don't think, gorgeous. I know."

Danica pursed her lush lips. "Go ahead and keep living in that delusion."

She got up, and so did he.

Rounding his desk, Gage stopped her before she waltzed out his office door, hand wrapping around her arm, pulling her back into him.

"Danica," he whispered by her ear, feeling her tense body give. "Here's what you're going to do. You're going to put that beautiful backside down in that chair you just jumped up from, let me eat my lunch, then I'll clear my afternoon, and go with you. End of."

Chapter Sixty-Six

"DANNY?" BERTA CALLED, waving at her as she crossed the parking lot, ready to go inside the fellowship hall for their monthly welcome committee meeting.

Her mind had been preoccupied with Gage and their trip to Seattle the other day, but she managed to say, "Hi" tugging the collar of her coat up a little more. "What's going on? Is everything okay?"

"Oh, fine. I'm fine. I just wanted to let you know John is stepping down as president of the chamber."

Danica put a hand to her throat. "He is? Why?"

"He's moving."

"To where?"

"Back to Ohio, where his parents are. I guess with their health problems, his youngest son's anger issues, and the divorce, he just felt it best to relocate."

"Is he taking Steve with him, or does his wife have custody?"

"Apparently, she gave up her rights. Can you believe any mother would do that?"

"No," she said, shaking her head.

"Well, she did. So, John's taking Steve to Ohio with him."

"Wow." Danica couldn't even wrap her mind around all of that.

"Listen. The reason I'm telling you this is, the board has talked, and we would like to offer you the position. Of course, you know it is a big job, but for a little town, I think the position pays well."

It did, but Danica couldn't believe her ears. "You want me?"

"Yes. You do so much for us and have filled in for John a few times, so you already know all the ins and outs. Plus, everyone loves you. Think about it for a couple of days and let me know."

"Al-All right. I will."

"Okay, sweetie. I'll let you get to your meeting. Talk soon."

Mind awhirl with the idea of becoming the Chamber of Commerce President, Danica hadn't been paying much attention, sad to say, during the meeting at church, and she was barely aware that she'd come home and was heading in the door.

"Danica," Mrs. Beil greeted, her face too serious.

"What's wrong? Is it the babies?"

"No, no. The kids are fine. I put them down for their nap."

Relief swept over her. "What is it then?"

"I'm sorry to do this, but I need to leave. My husband had an accident at work, and they've taken him to the E.R."

"Oh, no. What happened?"

"Something fell off or out of one of their shipment containers and hit him. They think he's broken his leg."

"Okay. You go on and take off. I'll pray for him."

"Thank you. I'll call you if, for some reason, I can't come tomorrow."

"Maybe you should go ahead and plan on staying with your hubby."

"Are you sure?"

"Yes." Danica shooed her. "Now, go, go."

Mrs. Beil placed a kiss on her cheek, saying, "All right," then out the door she went.

Putting her purse on the bar, Danica picked up the mail that had come, Mrs. Beil always leaving it for her. She sorted through sale flyers, the electric bill, the water bill, then went to a larger, what felt like a bubble wrap envelope.

Curious, she tore it open, peeked inside and frowned, tugging out a piece of paper. Just like the labels on the envelope, the note had been typed.

You sank your claws into both of them, but you couldn't keep them satisfied.

"What in the—" Danica pulled out black and white pictures, the sunlight sending a glossy sheen shooting over the first one, confusing her, not sure what she was looking at. Then, the image clicked in her brain.

Danica gasped, as she sorted through them—a man's naked torso, head tossed back as if in ecstasy, throat exposed. Feminine hands latched onto masculine hips—a small oval birthmark on the side of his rippled abdomen, by his navel.

She dropped the photographs, letting them scatter, ran to the kitchen sink, and retched.

Gage was on the phone, talking to the mayor when Dixie came to the door, face ashen. By the expression she wore, he knew something was wrong.

"Phillip," he said. "Can I call you back? Something has come up."

"Sure."

"Thanks. I'll speak to you soon."

Placing the handset down on the receiver, he asked, "Dixie, what is it?"

"I'm sorry to interrupt, but Danica called. She said she'd tried your cell phone, but hasn't been able to get hold of you."

"What's happened?" He rose from his seat.

"She was crying about something that arrived in the mail. She said she thinks the police will need to see, but she wants you to make the call on that."

"All right. I'm heading out."

"Chief?"

"Yes?"

"She's all torn up about whatever it is."

Gage nodded, grabbed his coat, pulled his cell phone out of his pocket, and sure enough, there had been six missed calls. He wanted to beat his head. He'd turned his phone down yesterday while in church with Danica, but never turned the volume back up.

Not willing to leave her alone, Gage had pretty much moved in with Danica, fishbowl and all, so he had a set of keys. Not slowing, he let himself in the house, going to the first place he thought to look—the family room. Sure enough, she was seated in that chair, facing the window.

"Danny?"

Her head swiveled to look at him. By the puffiness under her eyes and the redness of her nose, she'd been having a serious cry.

Striding over, Gage knelt by the chair, someplace he'd been far too much for his liking. He'd much rather he was there for happier reasons.

"I got something in the mail," Danny said, her voice low.

"Okay. Let me see it."

She produced an envelope and gave it to him.

Gage dumped the contents into his hand, read the note, scowled, then saw the pictures, coming to the last one which was of him, standing beside Jenny's car, telling her goodbye. That was taken a while ago, since the last he saw Jenny was when she came for a quick visit to tell him about moving to Seattle.

After confirming they got nothing in the way of fingerprints that would help them out with whoever it was who broke into Danica's home, and now this… well, the day pretty much blew.

"Marcus was having an affair."

Danica's hoarse voice drew his attention back to her.

"That's him. It might not show his face, but that's his body. His birthmark." The tears started rolling down her cheeks. "He was cheating on me."

Gage had never told her of his suspicions, but the pictures confirmed what he was hoping not to be true.

He took a deep breath. More than once, Gage wanted to strangle the man if he were still alive, and that feeling was very much present.

Tugging her up, he pulled Danny's body into his and hugged her tight. "I'm so sorry. I wish I could take away this pain for you."

"He, he, he cheated on me."

"Whoever sent those pictures, wants to lump Marcus' bad decisions in with me. Why else put a picture of me talking to Jenny in with them and say what they said in their note. This person knows you and me."

Danica tensed.

"Nothing is or has been going on between Jenny and I. Not since before I turned eighteen. We've kept in touch over the years, but only for her son's sake. I tried to be there for Justin as much as I could because I promised not to leave the boy hanging. It's not my story to tell, but how her son came to be isn't a happy one or even one of passion and love."

Danny was silent.

Gage blew out a breath. "I do speak with Justin. And someday, I would like you to meet him. But that's a discussion for another time. I want to focus on the right now. So, if even there is the slightest chance some of this hurt bombarding you is due to that picture of me, let it go."

She wrapped her arms around his waist and cried.

Chapter Sixty-Seven

"MRS. HARDING," DETECTIVE Rudd said, taking a seat on her couch. "I appreciate you taking the time to speak with me today."

It had been two weeks since Gage turned over the photographs that arrived in the mail to the detectives in Seattle who had been looking into Marcus' supposed suicide. Somehow, no matter what, Danica had a hard time believing he would kill himself.

"You're welcome." Reaching over for support, she took hold of Gage's hand, the man entwining his fingers with hers.

"I'm sure you're still in mourning, and what I have to say isn't going to be easy to hear. But, I'm afraid there's no way around this."

She nodded.

"We already believed your husband was having an affair, so those photographs only add to the mounting evidence we have collected since the time of his death. Computer records your husband kept indicate something we believe are meet dates."

"Meet dates?" she asked with a tilt to her head.

"Yes. Dates he met with or didn't meet with someone."

"R with a plus sign and R with a negative?" Gage inquired.

The detective nodded. "It is possible this indicates dates he met with a woman or possibly the dates he purchased or didn't purchase illegal drugs."

Danica closed her eyes and squeezed Gage's hand.

"Are you all right, Mrs. Harding?"

"Yes," she lied, returning her gaze to the stern man with eyes so brown they almost looked black.

"We think the large amounts of money missing from your accounts went to sustain his drug habit."

She shook her head. "But, my husband wasn't some addict. I would have known if he was, wouldn't I?"

"Autopsy results indicate prolonged drug usage, as well, forensic toxicology shows Marcus had a Molotov cocktail of drugs in his system."

Danica dropped her head, wondering if this were real. Something she'd pondered more than once.

"Mrs. Harding?"

She looked at him. "I'm sorry. This is all so…"

"I realize this is difficult."

"Do you need to stop?" Gage asked her, concern swimming in his silver eyes.

She did, but she had to face this. "Let's continue."

He nodded at the detective, who then asked, "Do you know your husband checked himself into drug rehab?"

Danica blinked rapidly. "No. How is that possible?"

"It was before your marriage to him. He completed the program in April a year prior."

She did the calculations, thinking about the first time she met Marcus. It was in the receiving line at WSU when she and Ryan danced in the final showcase in May.

"Danny?" Gage called, making her glance up at him. "Are you okay?"

"I don't know."

"Maybe we should take a moment? Perhaps step out and get some fresh air?"

She shook her head. "No. I don't want to waste Detective Rudd's time." Danica glanced back at the man. "Forgive me."

"No need to," he said. "As we spoke before, several weeks back, your husband was let go from the hospital."

"Yes. I had become aware of that before we spoke."

"What wasn't said at that time, drugs went missing from there. This took place before your husband was let go, and while the issue was investigated, it couldn't be linked to Marcus. However, it seemed to resolve itself once your husband left."

"You're saying he took drugs from the hospital?"

"It is a possibility. Some of what I'm speaking to you about I can't prove, but you might be able to help me."

She frowned. "How?"

"You might have met the person who supplied Marcus."

"You think he would have introduced me to a drug dealer?"

"I think it is very likely. But you need to drop any preconceived ideas about drug dealers looking like gangsters from the hood with gold teeth and dreadlocks. Most of the high-end dealers are people you would never suspect."

"I-I—" Danica licked her lips. "The only people who I didn't know, who my husband would have introduced me to, would have been colleagues of his at the hospital."

The detective nodded. "Was there anyone, a person he tended to visit with on a scheduled basis?"

"Not anyone I'm aware of. I didn't even know about that R thing on his calendar until Gage—" She cleared her throat. "I mean, until Chief Harrison asked me about it."

"It's okay, Danny. You don't need to call me Chief Harrison. Detective Rudd knows we grew up together and have been friends for years."

She looked at him, then back to the man across from her. "I have no idea what that R means, and if it was someone, who it would be."

"You might know it, but you aren't aware you do. Take some time. Think about some of your husband's acquaintances, and if you come up with anything, give me a call; or let Chief Harrison know and he will pass the information along."

The man stood. "Again. I'm sorry for your loss and for the difficulty of everything we spoke of today."

Chapter Sixty-Eight

FOUR MONTHS. WHILE not long in some ways, in others, it seemed like a lifetime. Danica still had difficulty believing Marcus was gone, that he'd missed so much. It was strange to think of how the world kept going on without him. How she had no choice but to keep on going too.

The twins had turned a year old, and Breck and Mase made a big announcement. *"We're pregnant!"* she'd said on Christmas Eve, glancing up at her husband with nothing but love and adoration. Danica shared in their joy, while at the same time swam in her sorrow. But the holidays came and went, and all had been quiet. No more bombshells or break-ins, just a peaceful time with her family and Gage, who still lived in her guest room. The two of them had become a weird amalgamation of their old friendship, their new friendship, his protective side, his tender side, and platonic roommates.

Danica was the president of the Chamber of Commerce. Her babies were talking with words more than sounds and walking, while she tended to hover, keeping an eye on them, worried they'd hurt themselves if they would fall the wrong way—her mother telling her not to be one of those helicopter mom's. And, then there was Gage. Always Gage.

At first, she wasn't sure what to think about the active part he played in her life, not used to having that from a man, she supposed. But after a while, Danica settled into the feeling of nice. Real nice. When he left work, he came home. Well, to *her* home, but he never left her hanging. Gage also helped her with the twins. The man, God bless him, would read to them, help with baths, change diapers. He'd even get on the floor and play with them. Aaron would roughhouse, his little frame doing body slams on Gage's muscled bulk—Ari more into sitting on him than wrestling around.

While things with Gage were great, things were also confusing. He'd been sitting in their room, reading the babies a bedtime story just moments before she excused herself, saying she'd be right back. What she didn't mention? It was too hard to watch him. Seeing how lovingly attentive he was with her children, tugged at her heart every time. And while she appreciated him, tremendously so, she was also frustrated in a 'woman loves man' kind of way that was never acted upon. And she wasn't sure if it ever would be. She still dealt with a mental tug of war over what was right and wrong, proper and improper for a new widow.

"Lord," she whispered, "is it wrong for me to have feelings for Gage?"

Admittingly, Danica was all jumbled up over loving Marcus, being devastated by him, believing she didn't know the man she married at all. Yet, she couldn't deny she'd loved Gage first. Once-upon-a-time, he'd been her everything.

"Aaah!" Needing to let her mind settle she left her en suite, knowing only one thing that would work and wandered into her home studio. Yes, it was a dance studio once again, thanks to Gage and Mase.

Glancing over her many music options, she pulled out an old CD, popped it into the player, toggled to the song she wanted, and pressed play.

When Jewel's sultry voice started, she began to move. Then she closed her eyes and lost herself in the feel of the music as it wrapped around her.

Gage went looking for Danny the moment the twins fell asleep, concerned because she'd never come back like she said she would. The first time she left him with the twins, saying she'd be back happened a few months ago, causing him to look for her then when she didn't return. He'd heard her voice coming from her room. At first, he thought she was on the phone, but soon figured out she was praying. For him. What she said hadn't been elaborate, but simple and to the point.

"Lord, please help Gage. Heal him."

He knew Danny hadn't been praying for physical healing any longer, but his spiritual one. Something shifted in him then—not a new faultline of anger and despair, but perhaps, the mending of one.

Coming to the hall, Gage heard the music and headed in that direction, stopping just inside the door to her studio.

She was still wearing her dark blue yoga pants and t-shirt combo, her hair piled on top of her head, but she had removed her socks and was swaying in a way that captured him.

Unable to move, he watched her, Danny's eyes closed, dancing as if she'd never taken such a long hiatus—the arch of her back, the extension of her arm, the bend in her leg as she spun. She was the embodiment of sensuality, grace, and beauty. It wasn't just physical beauty, but the type that shone from within and radiated from her smooth porcelain skin, making her glow.

Twirling across the floor, she was breathing hard. Heck, so was he. But no matter how much Gage tried to stay put, he couldn't. The mental chains he'd secured around himself so he could bide his time, snapped, and he went to her as she danced into him.

"Oh!" she spluttered, in a breathy pant, those eyes he loved opened, looking up at him from beneath her long lashes.

"Danica," he all but growled, taking her into his arms, lifting her off the floor, backing her into one of the mirrored walls, claiming her lips.

Just like their first and last kiss, he wasn't soft. He couldn't find gentle. And after a second, neither was she. His Danny wrapped herself around him—arms encircling his neck, those shapely legs around his waist. They had become mouths, tongues, teeth, hands, oh, her hands as she gripped his hair, giving him just as good as she got.

Every cell in his body switched to overdrive. His muscles bunched, his breathing was beastly, and Gage was going to do what he always wanted to do—take her.

Ding Dong!

"The door," she mumbled against his mouth.

"Ignore it." His tongue delved past her plush lips as they ate at each other.

Ding Dong!

"It's got to be the pizza I ordered. We'd better go, Gage." She'd said the words, but went back to kissing him.

Ding Dong!

"Gah!" Danica dropped her legs from his waist.

Worked up, his hair probably a fisted mess, he reluctantly let her go, then grinned.

"Why are you smiling like that?" Danny asked.

"You look…"

"I look what?"

Ding Dong!

With her hair half hanging from its restraint liked she'd been in a wind storm, her shirt askew, those eyes taking on that lust-drunk look, and her lush lips bee-stung from his heated kisses, Gage had a sense of secret caveman satisfaction.

"See for yourself," he said, tracing a fingertip along her jaw. "I'll get the door.

Striding down the hall, heading for the foyer, he knew the exact moment she looked at herself in the mirror, hearing her, "Holy buckets!" which made Gage smile. Huge.

Chapter Sixty-Nine

LETTING HERSELF IN, Danica entered her childhood home after the chamber meeting, where she had to pretend she and Gage hadn't gone at it with their mouths the night before.

"Chief Harrison," she'd greeted, shaking his hand.

The man dared to smirk and wink at her! *"Mrs. Harding. It's good to see you."*

She almost rolled her eyes, since she'd seen him a few hours before at her breakfast table.

"And you as well."

From there, it all pretty much went downhill when Courtney wanted to challenge her to a verbal smackdown. But Danica made Gage smile when she put the nasty woman in her place from the podium and moved on to other business.

Returning her focus to the task at hand, she yelled, "Mom? You home?"

"Yeah, baby-girl, I'm in the den!"

Going into the room that time forgot, Danica bent and hugged her mother around the neck. "Do you have a minute to talk?"

When she took a seat next to Mom on the couch, her mother leaned forward, grabbed the remote and turned down the TV. "I've always got time for you. You know that."

Danica nodded and bit the inside of her cheek.

"What is it?" Her mother's green eyes were wide.

"Nothing, and yet, at the same time, everything."

Mom took hold of her hand. "Tell me."

Danica gave herself a moment to gather her thoughts, trying to come up with the best way to say this, then just blurted out, "I kissed Gage."

Her mom blinked but didn't look at all shocked.

"Did you hear me? I *kissed* Gage, and not in the 'we're just friends' way." Danica stared at her lap. "The thing is, I want to do it again." She shook her head. "I'm so confused, Mom. I know Marcus did some horrible things, horrifying things really, but I loved him, and—"

"Baby-girl?"

Glancing up, she met her mother's tender gaze. "You have *always* loved Gage Harrison."

Had her jaw unhinged?

"Close your mouth, dear, before you attract flies."

Danica did what her mother told her to do. "You knew?"

She nodded. "Of course. I've always known."

"Then why didn't you ever say anything to me?"

"Because you weren't ready to talk about him. But now—" Mom grinned and patted her cheek. "You're ready, baby-girl."

Chapter Seventy

LOOKING UP FROM her desk, Paula walked into Danica's office at the chamber, saying, "Special delivery," as she put a massive crystal vase of crimson roses on her desk.

"Oh, my," she uttered, her hand going to her mouth. There had to be at least four dozen perfect blooms in front of her.

"I'd say you've got a pretty great secret admirer, Danny."

"Huh?"

The woman, who'd worked at the floral shop for as long as she could remember, winked then sashayed out.

Standing up to sniff a bloom, Danica bent, took a deep breath, then plucked the little envelope from the spike holding it.

It didn't say anything on the front.

Turning it over, lifting the tab and pulling the small card out, she read;

WILL YOU BE MY VALENTINE?

Her heart, which seemed overworked by the man, started beating wildly. No, there wasn't any signature, but Danica smiled. She would know Gage's big blocky handwriting anywhere.

Grabbing her cell phone, she typed out a quick text; *Valentine's day isn't until next week*, then hit SEND.

"We need to make sure and have an extra patrol working that night," Gage said to Officer Davis. "I hate being the one to decide who's going to pull extra duty, so you all talk among yourselves, and then let me know who is volunteering."

"Will do, Chief."

"Oh and—"

Tweedle-deet!

Gage held up a finger, indicating to hold on as he plucked up his cell phone, read Danny's text, and grinned.

"Sir?"

He put his phone down and looked at his officer.

"I don't think I've ever seen you take a call or a text while in a meeting," he remarked, with an almost smile on his lips.

"Things change."

"I guess they do." The man gave him a knowing look. "You were saying?"

It took Gage a second to get his head back in the game. "Make sure you guys do a few more drive-bys during the Sweethearts dance. Make your presence known. Maybe that way, if those knucklehead seniors see you, they'll think twice about getting in their cars and driving after knocking a few too many back."

"Agree, Chief. Anything else?"

"No. That's all for now, Davis."

The man nodded, got up, and strode out of his office.

Gage waited for a beat, then snagged his phone, thumb tapping across the too-small keyboard on his screen. *I know V-Day isn't until next week, but I'm asking early before anyone else does. You know the early bird gets the worm and all that. So, what do you say? Feel like being my Valentine?*

Danica grinned as she gave Gage a response, giggling as she pressed SEND.

Danny-D: *Worms are disgusting. What's in it for me if I say, yes?*

Gage chuckled. *I remember you telling me that every time I baited your hook for you when we were kids. As to what's in it for you? I think that's a loaded question.*

Keeping his eye on those little bouncing dots, made him giddier than a schoolgirl. It was ridiculous, he got that, but he didn't care.

Danny-D: *Eww… I still can't bait a hook. But as to your loaded question comment, your point is?*

"Oh, Danny, Danny, Danny," he said as he typed, *You're such a naughty girl. Do you know what happens to naughty girls?*

A second later, his cell phone rang, and he grinned. While they'd done nothing more physical than hold hands and make out like they were teenagers a few times, they did flirt. A lot. So maybe she wanted to move from flirtexting? *Is that a word?* Ah, well, he didn't know, but if she wanted to tease him with her sexy voice, then Gage was into that.

After tapping the icon and bringing his phone to his ear, he said, "Hello, beautiful."

"Gage, you need to come!"

He jumped up out of his chair, had his coat on, and was out his office door. "What's happened."

"I got something in the mail at the chamber."

"I'm on my way."

Pacing in her office, Danica wrung her hands. She'd absently opened the mail, more focused on Gage's texts than on anything else until a photograph slipped out of one of the envelopes and slid across her oak desk. When she glanced at it, terror struck her very bones. It was a picture of her and Gage, both of them walking side-by-side, each of them holding one of her twins as they left a park in Seattle on Saturday. It had been a super sunny day, a fun day, and now…

With shaking fingers, she'd turned the picture over and read one single sentence that chilled her to her soul.

"Danny?"

She spun around at the sound of his voice, not quite the absence of worry, but a sense of relief settling over her when she saw Gage. "It's on my desk."

Without any further discussion, he went, picked up the photo, scowled, then turned the picture over. That's when the muscle in his jaw started ticking.

"The Itsy Bitsy Spider," Gage read.

"You hummed that song while walking your fingers up Ari's arm, making her giggle that day," Danica said.

Going to her, Gage wrapped her in his strong arms, resting his chin on the top of her head, while Danica put her arms around his waist and held on for dear life. "From this point on, you and the babies won't ever be alone, not even for short periods."

"Okay," she readily agreed.

"I want Mrs. Beil to come here while you're at work. You have additional offices in this building that are empty most of the time. Set one up for the twins. I don't want her to be alone with them either. She may be at risk, too."

Danica nodded.

"I'll find whoever is doing this, Danny."

"I thought it was over, that those photos of Marcus were the end of it. It's been so peaceful since then."

Chapter Seventy-One

"HEY, BROTHER," GAGE greeted when Mase answered the phone. "I know you're at work, and I'm sorry to bother you, but I need to ask a favor."

"Shoot."

"I want to take Danny out tonight. She's always cooking dinner when she gets home, and I want to give her a break. The last we went somewhere was for Valentine's. Do you think you and Breck could watch the twins for us tonight?"

"Sure. No problem."

"I need to double-check with Danny first, make sure she doesn't have something scheduled. Then I'll call you back with a time."

"You bringing my niece and nephew over to the B and B?"

"Yeah. If that's okay?"

"Totally."

Gage smiled. "Great. I'll talk to you soon."

"Later, G."

Gage should be working, not on the phone making dinner plans, but another minute of non-grind to send a quick text wouldn't kill him.

Plucking up his cell, he typed, *Danny. I want to take you out for dinner tonight. Breck and Mase will watch the twins. Do you have anything going on, or can I make a reservation in Seattle and call Mase back with a time to expect the babies?*

After plugging in her dead cell phone, Danica went to wake up the twins. They had a late nap. Really late. Mrs. Beil went home early due to a bad cold, so without her, all their timelines were off, and she'd brought them on home. It was too hard to work in her office without someone to occupy her busy babies.

"Hey, cuties," Danica said, grinning at her smiling children as she stepped into their room. "You guys are wide awake."

"Go!" Ari insisted.

"All right, all right." She lifted her little girl out of the crib, kissed her neck until she giggled, then plucked up her son, placing a kiss on his forehead.

"Mama."

"Yep, Aaron," she said. "I'm your mama."

Leaving their room behind, Danica took the twins into the kitchen, put Aaron in the playpen then Ari next to her brother. Straightening, she asked, "Are you guys hungry?"

Ari nodded as Aaron rolled a ball around, making *vroom* sounds.

"You guys play nice while Mommy gets your dinner ready, okay?"

"'Kay," said Aaron, then tossed his ball over the top of the enclosure.

Going to grab it and toss it back, she paused, feeling a draft—there and gone. *Weird*, she thought as she placed the red and white ball into the pen instead of tossing it, then went to grab some mac-n-cheese from the pantry.

Box in hand, Danica snagged a pan from the overhead rack, put in the desired amount of water, and then placed it on the burner of the stove before she turned the heat on.

Humming to herself, she tore the top of the box open, then sat it on the marble counter. "Need butter," she told the twins.

"Butt," Ari said.

"Bu-tter," Danica enunciated, trying not to chuckle.

"Butt, butt."

"Bu-tter."

"But-rrr."

"Close, baby mine. Keep working on it, and you'll get it. Bu-tter."

Listening to her daughter chatter, she spun around, opened the stainless-steel refrigerator door, made a mental note that she needed to clean all the fingermarks and smudges off it, then plucked up the tub—

"Hello, Danny."

The eerie feminine voice came from behind her, making her jump, dropping the butter.

"Ouch!" Danica's hand automatically went to the side of her neck, where the biting sting came from.

"I've waited a long time for this," the stranger said, as fear spiked Danica with the realization, not only was someone in her home, but they'd drugged her.

"Do-don't hurt my babi..."

Danica was slurring her words, a fog overtaking her as she tried to turn, but an arm came around her chest—a steel bar.

Then everything shifted into nothingness

"Danica?" Gage called, striding into the foyer, then stopped.

The twins! They were screaming at the top of their lungs.

Gage had been worried before when she didn't answer his text about going out for dinner, then found out Danny wasn't at the office. But now, as he strode into the kitchen and saw Arianna and Aaron's red faces, bawling like little banshees, his worry transformed into panic.

Heading to them, he noticed something was still on the stovetop, and a box of macaroni and cheese was on the counter.

Going to turn the burner off before the pan scorched, he tripped over a tub of butter discarded on the floor. Picking it up, he put it on the counter, then made quick work of shutting the stove off before he went to the playpen. "*Shh*…I'm here. Gage is here, so quiet down."

"Dadda, Dadda." Ari tossed her arm in the air, squeezing her fingers together, making a fist then loosening, making a fist…

"Aw…sweet baby," he tried to soothe as he picked her up and patted her back. "I'm not your Daddy, but I sure wish I was."

With his free hand, Gage rubbed his sternum since it felt like something punched through his chest and was squeezing his lungs.

"Me, me, me," Aaron said through his sniffles.

"Okay, little guy." Gage plucked him up too, holding a baby in each arm, unsure of how to calm them when he wasn't himself.

"Where's Mommy?" he asked, attempting to modulate his voice.

"Bad," Ari said.

"Who's bad? Is Mommy bad?"

She shook her head, and if his arms weren't full, he'd wipe her glistening tear-streaked face.

"Danny?" he called again, listening, but hearing nothing.

No choice but to take the twins with him, Aaron glanced around while Ari rested her cheek on the top of his shoulder, nose pressing into the side of his neck.

Gage needed to get a grip; if for no other reason than to give the babies his assurance everything was all right. But who was going to assure him?

With giant strides, Gage went through the house, looking and calling, "Danica?" But she wasn't answering him.

"Do you know where Mommy is?"

"Bad," Ari said again.

Ready to head for the master suite, something skittered along the floor, then blew across his feet, making him glance down. It was a dead leaf, but…

He made his way to where the fresh April air was coming in, finding the French doors in the dining room that led out onto the back patio and over to the pool, wide open.

His miserable attempts at composure vanished.

Gage ran out into the waning light, yelling, "Danica!"

The babies started to cry again, clearly reading the fear in both his tense body and raised voice.

Chapter Seventy-Two

HER HEAD WAS pounding. Hard. Surly the bass drum section at Cedar Point High was over enthusiastically using Danica's brain for practice—shaking her.

"Wake up!"

"*Hmm?*"

Raddle, raddle.

"I said, wake up!"

"Hurt," she managed past what felt like numb lips.

Splash!

"Hu-u-uh!" An intake of air whooshed past Danica's parted lips, down her parched throat, and made her sit up in a quick burst of disorientating speed as water dripped from her eyelashes, trickled down her nose, and fell off her chin.

"Finally."

"What?" Head still hurting, and a crick in her neck, Danica swiped at her face.

Slowly, she glanced around, catching someone dressed in black, not too far away from her, putting a bucket on an old, dirty, hardwood floor with…*dead weeds sprouting from it?*

"Who are you? Where am I?" Then it hit her. "My babies! Where are my babies?"

"The little brats are where I left them."

Terror swelled her vocal cords, causing her to squeak, "Where did you leave them?"

"Where they were."

"In their playpen? You didn't hurt them?"

"Yes, in their *playpen*," she said, sounding exasperated. "No, I didn't touch them. I imagine someone will show up at some point and find the tiny monsters."

While being left alone at home wasn't optimal, at least this insane person hadn't harmed them.

Some of her panic subsided. "Who are you?"

"Well," said the lilting voice, "you sure do ask a lot of questions, but since I'm in such a generous mood, I'll answer them." Turning around, the woman shoved the hoodie from her head and smiled. "How are you, Mrs. Harding?"

It took her a second. The face seemed familiar, but, but… "Rosland?" she uttered astonished. "You're the nurse who worked with my husband. The one I met months and months ago at Canlis with Marcus."

"Ding, ding, ding," the woman said, sarcasm present as she clapped. "You win a gold star."

Attempting to stand, Danica was yanked back by the arm. Frowning, she glanced over to see her wrist cuffed to some kind of pipe. "Why are you doing this?"

"Because I hate you!"

"I don't even know you."

"Oh, but you do."

"I'd never met you until—"

"Miranda Burrell."

Danica frowned. "What?"

Rosland opened her mouth, tipped her head back, and yelled, "Miranda Burrell!"

"Miranda?" She knew the name, recognized it, but didn't recognize the woman at all.

Miranda dropped her head—burnt umber eyes slipping to her. "What's wrong, Danny? Don't you recognize me?"

"No. You look different."

"That's what a whole lot of cosmetic surgery does for a gal." She slid a fingertip down her face. "Nose job. Cheek implants. Collagen." Miranda tapped her lips. "It's amazing, isn't it?"

The woman ripped her hoodie off, her long strands of auburn hair going with the material, then tumbling around her shoulders before she grabbed her own breasts over the skin-tight t-shirt she wore. "These puppies were worth every single dime."

Blinking, Danica tried to keep herself calm.

Miranda smirked. "I know they're not the real deal like yours, but most men are too dumb to figure it out, or just don't care when it comes right down to it."

"Are you wearing my earrings?"

"These?" She grinned, posing, hand cupping her ear. "They are lovely, aren't they?"

"Rosland, I—"

The crazy woman kicked Danica's sock-covered foot with the toe of her chunky boot, making her wince in pain, jerking her leg away. "Miranda, you stupid cow!"

"Sor-sorry, Miranda."

"You're not yet, but you're going to be."

"I don't—" Pressing her lips together, Danica shook her head. "I don't understand. You were only here a couple of years, and we barely spoke to each other while you were in school."

"I know you don't understand. You never did, *Princess*."

"Mase," Gage said into his phone.

"You coming over to drop off the twins?"

"No. Listen. Danny never answered any of my texts, and when I went over to the chamber to find out what was going on, I was told she left early, took the babies home because Mrs. Beil got sick. I came home, and she's not here. The twins were screaming in their playpen, stuff was boiling on the stove, the French doors were open to the back patio, and she's gone. Something is wrong here. I need you guys to come take care of Ari and Aaron for me. Then I'm calling it in and heading out as soon as you get here."

"On our way now!"

That was it. Mase disconnected the call.

"Tell me what this is all about, Miranda." Danica wiggled her hand. The cuff was too tight.

"Everyone loved you. All the boys wanted to get in your pants. But you never let them, did you, Ms. *Goody-Goody*?"

Danica remained silent.

"I didn't care about most of them, but Gage? Now, *Gage*, I cared about." Miranda's face twisted into a mask of ugly. "But he was always too occupied with *you* to notice me. Even when I offered myself up to him, he turned me down."

That statement made Danica's eyes go wide.

"That's right, *Danny*"—she said her name like it tasted bad—"I went to his house one night, and shimmied out of my clothes. I mean, what hot-blooded male is going to turn that down, right? Oh, but he *did*. The guy didn't even cop a free *feel*."

Rosland/Miranda/Cray-cray shook her head. "It was always *you*. He couldn't keep his eyes *off* you!"

"He wasn't with me. He was with Jenny."

She scoffed. "He only wasted his time with her until he could have you. I would have given him everything she did, but no. Something about the older chicks did it for him, I guess."

Danica closed her eyes, not wanting to think about that.

"Aw…What's wrong, Princess? Don't like to hear about your boy toy getting on with someone else?"

"He wasn't my boy toy!"

"Yes, he was, but you played with him differently. Teasing, driving him mad with lust, but you never, ever put out." She clicked her tongue. "Such a shame, really. To drive the guy you loved into the arms of another girl."

"Stop it!"

"Ooo, I seemed to have hit a nerve with that one." Miranda grinned like a demented cat. "Let's see what other buttons I can press to make you twitch."

Gage was in his SUV, not sure where he was going; he just had to look for Danny. Do something. He'd called it in and had all his men out. Except for Stanley, who was going over Danica's house with a fine-tooth comb. He had instructions to call if he found anything to suggest where she might be, or who was involved with her going. No way would she have voluntarily left her babies behind, though. No way!

Driving toward the lake, for no other reason than once-upon-a-time he came upon her out there, he tapped anxious fingers on his steering wheel.

"God," he said. "I surrender. I know I've been a major screw up, and a huge disappointment to You. I blamed You for my mistakes, and for not fixing them for me. I've been mad at You for years, and I'm sorry. Leaving You out of my life hasn't helped me. I get it. I'm coming to You now because I need your help, and I hope You can forgive me for my past. But, no matter how much of an idiot I've been, you have always been there, waiting. You knew when and why I'd be coming to You. So please. I'm asking in your name, keep Danica safe, and show me how to find her. I love her. I always have. And there's no doubt in my mind she loves You. But unlike me, I'm sure she *hasn't* been a disappointment. Help her. Help me."

The bell tones of his cell phone started ringing, so Gage tapped the screen that was secure in its docking station to send the call over the speakers in his vehicle, answering with a blunt, "Harrison."

"Gage, this is Cooper."

"Coop, I'm dealing with some heavy stuff right now—"

"I know where your woman is," he said, making every hair stand up on the back of Gage's neck.

How does he know? "Where?"

"I came in tonight and started watching some old feed on my cameras, and I saw that person in black, only whoever it was, they weren't alone. The figure was pushing a wheelbarrow, and Danica was in it—unconscious."

"What?" Gage was gripping the steering wheel so tight, it felt like the skin over his knuckles was going to burst.

"By the time stamp, they have a good forty minutes on me, but I know where they were headed, so I'm going down there. I just wanted you to know."

"Wait. I'm a few minutes from your place. I'm going with you."

It was silent for a moment.

"Cooper?"

"Yeah?" he said. "I'm here. But, I'm locked and loaded, so no giving me hassle about my firearms."

"I wouldn't even think about it."

Thank you, God, Gage thought and pressed the gas pedal down.

Chapter Seventy-Three

"MAX," MIRANDA SAID. "You got under Gage's skin with that play. I'll give you that one."

"I wasn't playing."

"Yes, you were. You wanted to rub another guy in his face, and Max wanted to nail you. A win, win until you started liking Maxwell. That's when I went after him. Why should you have yet another guy drooling over you?"

The woman shrugged. "He didn't put up a fight, though. He was easy to seduce. Then you came storming in, and of course, Gage had to come running to your rescue after the prom." She pursed her lips. "You ruined my fun. Well, that night anyway."

"You're completely insane," Danica said.

"I know." Miranda studied her fingernails as if she were bored. "But it gets so much better, Princess."

"Better?"

Her eyes lifted as she dropped her hand, and one corner of her mouth quirked up. "Stealing Gage from me was bad enough. Whateva, I moved on. What's the saying? On to bigger and better things?"

The whacky woman started skipping across the cabin, like a child without a care in the world. And it was an old cabin Danica had realized, one that hadn't seen any TLC in years, judging by the rotting condition, the musty smell, and all the dirty debris around her.

"You know, he was mine first."

Danica frowned. "Who was?"

Miranda spun around. "Marcus, silly."

She tried not to gape, but Danica wasn't sure she accomplished it. "You're lying."

"Nope! He was *engaged! To me!* Then he decided to help a friend of his for some weird reason. That's when Marcus saw you dancing, and everything changed." Miranda scowled. "'I'm sorry'," she said, lowering her voice in a horrible imitation of Marcus, "'but I've met someone else'." She huffed. "Isn't that just great? He came home one night and told me that. Said our engagement was off!"

"I didn't know," Danica whispered, wondering what else she was clueless about when it came to the man she married.

"Yeah, well. It hurt—a lot. But I told myself I'd get over him and move on. Then I saw those photographs in his desk drawer."

"Photographs?"

"Those photos were of you! Seeing them made up my mind."

"Your mind?"

"To destroy you both, of course," she sang cheerily. "Oh, it took a lot of patience and planning. But the moment Marcus followed through with marrying you? I started on my revenge."

"Your revenge?"

"What are you? Polly parrot? Yes, Danny, my revenge. Let me tell you, graduating first of my class and becoming an RN wasn't easy. Neither was getting a job where our lovely Marcus worked. But once I made it past those hurdles, the rest fell into place."

Danica's heart was beating so hard she wondered if she were visibly shaking. Then again, she was wet, and the temperature was dropping. "The rest of what?"

"Marcus was an addict, you know. He started using in med school, needing something to keep him awake, keep him sharp. Then it turned into more and more to keep him going. So sad." She pouted. "But he decided to get clean for me, and he did it, but I guess, in the end, he got clean for *you*. I couldn't have that. No, no, no. That wouldn't do."

Cooper was making his way through the uneven terrain of the woods that made up the back of his property with the speed and silence of a phantom, but Gage was keeping up with him, no matter if he was feeling the strain in his back, making pain shoot down his right leg.

A few feet in front of him, Coop held up his fist, so Gage slowed and came to a stop right behind the big guy. "There's Danica's Escalade."

Gage saw it, parked next to a natural spring.

"There's a lamplight in that cabin," Coop whispered. "Go slow. Be quiet."

Gage wanted to sprint toward it, but fighting against his need to get to Danica, he deferred to the former Navy Seal, who knew every nook and cranny of Land's End.

He nodded.

"What do you mean?" Danica asked. She was going to keep on asking things, not only because she wanted to attempt to understand all of this insanity, but was also hoping the longer she kept Miranda talking, the better her chances were of Gage finding them. And he would—she'd silently asked God for him to come.

"There was no way you were going to get the best of Marcus when I didn't! *I* was the one who was there during his struggles. The one who *loved* him even in the bad times. So I *had* to do something."

"What did you do?"

The woman put her hands together and held them under her chin. "I got him hooked again. It was easier than I thought it would be. I started spiking his food and drinks. Then I told Marcus I had what he wanted. Oh, he resisted a bit at first." She cocked her head. "It didn't last long before he caved and came to me. But I had a price. On top of the money, I told him I wanted his body."

Danica's stomach churned.

"He fought it for a while. Even threw up after our first reunion between the sheets, but once he got mad and gave himself over to the inevitability of it, Marcus took me every which way—rough, hard, and dirty. Just how I like it."

Danica glanced down. *God, help me.*

"Ah…I hit a nerve again! But, I haven't made you twitch yet, have I?"

Miranda stomped her booted feet as she came to her, grabbed Danica by the head of the hair and yanked, making her scream.

That cry, Danny's scream, pierced his heart and had Gage moving past Cooper until the man grabbed him by the shoulder, pulling him back. "Keep your head," he whispered, so low Gage had a hard time hearing him.

Miranda produced a blade from…somewhere, and held it to Danica's face where she could see it, silver glinting in the portable camping light. "I've *dreamed* of messing you up. Making it so no man will *ever* find you beautiful again!"

"Please," Danica said in a soft lament. "Don't do this."

When the crazy woman let her go and backed away, she took a breath.

"I wouldn't get too comfortable if I were you. I'll hold out on the real fun until you've heard it all."

"Ther-there's more?"

"Marcus was looking into rehabs again. He didn't think I knew it, but I did. And when that happened, I had to intervene. So I made arrangements to meet him on his yacht, told him this was the last time I'd be selling to him. Told him I was getting out of the business. Too much heat. It wasn't true of course. If you only *knew* how much money I rake in with my little side venture, you'd be shocked. But, I digress."

Miranda sighed. "I knew the hook of that last time would make Marcus come running. I also knew he'd tell me anything I wanted to know once he started flying."

"How did you know?"

"He'd told me things before, like where he kept his money and his bank account numbers. You didn't think *he* spent all that cash on drugs, did you?"

Danica blinked, trying to let what was said to sink in.

"What a stupid, stupid woman you are. Yeah, he spent a wad on his habit, but I took, and took, and took from him, and more than his body." Miranda winked.

"You took our funds?"

"Yours? *You* didn't contribute. No, *not* the Princess. It was all *his* money, and he owed *me*."

"Because he broke things off with you?"

"Now, you're getting the picture. Your life should have been *my* life. But, no!"

The woman raced over, hauled off and slapped Danica, making her head jerk to the right.

"Payback for after prom!" She spun on her heel, giggling. "That felt good," Miranda said, going back to her position by the door, arms swinging. "I suppose we should finish our chat now."

The coppery tang of blood trickled into Danica's mouth.

"I went to meet him, let Marcus have a taste of what he was craving, then got him to tell me things like the security code to your house, and other stuff. Then, when he was tripping, I satisfied myself with your husband's body, put a gun in his hand and helped him pull the trigger."

Danica gasped, frantically jerking at the cuff around her wrist. "No-o-o!"

"Now, you're twitching."

Chapter Seventy-Four

GAGE'S RAGE WAS palpable. It radiated from him so much he was sure Cooper could feel it as they witnessed some insane, out of control woman with red/brown hair storm over to Danny—who was cuffed to an old plumbing pipe—and punch her in the mouth.

With his Sig Sauer aimed in front of him, he kicked down the flimsy door, yelling, "Freeze! This is the police!"

Keeping his eyes trained on the nut job, and away from his Danica, he moved forward until 'Looney Tunes' pulled a knife and put the blade to Danny's throat. "Put the weapon down."

"Oh, please, Gage. Like I'm going to do that."

She spoke as if she knew him, but then again, she was certifiable.

"Put-the-weapon-down," he said once again, with a bite to every word.

"How about I cut this cow's throat and put us both out of our misery?"

"I am *not* going to tell you again."

"Sure, you are. You won't pull that trigger. Not if there's a chance your darling Danny can get hurt in the crossfire. You'll do anything I want you to. See"—she drew the blade tighter, making a superficial cut into Danny's perfect skin—"Danica Dawn here is your Achilles heel. Your glitch. Your one true flaw. You know it, and I know it."

When a slight trickle of blood started to roll down the side of Danica's neck, Gage faltered, lowering his gun a bit.

"See." The woman smiled, toothy white. "You won't shoot me."

"But I will." Cooper's raspy voice came from the shadows, making the crazy woman jerk in the direction of the sound, knife lowering, giving Gage enough time to holster his weapon, rush her, and take her down—shoulder to the midsection.

She hit the floor with an *oomph*.

He'd rattled her momentarily, but she recovered and tried to stab him. Danica screamed bloody murder, though he couldn't focus on her to put her at ease. Gage was too busy knocking the weapon out of the culprit's hand.

Once the blade was gone, the female below him became a wildcat of hissing, cursing, and flailing. She might be going nuts, but she wasn't a match for his strength. Quickly, Gage flipped the perp on her stomach and had her hands behind her back, putting his knee into her lower spine as he cuffed the woman who was cursing him to Hades.

Chapter Seventy-Five

"DANNY!" GAGE HAD lunged for her the moment the woman was out of commission and started frantically inspecting her. He touched her face, her arms, her legs, then pulled out a set of keys from one of the many pockets of his tactical jacket, unlocked the cuff, taking it from her, then looking at the damage there. "Speak to me." He framed Danica's face between his hands. "Are you injured more than I can see?"

She'd been so terrified for his safety when Miranda tried to knife him, she'd lost her mind, although she could have gone astray earlier; it just took a few minutes to snap totally.

"Danica Dawn. Look at me."

She couldn't yank herself back together. She was unfocused, dazed, hearing Gage, yet pulling her hand up, trying to do something about the pain. Danica started rubbing her tender, bleeding wrist—the arch in her arm from being cuffed so long in a strange position made her shoulder throb too.

"Danny?"

Her eyes lifted. "Are you okay?"

Danica was aware her voice sounded far off. Flat. And on a strange level, she understood she functioned, but was detached.

"I'm fine. Not a scratch on me." Gage locked his silver gaze on her. "Besides the obvious, are you hurt?"

It took her a second to consider. *Am I?* Danica attempted to take inventory, finding the task too difficult, so she just shook her head.

Gage looked over his shoulder and said to someone she couldn't see, "Thanks," then tapped the com in his ear, giving the location where to find them and said they would need two ambulances.

That bizarre feeling morphed into something more tangible, causing Danica's teeth to chatter.

"Cooper," Gage said, "she's freezing. I need something to get Danny warm."

A second later, something soft hit him in the back, so he reached and tugged it around. It was the man's huge jacket.

Draping the coat over Danica, Gage willed himself to settle before sparing a glance for the crazy woman face-down on the dirty planked floor. Whoever she was, she would soon see what it was like to live behind bars—the knowledge of that sending satisfaction through him.

Danny was safe.

"I see no reason to keep you overnight, Mrs. Harding," the E.R. doctor said. "You have a few scrapes, bumps and bruises, but nothing broken. Your vitals are good. The drug in your system could cause nausea, so I'll prescribe something to combat that. While I wouldn't go as far as to agree with you about being 'fine,' I do believe you are fit enough to head home."

"Thank you"—Danica glanced at the name printed over the pocket of his white coat—"Doctor Wellington."

"No need for thanks. I'll get the nurse started on the discharge papers."

She nodded.

"And if I may? I can't say I knew your husband well, I came here only a few short months before he left Harborview, but I am truly sorry for your loss."

"I appreciate your condolences."

He bobbed his silver-head, then went out the door.

"Danny?"

Blinking, she looked over at Gage, who was seated beside her bed, his big, warm palm on her knee. "*Hmm?*"

"Are you really okay?"

"I'm…"

"Tell me."

"I'm going to be physically all right, but the things Miranda told me might take a long time to process, if ever."

"I get you've been through a lot; I do. But I will need to speak with you—on the record, officially."

She nodded.

Gage cupped her cheek. "I love you, Danica."

She loved him too, but she couldn't muster up the strength to say it. She couldn't do anything but let her head fall back on the pillow and close her eyes.

Chapter Seventy-Six

A MONTH HAD passed since the whole Rosland Strickler/Miranda Burrell incident, and Gage had found out so much it was hard to process it all. But the bottom line was this. When Miranda left Cedar Point her Junior year in high school, it was because her mother married a man named Dean Strickler, who adopted her. After she graduated from a private school in Seattle, she legally changed her first name, got a job for Marcus' father as a personal assistant, and then from there, it seemed she and Marcus entered into a romantic relationship. They were together for several years before he proposed to her, and soon after that, he checked himself into a rehab facility for the well to do—very Beverley Hills exclusive.

Once he completed their program, it wasn't long until he went to WSU, saw Danny dancing up on stage (the same dance Gage had watched), and Marcus met her in the receiving line Gage had walked away from. It became even more of a tangled web from there, Marcus pursuing Danica pretty hard, then finally he *paid* Ryan Fielding a half a million dollars to dump her. Danny had been oblivious as to why Ryan called off their engagement. Yes, the idiot accepted the money and walked! Marcus took full advantage of the opening he'd made happen, swooped in, and then the rest is well, history as they say.

"Gawonii?"

Danny's voice put a smile on his face as he buttoned Ari's pink coat. "Yeah?"

"My therapist called. She moved my appointment to Friday."

He turned to look at her. "Why?"

"Personal emergency."

Gage had talked Danica into seeing his therapist, the one who he still saw about his lingering issues surrounding what happened when he was in the FBI.

"Okay. Well, let's go to Seattle anyway. Make a day of it. I've already got the babies' coats on."

"Coat!" Aaron said happily, jumping up and down.

Danny grinned. "All right. Just give me a minute to grab my purse and stuff, and then we will go."

"Go, Donald's, Daddy!" Arianna exclaimed, that feeling of heartbroken and love hitting Gage at the same time he curled her into the crook of his arm.

"Sweetie pie… " He placed a smooch to her cheek, making her giggle. "We can go to McDonald's if you want, but Mommy and I have told you, I'm not your daddy. Marcus Harding was your daddy. I'm Gage. Your mommy's friend."

"My Daddy!" she insisted, shaking her blonde head. "No, Mommy Daddy."

Gage glanced up to see Danny watching them, her beautiful eyes taking on that shine; the one that said tears were imminent.

He gave his attention to the baby girl who held him in the palm of her little hand. “No. I’m not Mommy’s Daddy. Samuel is your mommy’s father. Your grandfather. I’m Mommy’s friend.”

“Sam-Daddy!” Aaron chimed in.

“Yes, Samuel is your mommy’s Daddy,” he said.

“Gage,” Danica called in her soft voice, drawing his attention. “It’s okay. Really. The twins will understand when they are a little bit older.”

“Love, Mommy,” Ari said, making him smile.

“Yes.” He kept his eyes on Danny. “We all love Mommy.”

Chapter Seventy-Seven

DRESSED IN A black suit, Gage adjusted his silk tie. Tonight was the night. She didn't know it yet, but he had every intention of making Danny *admit* she loved him. Next month he'd turn forty, and he'd had enough of the waiting. It was time. *Their time.* And since she'd permanently removed the wedding rings Marcus gave her, he wasn't going to waste another hour.

"What do you think about this whole retirement thing?" Danica asked later after he helped her out of the vehicle and then handed his keys over to the valet.

"I'm surprised Dad is actually going to retire, but I'm happy for him. He and Mom need to spend some quality downtime together."

Taking her hand, Danny gasped. "My ring. You're wearing it?"

"I am."

She glanced up at him, astonished love written all over her beautiful face. "Why?"

"It just felt right."

Silently, they walked into the snooty Seattle country club his parents belonged to, and then entered the smaller ballroom where people mingled, music played, chandeliers twinkled, and candlelight flickered.

"Hi, Chief Harrison." Felicia Sands sauntered up in a too-tiny dress, a big smile on her face.

Danica leaned closer to him—possessive.

"Hello, Ms. Sands," he said, trying not to let the fact Danny was up against him show by beaming.

The woman's gaze went from him to Danica, dismissing her, then back to his face. "I've missed you in the gym lately, so it's good to see you." She fluttered her lashes.

"Good to see you as well," Danica interjected, refusing to be ignored as she squeezed his fingers tighter with hers.

"I'm sorry. I don't believe you and I have been properly introduced." Felicia grinned, oozing fakeness, attention bouncing to Danny. "I'm—"

"The new owner of the antique store, Felicia Sands. And you and I *have* met. I'm Danica Lorry-Harding."

"Oh yes." Giggle, giggle. "From the chamber. *Now* I remember."

"Ms. Sands," Gage said, putting an end to the ridiculous woman's interference. "I hope you enjoy your evening."

Letting go of Danica's hand to put his palm on her lower back, Gage maneuvered them around the maneater and deeper into the room.

"Friend of yours?" Danny asked under her breath.

Her jealousy thrilled him. "Nope."

"Good."

Glancing down, Gage smiled at the woman he loved. "You ready for this shindig?"

Danny was looking up at him from beneath her long lashes, her blue eyes glittering. "Ready."

The dinner had been formal, but good. The food excellent—even Breckin thought so—and Gage was getting antsy, wanting to get Danica in his arms. Yes, for the third time in his life, he wanted to dance. But only with her. Only ever her.

His father stood, tapped his fork against his crystal glass, and said, "If I could have everyone's attention?"

Of course, he got it.

"I just wanted to say how honored I am you all came here tonight to celebrate another milestone with me. I've been so privileged to know all of you and to be able to do what I love for over thirty years. But, it's time now to pass the baton to the younger generation. So, while you all know we are here for my retirement, we are also here to celebrate the changing of the guard, so to speak."

His father glanced around, then said, "Starting next month, Doctor Caleb Novak, one of Cedar Point's very own, will be taking over the practice at the medical clinic. Caleb, will you stand?"

That was news. Gage hadn't realized Caleb was even there, was returning to Cedar Point, or that Dad had found someone to take over for him.

Two tables down, the boy he knew was barely visible in the man who stood, ran a palm down the front of his dress shirt, then smiled. "I'm honored as well, Doctor Harrison."

"Let's all show this young man our gratitude and appreciation, and when you see him around town, make him feel welcome."

A few cheers happened, along with a round of applause.

"Enough from me," Dad said. "I think the band is about ready, so, as my son would say, let's get this party started!"

Lightning cracked across the sky, sending a display of nature's fireworks into the room. The massive wall of glass framed God's picture show as Danica took the dance floor with Gage. This was only her third time dancing with him, yet, it seemed like it should have been so many more.

"You look beautiful tonight," Gage said in his sandpaper-smooth voice. "But you look beautiful every night."

A heated tendril of pleasure meandered over her skin at the compliment. "Thank you, Gawonii. You look very handsome yourself."

"I'm glad you think so." Placing his arm around her waist, his other palm holding hers up by his shoulder, Danica let him take the lead.

Looking into his silver eyes, she wanted to swoon, but instead, she pulled her gaze away, placed her cheek to his chest, and swayed to the music.

Dance after dance, the two of them stayed in their little bubble of contentment until the band started playing a song she hadn't heard in, she couldn't say how long.

Glancing back up at Gage, she grinned. "I love this song."

"After All?"

"Yes."

"I know you do."

"You do?"

"I know you, Danny."

It was such a simple thing to say, but it seemed to melt her into him. "*Mm…*"

When Gage placed his cheek next to hers, his breath tickled her skin, sending chills and fiery flames over her. "Danica?"

"*Hmm?*"

"Tell me you want me." He nuzzled his nose into the crook of her neck. "Tell me you need me." He placed his lips to the hollow beneath her ear and breathed, "Tell me you *love* me."

Oh, she wanted to. She longed to, but for some moronic reason, she remained silent. Then all too soon, the song ended.

When Gage let loose of her, the warmth left, only getting worse as he took a step back.

With a tilt to her head, Danica frowned.

"Okay then," he said, before, to her horror, he rubbed his tense jaw, turned, and walked away.

A horrible dread crept over Danica like sludge when she lost sight of Gage in the crowd of dancing couples. *Why didn't I tell him? He's leaving!*

Unsure of what to do, but knowing she needed to do something, Danica pressed her way through the couples, trying to be polite saying, "Sorry," and "Excuse me," then took the one step up to the stage where the band was playing and yelled, "Gage Harrison!"

The music stopped. The dancing ceased, and hundreds of eyes were on her.

"Gage Harrison!" she bellowed again.

The people parted.

"I need to tell you something!"

Like a dream, there he was, staring up at her, hands in the pockets of his suit pants, looking more handsome than ever before if that were possible.

"What is it?" Gage asked, not shouting as she'd done but loud enough the whole room could hear him.

"I want you!"

The corners of his lips turned up into his radiant smile.

"I need you!"

"You do?"

She nodded, tears welling up in her eyes.

"What else, Danny?"

"I love you, Gawonii. I've been in love with you my whole life."

"I know."

Coming to the edge of the stage in that pure male swagger, he held out a hand, and she took it, curling her fingers around his warm palm as he helped her down to the dance floor.

Danica's heart fluttered a specific pattern as it was wont to do in his presence. "Gage, I—"

He pulled her into his body with possession, slanted his mouth across hers, and proceeded to kiss her breathless.

There might have been clapping. Maybe even a few whistles. And Danica was reasonably sure she heard her brother-in-law shout, "It's about time!"

But she was way too busy kissing the man she loved to care.

Epilogue

Before

"SLOW DOWN AND hit your brake!"

Gage was yelling, though she didn't know exactly where he was. All she knew for sure? Her handlebars were swerving, the front tire going in the wrong direction, and she was panicking.

Danica screamed when she ran into the curb, let go of her bike, hand's going out an instant before she went airborne, having a major crash and burn.

"Danny!"

She heard him, but for a moment, she was addled.

"Are you okay?" Gage was there, by her side where she lay, her palms and knees a bloody mess—her new blue and white Huffy a bent street ornament. "Here."

She felt the warmth of him when he put his arm around her shoulders.

Trying not to hurt herself any more than she was, Danica let him help her right herself—the burning pain from her scrapes catching up, sending flames over her, making her cry.

"You're bleeding."

She knew it, but she couldn't stop watching him.

Gage took off his *Star Wars* t-shirt, wiped the tears from her face with it, then started dabbing at the cuts on her palm, making Danica wince and suck in a sharp breath.

"I'm sorry. I don't mean to hurt you."

She looked up at him, into his serious face as he tried to clean her up, struck how a lock of midnight fell over his right brow, the summer sun making a blue halo in his black hair. The way his skin was so much prettier than hers—those liquid silver eyes.

Danica didn't even realize the pain faded away as she thought, in her eight-year-old mind, *Gawonii must be an angel like the ones Mrs. Beil talks about in Sunday school.*

"Come on. I need to get you home." He scooped her up.

Danica rested her cheek against his chest, her knobby knees bent over his forearm, her thin arms going around his neck as he carried her. "I ruined my new bike."

She started to cry again, big fat tears over destroying her birthday present.

"*Shh…*" he soothed, "don't worry. I'll fix it, Danny. You'll see. Everything will be okay."

Eyelids fluttering closed, she listened to the *thrum* of Gage's heartbeat, instinctively knowing everything already was.

Bonus Scene

Before

"DO YOU NEED help with that?" Mason asked as Danny pulled a camping chair out of the trunk of his Mustang.

"I'm good. I've got it." She wanted to keep herself busy, not stare at Gage, who was coming their way, holding a blue cooler. There was nothing she could do about the flutters happening in her tummy.

"Hey, guys," he greeted them, his voice deep, velvety, yet rough around the edges—sandpaper-smooth.

"G! Glad you're here," Mason said, the two of them bumping fists.

"You want to go over by the dock?" Breck asked, plucking up some blankets.

"Sounds good to me," Mason said.

Handing a quilt to Mase, her sister asked, "Did anyone see if Jake and Maggie are coming?"

"I did," Gage said. "I'm sure they are on their way."

Their arms loaded down with stuff for the afternoon—blankets, coolers, bags of towels, sunscreen, and bug spray—they headed toward the lake.

In the distance, Danica noticed a little boy sitting on the end of the pier, his legs swinging over the edge. She thought it was Cooper, old man Kane's grandson who came to visit for the summers. Then all thoughts turned to Gage, who stepped beside her.

Looking up at him, she grinned.

When he returned the smile, bumping his shoulder into hers, her heart soared. "You going to swim?"

"I don't know. I might just enjoy the sun, work on my tan."

"I've brought some floats from home. When we get settled, I'll go back to my car and get them."

"Okay. Thanks."

Side-by-side they went, stepping onto the end of the dock, Gage yelling, "Hey, Coop!"

The boy put his fishing gear aside, scrambled up, brushed his hands together, looked at them then waved. "Hi, Gage."

"You getting ready to call it a day?"

"Yeah. Fish aren't biting." He bent and got his pole.

"Really?" Mason put down the bags he'd been holding. "The fish in this lake always bite."

"Not today. I think it's too hot."

"That sure is a nice pole," Gage said.

Cooper smiled. "I got it for my birthday."

"Oh, yeah? When was your birthday?"

"Last Tuesday."

"Well, happy late birthday then."

"Thanks!"

"How old are you now?"

"Eight."

"Wow," Breckin said, "you got a girlfriend yet?"

Cooper's little face scrunched up. "No way! Girls are gross!"

Mason laughed and curled his arm around her sister's waist. "You might think that now, but trust me. One day, you won't."

"Danny." Gage stepped back to her, a frown on his brow. "I'll carry that for you," he said, reaching for the large canvas bag she had.

She'd stopped going over a new dance routine in her head and smiled at him. "It's okay." Danica swiped some hair from her cheek. "I'm fine."

"Hi, guys!"

Everyone turned to see Jake and Mags coming their way.

"Hey, Maggie!" Danica wiggled her fingers.

"Did you bring the stereo?" Breckin asked.

Jake lifted the boombox proudly. "Yeah!"

"I hope you remembered to check the batteries," Mason said, "last time it died."

"During one of my favorite songs," Breckin added, rolling her green eyes.

Jake shook his head. "I replaced the batteries before we came."

"Hi." Mags bent toward Coop. "And who are you?"

"Cooper," he muttered, dropping his head, glancing down at his feet.

"Cute name. I'm Magdalene, but everyone calls me Maggie."

He nodded as he looked back up at her, appearing to be in awe.

"Has anyone ever told you, you've got great eyes?" Mags asked him.

His cheeks turned berry-red. "No."

"Coop there, he's going to be a real heartbreaker when he grows up," Breckin commented.

"Are we going to eat or what?" Jake groaned.

"Seriously?" Maggie lifted her gaze toward the sky, irritated, then straightened. "We just got here."

Gage held up his cooler. "We just need to start the grill."

"Let's do it, I'm starving," Jake complained.

"You're always starving," Maggie said, then winked at little Cooper.

"Got to go," he blurted, then took off like a shot.

As if they were in the choir, their group all sang, "Bye, Coop!" at almost the same time.

"I think someone has a crush on you, Maggie," Breck said, then chuckled.

Jake tossed his arm around Maggie's shoulders. "Yeah, well, she's mine."

"Really, Jake? Cooper's a little boy, no need to get all caveman possessive."

The two started their squabbling, so Danica decided to head on down the dock, flip-flops *thwap-tapping* the wood.

Gage was pulling food out of the Colman cooler when he came to a dead stop—a package of hotdogs slipping from his grip and tumbling back into the ice. Backlit by the sun, Danny lifted the NSYNC t-shirt she was wearing over her head, those golden strands of hair going with it, then tumbling down around her bare shoulders as she dropped the material at her bare feet.

He swallowed hard when she started shimmying out of her shorts, exposing a whole lot of perfect, creamy-white skin.

Heaven help me, she's wearing a tiny pink polka dot bikini.

Gage wanted to gawk, though he was pretty sure he already was. He blinked, hoping he wasn't drooling, catching both Phillip who had joined the party, and Jake, looking at her. He didn't like it. At all!

A heated spike of anger pierced him as he considered going to Danny and covering her up. But if he did that, it would cause a scene. So he left his job at the cooler and headed her way, intent on getting her into the water where no one could see her beautiful body. Though, the idea of her soaking wet and glistening did things to him.

I'll just make sure to wrap a towel around her when we get out.

Yes. Gage had a plan.

Grinning wickedly, and fully clothed, he jogged down the pier, his sandals *thudding* a rhythm.

Danny was adjusting the little string on her hip, then glanced up, blue eyes wide. "Gage, what are you—"

"Got you!" He picked her up and jumped—the two of them making a huge splash.

About the Author

D.L. Lane is a wife, musician, a graduate of Liberty University, and a member of American Christian Fiction Writers. In 2010 she walked away from the day job and started a writing career using a pen name. As far as the world was concerned, she was very successful writing romances, however, success aside, she knew she wasn't on the right path but stubbornly kept on going for nine years. Although a Christian and raised in a religious home, D.L went her own way, leaving God out of her choices until He said, "Enough."

Weary and seeking guidance, she finally listened and left the course she was on as an established novelist to take a new path—putting God first in her life where He always should have been.